PENGUIN BOOKS

DEAREST DOROTHY,
WHO WOULD HAVE EVER THOUGHT?!

Charlene Ann Baumbich is a popular speaker, journalist, and author. Her stories, essays, and columns have appeared in numerous magazines and newspapers, including the *Chicago Tribune*, the *Chicago Sun-Times*, and *Today's Christian Woman*. She is also the author of the first three books in the Partonville series, *Dearest Dorothy, Are We There Yet?*, *Dearest Dorothy, Slow Down, You're Wearing Us Out!*, and *Dearest Dorothy, Help! I've Lost Myself!*, and six books of nonfiction. She lives in Glen Ellyn, Illinois. Learn more about Charlene at www.welcometopartonville.com.

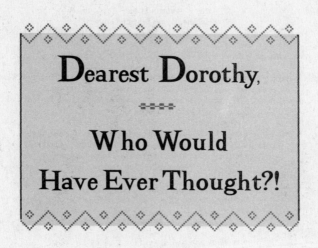

Dearest Dorothy,

Who Would Have Ever Thought?!

Charlene Ann Baumbich

PENGUIN BOOKS

PENGUIN BOOKS

Published by the Penguin Group

Penguin Group (USA) Inc., 375 Hudson Street, New York, New York 10014, U.S.A.

Penguin Group (Canada), 90 Eglinton Avenue East, Suite 700, Toronto,
Ontario, Canada M4P 2Y3 (a division of Pearson Penguin Canada Inc.)

Penguin Books Ltd, 80 Strand, London WC2R 0RL, England

Penguin Ireland, 25 St Stephen's Green, Dublin 2, Ireland (a division of Penguin Books Ltd)

Penguin Group (Australia), 250 Camberwell Road, Camberwell,
Victoria 3124, Australia (a division of Pearson Australia Group Pty Ltd)

Penguin Books India Pvt Ltd, 11 Community Centre,
Panchsheel Park, New Delhi–110 017, India

Penguin Group (NZ), cnr Airborne and Rosedale Roads, Albany,
Auckland 1310, New Zealand (a division of Pearson New Zealand Ltd)

Penguin Books (South Africa) (Pty) Ltd, 24 Sturdee Avenue,
Rosebank, Johannesburg 2196, South Africa

Penguin Books Ltd, Registered Offices:
80 Strand, London WC2R 0RL, England

First published in Penguin Books 2005

1 3 5 7 9 10 8 6 4 2

Publisher's Note
This is a work of fiction. Names, characters, places, and incidents either are the product
of the author's imagination or are used fictitiously, and any resemblance to actual persons,
living or dead, business establishments, events, or locales is entirely coincidental.

LIBRARY OF CONGRESS CATALOGING-IN-PUBLICATION DATA
Baumbich, Charlene Ann, 1945–
Dearest Dorothy, who would have ever thought? / Charlene Ann Baumbich.
p. cm. – (Dearest Dorothy; bk. 4)
ISBN 0-14-303619-X
1. Older women–Fiction.   2. Illinois–Fiction.   I. Title.
PS3602.A963D44 2005
813'.54–dc22   2005048743

Printed in the United States of America
Set in Berthold Garamond

Dedicated to:

Bridget Ann Baumbich

Acknowledgments

To Danielle Egan-Miller, Browne & Miller Literary Associates, who ROCKS. Thank you for caring so very, very much and so very, very well.

If you want to be proud of your book (not prowd of your booc), have the good fortune to fall into the capable hands (not fell into the culpable sands) of a Most Excellent Production Editor and Copy Editor, a duo with superb sight (not site—which they thankfully corrected a million and forty-two times). Thank you, Sharon L. Gonzalez and Diane Turso, for making me look good (or is it well, or swell, or . . . SAVE ME!). Bless your meticulous and keen minds and eyes, your pursuit of (or is that for?) excellence and for helping the readers to have more than a CLUE as to what folks in Partonville are talkin' 'bout, as Arthur would say. And thank you for letting him talk like that.

Here's what Good Editors do, at least mine: she edits me (forces me to go deeper, try harder, clear up the fog, unleash the possibilities, stay true to the story, stop rambling, trust my gut, not hang myself with stupid stuff). She gives me space and time to move from detesting her rewrite letter (eleven pages, *single spaced*!) to realizing she's a genuine genius who guided me, even when I thought I didn't need to be led. She laughs with me, assures me, puts her foot down and makes me a better writer. Thank you, Carolyn Carlson, for your faith in my gifts, your honesty, your time, your gentle heart and nature.

Thank you, my Honey Bunny of a husband, for sticking with me, even after I put a rearview mirror on my computer monitor so I could catch you standing in my office doorway looking at the back of my head when I was trying to write—and then YELLED at you for being so intrusive. I love you, even when you threaten to write a book about what it's *really* like living with an author. (Hopefully, my herewith True Confession has beat you to the punch ;>)) XOXOXOXOXOXOXOXOXOXOXO

Thank you, Dear Readers, for trusting everyone—including me—who helps to make a book a book. May the band of merry folks (including Acting Mayor Gladys McKern) you discover within these pages stir your heart, tickle your funny bone and whisper a word of faith about LIVING LIFE TO THE FULL!

Introduction

To be seventy years young is sometimes far more cheerful and hopeful than to be forty years old.

–Oliver Wendell Holmes

And now, welcome to Partonville, a circle-the-square town in the northern part of southern Illinois, where oldsters are young, trees have names and the obvious sometimes isn't.

1

Jessica withdrew her arm from beneath the cozy covers and clamped her hand over her shut-tight hazel eyes. The light, which was barely a muted glow seeping through her handmade, roman shades, felt like a Halogen high beam aimed at her pupils. *NO! It can't be morning already!* After wearily listening for a few moments to Sarah Sue's five-month-old chattering in the next room, Jessica could sense that her daughter had been awake for a while. She was reaching the familiar stage that teetered between happy gobbledy-gook and crankiness. The tiny plastic ball with bells inside, one of Sarah Sue's favorite toys, tucked nightly in her crib so it would keep her occupied during her early-morning wakefulness, banged to the floor. *Drats! It won't be long now. I am so tired.* She rolled onto her side away from the light and pulled the covers over her head. Snuggling into a fetal position, she tucked her hands under her chin. *Please, Sarah Sue, go back to sleep. Please.*

"WHAaaaaa! WHAaaaaaaaaaa!" It sounded like somebody had stuck her daughter with a pin, so sudden and piercing was the wail.

"PLEASE GO BACK TO SLEEP!" Jessica bellowed from beneath the covers. It wasn't like her to yell. It was such an unfamiliar sound, in fact, that Sarah Sue stopped mid-squawk. *Bless you, child of mine. Bless you.* During the quiet lull, Jessica wished it were the weekend and Paul could take over. She felt a selfish pang of guilt for thinking such a thing, for as much as she longed to go back to sleep, she also hoped that the twelve-unit motel they'd stretched their time and finances to buy would one day make enough money to allow him to quit his coal miner's job, even if he had to find a part-time position elsewhere. Maybe something outdoors so he could drink in enough fresh air to make up for all his underground labors.

"WHAaaaaaaa! WHAAAAAaaaaaaaa!" Sarah Sue was cranked up for good this time and Jessica knew there would be no stopping her until her child—The Squawking One she'd just blessed—was rescued not only from her solitude but probably from her amply loaded diaper as well. Jessica wiggled around just enough to peak at the clock. It was 8:45 A.M. "Goodness," she said as she flung back the covers, exposing her floor-length, white flannel nightgown with a teddy bear print on it. After sitting on the edge of the bed for a moment to fully claim her wakefulness, she stood, the soft gown unleashing its collected warmth as it unfolded around her long lean legs. Paul had been gone for hours already and Sarah Sue was usually done with breakfast and ready for a morning nap by now. "This is a record!"

Her body felt more like a shipwreck than one of a fit woman in her late twenties. Partonville's annual Pumpkin Festival had ended a few days earlier and the motel, which had been booked solid for the weekend, was at last blissfully empty. Even though they could use the money she was glad for the respite. Between check-ins and daily service, running the switchboard, readying her crafts for the sale, building and decorating a special arch for Acting Mayor Gladys McKern's pronouncements (what had she been thinking about getting on *that* committee?)—not to mention caring for a husband and a teething baby—she'd worked from the crack of dawn until nearly 1 A.M. for days on end. She'd been so tired yesterday that she hadn't even finished cleaning all the vacated rooms and instead took an afternoon nap when Sarah Sue went down for hers.

She slowly lumbered toward her daughter's room. Sarah Sue immediately quieted at the sound of her mother's feet padding down the hall. Just before Jessica entered, she realized she needed to hit the bathroom herself before she could deal with what, even through the closed door, was a for-sure loaded diaper, so she whirled on her heels. A queasiness rolled through her stomach. *No whirling. Too tired.* Next she was hit by an onslaught of lightheadedness. *Definitely no more whirling.* Sarah Sue made that annoying half-whine, half-cry sound when her door didn't open the way she'd expected it to. As soon as Jessica entered the bathroom, a severe wave of nausea overcame her and the next thing she knew she was retching into the toilet.

"WHAaaaaaaaa! WHAAAAAAAAAAAA!" Jessica started to holler "I'll be right there," but before a sound could escape her throat, her head was back in the toilet bowl. When she was done, she rocked back on her heels until her buttocks hit the floor, legs bent up in front of her, feet flat on the floor. With a few moist strands of brunette hair clinging to the side of her face, she leaned back against the bathroom wall and closed her bloodshot eyes. In spite of her exhaustion, her mind wandered over the events of the last few days.

The decorations at the Pumpkin Festival dance had been remarkable, as had the atmosphere, the band, the DJ. . . . She saw herself dancing in their midst while resting her head on Paul's shoulder, Sarah Sue dangling between them, strapped to Paul in that baby sling contraption they took turns wearing. While she'd yawned and wondered if it were possible to fall asleep standing up swaying, she'd felt a deep contentment. She was dancing with her husband, in whose arms she always felt safe. And he was looking so handsome in his simple yet, to her, sexy outfit. Paul, smelling like Dial soap (as close as he got to cologne), was wearing a new (the dressed-up part) plaid flannel shirt over a long-underwear top, jeans that were slightly frayed around the cuffs and his new (*excessive* dress up, Jessica had teased) black Converse (the only brand and color he'd worn since high school) high-top gym shoes. The total ensemble created what they both referred to as his above-the-ground uniform. He had stroked the back of her head and whispered in her ear, "Just think, honey, we're almost back to normal. All the big doings are winding down as we dance, and Sarah Sue is finally sleeping through the night on a regular basis."

But now, before she had a chance to further contemplate their blissful return to normalcy, she bolted back onto her knees, leaned over the toilet bowl and was racked by a few more dry heaves. Wrung out, she curled up on the cold floor and half covered herself with the fluffy white oval bathroom rug. While Sarah Sue wailed, Jessica Joy moaned a short prayer. "Say it isn't so." The phone was ringing in the background but she couldn't bring herself to get up and answer it. Soon she heard her own perky voice on the answering machine saying, "The Lamp Post motel. Your call is important to us and we're sorry we missed it."

"Your call isn't all I've missed lately," she mumbled with a groan.

Katie Durbin sat at the table in Dorothy's cheery kitchen. Dorothy's erect back was toward her as she stood at her kitchen counter slicing fresh lemon wedges for their large glasses of water. Katie locked eyes briefly with Sheba— Dorothy's black-and-white mutt—who'd suddenly sprung up from beneath the table with a bark and plunked down in front of the heating vent near Dorothy's feet. Katie had decided to stop by Dorothy's on her way home from a shopping trip to Hethrow. She'd gone to nearly a half dozen stores before finally settling on a couple of rugs: a short-bristle mat for the back porch and a nappy woven rug for just inside the kitchen door. Maybe between the two of them her floor would stay tidier. She was tired of Josh tracking in debris from the pasture, the barn and everywhere else he'd tramped. Although she'd tried to train him to take his shoes off on the porch—something she'd never had to think about when they lived in the city—it seemed he was in the kitchen with his head stuck in the refrigerator before her repeated request ever registered. You'd think by sixteen years of age he'd just know better.

"How did you ever keep the farmhouse clean when you had three children running in and out all day, Dorothy?" Dorothy smiled at Katie as she set two glasses of water—a lemon wedge perched on the edge of each—and a small bowl of backup lemon wedges between them. The feisty 87-year-old seated herself, pushed the sleeves of her pink (her trademark color) cardigan sweater up to her elbows, took a big swallow, then broke out in a grin.

"HA! Clean? Clean, with three children, a husband, miscellaneous mutts, stowaway barn cats, mice and dust from the gravel road? I doubt that house was ever clean until the day I moved out a few months ago. Now by the end of *that* day, I finally had a clean house."

"Mice?" Katie held her lemon wedge mid-air.

Dorothy took note of Katie's surprised face while Sheba moved from the vent to underneath the table to curl up next to her feet. *Such a city girl.* "Mice," Dorothy said flatly. "Lots of mice. Which is why we always kept so many barn cats around. Of course, since I am a dog lover to the core, much to my chagrin one child or another would drag one of those barn cats into the house if it didn't claw them to pieces first—and boy that happened more times than I'd care to remember—and they just never seemed to leave. Although I by no means much took to those cats, I was always grateful when one or another of those scraggly things would turn out to be a good house mouser."

"House mouser? Are you telling me that the farmhouse might have mice?" She finished squeezing the lemon, slid the rind into her glass and picked up another wedge.

"No, dear."

"Well, that's a relief!"

"I'm guarant*eeing* you the farmhouse has mice. Then, and now. Throughout the generations. Families of mice, especially this time of year. You don't live on a farm without mice, dear; you just learn to set lots of traps, or get mouser cats or . . . cohabitate."

Katie mentally ran through Dorothy's brief list of rodent antidotes. When she spoke, her voice held an edge of frustration. "A, I'm severely allergic to cats, Dorothy. Most animal dander, in fact, so cats are out. B, after witnessing way too many rats in and around condemned demolition properties in Chicago, I have no tolerance for any size rodent. And C through Z, I'm not sure if I can *take* many more surprises!"

"Just get you a goodly amount of traps and set them along the edges of the kitchen floor, and under the sink, of course . . . and down in the basement and perhaps along the back of the counter splashboards, if you should find evidence they've been in your silverware drawers, and . . ."

"In my silverware drawers? *Evidence?*" Dorothy couldn't contain herself from bursting out laughing at this hard-nosed commercial real estate tycoon who looked on the verge of unraveling at the thought of a few little critters in her house. She reached over and patted Katie's hand, still chuckling.

"Traps. That and a little poison, if you . . ."

"STOP! I can't *hear* any more about this right now, Dorothy!" As if to wash this whole conversation away, Katie squeezed the wedge in her hand, plunked it into her glass and took another sip of her water, then screwed up her face again.

"Are you alright, dear?"

"Just a little too much lemon, I guess."

"I've got a better idea. I've been having a hankerin' for iced tea anyway, I don't care if we have flipped our calendars to November. Iced tea is a year-round beverage in my book." Dorothy picked up their glasses and set them in the sink. Then she pulled a dented, two-cup, aluminum saucepan from one of her cabinets. While she filled it with water and put it on her stove, Katie's breath hitched at the sight of the pan. Dorothy rummaged through her cabinets and retrieved the box of Lipton's tea bags. For the first time all day, she noticed the hands on her teapot-shaped, battery-operated kitchen wall clock. It was well past lunch. "Are you hungry? I can fix us a sandwich to go with this tea. I'm sorry I didn't notice the time when you first dropped in."

Katie thought on it for a moment, then decided she *would* like a bite to eat. "Just something small would be nice, maybe a few crackers, if you have any. After all, I did drop in unannounced."

"Pish-posh on announcements! Since when does a friend need an appointment to see a friend? And, Katie, I know you better than to think a few teensy mice have turned your stomach enough to need soda crackers to settle it!" Katie chuckled at Dorothy's dose of welcome perspective. "I have a brand-new loaf of rye bread and a half pound of that good smoked turkey from Your Store. It'll just take me a minute to whip us up a quick lunch."

"I couldn't believe it when I saw you get out that pan. Is that a Pardon-Me-Ville thing?"

"This pan?" Dorothy asked, pointing to the pan on the stove, as though she had a dozen of them lined up on the counter. Katie nodded an affirmation. "Well, I don't know about it being a Pardon-Me-Ville thing but it sure is *my* thing. This old pan is the one Mom used when she made her sweet tea. Even though ice was pretty sparse in the warmest months, after she'd brew and sweeten, she'd usually manage to have just enough ice to chill it. But when we were out of ice, our good, deep well water always ran a refreshing temperature. Although it wouldn't be nice and cold the way I like it today, it sure did wet our whistles plenty fine."

"I have to admit," Katie said, "that cold well water is one of the things I do love about the farm. The reason I asked if that pan was a Pardon-Me-Ville thing is because my mother used to make tea that exact same way, in a little beat-up pan that could be that one's twin," she said, pointing with her eyes and chin. "I hadn't thought about it for years until I saw yours. She used to make me warm tea with honey when I wasn't feeling well and iced tea in the summer, mostly. I wonder what happened to that old pan? So many pieces of her life I just gave away, let them go after she died." Her face washed over with regret.

"Don't look back, honey. We do what we do, and then we move on. Sometimes we've got nothing more in us than to let go." Dorothy put the tea bags in the water to steep, then went about making the sandwiches.

"Thanks. I needed to hear that." But even so, she couldn't help but wonder briefly if her mom's pan had gone to the garbage, the giveaway box or if it might even be in an antique or resale store somewhere. Although she wasn't much for antique stores (they often smelled odd and her taste ran decidedly toward the contemporary), she pictured the little pan set proudly on a shelf with a price tag worthy of its memories.

After a brief silence Katie said, "Hm, it's kind of surprising."

"What's that?"

"I don't recall noticing any antique stores around here."

"You mean to tell me you haven't been to Swappin' Sam's yet?" Swappin' Sam's was one of Dorothy's favorite haunts.

"Hardly. Just driving by it is ghastly enough. What an eyesore right there at the mouth of town." Her Realtor's eye had cringed more than once at its location. "That's just a junk store anyway, isn't it?"

"I'll have you know that Sam Vitner considers himself to be quite the aficionado of *all* things, collectible or otherwise." Dorothy lowered her chin and raised a playful eyebrow.

"How long has his place been around? From the looks of the length of grass grown up around some of those things out in his yard, I'd say too long."

Dorothy cut the sandwiches in half, arranged them on paper plates and began to sprinkle a few potato chips first on her plate, then Katie's.

"No chips for me!"

"Leaves more for me then," Dorothy said smiling. She got out a jar of midget sweet pickles and set them on the table for Katie to open. "Your hands will deal with that easier than mine." Dorothy flexed her arthritic fingers open and closed a few times. Soon they were both served and seated. "Would you mind if I say a quick prayer, honey?"

"Go right ahead." Katie bowed her head, took a deep breath and released it, readying herself for one of Dorothy's earnest outpourings. Dorothy could switch between easy chatter with friends and talking to God as naturally as a lightning bug turns its glow pad on and off.

"Dear God, THANK YOU! Amen." Before Katie could lift her head, Dorothy had popped a chip in her mouth and was picking up a second. She noticed Katie's hands were still folded. "Sometimes a hearty thank-you pretty much says it all!"

Katie smiled and spread her paper napkin on her lap. "So how long *has* Vitner's place been there?"

"Oh, I'd say at least a good forty years or so. He was quite successful from the get-go, no matter what the economy. Like it says on his sign out front, 'If you've got the time, you'll make the find.' I can tell you I sure have found some goodies! You might find this hard to believe, but folks come from miles around to prowl through his place, sometimes stopping there before heading on to the hardware store, just in case. He keeps his finer collectible pieces in that main building farthest from the road; what I'd call the good old stuff in the two smaller buildings to the side; hardware parts and such are in a couple of truck trailers out back—I'm sure you've noticed those. Of course, how could anybody miss those toilets out front! Most of the larger unrustable things just seem to end up sprawled around here and there outdoors."

"Thus the eyesore."

"Well now, Ms. Katie Durbin," Dorothy said with a twinkle in her eye, "perhaps you forgot that my guest poster bed is partially made out of old dining room table legs from that eyesore of a place, and I'd say at least another six items in my house are either totally or partially fashioned from treasures I've found at Sam's. One woman's eyesore is another's golden nugget." She took a bite of her sandwich, chewed, swallowed. "I guess that's how it is with all of life: it depends on how you look at it—whatever the *it* may be!"

"Duly noted," Katie said. "I remember you telling me Edward Showalter helped you create that beautiful poster bed. However, Ms. Dorothy Jean Wetstra, no matter how I might or might not be forced to look at a mouse—and believe you me, I do not *want* to look at a mouse—it will still look like a mouse."

"Here's to a very astute woman!" Dorothy said, picking up her iced tea and holding it high in the air. It was hard to tell which was louder, the clink or the laughter.

2

As soon as Katie arrived back at Crooked Creek Farm she began to fuss with the rugs, temporarily ignoring the blinking light on the answering machine. Josh's bus would soon be dropping him off at the end of the one-eighth-mile lane, which meant Josh would be barreling into the tiny enclosed back porch, then on into the kitchen. The rug with the bristles was aesthetically too large for the back porch area but Katie decided in some ways that was good since Josh would *have* to walk on it in order to reach the stairs. Although she liked the nubby texture of the other rug, which fit right in with her color scheme, the door wouldn't clear over its lush pile. She scooted it this way and that with her foot, trying to decide how it might look away from the swing of the door. The more she looked at how well it matched her décor, the more she wanted it to work but the bottom line was that it didn't, not even in front of the sink since she found herself tripping on it twice just moving it around. Disappointed, she rolled it up and shoved it back into the bag with the receipt.

As annoying as it was to put the same task back on her to-do list, she was, truth be known, happy to have anything on her list lately. Even though she was financially secure— enough money in the bank so that she never really had to work again—the loss of her corporate job in commercial real estate development combined with the move from Chicago to Partonville had left her with lots of free time. Too much free time, she was beginning to realize. She'd never in her Type A life been idle enough for boredom to strike. Perhaps "the 'B' word," as one of her clients had once referred to boredom when explaining why he was developing a huge amusement park at age sixty-seven, was quickly becoming a serious possibility. The simple fact was that she missed a good challenge.

She approached the answering machine mounted on the wall, pushed the button and turned to get the scissors to cut the tag off the bristle rug she'd decided to keep. "Kathryn Durbin, Colton Craig here." Katie stopped dead in her tracks and moved swiftly back in front of her machine to stare at it, even though his strong deep voice was plenty loud enough to hear all the way on the porch. "I'm sure you're surprised to be hearing from me, but then again, maybe you're wondering what's taken me so long." Surprised? Flat out *stunned* was more like it! "I'd like to get together for lunch soon. Perhaps next week? Give me a call at my office." Katie was racing across the room to retrieve a pencil, irritated with Josh for always walking away with the pens, pencils and notepads she left near the machine. She whipped open the drawer just as he was reeling off the number but she didn't hear a digit since what she saw was . . . yes, *evidence*. Mouse-in-the-house evidence. She winced as she struggled to jimmy shut the old wooden drawer that refused to glide.

"I look forward to hearing from you soon," Colton said, his voice as smooth as she remembered it. "I hope you're having a good day." Click.

"If any two things could have turned my otherwise mediocre day bad," she said aloud to the machine, "I've just received notice from both of them: the mouse *and* the rat!"

◇△◇

Jessie Landers slammed the phone down in its cradle. "The nerve of them!" she shouted from the kitchen to Arthur who was sitting in his La-Z-Boy recliner in the living room. "The *nerve* of them."

"What are ya yelpin' 'bout, woman?" Arthur had the television turned up so loudly it seemed to her it would have been impossible for him to hear a tornado had it been ripping through his own hair. Jessie came storming around the corner, grabbed the remote out of his hand and turned the annoying thing off.

"Arthur Landers, you have got to get yourself some hearing aids."

"Is that what yur yelpin' 'bout?"

"It is now!"

"What was it before—although I'm sure I don't *really* wanna know."

"Your relatives."

"What relatives?"

"Your Indiana cousin and his wife. At least that's what you've been telling me he was all these years—although I'm beginning to suspect they both descended from a band of gypsies."

"Well then, so did I! Give me that remote, if that's all yur crabbin's 'bout. I can't do nothin' to change them kind of genetic details."

Jessie put the remote behind her back so he couldn't snatch it out of her hand. She knew it would take an act of God to rouse him out of his ever-loving chair. "Herm and Vera said they'd like to come for Thanksgiving . . ."

Arthur cut off her sentence. "You knew that. You invited 'em, woman. You goin' daft?"

"They said, Arthur," and Jessie spoke through a tightening jaw as she worked to calm herself down, "they said they'd like to come a little early."

"Like how early?"

"Like two weeks and three DAYS early, which means, Arthur, on MONDAY, which is only six days away!"

"I thought ya liked Vera," Arthur said, staring at the television like it was still on.

"I do like Vera—in small doses. As you well know, I don't like much of anybody if I have to be stuck with them over three days in a row." What this implied about their nearly six decades of a mostly stormy marriage was not explored, but Arthur rolled his eyes to acknowledge he'd heard what she'd said, even though she hadn't said it. At least this time.

"Did ya jist tell 'em no? N-O? Jist come on Thanksgivin' Eve?"

"Have you ever tried talking to somebody who doesn't stop to catch a breath?" she asked, hands on her hips. He raised an eyebrow at her; she replied with a defiant squint that dared him to say more. "There's no way I can get this house clean by Monday, Arthur, unless you help me, and since it's your relatives . . ."

"What's ta clean?" he asked, lifting the television schedule up off the end table next to his chair and finding nothing. "See? Clean as a whistle under there!"

"You are not funny. This place is a pigpen, thanks to you. It's bad enough the Happy Hookers are coming to our house for bunco before Thanksgiving, but now to have to be ready for out-of-town company weeks ahead of schedule. . . . That means I now have to clean the back bedroom before bunco, too." (That's where she usually threw everything when she was cleaning for the Hookers.) She sighed and turned in a wide circle, taking in the challenge before her, already dreading the smell of cleaning products. She'd rather clean a horse stall than have to dust. She'd once seen a plaque that said "Nobody ever died from oven crud," and she'd emitted a big A-MEN right out loud, right there in the department store. She'd wished on more than one occasion she'd have bought the dang thing and hung it on her front door, just for a fair warning.

"Arthur, I'm putting you in charge of cobwebs. You can use some of your old shop rags to cover the head of the broom. How about you get right to it."

Arthur stretched back, reclined in his La-Z-Boy, cradled the back of his head in his hands and closed his eyes. "Right after my nap," he said. Right after jackrabbits fly, he thought.

Jessie looked at the digital clock on the video machine. It was 3:25. "I'll give you until three-thirty, then I better see you moving, buster!"

"You'll see me movin' alright, woman. Movin' right out the back door, down the driveway all the way to Ca-li-for-nI-A!"

"Well, don't forget your precious La-Z-Boy when you go. One less thing I'll have to clean around."

"Been shopping again, huh, Mom?" Josh hollered as he leapt over the new bristle rug onto the first step of the back porch, figuring his mom wouldn't want him getting her new purchase all dirty. By the time Katie came down from her bedroom and got to the kitchen, Josh's backside was already sticking out of the fridge. Mud smears dotted the floor. She sighed, counted to three and turned her internal hot-switch down a notch. "Look at the floor, son." Josh, can of soda in his hand, backed out of the fridge, closed the door and turned to greet his mom's disgusted face. "Sorry. Toss me the roll of paper towels. I'll clean it up."

"Did you not see the new rug on the porch?" she asked as she tossed him the roll.

"Yup. I didn't figure you'd want me to mess it up."

Katie just shook her head. *Oh, well. He was* trying *to be considerate. 'One person's golden nugget . . .' Isn't that what Dorothy'd said?*

Josh leaned over and dabbed at the mud smears with a huge wad of toweling. "You won't believe what happened in biology today. See this black swirl right here?" he asked, pointing the toe of his shoe at a muddy dollop before wiping it up. "In a *way* misguided flirting attempt, Sasha Kramer, one of our entire class's most brainiac students, dared Kevin Mooney to mix these two vials of chemicals together, and he was just showoff enough—and dumb enough—to do it. BLAMMO!" Josh simultaneously tossed the soiled paper towels into the air when he discharged the word. "This brownish-black swirl of foul-smelling stuff spewed everywhere."

"Oh, my! Was anyone hurt?"

"No. Unless you count Sasha's feelings when Kevin accused her of knowing exactly what she was doing, which of course she did since she's never received anything less than an A+ in any class she's ever taken." He collected the toweling, bunched it up and tossed it in the garbage.

"What did she say?" Katie asked, retrieving a towel wad he'd missed.

"She said she was sorry, that she thought he could take a joke and that she didn't know it would be *that* explosive."

"And he said?"

"'I *can* take a joke, when it's *funny*.' And then he asked for a hall pass to go to the bathroom to try to get the mess off his clothes. But the teacher made him use the lab sink, so we all got to watch the slimy circle over the OLD in his Old Navy sweatshirt get bigger and bigger and his face get redder and redder and he didn't even attempt to get it off the front of his pants and then Sasha started crying and then the bell rang."

"Did anyone comfort Sasha? Poor girl."

Josh gave her a double take. He would never understand women. "I can tell you it wasn't Kevin!" Josh said. "Anything that exciting happen with you today?"

"Exciting would not be the correct word. Disturbing, perhaps. I stopped by Dorothy's today and ended up having a bite of lunch with her."

"Since when is that disturbing?" He knit his eyebrows together in puzzlement.

"It wasn't the visit that was the issue; you know I enjoy Dorothy. It's what I learned while I was there and then what was confirmed after I arrived home. Here, take a look." She walked over to the drawer that held pencils, pens, paper clips—evidence—and other stuff people usually kept in their junk drawers, although she didn't own any such junk and what she did keep around was organized with neat drawer dividers. "Go ahead. Open it."

Josh pulled open the drawer and stared. "What?"

"Look closely, Josh, then go wash your hands."

He studied the drawer, then shrugged his shoulders. It occurred to her that her son might not have any idea what mouse evidence looked like. Before she spoke, she spent a quick moment, as disgusting a moment as it was, trying to recall why *she* did. *That's right.* When she and Josh's dad, her ex, had first gotten married, they were so broke they'd briefly—very briefly—rented a crummy place with mice and cockroaches. No wonder she doubly hated the squeaky things; they brought back all kinds of bad memories. She walked next to her five-foot ten-inch son, reached up to put her hands on his shoulders and moved him aside to stare in the drawer. With her index finger she pointed. "See that?" Josh stuck his head nearly in the drawer to see what could possibly be in the corner where her fingertip was aiming.

"These little black things?" he asked as he started to reach for one.

"DON'T TOUCH THOSE!" Josh quickly withdrew his hands, visions of the biology class episode rifling through his mind. Katie drew a breath and loudly exhaled. "That, Joshua Matthew Kinney, is mouse evidence."

"Mouse evidence?"

"Exactly."

Josh stood in silence shifting his eyes from her to the evidence and back again until he finally put it all together. "Oh! Mouse twerps! Mouse doo!" He busted out laughing, just like Dorothy had. "Mouse *evidence.* You crack me up, Mom!" He doubled over with laughter this time.

"Yes, mouse *evidence.* And just what you and Dorothy both think is so funny about filth and disease, not to mention the idea that disgusting mice are creeping around our home while we sleep, is beyond me."

"Dorothy's seen this?"

"No. But she knows the farm has mice—a little detail she neglected to mention when I talked about buying this place from her."

"Mom, it's a farm! Animals are supposed to live on farms so why wouldn't mice? All we need is a few traps, I'm sure. No biggie."

No biggie. No biggie she lived miles away from civilization. No biggie she practically had no friends. No biggie her house was infested with mice. No biggie she was bored to tears. No biggie she had recently become more a talk of the town than a member of it, due to discovering she'd been conceived out of wedlock and her father never learned of her birth.

"Right. Mouse evidence is no biggie—for me," she said beginning to smile. "I'd say it's just the right-sized task for you, though. The 'no biggie' (she drew air quotes around the phrase) needs to be cleaned out of all drawers and cabinets, then you need to scrub them down, shop for mousetraps and set them and dispose of . . . whatever, should they actually catch something. 'No biggie,' no arguing. Alrighty?" *Big* smile.

Josh laughed. "Alrighty!" He whirled on his heels and said he was going to change his clothes and that he'd start thinking about the 'no biggie' (his own air quotes, only more dramatic) project after he checked his e-mail, and by the way, he'd need the SUV to go get the traps. And by the way, she said, no he couldn't have the car tonight because she was going out to run her own errands. Well then, if Shelby (His sweet Shelby!) wasn't too busy, could he call her to take him? Well then, even though there was absolutely no dating on weeknights allowed, she guessed he could, but only to run the errand, and Shelby could not come in the house. "Understand?" "Understood." "And no going in the barn either when I'm not home. Got it?" "Got it." (All discussions were moot because Shelby couldn't come anyway. Unbeknownst to them at the time, day after day would go by without traps. The only thing that would change would be their continued discoveries of more evidence, Katie's ever-growing disgust with the mice, Josh's amusement that his mom could get so freaked out every time she discovered more evidence, her exasperation that Josh wasn't handling his chore and his continued bemoaning that he never had the wheels to get the chore started.)

As soon as he'd disappeared up the stairs, Katie listened to Colton Craig's message for the fifth time; each time she had started to delete it, but didn't. This time she wrote the number down. Maybe it was the perfect moment to explore just how valuable her land was to the guy who more than anyone else on the planet, she was sure, wanted it for development. The guy who was tangentially related to how she'd lost her job. Well, perhaps he could have it, mice and all. She could kill two birds with one delicious stone by not only getting herself out of this B-word of a mouse-laden place but by watching her biggest professional enemy grovel for the gem for which he lusted: that which was contingent to Hethrow, the town Craig & Craig (as in Colton Craig and his brother) Developers had transformed from a sleepy little stop along the way into a sprawling metropolitan success.

Herm and Vera stuffed their giant old green vinyl suitcase until they couldn't squeeze in one more pair of underwear, even though they each had two pairs to go. "Won't matter if we take all our skivvies anyway," Herm said. "My cuz is got a washin' machine, I'm sure."

"Good point," Vera replied as she flung her winter hat and gloves—just in case—into a cardboard box they were preparing to toss in the back seat of Henrietta, their old Buick sedan. (If Jessie had thought about it, she would have known Herm was for sure a blood relative since with the Landers men, it was Buicks or nothing.) Even though Herm and Vera weren't leaving for a few more days, they knew they'd both feel better knowing they were ready to fire up Ol' Henrietta and head toward Partonville! It had been six years since they'd all gotten together, which is why Jessie had invited them in the first place.

Six years, it turned out, had been just long enough for everyone to forget the misery brought on by their last visit.

Although the washer and dryer were still whirling with the final load of sheets, Jessica, after working like a dog all day (which is how her mom would have described it), was at long-last finished cleaning all the rooms at the Lamp Post motel. Never had she stretched such an important bevy of tasks over so many days. She'd also at last taken the time to count the money Wanita had collected for the bookmarks Jessica had crocheted for the Pumpkin Festival craft fair—all thirty-seven of them—and given to Wanita to sell in her booth. Wanita ("Yes, that's the way you spell it," she'd had to say over and over her entire life) was a good egg to keep the finances separate, even though a few buyers had whined. Wanita had handed the envelope to Jessica at the festival dance. Jessica had tucked it in her purse where it had remained until today. She wanted to give Wanita a portion of the funds for her trouble. "You know," Jessica had said, "like a commission fee." Although Wanita had said that she didn't feel right about taking money from her for such a small favor, Jessica could see her warm to the idea when she'd brought up the word "commission" and proposed that it be a flat five percent of the take. Wanita had acquiesced while her three-year-old twin boys each held on to one of her plump legs with one hand while socking each other with the other, causing her body to jerk this way and that. "Well, that se-ems fair e-nough, and if it m-akes you feel ha-appy," she'd said, her words bumping out of her mouth as her head jerked.

What made Jessica feel the happiest about sharing her extra income was knowing that Wanita would have a few more dollars to buy her children shoes and it was obvious they needed them. Wanita's husband had, not by choice, been unemployed for at least two months. The mines had had a serious round of cutbacks, Paul and Jessica having held their own breath more than once. Since folks had purchased every last one of the bookmarks, the commission added up to more than either of the women might have expected. Wanita had described to Jessica how some women bought five and six at a time for Christmas gifts; it was all a good sign for the Spring Fling craft fair in March, they agreed. Jessica was already visualizing how she could decorate the bookmarks with pastel yarns and buttons.

But for now, the last remaining chore from the Pumpkin Festival was to drop the money off to Wanita since it was finally tallied. "Maybe tomorrow. I need to go to bed early," she told Paul after recapping the financial and creative tidbits. But that's all she told him. They were so financially strapped (hence his above-the-ground uniform—although she speculated that even if he were a millionaire, that's what he'd want to wear, which was fine with her since she adored his rustic manly look), and he worked so hard already, he didn't need something more to worry about, especially since she continued to hold out hope that there would be nothing else to tell, even though a mild nausea had consumed her most of the day. The kind of nausea that she'd experienced too recently to forget.

Wanita once again thanked Jessica for the commission fee. "If you ever want me to do this again, don't hesitate to let me know. And if you ever need help cleaning rooms or anything and if you wouldn't mind if I brought the twins along, maybe I could give you a hand once in awhile. I've been thinking about these few extra dollars. . . ." Jessica sure understood the need for extra dollars, which is why she'd put in all the late hours crocheting to begin with. But as much as she wished she could offer Wanita a steady part-time job, she was sure that wouldn't be financially possible. Maybe with the holidays coming, she might need her. When the Lamp Post had been steadily booked in the past, Jessica had, on occasion, hired somebody to give her a hand. But then visions of Wanita's rascally twins throwing toys in the toilets, drawing on the walls and pummeling each other—which they were constantly prone to doing—with pillows until the stuffing flew every which way, sprang into her head. "I'll keep that in mind," Jessica responded. But about the only thing that would stick in her mind at the moment was her need to toss her cookies again.

3

Arthur waited in his truck for Lester to flip the sign on the door to Harry's Grill from CLOSED to OPEN. He'd been waiting since 5:25 A.M., about a half hour after he'd woken up. Even though he usually hit Harry's at 6 A.M. when the grill opened, more than ever he'd wanted to get out of the house this morning before Jessie got up and started bossing him around again. He recollected that company had always thrown his mother into a tizzy, too, but today things had reached a fevered pitch with his spitfire of a wife. For the last few days she'd nearly worked him to death—literally. Between fumes from the cleaning products, having to crawl up and down the ladder to wipe down shelves so high in closets that nobody would ever see them ("And may I ask you, woman, what is the point of *this*?") and sending him to Your Store to buy bathroom deodorizers she'd seen advertised on TV ("We've never needed smell-good before so why do we need it now?"), he was plumb worn out—not to mention she'd nearly accidentally, he hoped, knocked him cold when she'd tossed the plastic gallon bottle full of bleach at him thinking he was ready to catch it, which he had not been. (Thank goodness that when the bottle landed on the floor the impact didn't knock the cap off; she'd have probably blamed that on him, too!) But worse yet, she'd expected him to clean the bathtub floor with the horrible stinkin' stuff.

Yes, siree, boys and girls, it had been time to vacate the premises before that "maniac of a gol' dern crazed woman" woke up and opened her mouth.

Arthur watched the six-day-a-week usuals gather outside the grill's door. Acting Mayor Gladys McKern always bustled her way to be first in line. Eugene Casey, owner of Casey's Funeral Home, was much appreciated as a regular since the *Partonville Press* only came out twice a week and breakfast-goers would be the first to know of any passings in the night before the grapevine had a chance to spread the news. And speaking of the grapevine, there came Cora Davis, the very taproot of the grapevine, right on time. Heaven forbid somebody should nab her seat in the window. Unless it was print day, Harold Crab, publisher and editor of the newspaper, was an early bird as well. Of course, others like Doc Streator and Sam Vitner frequently showed up, too, just as they did today. Arthur leaned on his steering wheel waiting until the "line of characters takes a load off," then slammed the door to his truck and made his own way to *his* usual stool. Before either his backside landed or he'd said a word, Lester slid a mug of high-octane coffee in front of him. "You can't even imagine how much I need this today, Lester," Arthur said with a dramatic sigh.

"I've got plenty more interesting things to imagine than that," Lester growled. It usually took Lester a good half hour to speak nicely to anyone, and then the level of niceness in his tone of voice was still debatable—although everyone knew he had a heart of gold. He was a man of few words, at least way fewer than Arthur. (Then again, most people were—aside from Gladys.)

"Jessie's on a cleaning rampage!" Arthur spouted to Lester in a voice one might use to "interrupt this program with an important announcement."

Lester was going to say "Did I ask?" but instead, sounding like he could not care less, he more or less grunted "What does a cleaning rampage look like, Arthur? I have no earthly idea." Without waiting for an answer, the lifetime bachelor turned his back on Arthur to face the grill, grabbed two eggs out of the large green bowl, one in each hand, and simultaneously cracked them on the edge of the well-worn Formica ledge around the griddle. He separated his fingers enough to open each shell and unload the contents onto the heat, a finely honed skill with decades of experience behind it. Pleased himself with the maneuver every time. The familiar sound of the sizzling eggs and bacon was music to Arthur's ears, especially after enduring Jessie's relentless commands.

"What does a cleaning rampage look like?" Arthur repeated Lester's question. "Look-ee here for a minute." Lester obliged by peering over his shoulder between flipping the eggs. "It looks like this." Arthur slid off his stool and stood behind it. He drew up his hands to waist-high, rounded his shoulders and held his breath until his face turned red. Then he exhaled with a whoosh and said, "It looks like that."

Lester didn't give Arthur the satisfaction of a smirk, even though he knew that Arthur's exaggerated pose probably wasn't much of a stretch since everybody knew Jessie had a temper. But Harold Crab burst out laughing while Arthur sat down again, obviously pleased with his theatrics. Gladys gave a loud harrumph that served as her judgment about making fun of women, although what she was really thinking was that the last she'd seen, the Landerses' house was past due for a good cleaning and she for one was happy it was taking place before their upcoming Hookers' meeting.

Harold spread his paper napkin on his lap. "So what brought on this rampage?"

"The Hookers are meeting at their house this month," Gladys said. Gladys had been a member of the Happy Hookers since their inception decades ago. The eight ladies had originally gathered to hook rugs (and thus the name Happy Hookers), but one day they tired of hooking and took to playing bunco, a raucous, mindless dice game that offered a great opportunity for gab, prizes and dessert.

"Oh, but that's only a part of the story, Queen Lady." Arthur spoke loudly knowing full well it would attract Cora's attention, which was why, of course, he offered no more. When Arthur glanced over his shoulder at Cora and grinned, she realized she'd been baited and therefore let herself settle back on her seat after having leaned his way. Of course, she tried to make it look as though she was just resituating herself, but they both knew better.

Turned out the bait-and-switch ended up on Arthur, however, because nobody asked him what else was happening, which left him no alternative but to just go ahead and tell. "Herm and Vera are comin' in from Indiana fer Thanksgivin'."

"Gonna be a long rampage," Harold said. "Thanksgiving is not for . . ."

"The rampage kin only last three more days since they're gittin' here Monday. They're comin' in a little early so as we kin have us a nice leisurely-like visit. Haven't seen 'em for years, ya know."

Gladys leaned back when Lester slid her breakfast in front of her. She picked up a piece of toast and bobbed her head back and forth like she was counting, which she was. "Do you mean to tell me they're going to be here for more than two weeks?"

"Yes, Mizz Mayor and math wizard extra-or-di-naire." Arthur bit into his toast looking very satisfied with his own cleverness.

"Poor Jessie," Gladys said. *The cousins AND you,* she thought, shaking her head in sympathy.

It was mid-Sunday afternoon when Dorothy decided to get up off the couch and take Sheba for a walk. It was shocking just how easy it was to become a couch potato. Before rising, she'd taken a gander at her stomach—two more pounds on the scale—and decided she'd morph into a bowl of couch *mashed* potatoes if she didn't get more exercise. "Let's get ourselves moving, Sheba!" Sheba was at the door before Dorothy had her coat buttoned and off they went. When they got to the first corner, however, Sheba turned and headed straight for May Belle's. Lickety split, she'd run up on May Belle's porch as fast as her skinny legs would deliver her. Earl, who was often watching out the window, had the door open before Sheba even had a chance to give it her customary pawing. Earl gave Dorothy a wide grin as she came up the stairs and announced to his mother that his Dearest Dorothy and Sheba had arrived.

"My, don't you look handsome today, Earl! I meant to tell you that in church." Dorothy peeled off her coat and handed it to Earl who hung it in the front closet. He was wearing a pair of dark gray pinstriped wool pants and a light blue, long-sleeved dress shirt with a dark blue sleeveless hand-knit vest buttoned over the shirt. Although the garments were worn thin, especially the pants, they were spanking clean and crisply pressed. May Belle, Earl's mother and Dorothy's best friend since childhood, had always been meticulous when it came to Sunday clothes, which Earl left on the whole day. Earl knew these very same dress-up clothes had been worn by his dad and it made him feel good when his mother said he looked just like his handsome father when he wore them. Earl's hair was slightly tussled, probably from removing his baseball cap when he got home, and anyone with less consideration for a forty-five-year-old with limited mental capacities might have reached up and smoothed it. Dorothy, however, respected Earl as the grown man he was. She wouldn't have just reached up and fixed Arthur's or Pastor's hair, so why would she do that to Earl?

After Earl closed the closet door, he responded to her compliment by casting his eyes toward his feet, but nonetheless, she saw the corners of his lips turn up ever so slightly. He leaned down and brushed a smudge off the toe of his left shoe.

"You look nice too, Dorothy," May Belle said as she rounded the corner, Sheba at her heels. May Belle fingered Dorothy's pink silk scarf tied around her neck, which set off her navy blue pant suit. Dorothy hooked her arm through May Belle's and said, "Where shall we sit our little mutual admiration party today, dearie?" She leaned her head toward May Belle's silver hair, who did the same in return. Even though Dorothy was a good several inches taller it was a gesture they never tired of sharing. May Belle didn't bother to answer Dorothy's question since Dorothy headed straight to her usual seat. "Guess I can become mashed potatoes on *anyone's* couch!" she exclaimed, patting her belly as she sat. Sheba jumped right up on her lap and rested her head on Dorothy's knee. "So much for our exercise," Dorothy said to her, giving her a good scruff behind the ears.

"How about a cup of coffee? I've got about one cup left," May Belle offered before seating herself in her favorite place, her green wing chair with hand-crocheted doilies on the arms.

"I'm coffeed out. A nice visit with good friends is all I need. And do not even *think* about getting me any sweets. You know you're my favorite baker in the universe, but I have got to get more exercise if I'm going to keep dropping by your house—which I am. Just being able to pop in is one of the best perks about my move from the farm."

May Belle suddenly clapped her hands together. "Say, somebody I know is in her birthday month!" May Belle loved birthday celebrations so much that she thought of any way she could to stretch them out. She especially loved making a fuss about Dorothy's birthday, which often got lost in the rush of holidays since it sometimes fell on Thanksgiving (which it did this year), so May Belle and Earl usually threw her their own private party either before or after. "If an elf were to ask me what you wanted for your birthday, what do you think I should tell him?"

"An elf, huh? Let's see . . . What should you tell an elf? What do you think your mom should tell an elf, Earl?" Earl shrugged and Dorothy winked at him. "Well, even though I don't need one more grain of sugar, since it *is*—or will soon *be*—my birthday, as the birthday girl, I'd tell an elf I wanted a lemon chiffon cake for an appetizer, a dozen double-chocolate brownies for the main course, three snick-erdoodle cookies for dessert and my good friends Earl and May Belle to share them with me."

"If an elf asks me, then that's just what I'll tell him," May Belle said, nodding her head with satisfaction. The ladies sat in silence for a few moments, thankful for their comfortable friendship.

"I declare," May Belle said, "Gertrude played her heart out in church this morning, didn't she? Her playing seemed to inspire the choir and *all* of us to sing so energetically! It made me feel so happy inside!" Gertrude Hands was United Methodist Church's faithful organist and the electronic keyboard player for the Partonville Community Band.

"And I believe more of us than ever—discounting you and me, of course—even hit the high notes," Dorothy said with a smile. "A Baptist friend of mine used to talk about raising the rafters at praise and worship meetings. I'd say we mild-mannered Methodists did a good job of at least coming close to those rafter-raising Baptists this morning." May Belle drew her hand over her mouth and laughed. She loved Dorothy's way with words.

"Well, I don't know about raising rafters, but I've got to take down my bedroom curtains and give them a good wash," May Belle said. "I had all intentions of doing that right after church today, but while you headed off with the altar guild to set up the Thanksgiving decorations, I came home and plopped myself in my chair. And *still* I feel like I could use a nap. Honestly, I think I'm still worn out from all the baking for the Pumpkin Festival and Centennial Plus Thirty festivities. I bet you are too. How'd it go with the decorating today, by the way? I can't wait to see it." Dorothy had confiscated leftover Pumpkin Festival garlands and grapevine wreaths and such before they'd been tossed into the garbage—something she'd bemoaned she hadn't done last year.

"It went. It would have gone better if Jessica Joy had been there to lend us her decorator's eye. Point out what would go best where. You know how gifted she is at that sort of thing. I'm sure you noticed she wasn't in church today. Paul, who had our adorable Sarah Sue strapped to his chest, said Jessica was feeling a little under the weather. Touch of something, I guess."

Katie walked through the farmhouse carrying a notepad, her Realtor's sensibilities in high gear. She was taking stock, trying to decide if the structure had any historical value, something she'd not previously considered. She'd just assumed that when the land was eventually developed, this old mice-laden house (as she'd recently come to think of it), along with the rest of the out buildings, would be bulldozed to make way for new homes (that's the way it happened!), maybe even a gated community and school, a shopping center, the works. No doubt those had been Colton Craig's visions when he'd made his under-the-table offer to Dorothy for her beloved Crooked Creek Farm last April, the sale Katie beat him to.

Since Dorothy had confided in only one person about his proposal and that had been Katie, Katie had, in a moment of—she had never been sure what all that moment had been about, although Dorothy kept referring to it as her answer to prayer—bought the place with full knowledge it was a gold mine. She had, just as under-the-table, overbid her arch rival and signed the deal, but not before assuring

Dorothy that at least twenty acres of the one-hundred-sixty-acre farm (the specified twenty including the swimmin' hole, Weeping Willy, Woodsy and Willoway, the trees Dorothy had long-ago named) would be donated to the conservation district for the development of Crooked Creek Park. Something to keep Dorothy's family heritage and fondest memories alive. Katie had been true to her word and in fact helped draw up the gift papers. She was also no fool (and she knew the action had caused Colton to sit up and take notice); any development around a park would considerably up the price of the land surrounding it. She hadn't been referred to as Kathryn Durbin, Development Diva, for nothing!

If Mr. Craig had thought about all the obvious angles—and he no doubt had—she would simply have to discover a few more before their luncheon. She was also absolutely sure he'd been lathered up about golf course possibilities when he'd made his original offer. Of course, that was before those twenty acres—twenty prime creek-access acres—had been donated. Nonetheless, she'd spent a goodly amount of research time chasing those options anyway. A stone unturned might have dollar signs pasted to the bottom of it. However, her research confirmed her initial suspicions: sans those twenty acres, there now wasn't enough land left for a regulation course (too bad Arthur and Jessie weren't ready to sell—or were they?), and Colton had already saturated the area with shorter executive and nine-hole courses. She'd checked "golf course" off her brainstorming list.

But what if she could also manage to build a lake? Would there be enough water to maintain the creek in the park and an upstream—or would it be downstream—lake? Lakes added development value. Something else to explore.

Still, she had the gut feeling (and her intuitive business gut was almost never wrong) there was something less obvious that made this land more valuable than met *anyone's* eye. One of the things she'd tapped into while Internet browsing—the thing that was inspiring her walk through the house, notepad in hand, competitive juices flowing—was the idea of a farm preservation project of some sort. What if she now donated the five acres that held the house and barn for a museum or something, maybe even set it up between the park and a lake? She'd heard about a couple of "working farms of the past" they called them. People in period costumes making apple butter and milking cows and such. As opposed to the plethora of golf courses already in place, she'd discovered there was no historical drawing card within a relatively large radius. Or maybe the barn could be transformed into a banquet center, health spa, artist's retreat center or. . . . That would still leave one hundred thirty home-buildable acres resting between a natural park and a point of interest. *Yes!* Another piece of possibility for her lunch date, if for no other reason than to simply dangle it under his nose as part of a bigger picture.

Oh, how well she remembered Keith Benton getting her ousted from her position. Oh, how well she remembered that he had often paired up on investments with the pompous Craig brothers. But when Colton had become a certified rat in her personal world was when she'd learned he'd single-handedly manipulated some foreign investors to throw their money behind Benton, which—in a chain reaction of events—ultimately led to her job loss. Although underneath it all she *admired* Colton's cunning, oh, how sweet were the possibilities for her single-handed revenge.

4

"Isn't this beautiful country, Herm?" Vera had her nose all but pushed up against the passenger window. They'd been driving along in silence for about twenty-five miles, which was a record. Normally Vera would have been chatting non-stop, same as Herm. They often talked at the same time, neither seemingly noticing the other was not only not listening but blabbing away too.

However, this time some mysterious force just seemed to have sealed their lips for a spell. Perhaps the silence was due to the fact that neither of them had slept well the last two nights, so excited were they to be setting out on a journey. They hadn't left their Indiana neighborhood since the last time they'd visited Partonville—unless you counted the two-night stay in Ohio when they attended that funeral—and they were long overdue for a change of scenery. Or maybe their odd silence was because of the full moon. Maybe it was just that they were saving up words for the visit.

"Did you say something?" Herm asked.

"Yes, Herm." She paused a moment until she remembered what it was. "I said isn't this beautiful country?" Vera thought the horizon—a wonderful blue-gray sky zip-locked to the black Illinois earth, a few trees hiding the seam—was stunning in its starkness.

Herm quickly checked Henrietta's rearview mirror to make sure nobody was coming up on him before he took his eyes off the road for a second to survey the beauty Vera was talking about, since surely it wasn't what was ahead of them: a vast flatness. Since she was looking out her window, he jockeyed his head around to get her point of view. Flat nothing. It was everywhere. He chose not to answer, hoping she wouldn't notice, which she didn't. She simply sighed a sigh that exuded the sound one makes when beholding grandeur, leaned her head back against the headrest and within a few moments was snoring, her mouth hanging agape.

Herm allowed his eyes to rest briefly on her profile. "Oh yes, it's beautiful alright. Plumb gorgeous. But no matter, I love you, my sweet pea," he whispered.

Jessie had been throwing things all morning. Since she'd been a champion semi-pro, fast-pitch softball catcher in her heyday with the best pickoff arm in the league—and she still played ball now, serving as the pitcher (knees too worn to get up out of the catcher's squat) for the Wild Musketeers, Partonville's mostly senior citizens' softball team—she still had quite an arm. It just came naturally to her to let it rip, it being anything she could get her hands on.

It seemed she'd been born with her internal engine constantly revving, making it next to impossible for her to sit still. Her inability to settle, coupled with an upbringing that, for the most part, trivialized "feelings" ("Obedience is what matters, Jessilyn," her parents would say when they sat her in the corner time and again for fidgeting), diverted her from a healthy exploration of such "feelings" as emotional frustrations and wounds, so she had early on learned to vent them outwardly—by winging things. Sports, baseball in particular, had been a positive outlet for pent-up emotions. But when frustrations arose and she wasn't on the playing field. . . . So far among the things she'd launched this morning was the remote control straight into the garbage can. *He gives more attention to the TV than to me.* Next she'd zinged the can of snuff she'd found hiding in the corner of his La-Z-Boy out the back door. *That rot can't be good for his gums or his gizzard!* (Unbeknownst to her, Arthur had not only retrieved his beloved items but hidden them from further abuse.) Her next frustration came in the form of his oldest and favorite pair of coveralls that were never hung up and were worn so thin she claimed, as she launched the wadded-up mass right at him, "I can nearly see your butt crack through these things! *(He asked for it!)* I don't ever want to see them again," she belted, "hear me?"

Since he'd been in motion when the pants came his way, he just grabbed hold of them, bundled them to his chest and kept on marching, right out the back door all the way to his pappy's old outhouse (stomping to burn off steam) where he changed into them. *Ya think yur so gol' dern smart; well, watch this!* Within a flash he marched back into the kitchen.

"I thought I told you . . ." Jessie started to say when she saw what he was wearing.

"You have done told me yur last thing, woman!" The volume of his bellow took her by surprise, which caused her to draw a deep breath and stiffen herself for the battle. For better or for worse, the Landerses' love language could best be described as snarking. As loud and exhausting as their noisy diatribing could be, it had, over the decades, simply become their communication default mode.

Arthur tossed the coveralls he'd changed out of onto the kitchen table, marched right over to his La-Z-Boy and disassembled the back of the chair from the seat. *Handy the way they make these so portable, which is one more reason I love 'em more than women!* It was such a pure and grateful thought that he actually patted the seat a couple of times like it was a giant St. Bernard sitting there at his feet. Then out the door he marched with the back of his beloved chair, straight to his pickup truck where he gently laid it in the bed. Jessie just watched, figuring he was finally going to get rid of that thing, which was nearly as old as his see-through coveralls. He marched back in and picked up the bottom of the chair, then proceeded to deposit it in the truck as well. But rather than coming back in to help her rearrange the furniture, which she was already doing to fill in the gap left by the chair's void, he marched back outside and climbed into the bed of his pickup and reassembled his chair. Then he got behind the wheel, fired up the engine and drove across the lawn right up to the back door where Jessie was now standing, having scurried there when she heard the engine turn over. "I'll be back when I return," he said with a note of finality.

"I don't know why you bothered to reassemble that thing just to take it to the dump."

"Is that what ya think I'm a doin'?"

She studied his face—his familiar, bold-featured face—through the screen door, through his truck window. Even though she was feeling a little guilty about throwing things *at* Arthur (although that never stopped her), her dander was up. She was sure he'd asked her a trick question so she chose not to answer; she just glared at him.

"I've been workin' nonstop for days," Arthur said more matter-of-factly than angry, "and I'm tired of bein' bossed around. It's time I git me some rest and the only way I see that happenin' is to git out of your rampage. And since ya told me to take my chair with me when I went, that's just what I'm a doin'."

"Arthur Landers, *your* cousin and his wife are due here within the hour. Now get yourself right back in here and help me finish up!"

Arthur's foot hammered down on the throttle. Gravel spit from behind his wheels, which kept him from hearing her uncommon and desperate "PLEASE!" and away he went. When he hit the ruts in the lane the La-Z-Boy bounced up and down like it was happily cheering to be going on a road trip. Since there was nothing Jessie could do to stop him, the best she could do was to throw something toward his back draft. The first thing she set her eyes on was a can of furniture polish. She was sick of cleaning anyway, so away it sailed.

Arthur plunked down in his La-Z-Boy, which was still in the bed of his truck, settled back with a smile and snapped up the footrest. He reclined and contemplated the fact that no chair in the whole world could or would ever fit him better; the fabric and padding were worn just where he was. "Can't even *see* my butt now, woman!" He'd pulled his truck under a tree in the back picnic area of the park. Not another soul was around. "Perfect," he said as he gazed up at the tree branches directly above him. The only thing that would have been more perfect was The Tank, Dorothy's now kaput 1976 battle-worn Lincoln Continental. Tinkering with engines—and oh, how The Tank always seemed to need a tinker or two—used to be Arthur's labor as well as his relaxation and thinking time. Now all that seemed left to distract or entertain him was breakfast at Harry's, a walk down to the creek or out to the ancient outhouse (out of service but filled with memories), mastering a new song on his Hohner harmonica or a rest in his La-Z-Boy. And when he didn't want to think at all—which seemed to happen more often than not lately—he turned on the TV. And he sure didn't want to think right now, especially about his hysterical wife; he just wanted to enjoy the silence.

I'll have to remember this spot when the leaves are back next summer. He pulled his pocket watch out of his good ol' coveralls and took note of the time. He figured he had just enough of it to take a short nap and get back before Herm and Vera arrived, which would undoubtedly be right on the dot since Herm kept a steady pace and had always been good at calculations like arrival times and such. He also guessed his absence would be just long enough to appropriately make his point with Jessie, whatever his point was.

Dorothy and May Belle sat at Dorothy's kitchen table nibbling on the last of the orange and black jelly beans left over from Halloween. Since May Belle didn't like the black ones, Dorothy picked through and ate those, leaving May Belle with her favorite flavor. Not only was orange May Belle's favorite of the Halloween colors, but out of all the jelly beans eaten by mankind. May Belle put her hand over her mouth and laughed when Dorothy stuck out her tongue, which had turned an awful putrid shade. "I would only make this sacrifice for my best of friends, May Belle."

"You don't fool me for a second, Dorothy Jean Wetstra. Your favorite jelly bean flavor has *always* been licorice! You're just pleasing yourself and we both know it."

"Busted! You know me too well."

"Yes, I guess I do—although after all of these years you can still surprise me."

"Oh, like when have I surprised you lately?"

"When you asked for a lemon chiffon cake for your birthday instead of angel food."

Dorothy studied the empty jelly bean bowl. "I am too full, May Belle. Why on earth did you let me eat all of those?" May Belle laughed again knowing full well that if Dorothy made up her mind to do something nobody could stop her. She watched Dorothy walk to the kitchen window where she stood gazing into the back yard for a moment. May Belle knew she was watching Earl tidy up her yard by the way she smiled.

"How's this for another surprise!" Dorothy exclaimed. She turned to face May Belle. "I think I've just had me an epiphany!" She laughed, having reminded herself of a television evangelist she'd heard recently. "Do you *know* how many people don't have enough of *anything* to eat in this world—dare I say right here in Partonville—let alone their choice of dessert? Plenty. And here I am fighting my weight and asking for more! What if I could turn my eating thoughts into feeding actions? Maybe something like a community Thanksgiving meal on Thanksgiving Day. A gift of thanksgiving." Like a runaway train picking up a head of steam, her enthusiasm was mounting with each turn of her mental wheels. "Sponsored by our church! Now wouldn't that just be the berries?"

May Belle instantly took to the idea, which Dorothy knew she would. "I wonder, though," May Belle said, tapping her index fingers together after rubbing the small of her back, "do you think any of us will have the energy to tackle this kind of an undertaking so soon after the Pumpkin Festival? Like you very well know, I for one am still recuperating."

"Good question." Dorothy sat down. She knew herself well enough to know that sometimes her spontaneous ideas needed to be reined in long enough to give her common sense time to catch up with her enthusiasm. They sat and stared at each other. It was true: they'd *both* pretty much worn themselves out for the festivities—although every speck of energy had been worth it. "Well, we still have awhile to refresh ourselves," she said with a tone of caution. "I wonder if St. Augustine's might be interested in cosponsoring such an event with our church? You know, share the responsibilities as well as the blessings." Her enthusiasm was taking over again. "And why does it have to be complicated and take a big bunch of doings? Just get a few people to volunteer to cook an extra turkey. Maybe Lester could do up a big pan of dressing, he's *always* so good about those kinds of things." Her mental wheels were now churning full throttle again.

"Well," May Belle said, a note of optimism in her voice, "I guess I could bake some pans of spice bars, which would be cheaper and easier to serve than pumpkin pie but still have the seasonal flavor."

"I think the boys are coming home for Thanksgiving and we Wetstras could take charge of potatoes. It would be a good transition too since for the first time we won't be on the farm for Thanksgiving." Dorothy's smile flattened out.

It had been only a matter of months since Dorothy had gotten the surprise offer by the Craig brothers, the farm had subsequently been sold to Katie Durbin, an auction had been held and Dorothy had moved from the place of her birth—the only home she'd ever known—into town. She'd moved into Katie's Aunt Tess's old house, which Dorothy had redecorated and made her own. And yet . . . would any home *ever* feel as much a part of her very soul as the farm? In all honesty, she wondered if the idea for the Thanksgiving dinner hadn't at least in part sprung to life because, try as she might, she couldn't stop feeling sad at the thought of not having Thanksgiving dinner at the farm. May Belle knowingly patted the top of Dorothy's hand. Dorothy's move into town hadn't been an easy one and May Belle knew that no matter how much she tried to hide it, Dorothy still pined for the land she loved. If there were a way May Belle could help with the transition, she'd do it.

"Dorothy, I *think* we could manage, Lord willing and our bodies hold out. It always makes me feel so good to feed folks," her voice strengthening at the possibility. "Yes, I'm plenty worn out right now, but like you say, we've still got some time, and it wouldn't be that much work if we shared the load. Just an extra turkey and some trimmings. . . . Certainly nothing like the Pumpkin Festival—especially if we *could* team up with St. Augustine's. We don't have that many younger folks in our church to pitch in, but even though I've heard tell their membership is going down just like ours is, they do."

"Maybe," Dorothy said somewhat tentatively, "we could just present the idea and see if they might fly with it, spare us old geezettes. I reckon the younger ones will have their own ideas about how things should be done anyway. Instant everything! Hard telling what all they know how to micro-wave these days."

"Before you volunteer your boys, Dorothy, are you sure they'll want to come home for Thanksgiving and get involved with something like this? The last time they were here you all worked so hard on the farm auction and you don't get to see them very often . . . might they just want to come relax and spend time with *you* this trip?"

Dorothy screwed up her lips. "I can't even *imagine* they won't like the idea. Those boys grew up watching their father volunteer for just about everything. I'm not sure if my grandsons will get to come. Last I heard, Vincent and Joan were still fussing with each other over how they were going to split their time with the kids for the holidays this year." Dorothy's younger son, Vincent, and his wife had been divorced for a couple of years, a continuing grief for everyone. Never had Dorothy imagined divorce would be a word that applied to anyone in her family, but so it was. *Lord, let them get over their pains and egos and make* kind *decisions for everyone!* she prayed each time she thought about them.

"We'll need to talk to Pastor, of course," May Belle said. "Think he'd mind if we used our church basement? I don't think more people would come than might fill that up, do you?"

"I'll give him a call later today. But let's not get ahead of ourselves. The St. Auggie's folks might not be as interested as we hope, in which case maybe we should just let it go this year, maybe start planning something a little earlier for next year. Let's take it one step at a time."

5

Jessie heard Henrietta's horn tooting from a quarter mile away. It was tradition among the Landerses to toot their horns when arriving and departing; it's just what they did, everyone hanging out windows or standing at their doorways flailing their arms like there was no tomorrow. *Where are you, Arthur Landers!* She peeled off the rubber gloves she'd been wearing to clean the toilet, which she gave a good flush, hoping the smell of the bleach water would disappear down the hatch too. But just in case it didn't, she spritzed the new bathroom deodorizer and quickly gave the air a sniff. *Doesn't smell like baked apple pie to me!* She made fast tracks to the kitchen, tossed the rubber gloves in the cabinet under the kitchen sink and walked outside to wait. She let out a big sigh realizing that whatever wasn't cleaned by now was just going to have to stay that way and that made her happy. She could see the dust kicking up at the end of the driveway as Henrietta's nose pointed right at her. Within moments Herm and Vera were, kink by kink, unfolding themselves out of the car. Since Jessie wasn't the hugging kind and everybody knew it, both Herm and Vera extended their hands in a greeting.

"Jessie!" Vera exclaimed, clapping Jessie's hand between hers. "You haven't aged one wrinkle!"

Jessie smiled and studied Vera's face as she readied to return the compliment, then realized she couldn't unless she told a whopper. She wondered if Vera had just done exactly that. Jessie had never been one to spend much time studying herself in the mirror. If you kept your hair cut short (she cut it herself) and didn't wear makeup, what was there to look at? She'd much rather spend her time either playing baseball or listening to sports (*especially* baseball, no matter which league or team—although she was partial to the Pittsburgh Pirates) on the radio (she'd needed distance glasses for a couple of years but didn't want to spend the money, so she'd purchased those cheap reading ones from Wal-Mart, which of course didn't do a thing to help clear up the fuzzy TV), digging in the garden, working crosswords or 500-piece interlocking puzzles (both of which her Wal-Mart glasses did help) and—of course—winging whatever.

"Herm," Jessie said nodding her head in a greeting. Herm shook her hand up and down so vigorously and for so long she thought he might rattle her brains loose.

"Hermie, honey! Settle down before you dislocate her pitching shoulder!"

Herm looked around Jessie toward the kitchen door, then surveyed the yard toward the shed but the shed doors were closed. "Where's that ornery husband of yours?"

"To tell you the truth, he's . . . um . . ."

Just then they heard a horn begin to honk. They turned to find Arthur's pickup tearing down the gravel road, then watched it rush up the drive. Arthur slammed it into park and hopped out. Herm took note that Arthur could still move pretty quickly for an old coot.

"Talk about the devil," Jessie said. Herm and Vera laughed; Jessie did not.

"Herman the Vermin!" Arthur said as Herm hobbled toward his cousin, his bad knees working as best they could. The men hugged each other so hard it made them both grunt.

"Arthur the . . . ," Herm shook his head and laughed. "Never could think of a good rhyme for that one, not in all the decades I've known ya! Maybe one of these days."

Arthur next hugged Vera with only a little less enthusiasm than he had shared with Herm. "So yur still married to him, huh? Only a saint of a woman would put up with the likes of such a rascally fella, Vera Landers."

"Ain't it the truth," she said while winking at Herm, the love of her life.

"What are you doin' with your La-Z-Boy in your truck, Arthur?" Herm had walked over to the pickup to see what he first imagined must be a new chair. It didn't take him long to recognize the old one: aside from the color of the fabric, its identical twin was safely and blissfully parked in his very own living room.

"Just airin' her out," Arthur said matter-of-factly. "Just airin' her out."

Herm looked out over the field far enough to spot his uncle's old outhouse. "See the shrine is still in place," he said. "We sure had us some good times in there when we was young, didn't we, Art?" Herm slapped Arthur on the back.

"I reckon we surely did." The two men stared out yonder like they were viewing a visitation from the Queen of England rather than staring at an old outhouse.

"How about you and I go into the house and find something more interesting to look at," Jessie said to Vera. "Like how about a nice cold root beer?"

"Sounds good to me!"

If there's one thing Vera had always been, Jessie thought, it was agreeable.

Vera and Jessie drank their root beers—Jessie swigging hers out of the bottle and Vera having hers over ice—and caught up on the daily things of life. Arthur and Herm strolled on out to the outhouse for old time's sake. Once there, Herm stepped inside the door and said, "Look-ee-here, Art." He was grinning from ear to ear. He unbuttoned the middle pocket of his coveralls (an unbreakable love for coveralls was as tightly knit into the Landers men's genes as was their love for Buicks and La-Z-Boys) and withdrew two cigars. Arthur's eyes lit up; it had been a long while since he'd enjoyed a fine cigar. Even though Jessie had bugged him for years to give up the "nasty stinking cigar habit," in the end he hadn't done it for her, which he surely never admitted. He'd watched some health program he'd seen on TV one night. A group of doctors was performing an operation on a guy with lung cancer and it was so gruesome it turned his stomach. Even though he didn't used to inhale his cigars and even though he used to smoke only about three of them a week, he couldn't get the images out of his mind. Not only did he give up cigars right then, he vowed to never watch that health channel again. But what the heck, one cigar every year or so, along with a little snuff now and again, wouldn't kill a man. And now here they were about to hide in the outhouse to smoke, just like when they were kids. Funny how the old feeling of hiding out—especially with a cigar in his hand—resurrected itself in his racing heart.

Arthur, Herm and their other two scalawag cousins used to take turns hiding in the outhouse and get in all kinds of trouble, especially when the leaves were on the trees and the outhouse wasn't so visible from the farmhouse. Not only had they smoked cigars and some of his dad's cigarettes in that tiny structure, but they'd repeatedly gone through one or another of their sister's diaries, hunkered down over a Sears catalog in which some of the models wore nothing but brassieres and girdles, and for various reasons tortured one another by holding someone's head down the hole until they swore they'd never tell—which they had not. Would the two stout men be able to fit inside, or would they have to be pried out, they wondered? The Landers cousins didn't last long in there this time, but nonetheless, it's where all of the day's favorite stories began after those first few silent and bliss-filled puffs. There was just something satisfying, they each realized without expressing it—which wouldn't have been very "Landers Man" at all—about being with someone who knew your stories and could nod a knowing head at you when you told them again anyway. In celebration, Arthur whipped out his Hohner harmonica and played a few bars of "Memories," a song he'd just mastered. They were sweet enough notes to bring a tear to Herman's eye. Although he couldn't imagine an entire play about cats, he had loved the words to that song since the very first time he'd heard it on the radio.

An hour later, the women, who were still at the kitchen table, heard the men approaching the house. Jessie had just finished telling Vera about the day's La-Z-Boy escapade and they were both laughing. Even though Jessie told the story without a hint of humor, Vera had found the whole thing hysterically funny and erupted in laughter. Although Jessie still didn't think it was *that* funny, recounting it and watching Vera's face light up lightened her up about it, too, and next thing she knew, she was laughing as well. Vera's ability to be happy about nothing was one of the reasons Jessie had taken to her the first time they'd met. Before the men entered the door, though—each carrying a half of the chair they'd retrieved out of the truck—Jessie told Vera she couldn't tell Herm about the Runaway La-Z-Boy, as Vera kept calling it, and Vera nodded her head in agreement. Although the menfolk had agreed to keep their little cigar escapade a secret, they knew from the gals' sniffing that they'd been discovered.

Late that night after they'd all gone to bed, Jessie heard Herm laughing like a hyena, Vera shushing him loudly as he laughed.

Vera had blabbed. Of course.

Katie was exhausted. She'd spent the entire late afternoon and part of the evening driving around the outskirts of Hethrow surveying the lay of the land, trying to put herself in Colton's head to imagine what he might be envisioning for his next move *(What else is he going after?)*, as he'd lost his prime expansion opportunity when he lost Crooked Creek Farm. Since he wanted to have lunch with her, however, she assumed he was making his move for his second chance at the farm.

To entertain herself between bouts of collecting stats, Katie mentally laid out the house of her dreams, the one she'd always wanted to build for herself, picturing it being the largest in the new Crooked Creek development, and of course the one located on the prime plot. *Where would that be? Backed up to the park where the view would always be one of green . . . but not too close to the historic site? Or health spa? Or . . .*

After it turned dark, she'd visited the library to look up old maps, scout newspapers and search survey results on population growth—many of the same things she'd done before making Dorothy her offer that had landed the farm. She was stunned when the library made the announcement they'd be closing in fifteen minutes, which would be 9 P.M. This morning she'd told Josh to do his homework when he got home and to go ahead and make himself a sandwich if she wasn't there in time for dinner; she never expected she'd be this late. When she'd phoned at seven, she'd gotten the machine. She figured Josh was down at the creek where he'd been spending much of his time lately. *He sure won't want to move. But he could still hang out at the creek; after all it will be open to the public during park hours as soon as the conservation district gets things in place.* He'd either be there or in the barn, a place of solitude he'd become as attached to as Dorothy. *And if there's any kind of farm preservation, he could even visit the barn. Just so he doesn't have to change schools—unless they build a new one in our development.*

Our development, she'd caught herself thinking again on her way home. Oh, my! Was she beginning to feel more at home in Partonville than she realized—mice, boredom and all? *Somebody spare me!* Gads, her mind was already a couple of years ahead of the clock. Either that or she'd completely lost it.

When she pulled up the lane she noticed the only light glowing from the house radiated from Josh's bedroom window. It was the familiar flicker of a television. She turned off the SUV's engine, grabbed her handbag and briefcase, then headed for the back porch. She was happy to see Josh had actually left his muddy shoes on the new rug. *Will wonders never cease!* She didn't bother flicking on the kitchen light; the glow of the back spotlight through the porch window was just enough for her to make her way to the kitchen table to deposit her items. She shed her coat, draped it over the back of a chair and, not unlike her son, walked directly across the floor to the refrigerator. She was starving; she hadn't even stopped for dinner. She reached for the fridge door and *SNAP!*

"OH!" she exclaimed as she jumped sideways and crashed into the counter. *SNAP!* near her elbow. *SNAP!* "OOOOOH!" As much as she wanted to lurch again she made herself stand perfectly still, her back plastered against the counter.

"JOSH! JOSHUA MATTHEW KINNEY! GET YOURSELF DOWN HERE RIGHT THIS INSTANT!" When the kitchen light suddenly flipped on, she threw her hand over her eyes.

"Mom! What are you doing down here in the dark?" He scanned the tripped mousetraps surrounding his mom on the floor and countertop. "OHMYGOSH! Did any of them get you? Are you all right?" His mom was as stiff as a board, like somebody had yelled FREEZE during one of those old yard games.

"I *am,* Joshua . . . I am . . . Thank goodness I didn't take my shoes off! I am. . . ." And then she doubled over laughing as she spied the multitudes of mousetraps that lined the baseboards and countertops. "I am trapped!"

"No, Mom, Shelby did not come in the house or the barn. Shelby wasn't involved at all; Kevin took me shopping and brought me home."

Dear Alex and Outtamyway (a.k.a. Original Bearer of Mouse-in-the-house news),

What a night it was last night! You haven't heard all of this, Alex, but here's the recap: Dorothy told mom there were mice on the farm and mom then found "evidence." She has yet to call "it" anything else. (Come on mom, just one time at least call it DOO!) Since I thought it was so funny (and mom said you did too, Dorothy), she told me I was the one who had to clean "the evidence" out of the drawers and deal with the issue, disposing of anything the traps might catch.

Good thing the "anything" that tripped a few traps the first night they were set didn't get caught in one of them because otherwise I'd have to be getting rid of . . . MOM!

If either one of you come to visit, BEWARE! (And Alex, when *can* you get down here from Chicago again? And Dorothy, when are *you* coming to the farm again so we can get in one last crawdad hunt before it gets too cold? And Alex, that crawdad hunt invite goes for you too, man! And Dorothy, think your grandsons are gonna make it for a visit before the snow flies? Questions. I've got questions.) Mom seems to think I went to the extreme, but I say if you want to catch ALL the mice, set a ton of traps. It didn't seem to me like a dozen in the kitchen was too many since those things are so cheap to buy! The expensive part is the cheese since the only stuff we had on hand was mom's gross cheese from the health food store in Chicago. (I didn't think the mice would even like it but it's all we had.) Not sure which made her madder: "the evidence," getting snapped at by traps or seeing what I'd put in them. Poor mom . . . Believe it or not, though, we did end up sharing a good laugh. (Score one for the momster!)

Later, you guy and guy-ette. Gotta do homework.

Joshmeister

Josh,

What will you think of next for entertainment down there on the farm? Trust me, there's nothing that exciting happening here in the city. Unless you count the fact that Jennifer (yes, THAT Jennifer) smiled at me in the hall yesterday. I might try asking her out—again. Speaking of women, say hi to Shelby for me, you love-struck sap. Later. English exam tomorrow.

Alex

PS I'm talking to mom about maybe coming down there. Will let you know what she decides. She probably won't say until after she gets my latest English exam grade. Don't hold your breath.

Dear Joshmeister (and Alex too),

BUDGET HINT: mice really like peanut butter. But it

sounds like they don't stand a chance unless they learn to fly. Now wouldn't that be a sight! (They could dive-bomb us with "evidence.")

As for a crawdad hunt, I'm ready when you are. Don't answer me tonight since you're supposed to be studying, but how about this Saturday morning? If we can believe the weatherman (which we usually cannot), it's supposed to be warmer this weekend.

Now get back to the books. Both of you. And Alex, "i" goes before "e" except after "c" . . . then again, sometimes that doesn't apply either. HA!

Outtamyway

6

"I just can't imagine why someone in town hasn't thought of this before," Dorothy said as she leaned in toward Pastor Delbert Junior who was sitting across from her at his desk, "especially since times have been a little tough for so many folks the last couple of years, what with the mine layoffs and all. Come to think about it, though, I guess there've always been folks who are alone on holidays. Folks whose families are scattered hither and yon or who've passed on."

"Isn't that often the way of it, Dorothy? Every time I use the plastic squeeze ketchup bottle I wonder what took us so long to come up with it."

Dorothy hesitated a moment, shifting gears from Thanksgiving to ketchup. She figured out that he was talking about the simplicity of just squeezing the plastic ketchup bottle versus pounding a glass one to death. She nodded her head in agreement. "Do you think folks at St. Auggie's will be interested? I know you and Father O'Sullivan are good friends. Should you run it by him or should I? Or is there . . ."

"Whoa, Dorothy! One thing at a time. Have you presented this idea to our own Social Concerns Committee? Sounds like something under their jurisdiction. I know you're on the committee, but what do the others think?"

Dorothy sighed. The last thing she wanted to do was activate Gladys, the head of the committee, and, in Gladys's own opinion, the boss of the town—if not the universe. No sirree, if they were trying to keep things simple, giving Gladys the reins would not be the answer. She liked May Belle's thoughts about the younger women at St. Auggie's maybe running the show. But how to get Gladys to go along with *that*?

"No, I haven't talked to our committee yet. I will, though, before we contact anyone at St. Auggie's." Pastor straightened his glasses from right to left, then left to right as he studied her. "You look like you're not at all sure about this, Pastor Delbert. What are you thinking?"

"I'm thinking, Dorothy, that there isn't much time to prepare. I'm thinking that you'd have no idea how many folks might show up, so how could you plan? I'm thinking my glasses are making me crazy and I'm wondering if I made a mistake not even attempting to try contact lenses. I'm thinking, Dorothy, that I am not concentrating very well today."

Dorothy relaxed her eyebrows, smiled and nodded her head up and down. "My moment with the Big Guy went just about like this the other night. I sat down in my prayer chair next to my bed, picked up my Bible, said 'Good evening, Lord,' and the next thing I knew, I was picturing myself in the barn staring out the window at the harvested fields. 'Sorry,' I said, and started praying again. Wouldn't you know that within five seconds my mind had wandered off again? I can't imagine being God, can you?"

With a punch of determination Pastor rammed his glasses up on his nose as though if he pushed hard enough they might stay there for more than ten seconds. "Dorothy, sometimes I can't even imagine being *me* and this is turning into one of those moments."

"You know, Pastor Delbert, I think you could use a vacation."

"Dorothy, you sound just like my wife. She's been telling me that for months."

"She's right, you know. But before you go on vacation, how about we finish discussing the possibility of a Thanksgiving dinner."

"Why don't you go ahead and give Father O'Sullivan a call yourself. He'd be delighted to hear from you anyway. He always asks about you when we get together for coffee. But don't forget: you need to get approval from *our* committee first."

"If we *can* get this worked out, do you think we could hold it in our church basement?"

"I don't see why not."

"At least that's one detail off the list!" Dorothy stood and Pastor followed suit. As usual, he stood so quickly that his well-worn office chair rolled back away from him and crashed into the wall, leaving its next notch in the paint.

"I'll keep you posted!" Dorothy whirled on her heels and began chugging up the stairs to the narthex before Pastor had even said good-bye. She was on a mission. Within thirty minutes after she'd returned home, she'd made all the calls.

◇◇◇

Sarah Sue chewed on her fist, then on her teething ring, then on her other fist. She was lying on her back in the portable crib Katie had purchased for Jessica as a baby gift a few months earlier. Although Katie believed it to be a practical gift, she'd also selected it with slightly selfish motives knowing it would enable Jessica to feel more secure coming out to the farm for a visit since she'd have a place to safely hold Sarah Sue captive once she started to roll and roam a little.

"Why is it so entertaining to watch a baby chew on things?" Jessica mused more than asked. Sarah Sue's heart-shaped mouth was an exact duplicate of her mother's and they smiled at each other with adoration.

"Because it means you're not doing something else more taxing and because babies just naturally make us happy," Katie said, never once removing her eyes from Sarah Sue's wet chunky fingers that thrashed through the air as fast as her little legs were kicking.

"Yes," Jessica said flatly as she leaned back in her chair and gazed out Katie's living room window, "babies make us happy."

"You say that like you're not sure today. Was Sarah Sue up last night?"

"Nope. I was, though."

"Bad dream?"

"You might say that." Jessica was still staring out the window wishing her stomach would stop rolling while at the same time being grateful it didn't feel like it was rolling quite hard enough to make her sick—at least not at the moment. Katie stared at her friend, waiting for further explanation, but none came. She bent down, scooped Sarah Sue into her arms and planted a kiss on her forehead.

"So," Jessica said as she folded her hands over her abdomen, "tell me about the great mousetrap adventure. You said you had quite the story to share."

"How about I get us something to drink first." Katie gave

Sarah Sue one more kiss, this time on her left ear, then passed her to her mother who'd raised her arms. "Want water, iced tea, diet cola, maybe a glass of wine?"

As tempting as a glass of wine sounded, Jessica knew she better take a pass on it, just in case. "I'll have an ice water, please." She wasn't one for much imbibing, but every once in awhile a small glass of wine did her good.

"Be right back. Hold your places," Katie said over her shoulder.

Jessica put Sarah Sue back in her portable crib, then re-arranged herself on the couch in slow motion as though doing so would keep her body from stirring up trouble. She grabbed hold of a lock of her hair and began twisting it around her finger while she stared at her daughter, trying to imagine what it would be like to have a newborn too. How old would Sarah Sue be when the baby was born? *Gads! Barely over a year!* She put her hands on her abdomen again and groaned. It just couldn't be. That's all there was to it. Financially it would be a disaster, although she was sure, like always, God would help them find a way. But emotionally . . . she just wasn't sure she had it in her.

Katie came back with their drinks and the two of them chatted for another hour. Jessica barely took a sip. When Katie had to repeat a couple of things to her, Jessica finally realized she was now spending more time fretting she might get sick than listening. "I gotta get going," she said, picking Sarah Sue up and settling her on her cocked hip.

Katie picked up the diaper bag and slung it over Jessica's shoulder for her. "Thanks for coming out. Want the crib?"

"Nah. Just leave it here again. This is the only place I bring it anyway, since I get so few breaks." The two of them passed through the kitchen, Jessica having parked her old compact car near the back door where everyone always parked. Her eyes landed on the plastic bag with the rolled up nubby rug sticking out the top. She walked over for a closer inspection, fingering the texture with the hand that wasn't wrapped around her daughter. She turned and looked at the kitchen, then back at the rug.

"Perfect colors! Perfect. And I love the feel of it. Where you gonna put it?"

"Back on the store's shelf. I bought it for inside the back door over there but the door won't clear it. I tried putting it in front of the sink but it's too bulky there. I just love the looks of that thing, but it just won't work."

Jessica walked over to the back door and squinted her eyes around Katie's kitchen. "Oh! You know where it would look wonderful? Across your kitchen table. Either direction. If you ran it the short way it could serve as two placemats. If you ran it lengthwise," she said, walking toward the table, "you could put a centerpiece on it and . . ."

Katie squinted her eyes like Jessica was doing. It was a mystery to Katie how Jessica could "see" this way. All she saw was a rolled-up rug sticking out of the top of a bag and an empty kitchen table. "Think? I don't see it."

Jessica plucked the rug out of the bag and tried to place it on the table while still holding her daughter. "Here," Katie said, taking the rug, "let me do it." The minute the rug hit the table she knew her friend was, as always, precisely right about anything having to do with decorating. "You, my dear, are a genius. This makes the most perfect table runner! I swear, there isn't a problem you can't fix!"

"Yes, there might be," Jessica replied quietly. But that's all she said before she left.

The Landers clan didn't arrive at Harry's until 8 A.M. After they'd all agreed that breakfast out would be nice, Arthur had stated the night before he always arrived when the doors opened at exactly 6 A.M. "It's good to get there at the crack of dawn," he'd said, to which his cousin had responded, "Sometimes, Arthur, dawn don't crack until later than you think. Kind of like an optical illusion." Three of them had laughed; Arthur had just grunted but he'd also hoped Herm and Vera would awaken earlier than they'd *been* getting up, which was later each day. Somehow since their last visit he'd managed to forget their penchant for sleeping in since, well, it just wasn't like a Landers to sleep in. When they'd finally arrived at Harry's, there wasn't room for the four of them to sit at the counter together so, with a sigh, Arthur made the sacrifice and bypassed his stool. They sat at Cora's usual post at the window table since she had already come and gone.

"What'll it be?" Lester asked as he whipped his pad out of the pocket in his makeshift apron, which was really a large dishtowel doubled in half and tied around his slim hips. Although he usually donned an ugly stained apron, when he looked through his freshly washed apron inventory today—all two of them—he'd decided to toss them both in the rag bag. He'd decided that sometimes a guy could be too frugal and made a note to call the restaurant supply place tomorrow.

"Could we see a couple of menus, please?" Vera asked. Arthur gave Lester an apologetic shrug. Lester pointed to the sheet of paper standing between the salt and pepper. The makeshift menu was hand scrawled and tucked in a plastic page protector. Vera picked it up and began to read it out loud to Herm. "Two eggs, two strips of bacon, home fries, toast and coffee for . . ."

"I don't care how much it costs, Vera. We're on vacation!" A tone of happiness wrapped his words.

"Right, Herm," she said, reading the rest to herself, only her lips moving.

"That'll be separate checks," Herm said to Lester while pointing two fingers first at himself and Vera, then at Arthur and Jessie. Although they might be on vacation, he wasn't that big of a spender. Jessie kicked Arthur under the table to stop him from saying what she knew was on his lips.

"Whatcha kickin' me for, woman?"

Jessie's face darkened. She should have known better. "I was just trying to cross my legs, Arthur."

"Jist bring us one check," Arthur said to Lester. "I guess I kin afford to buy my cuz and his wife a breakfast. After all, we ain't seen 'em for a long spell. That and I figure he kin buy the next meal—or several."

Vera tapped Herm's leg under the table, figuring she knew what he was about to say.

"Rather than working to keep track of whose turn it is, let's just keep things separate this trip, okay?" Herm looked back at Lester and repeated his two-by-two gesture. Lester grunted and flipped his pad back to the previous page again. Lester remembered Herm all too well from the last time he was at the grill. He just wanted to get their orders and be done with them.

Both women sat in stunned silence since neither of their husbands had said what they'd expected they would, even though neither had been able to take a hint. Jessie thought

Arthur was going to tease—or should she say chastise?—Herm about it being his turn to buy since Arthur was buying all the meals out at the farm, even though she was cooking them, and Vera thought Herm was going to remind Arthur that he and Vera had bought that fancy dinner out at the country club the last time Arthur and Jessie came to visit them, since he'd brought it up a time or two before. What neither woman expected, however, was what Herm said next, and that was what he said to Lester, which sadly reminded them all of what they'd forgotten since last they were together.

"Correct me if my memory serves me wrong here, Lester," Herm said (feel the unleashing begin!), "but ain't you the guy ol' Arthur stole Jessie from?" (ShaZAM!) This time the women responded like a professional wrestling tag-team, simultaneously hiding nothing and whapping their husbands on the arm above the table (well, Jessie whapped and Vera tapped). They did so in hopes it would snap some sense into them before they said anything else and this age-old sore spot revved up again. Although Arthur and Herm seemed to think it was just old water under the bridge and something to poke fun at, it seemed perfectly clear to the women that by the look on Lester's face, it was not a topic for open season. Water under the bridge? Yes. Funny? No.

"I'm just here to take your breakfast order," Lester said with disgust as he folded his pad closed and stuck it back in the folds of his makeshift apron. "Let me know when you're ready. I got people to feed." He spun on his heels and was back behind the U before either of them could open their mouths.

"Still a sore loser, is he?" Herm said to Arthur with a chuckle.

Arthur gave Jessie a sideways glance and sucked air through his teeth. "Some days, Hermie," Arthur said way too loudly, "I ain't sure if I won or lost!" Arthur slapped Herm on the back and the two of them guffawed. Vera's face turned red with embarrassment for Jessie (the line was thin between teasing and torture, she thought) and Jessie's face turned red with anger—although by some miracle of the moment she didn't knock Arthur to the floor with the windup and uppercut she was envisioning.

Herm and Arthur were talking about Buicks by the time Lester was back to take their orders, which took place without further conversation or incident. Even if somebody had tried to chat with Lester about anything other than food, he wouldn't have stayed long enough to hear it. He was busy cooking up a giant batch of green beans with bacon and onions to accompany the evening's liver special and they needed lots of stirring. Besides, those old "remember when" conversations were fine—unless they involved the era when he and Jessie were sparking. Then he hated them and always did his best to nip them in the bud. There was nothing funny about it, he thought, and everyone, especially in that Landers clan, should know better by now.

Truth be told, Lester spent a few hours each year—no, not days, weeks or months but nonetheless concentrated hours—allowing his mind to imagine what his life might have been like had *he* proposed first to the woman for whom his young heart so strongly yearned nearly six decades ago. More often than not, the what-ifs rolled around at the holidays; since he'd never married he'd had to train himself to live with a brief, dull, lonely ache when it snuck up on him.

Even though Partonville was small, he didn't see Jessie that often since Arthur usually came to Harry's solo. But when he did see her, every now and again—just for a moment—his heart still skipped a beat. No matter that her once long and thick black hair was now neckline short, thinned and snow white, her eyes still held that mischievous fire that had first captured his attention clear back when they were in sixth grade. He noticed it most during baseball season when Jessie took to the mound and strutted her stuff. Her hazel eyes with prominent orange flecks still flashed a captivating hue when her adrenaline was pumping. This past summer when, thanks to her pitching, the Musketeers had beat the Palmer Pirates for the championship (of course, an opponent's arthritis and somebody's recent cataract surgery hadn't hurt either), he'd suffered a brief bout of what-ifs just recalling the spark in her eyes and the ancient longing in the pit of his belly as she'd bared down to clinch the win, especially when he'd seen Arthur kiss her right on the lips afterwards—an episode that had stunned everyone who'd witnessed it, including Jessie.

It wasn't that Lester was jealous of Arthur; Lester had neither a jealous nature nor a bent toward severing long-standing friendships. And it wasn't that Lester still pined for Jessie. No, he had long ago determined that woman would have plumb worn him out and that Arthur had saved him a heap of trouble learning that—the hard way! And Jessie, well, she'd never given Lester so much as a flirty glance once she'd said yes to Arthur's surprise proposal and their runaway marriage, but then she'd never been the flirty type to begin with. No, she'd faithfully stuck with her crabby old coot of a husband through thick and thin. But in spite of it all, when that old feeling did visit him for a spell, said visiting time was most often spent replaying the moment he learned the love of his life had turned to another.

Even when the She-Bats were out of town, word always got back to Partonville if the traveling league's most renowned catcher with the fiercest pickoff arm (1942 Golden Glover, she was) had changed the momentum and the She-Bats had come away the victors. Harold reported every detail in the *Partonville Press*. While farmers tended their crops and critters, coal miners picked and shoveled away, kids played and the womenfolk pickled beets and did the laundry (and Lester K. Biggs opened the grill at precisely 6 A.M. and closed at precisely 6 P.M. six days a week, flipping burgers and cooking up meatloaves while pining for his heartthrob to return), Jessie played her heart out. Everyone would drop whatever they were doing and cheer when news came down the pike about Mugsy McGee (later to become Mugsy Landers), their hometown hero. Partonvillers followed her career as though she played for the big leagues, which in their eyes she certainly did since she was a reason for pride, a constant source of hope. ("Yup, corn is down, but did you hear who Mugsy's playin' this weekend?) Although Jessie had hinted a time or two—and on occasion just flat out barked—that she'd sure like it if Lester, her steady beau (although Jessie didn't think in terms of such flowery words or romantic notions) for the last two years, could shut the grill just *once* and come root for her, alas, he couldn't. "Won't," she would say. "Can't," he would respond. And then she would shake her head and pack her bags for the upcoming road trip while Lester prepared the next day's menu.

One sweltering mid-summer day Jessie returned to town after the She-Bats had finished playing back-to-back, out-of-town tournaments. Word had already spread she'd batted .400 in the first one! Lester had watched the clock all afternoon. At the click of the closing lock he scurried to get dishes and counters washed up, prepare a few things for the morrow, take a quick shower, splash a few drops of Old Spice (an extravagant but worth-it expense, he'd decided, especially if Jessie noticed) into his hand and smear them on his cheeks and neck and head out the door. He all but jogged to Jessie's house, arriving by 6:54 P.M. (he'd checked his watch just before turning the corner) only to find her sitting on her front porch stoop, Arthur right beside her. They were both laughing so hard their heads were thrown back as though they were looking at the sky. Lester slowed his gait, stuffed his hands in his pockets and walked up the sidewalk. He worked to steady his labored breath—from both the hustle and a sight he did not like, not one bit. This wasn't the first time he'd found Arthur at Jessie's house but it was the first time Arthur hadn't offered an excuse as to why he was there, like "I had to return a bat I borrowed last time she was in town," or "I was just passin' by when I saw her pull up," or "Just keepin' her company till you got here." Lester also didn't remember Arthur sitting this close to Jessie before either.

Even though Lester and Jessie had been dating for a long spell and they were, after all, in their mid-twenties, which was pretty old for single folks in those days, they'd never talked about a future together—although most in Partonville, especially Lester, assumed they had one. Lester was waiting until he felt more financially secure, having recently purchased Harry's Grill from Harry Schwartz after Harry's painful rheumatoid arthritis finally locked him up more often than it let him go. Lester had visions of his name over the coffee cup sign above the door. LESTER'S GRILL. He didn't have the finances to change the sign right away, but when he could put his name above the door then he figured he'd finally have enough to offer Jessie before he popped the question. Something that would cause her to want to settle down, give up all that traveling, stay home and start a family. Maybe as a wedding gift he'd even rename the grill "Lester and Jessie's." When he really allowed himself to dream, he envisioned their children running the grill long after their parents were gone.

But there was Arthur, sitting so close to her. *I should have popped the question right then,* he'd said to himself on more than one occasion. Instead he stood awkwardly waiting for Arthur to get up and leave so he could sit down beside Jessie. But Arthur didn't get up. Lester waited for Jessie to scoot farther away from Arthur and pat the cement between them, signaling Lester to take his place by her side, but she did not. The two of *them* sat side by side and he stood before them until dusk turned to dark and both men went home. He'd never once gotten close enough to her for her to even get a whiff of his new cologne.

Jessie was a passionate woman; he shouldn't have been so decent, waiting so long to kiss her, then being so polite about it when he had given her that initial peck on the lips. He should have swept her up into his arms, pulled her close and held her there, whispering his earnest love into her ear then out into the world.

He should have seen it coming.

Within two days Jessie was back on the road again, Lester was making what would become his famous signature smashed taters and Arthur was driving his first Buick (used as it may have been) down the hard road as fast as it would go straight toward Jessie. When the game was over, Arthur waited for her outside the ballpark gates, told her she'd played a wing-ding of a game, gave her a big smooch and just like that he'd said, "Woman, let's get hitched." Just like that she'd said, "Why not?" Rather than Jessie going back to her motel room with the rest of the team, she'd hopped in the front seat next to Arthur and they'd driven fifteen miles to a justice of the peace and just like that they were married. Arthur stayed to cheer her on during the rest of that road trip and for many more to come.

Two days after their marriage, while Arthur and Jessie honeymooned around the tournament schedule, Lester was chopping and peeling for the day's beef stew special. Harold Crab came into the grill, sat down at his usual spot at the U and began pretending to read a magazine while tapping the fingers of his left hand on the tall metal napkin holder and his right fingers on the countertop. Lester and Harold were the only ones in the grill.

"You got the jitters today?" Lester asked Harold as he poured him a cup of coffee.

"You heard from Jessie the last couple days, Lester?"

"Nope. But I'm expecting her home on Thursday." He beamed at the thought.

Harold moved his magazine aside and began to re-arrange the salt and pepper shakers in front of him, then he moved them to the other side of the metal napkin holder. He blew on his coffee but didn't take a sip. He set the cup back down in the saucer, moved the saucer slightly to the left, cupped his hands around it, then sat perfectly still staring at the counter for a minute. "Lester," he said to Lester's back while he dumped the onions into the pot, "I've got something to tell you. As much as I don't want to be the one to tell you, I reckon somebody's got to, and I'd rather it was me than . . ."

"For crying out loud, Harold! You're acting like a girlie-girl!" Lester grinned as he picked up the cutting board and scraped the carrots into the pot with his big butcher knife. He turned to face Harold, knife still in hand, and leaned on the counter in front of him. "Go ahead and spill your beans but make it quick. I've got stew to stew."

Harold looked straight into Lester's eyes. "Arthur and Jessie got married two days ago, Lester." Lester stared at him unblinking. Harold pulled in his lips. Having married the love of his life the year before he couldn't imagine receiving this type of news himself. It must have sliced right through Lester's heart as though the giant knife he held had driven through him, although Lester's expression never changed.

Lester suddenly and silently turned back toward the grill, his back to Harold again, and dumped the potatoes into the pot. There was no need to question this information; Harold was a newspaper man who always got the story straight. Harold stayed for two coffee refills waiting to see if Lester might want to ask anything, say . . . anything, but he didn't. It was the same nothing everyone said to Lester about the situation from that day forward, for what was there to say?

But now, Herm had said it in black and white. Again.

". . . aren't you the guy ol' Arthur stole Jessie from?" In a repeat performance of his last visit, unbeknownst to Herm, the loaded words had flown out of his mouth straight into Lester's vulnerabilities—and right before the holidays.

For a month after Herm had last asked Lester that question, Lester hadn't thought to put a collection jar out on his counter for this cause or that, his charitable spirit having temporarily been knocked out of him. (Even Gladys, who could be as hard as nails, thought she knew what must have instigated that lapse since she'd been within earshot of the episode, and the only other time Lester hadn't put out the jar for a long spell was after Jessie had married. *Both of those Landers men are as dumb as rocks!* she'd thought.) Since that fateful wedding day Lester had swallowed his private wounds (and time, the great healer, had done its job) and he and Arthur (who assumed Lester hadn't really cared *that* much about Jessie to begin with or he'd have made his move long before Arthur did) had continued to engage in their usual friendly bantering. When the passing dark cloud arrived during Herm's last visit, their bantering took an ugly turn that quickly mutated into out-and-out caustic barbs, causing discomfort to many who sat at the U. The barbs were never direct hits at temporarily opened wounds, but nonetheless, they were ugly barbs. "Settle down, you two," Harold had said on more than one occasion. "You're giving me heartburn!" Eventually the whole hullabaloo passed and things got back to normal. Arthur never had been entirely positive what had gotten Lester so riled, but surely, Arthur thought, Lester had gotten over *that*. And if he hadn't, well, there twern't much to be done about it now, was there? All's fair in love and war. Marriage was marriage. Water under the bridge. End of story.

◇◆◇

On the outskirts of town, Jessie fumed. Arthur's insensitivity at implying he might have *lost* to Lester when he married her—probably loud enough for Lester to have overheard, and in front of Herm and Vera, the consummate lovebirds!—made her . . . furious. Furious because furious was much easier to deal with than wounded. Furious was at least active! Although she'd never once (including now) wished she'd married Lester instead of Arthur, on a day like today when Arthur acted like such a hyena, she found herself briefly speculating about a few things, like what her life might have been like if she'd have been the least bit willing to give up baseball (something Arthur had never asked her to do) to become the wife of the ever steady, ever sensible Lester K. Biggs.

7

Dorothy, Gladys and May Belle sat around May Belle's inviting dining room table (Sheba curled up under it), complete with doilies, a silk-flower fall centerpiece (a gift from Dorothy several years ago) and May Belle's good tea set. They were the only ones on UMC's five-strong Social Concerns Committee who could make it for the makeshift meeting. Nellie Ruth and Jessica had phoned at the last minute, Nellie Ruth saying something personal had come up—although they suspected it was some*one* personal and his name was Edward Showalter (those two seemed to be quite the item lately)—and Jessica just announcing she wouldn't be there. She didn't offer an excuse. The committee usually held their monthly meetings at church, but since this was a special gathering and May Belle and Dorothy wanted simply to get Gladys's approval (which would make for a committee majority), May Belle had suggested neutral ground for the meeting might be best. "Gladys isn't used to presiding over my dining room table," May Belle said to Dorothy with a chuckle, "although I'm sure she'd like to." May Belle didn't bother telling anyone her back had been aching all day since she'd climbed on and off her step stool hanging freshly washed, starched and ironed curtains in both the bedrooms, not to mention her back had still not quite recovered from all the baking for the festival. ("Ovens are not designed for the lower back," she'd said to Earl in the midst of her baking marathon.) Although Earl had done what he could to help with the curtains, it was usually too hard for him to get the right hooks in exactly the right rod slots so she did that part herself. No, she hadn't mentioned her troubles; she just said she'd be delighted to host and agreed with Dorothy's comment that it would be easier for her to serve her customary refreshments right there in her own home for a change. And no matter how poorly she might have felt, it never occurred to May Belle not to bake since baking was her gift, her hobby and her passion. This morning it had been a caramel pecan coffee cake, one of her personal and irresistible gooey creations.

Gladys started to call the "emergency meeting" to order but Dorothy jumped in and said since it was neither an emergency nor an official meeting she could dispense with the formalities. "This is more of a bat-around gathering to see if we're interested in supporting *(Yes! Dorothy thought. We will play a* supporting *role!)* a new community project. But we have to first determine if we're even up to such a thing so close after the Pumpkin Festival and Centennial Plus Thirty. I know we just about wore ourselves out and the older we get the longer it takes to get our spunk back!"

"Speak for yourself, Dorothy. Even as the Acting . . ."

"Aside from *you,* of course," Dorothy said, interrupting her highly esteemed and fully combustive Acting Mayor Gladys. Dorothy went right on to share the idea of a community Thanksgiving dinner and assured Gladys they already had Pastor Delbert's approval. Like a politician ever aware of sound bites, Dorothy kept referring to the key phrases of "younger women," "shared responsibilities" and "our *supporting* role." May Belle jumped in to talk about bringing different faiths together in a cooperative role, knowing Gladys would take to that idea since her son and his family were members at St. Augustine's. Dorothy said she'd be talking to Father O'Sullivan as soon as they had consensus. Dorothy and May Belle hoped they were talking fast enough to steamroll Gladys before she had a chance to get wound up, which, much to their surprise, worked. Almost.

"I think we'll need another pot of coffee to dig into the details, May Belle," Gladys said, trying to gain authority. May Belle's eyes darted to Dorothy, who shrugged.

"One thing I don't think we'd lack," May Belle said as she slowly (and painfully) stood to gather the empty plates, "is volunteers to help cook and serve. Oh, and clean up of course." Just then Earl passed by the table. "Earl would love to be on the setup and cleanup committees, wouldn't you, Earl? You did such a wonderful job with the festival duties." If his mother thought it was a good idea, then so did he. He nodded his head and kept walking.

"Earl," Dorothy said to his back, "I'm so glad we can always count on you." He turned his head just enough to receive her warm smile.

"I'm not as confident as you are about finding enough volunteers, May Belle." Gladys was frowning as she spoke. "You know the folks who don't need to come for a handout will be engaged with their own families."

"Gladys, providing a handout is hardly the spirit of this endeavor," Dorothy said.

"What else can you call offering free food?" Gladys wanted to know. "Or are we planning on at least charging a nominal fee?"

"That's the beauty of a supporting role and a cooperative effort, Gladys. *We* do not have to figure all of this out! But for the record," Dorothy said aloud and silently prayed, *Lord, help me find my nice,* "an offering of thanksgiving is what we'd be giving and you don't receive payback when you are the one giving, Gladys. Dear. It would be the churches' way of thanking God on Thanksgiving in a physical and practical way."

"How on earth does that thank God? Seems to me it just helps breed dependency."

Dorothy squeezed her hands together until her fingertips turned white. *Lord, in the spirit of thanksgiving, help me be thankful for Gladys.* In God's perfect timing, May Belle had finished clearing the dishes and returned from the kitchen with a filled decanter of coffee. She put one hand on Dorothy's shoulder and gave it a gentle squeeze as she leaned—with a slight wince—over her other shoulder to pour Dorothy a refill and said, "Like the good book says, Gladys, if we extend generosity to anyone, it's the same as if we've extended it to Jesus."

"Right and amen," Dorothy said. She sighed with relief at her friend's ability to say what was important rather than combative.

Gladys sipped on her coffee. As much as she wanted to argue about this whole idea she knew that to do so now would make her sound heartless and unspiritual, which she certainly was not. Although in general she had no trouble arguing with anyone about anything, she found it frustratingly impossible to argue against God. At least out loud.

"You know how much I hate to admit this," Gladys said reluctantly, "but it is true. I *am* still tired from our recent big doings." She seemed to forget her mayoral status long enough for her shoulders to slump. "Day before yesterday when Caleb's wife phoned to invite me to their house for Thanksgiving dinner this year I was so happy! I know she expected an argument from me, but the truth is, I'm glad for somebody else to have all of that trouble, especially since Jake's

been gone. To tell you the truth, I don't want to have anything to do with cooking for this event if we have it, *especially*
since I don't have to even do it for my own family this year."
Although all three ladies were widows, Gladys's loss was the
freshest, Jake having been killed in a truck accident less than
five years ago. Caleb was Gladys's only child and he lived in
Partonville, as did her brother and his family, who had also
been invited to Caleb's home for the Thanksgiving holiday.
Their family was all taken care of, thank you very much.

Dorothy nearly fainted dead away. What an opening! Was
it possible Gladys was *relinquishing* control of something? She
jumped right in. "I thought maybe Lester might want to chip
in with a big pan of dressing," Dorothy said. "Turkeys cook
faster when they're not stuffed and he's got those big pans
and that large oven at the grill. And . . . OH, MY! Do you
think Lester ends up spending holidays alone after cooking
for everybody else all year? He might be thrilled to pieces to
come to a big gathering! I sure hope this all works out!"

"I can tell you if I cooked every day of my life, the last
thing I'd want to do on a day when I didn't have to cook
would be to cook." Gladys grabbed hold of the fold in her
blazer that had ridden up under her ample bosom and gave
it a yank.

"You know, Gladys," May Belle said quietly, "I appreciate what you're saying and that's very kind of you to be so
considerate of Lester." And she meant it. "But the truth for
me is that I could bake every day of my life and never tire
of it. It makes me feel useful. Content. Maybe Lester is the
same way with his cooking."

Dorothy smacked her palms on the table, causing Sheba
to jump up, appear out from under her legs, take a quick
look toward Dorothy then run to the front door, the sound

somehow signaling her it was time to go. "So, Gladys, *(Hustle, Dorothy, keep hustling along!)* I'm glad you agree we should join forces and serve the community in the same fine way you are used to doing as mayor!"

"Well I . . ."

"When I get home," Dorothy barreled on, "I'll phone Jessica, although she might be out running errands since she couldn't come to our meeting. May Belle, you get a hold of Nellie Ruth. *(GOODNESS! There's another one without family in the area!)* Gladys, you can look forward to spending Thanksgiving with your family as well as knowing you have contributed to a fine event! Splendid! And I really appreciate your forward thinking *(one of Gladys's favorite phrases)* about us taking good care of ourselves! You are absolutely right, dear, in that we need to rest when we have the chance. I'll let you know what Father O'Sullivan says as soon as I talk to him—or whoever he turns me over to. Earl, honey, would you get our coats, please? I'll also stop at the grill on the way home and run this idea by Lester. See how he might react to making the dressing. St. Auggie's will have to make their decision by tomorrow, though, because if it's a go, we have to give Harold a chance to get a notice in this Sunday's *Partonville Press*, and the Wednesday edition, since those would be his only chances. Of course, I'll remind both churches they'll want to get it in their Sunday bulletins this week and make announcements from the pulpit."

"May I remind *you*, Dorothy," Gladys said, using her best mayoral voice, "that these are *not* our responsibilities if we are in a *supporting* role!"

Point well taken, Dorothy thought. She made herself zip her lips so Gladys got in the last word—aside from the *Amen and THANK YOU, Jesus!* she said under her breath.

8

Clothes were flung all over Katie's bedroom. A neat-nick, she hardly ever had more than one item of clothing off a hanger at a time, but she was running late (a definite no-no in her business book) and trying to maneuver in her small bedroom, so a pile had accumulated. She'd narrowed her choices down to six outfits, holding each up in front of her as she stood before the full-length mirror bolted to the outside of her closet door. Back in her brownstone in Chicago, she'd not only had two walk-in closets, but a freestanding mirror mounted in a beautiful swinging frame that she could move and tilt this way and that. No room for such luxuries in this teensy mouse house. She moved like a windup doll as she rifled through the choices. Black suit: too severe for lunch. Blue tailored dress: V-neck too low for Colton, who wouldn't hide the fact he was noticing.

After tossing a few more ensembles aside before even holding them up again, she finally came to the emerald green semi-casual suit, the last thing on her bed. She decided it was the perfect blend of Development Diva and flattering. Mr. Craig definitely liked the ladies; a smart business woman played all her cards. She'd often been told that the emerald color made her Paul Newman–blue eyes stand out. The memory of those comments gave her a momentary flashback to the instant she'd first noticed her eyes were a mirrored-match with those of her newly discovered half brother, Pastor Delbert. A brief bout of "illegitimate child" careened through her but she immediately buttoned up the temptation to fall prey to her "back story," as they say in books and movies. She couldn't imagine how Colton could know about it anyway, but the truth always proved that what matters most is how you feel about yourself. She'd read that in one of her get-a-grip-type books after her divorce from a husband who'd left her for a younger woman. She squared herself up and tossed any personal insecurities aside. Even though Colton was definitely not her type, he was a player and she knew it. This would not be the time to go in with her guard even partially down. *Men deliver such a mixed bag of trouble.*

Katie hadn't once been in a serious relationship since her divorce from Josh's dad, Bruce Kinney, over a decade earlier. In fact, she hadn't dated anyone even semi-seriously. Okay, truth be told, to call any of her social engagements an honest-to-gosh date was even a stretch. She had instead put all of her emotional energies—whirlwinds of anger, avalanches of grief and a brief bout of paralyzing insecurity about what caused her husband to choose a younger woman—into her work. Into beating every man at the deal-closing table. She'd so occupied herself with business that she'd left no room for a personal life and while she wasn't looking, she'd lost her way with her son. It wasn't until they'd come to Partonville to deal with her aunt's estate, the house Dorothy now lived in, that Dorothy had helped shine a light on what she was missing. Although they still had a ways to go, even in the midst of normal teen–parent traumas and dramas they were thankfully making headway.

After buttoning herself up and checking the mirror several times, first moving up close, then backing away as far as possible for the long view—which wasn't that long since the room was so small, so she had to get up on the bed, and when she stood on the bed she couldn't see her face in the mirror ("I swear, this place is shrinking by the minute!")—she opted for the higher heels and smaller earrings.

Katie drove down the lane in her large, cashmere beige SUV, a Lexus LX470. She was glad to once again be heading out of Partonville in it, although to be behind the wheel of the newest model Blue Vapor Metallic 470 she'd test-driven on her last venture to Hethrow would have been even better. She'd come within a breath of trading up for it, right on the spot. Then she'd pictured the heads at Harry's turning and the mouths wagging when she circled the square. She'd already heard enough whispers about her "fancy vehicle." Not that she needed a new SUV, but she'd been used to trading every two years and it was time. When she drove away from the dealership with only a business card in her hand, she couldn't decide which bugged her more: the fact that she wasn't driving the new SUV or that she'd let the opinions of a grill full of Pardon-Me-Villers affect her. For the second time in the last hour, she bucked herself up and straightened her spine. This time she grit her teeth as well. The entire town was suddenly on her nerves.

Although Colton had suggested they meet at his office, in order to level the playing field, Katie'd said, "How about we meet at Fedora's on the corner of Central and Third." She'd said it like she'd been there a million times in order to demonstrate familiarity with Hethrow. During her previous explorations she'd discovered the trendy place on the opposite side of town from his offices, which she'd also driven by. (He had quite the empire; even the exterior of his office building reeked of his success.) She'd popped into the restaurant and checked the menu: plenty of salads and sparkling waters. *Perfect.*

She'd recommended they meet there at one thirty, after the lunch crowd had departed, and said she'd make the reservation. She didn't want to be stuck with him any longer than she had to so fast service was a must. She had not planned on being ten minutes late—*definitely* not her M-O—when she entered under the striped awning.

"I have a reservation for one thirty. Durbin. I'm assuming my guest has already arrived and been seated."

The hostess ran her finger down her reservation sheet. It stopped at her name. "No. It doesn't look like it. Would you like to go ahead and be seated?"

"Yes. That would be fine."

"What is your guest's name?" the hostess asked as they walked toward the back of the restaurant. "I'll send her to your table when she arrives."

I don't look that *out of practice!* It frosted Katie that the woman just assumed she was waiting for a girlfriend. "Him. His name is Colton Craig."

"Oh! Mr. *Craig*!" she said as she pulled out Katie's chair, seating her on the side of the table that looked toward the middle of the room. With suddenly rosy cheeks the hostess gushed, "I'd be happy to show him to your table when he arrives!" Even though Katie hadn't seen Colton Craig for a long while, it was now clear he had not lost his charm.

When the hostess turned around she ran smack into him, full force. He grabbed her by the shoulders to steady her. "I am so sorry," he said, his low voice winding around her as his hands drew her just a hair closer. (The man is shameless, Katie thought.) "Are you alright?"

"I'm fine, Mr. Craig. I'm the one who was moving too quickly."

Colton dropped his hands from her arms, said that no, he owned the full responsibility for disrupting such a beautiful lady. "And speaking of beautiful ladies . . ." He looked around her to Katie, moving toward her with his hand extended, perfect pearly whites gleaming through his tan, deep green eyes flashing streams of sparkles right at her.

Since Dorothy had worn her pink wool sweater over her blouse and under what she referred to as her boring beige windbreaker, she felt plenty warm during the short walk from May Belle's to Harry's—with a short stop at her home to drop off Sheba. Although Lester liked Sheba, both Dorothy and Lester believed dogs didn't belong in diners. The breakfast crowd was gone, including the Landers clan, and the lunch crowd was in full swing. Lester scurried from here to there, clearing dishes, flipping burgers and pages in his order tablet, and serving up refills. Dorothy sat at the U in the last stool near the wall, right alongside the grill, which the U wrapped around. When Lester removed the lid from the pot of beef stew—she could tell by the glorious smell of his lavish use of bay leaves—to give it a stir, she seized the moment to toss the Thanksgiving idea at him before he poured her a cup of coffee, which she was going to decline since after May Belle's she was once again caffeinated and sugared up enough for the whole week.

"Lester, I've just been meeting with the Social Concerns Committee and we've been discussing the possibility of having a Thanksgiving dinner at the church for anyone who would like to come."

"And?" He did not look her way while he stirred.

"I wondered if you might like to participate."

"By?"

It suddenly occurred to her that maybe Gladys rather than May Belle was right: maybe Lester would be grateful not to cook when he didn't have to and maybe she should just let the idea of him bringing anything slide. "By, well, joining us."

"Think I got nothing better to do?" he said flatly. *Just because I'm a bachelor.* His response caught the attention of Doc Streator who was sitting right next to Dorothy, who wasn't sure how to respond.

"I think, Lester," Doc said in his kindly voice, "Dorothy just thought you might like to join in the festivities along with other folks." He swiveled on his stool to face Dorothy. "Right?"

"Right," Dorothy said somewhat sheepishly, since it hadn't been officially determined there was going to be a festivity. But if there was, Doc's wife had been gone for years and perhaps he, too, spent Thanksgiving alone, although she thought his daughter and her children invited him to their house about an hour away. Then again, she wasn't sure.

"This is the first time I've heard about a dinner at the church, Dorothy. I haven't seen anything about it in the Sunday bulletin." Doc turned back to his plate and took a bite of his BLT.

"To be honest with you . . ."

"Probably something they've cooked up for the lonely hearts' society." Lester slammed the lid back on the stew, emptied a batch of fries onto the plate with a hamburger, tossed two slices of sandwich pickles on top and strode off to serve it up.

"You know, Doc," Dorothy said, sliding off her stool, "I've got another stop to make so I think I'll just head on. I believe Lester's got his hands full right now. It was inconsiderate of me to bother him at the height of the lunch hour." She patted Doc on the shoulder and left without another word. As she walked by the front window she saw Lester back at the grill and Doc leaning forward to talk to him. *Lord, I don't have a clue what that was all about, but I'm sure You do. I think something—or somebody—needs fixing. If it's me, let me know before I get in more trouble, okay?*

Walking felt good. Although she did walk to Your Store, May Belle's and around the square every once in a while, it wasn't with the same vigor as when she used to head down to the creek each morning, or ascend the ramp up into the barn, or climb the stairs to her office and bedroom. Yes, she had to admit she was grateful for the conveniences of town and the lack of stairs for her arthritic joints; she was especially thankful when she had to occasionally pop a nitroglycerin tablet for her heart and didn't have to run either up or down the stairs to get one if she didn't have one on her. But it seemed more obvious lately (the Big Guy often got her attention through repetition) that she wasn't getting near the exercise she used to and that simply was not good. She decided before heading home she'd just keep walking the few extra blocks right on over to the Lamp Post and see what was up with Jessica Joy. Give that sunny daughter of hers a sloppy kiss, if they were home.

As Dorothy strolled along she recalled how her grandmother would sometimes remove her upper and lower plate and chew on Dorothy's neck. She'd scream and protest but in truth, she'd loved every minute of her feisty granny's attention. She smiled now, recalling the warm feeling of gums on her skin. By the time the memory began to fade she was entering the Lamp Post's office and ringing the bell on the counter. After waiting a few moments, she rang the bell again, only louder this time. She figured if Jessica weren't home she would have locked the office doors. If she was cleaning rooms, she usually left a plaque out saying so and instructing guests to "Please come and look for me!" She'd hand-painted the little instructive sign, trimmed it with a border of flowers and had Paul mount a special decorative hook on the door for just this purpose. But no such sign was there today.

"Just a minute!" Jessica yelped from the bathroom where she was wiping a cold rag over her face, her head having been in the toilet again. Pretty soon the door between the office and their home opened and in she came. She was carrying Sarah Sue on her hip and they both had red eyes, as though they'd been crying.

"Dorothy! I'm so glad you stopped by!"

"Am I interrupting anything? You look . . ." *Now who would want to hear that! Don't go causing more trouble!* "You look as beautiful as ever."

Jessica's face turned crimson. "You're too kind, Dorothy. I know for a fact I do not look beautiful." She gave a lame smile but it was clear she'd had to work at it. She turned her head toward her daughter. "Now there's a beautiful face, even when it has snot running down its nose." Jessica sighed, grabbed the bottom of her sweatshirt and swiped Sarah Sue's nose, causing her daughter to have yet another hand-batting fit, which she'd been doing all day. Jessica invited Dorothy to please come in to her home and sit down. "I'm sorry the place is such a mess," Jessica said as she preceded

Dorothy into their living room, moving a couple of items from here to there on her way.

"Don't go to a lick of trouble, honey. It's you and Sarah Sue I stopped to see anyway, not your place. Besides, I rather prefer a rumpled nest myself. Suits me just fine! Says, 'Somebody LIVES here!'" Dorothy plunked down in Paul's chair realizing she was winded. Jessica put Sarah Sue down on the floor on her tummy, pulled a few toys in front of her, then sat herself down on the couch. Although Sarah Sue wasn't quite old enough to sit up by herself or crawl after anything, she liked grabbing hold of the toys and banging them on the floor.

"Would you like something to drink? Or maybe a bite of lunch since it's nearly noon?" The thought of putting anything in her own mouth made her stomach roll.

"No, thank you. I'm still filled to the brim with two doses of May Belle's caramel pecan coffee cake and about a dozen cups of coffee." Suddenly the unasked question about Jessica's absence at the meeting hung awkwardly in the air. Jessica's neck turned red and she diverted her eyes in embarrassment. There was no good excuse to offer without telling the truth, since there weren't any guests at the motel. But she wasn't ready to accept the possible truth herself, let alone share it, especially since she hadn't told her husband yet. She'd just kept telling him "I think I have a touch of the stomach flu." When he'd left for work this morning, which he did before dawn, he'd kissed her forehead as she'd laid in bed then whispered "If you don't feel better today, honey, I want you to call Doc Streator. Hear me? I'm beginning to wonder if you don't have food poisoning or something." A quiet uh-huh was her only response. She groaned after he was out the door. Not only did she feel physically lousy but now her conscience bothered her for holding back. But first she had to be sure. *Please, God!* No sense both of them being crazy, especially if it turned out not to be true. *PLEASE, God!*

But how could it not be when here came another wave of nausea so powerful she knew she had to run to the bathroom. "EXCUSE ME!" she yelled as she ran down the hall. Sarah Sue started to pucker up in the wake of her mother's sudden departure. Dorothy quickly pulled the sleeve for the armrest off the chair and began playing peek-a-boo with it. Some age-old tricks never lost their ability to work. Soon Sarah Sue was giggling and so was Dorothy. They were sure making happier sounds than Dorothy heard coming from the bathroom.

Jessica finally entered the room, her face blotched from retching and red from blushing. "Goodness, Jessica! Is that why you weren't at the meeting? And come to think of it, you weren't at church on Sunday either. Oh, honey, how long have you been sick? And here I am just dropping in on you . . ."

"I'm not sick." Jessica stared at Dorothy, tears welling in her eyes. Her bottom lip began to quiver so she bit it, hard enough it actually hurt, which made her eyes pool all the more.

Dorothy studied the tear spilling over Jessica's lower right lashes, took note of her lip, thought about the retching. And she knew. She knew what Jessica was unwilling to admit. "Oh, *honey*!" Dorothy moved toward Jessica and simply opened wide her arms. Jessica rushed right into them and sobbed on her shoulder, which caused Sarah Sue to start bawling. Dorothy held Jessica and gently patted her back, stroked her hair, spoke words encouraging Jessica to just let it out, which freed her to unabashedly wail and so she did.

"It just can't *be*," Jessica finally whimpered after her sobbing subsided, although Sarah Sue's had kicked into full volume. She picked up her daughter and plopped down in the chair with her. Although Jessica had looked at Dorothy when she'd spoken, she couldn't maintain her eye contact without breaking into more tears. She lifted the bottom of her sweatshirt and wiped Sarah Sue's nose as well as her own. "Oh, Dorothy, I'm a mess in more ways than one."

Dorothy held out her arms and Sarah Sue came right to her. She backed up and carefully seated herself, her balance not being what it used to be.

"Let me go get some tissues first," Jessica said as she popped back up and disappeared into the bathroom for a moment. She returned with a wad of four or five of them bundled in her fist. She sat down, selected one and blew her nose. Then she handed another to Dorothy for Sarah Sue.

"What am I going to *do*, Dorothy?" Jessica blew her nose and actually contemplated the question now that it was out there.

"Why, you're going to have a baby! Partonville is going to have a new citizen and I just know," Dorothy said, swiping at Sarah Sue's face and chin while Sarah Sue batted at her hands, "that he or she will be just as sweet and as beautiful as this little cherub." Sarah Sue beamed at Dorothy then suddenly buried her head in the crook of Dorothy's neck. Dorothy wrapped her arms around the warm wiggly bundle and held her close. "What does Paul have to say? I'm sure he's happy. It's just so clear when I see you how much he adores the both of you."

"He doesn't know yet," Jessica whispered. Dorothy

raised an eyebrow and Jessica's face and neck turned red again. "I haven't been to the doctor yet, but I've known it in my heart of hearts for some time. I haven't had the courage to tell Paul. Honestly, I kept hoping I'd wake up and find . . . But all I'm finding is more assurance that it's true. I can't put off telling him much longer, though. He's worried I'm really ill with more than a touch of the flu."

"How far along do you reckon you are?"

"Just far enough to be sick. With Sarah Sue, the nausea began about a month into it. I think the worst of it lasted about two more months, which is sure terrible timing with the holidays coming and business always picking up then. I tell you, I just now got caught up from the Pumpkin Festival weekend when we were all booked up."

"You need to ask for help, honey, at least until you get through this phase."

"We can't afford anyone right now. We just bought that new neon sign out front. Did you see it? (her face brightening for a moment), and an answering machine and . . ."

"Your new sign is just perfect, Jessica. Why it would make anyone want to stay here. And I'm sure we can figure something out to get you some help. Don't fret yourself now. Just be good to yourself. Do the best you can, honey. That's all any of us can ever do anyway."

"This is going to be a huge financial mess." As quickly as Jessica began to look hopeful, she'd deflate again as another piece of reality hit. "And where are we even going to put another child in this tiny place?"

"I remember one single momma I knew who set up a crib right in a closet. I always thought the baby looked so cozy in there, surrounded by all those colors, soft fabrics. . . . Sleeves of the arms that held her so safe dangling right above her. . . . I've never forgotten those images. And think how happy Sarah Sue will be to have a little sister or brother."

"And think how she won't even be potty trained before this one gets here. I mean, good grief! I'm still nursing! I didn't think I could get pregnant while I was nursing." Jessica's shoulders slumped so low she'd nearly rolled into the posture of a lifeless slug.

"How about we don't think anymore at all right now. How about we just have a little prayer. Okay?"

"Okay." Jessica straightened a fraction and folded her hands together.

"Lord," Dorothy said, bowing her head, "here we are, just as we are." Sarah Sue grabbed hold of a few strands of Dorothy's fine hair and gave it a yank. Dorothy kept her eyes closed but reached up to untangle the pudgy little fingers. "We are all Your children, so how about You remind us about that, especially Jessica as she struggles to come to grips with the idea she's growing another child of Yours in her womb right as we speak." Jessica put her hand over her abdomen and tried to will herself to ponder a child of God within her rather than a complication. "How about You give her an extra dose of peace, even in the midst of . . ."

Jessica flew up from her chair and bolted back to the bathroom. Dorothy heard the sounds of retching again shortly after the bathroom door slammed closed. Sarah Sue was too distracted with Dorothy's fine hair and pink scalp to notice her mother was gone. "Sometimes, God, things . . . kids, are not as easy as they seem. But then You know all about that because look at us, and we're Your kids! I'm trusting You to give us all what we need, and that includes giving Jessica the courage to tell Paul. Please soften his heart to receive the news with grace and comfort for his sweet wife. I don't know what else they're going to need, but I'm trusting You to supply it." Sarah Sue was now sticking her fingers into Dorothy's mouth, making it difficult for her to speak out loud. Dorothy, eyes still closed, heard Jessica return to the chair across from her. Sarah Sue giggled as she hooked a finger into one of Dorothy's nostrils before flinging her hands toward her mother. Dorothy opened her eyes and looked at Jessica. With a smile and a wink she said, "I covered your back while you were gone." Jessica gave a light chuckle, which, under the circumstances, felt mighty good. "I reckon there's nothing left to do but say 'Amen,'" and so they did.

As happy as it made Dorothy's heart to learn about Jessica's news, her heart was also pierced by the thought of all that was lost when her daughter had succumbed to breast cancer ten years ago. Dorothy adored Vinnie's boys, her grandsons. But *OH, LORD!* How she would have been blessed to watch Caroline Ann, her only daughter, become a mother, had it been in God's will for her to do so. Jessica was sweet spirited like her Caroline Ann had been. A quietness, yet so many gifts. . . . Never a day went by when Dorothy didn't ache with the loss of her only daughter. She'd once heard someone say you never got over the loss of a child but that you eventually learned to live with it. So true. *Lord,* Dorothy said, brushing a tear from her eye as she walked toward her home, *hold me close to Your heartbeat since I know that's where Caroline Ann's head is resting right now.*

9

"**E**dward Showalter, you sure do know how to treat a lady," Nellie Ruth sighed, her eyelids all but batting. The two of them were seated across from each other at a table for two complete with a "*fabric* tablecloth and napkins," she told Dorothy the next Sunday when they were setting up the altar for church.

Edward Showalter had phoned Nellie Ruth bright and early on her day off saying he could use a ray of her sunshine on such a cloudy day, tempting her to bow out of the Social Concerns Committee meeting, which she had—a scandalous first for the ever-responsible Nellie Ruth McGregor. When he suggested either a late breakfast or an early lunch, Nellie Ruth asked him if they might try this new little place she'd recently heard about. Turned out Edward Showalter already knew it firsthand: a buddy of his owned the little café just down the street from the Now and Again Resale shop on the outskirts of Yorkville.

Nellie Ruth had first heard about A Little Piece of NYC ("Isn't it cute how it rhymes!" Jessica had chirped) during the last Happy Hookers' meeting when Jessica (before the mere thought of food made her stomach roll) mentioned she'd spied it during her recent visit to Now and Again Resale, which was her favorite place to shop along with Swappin' Sam's, of course—but he didn't have a dedicated crafters' corner. Although Jessica hadn't actually been to "the Piece," as it would quickly go on to be nicknamed, she described in great detail each clever nuance of the attractive look of the place, from the window flower boxes filled with fall foliage—but she was sure there would be geraniums in them come spring—to the romantic shadowed wooden cutouts of a couple mounted on the exterior. They were sitting at a table, forks to their open mouths. There had been quite the discussion during bunco as to what kind of food they'd find at this NYC place. "Maybe a glorified hot dog stand." "No! It's Chicago that's famous for hot dogs." "Could be bagels. Lox. Things like that." "I think that's ethnic, Jewish to be exact. Yes, my friend Sylvia is Jewish and she likes bagels and lox. But maybe it also implies New York. Not sure." "Maybe it's those sandwiches with the steak and onions, cheese and . . ." "You mean a Philly Cheesesteak? Well, that definitely isn't New York. It's New Jersey!" "Maybe the waitresses are just rude. Aren't people in New York always rude? I've heard they're rude." Nellie Ruth's curiosity had been aggressively piqued at that meeting, but now she would learn firsthand what "it" all meant.

Edward Showalter and Johnny Mathis ("No, not that one!") had first met in a tavern "some plenty odd years ago," they'd tell folks. It was hard to determine which one was more skunked that evening; they'd both spent the afternoon on their stools, neither employed, each having lost his job due to the bottom of countless bottles. They got to meeting up just about every afternoon until one night Johnny rolled his car on the gravel road, breaking four ribs, a leg, an arm, rupturing his spleen and peeling back his nose before the car settled on its roof and rocked to a halt in a cloud of dust. His wife, Mary, looked at him wrapped from nearly head to toe in the hospital and said, "Johnny, you either get help before you drink yourself to death or kill somebody, or I'm leaving. In fact," she said, swallowing hard on her way out that evening when visiting hours were over, "I won't be home when you get there. It's time I stop paying the bills, picking up the pieces and replacing totaled cars. (This hadn't been the first.) I'll be at my mother's house. You can let me know what you decide. And if you do decide you want me, then you have to first prove to me you can stay sober for more than a few weeks." Her heart felt like it was shattering into a million pieces, a few of them dropping to the floor with each step she took away from the man she loved.

By the time Johnny left the hospital, which was going on two weeks later, he hadn't heard from Mary; she would neither receive nor return his calls for fear the sound of his voice would erase her resolve to stay away. He'd decided if he could stay sober this long he had a fighting chance to conquer what had surely become a demon in his life. But as his addiction would have it, he went straight to the tavern the evening of the first day he was home since he didn't know where else to go. His house was too quiet without Mary who had, this time, meant what she'd said. At least he could count on his friends. When he swung open the tavern door he was greeted by the familiar strains of country western music wafting from the jukebox. The bartender nodded a greeting and automatically started to draw him a beer. Johnny waited a moment for his eyes to adjust to the dim lighting before he headed toward his usual stool. He was aware of every sore bone and muscle in his body as he climbed up and he didn't even attempt to hide the painful grimace on his still somewhat black-, blue- and yellow-bruised face. Although the doctor had warned him about drinking while taking the medications, he figured a beer or two wouldn't hurt. In fact, he figured they could probably do a better pain-killing job than the drugs anyway.

"Welcome back," Edward Showalter said, raising his mug in a toast before gulping his last drops and ordering another. As the bartender plunked a cardboard coaster down in front of Johnny and set his beer on it, Edward Showalter instructed him to "Put the gimp's on my tab." He winked at Johnny who picked up the beer and lifted it to Edward Showalter in a thank-you salute. Johnny thought about how good that beer looked: perfect head, golden wheat color, enticing fragrance . . . he could hardly wait until that first refreshing swallow slid down his throat and he could lick the delicious froth from around the corners of his mouth. They clinked glasses and simultaneously said, "To liquid gold." The two of them had come up with the familiar toast—and countless life-altering inventions they would never pursue—shortly into their daily ritual.

Before the brew was to Johnny's lips, out of nowhere an image of his wedding day flashed into his mind. Mary was looking at him with adoring eyes. "For better or for worse," he heard her saying in his head, "but Johnny, I never thought it could get this bad." He shook his head to clear it. His sweet Mary, gone now, unless . . . He started to again raise the glass to his mouth, but she was still in his mind's eye, her sorrowful eyes shooting unspoken pleas his way while she choked back her tears as she left the hospital room. He looked at the mug perched in front of his face, licked his lips and swallowed down his own spit.

"To *hell* with liquid gold!" He slammed the mug down on the bar sending a geyser of beer into the air causing Edward to jump and the bartender to reach for a bar towel. There would be no easy wipe-up, though, since Johnny next shoved the mug away from him and it skidded sideways through the spill until it fell crashing to the floor.

"NO MORE!" he shouted. He slid painfully off his stool and limped out the door before he had a chance to change his mind. Edward Showalter tossed a ten-dollar bill on the bar and chased after him. It just so happened that that very morning Edward Showalter had awakened on the edge of a wet, plowed field. He was covered with mud, one shoe missing. How he got there he had no earthly idea. His car was parked along the side of the road, the driver's door still open. Apparently he'd left it running since it was out of gas and the battery was dead. Although it wasn't the first blackout he'd had, it was to be his last since that very evening he and Johnny made a pact to leave the bottle behind. They believed something bigger than the both of them had brought them—together—to that moment. It hadn't been an easy road, Lord knew, but having somebody to walk it with had bonded them for life. They still held each other accountable, in and out of AA meetings, both believing that only the will of God, prayer, their AA sponsors and dogged determination had kept them sober for this long. It would only take one slip, they would remind each other. "Having a beer is probably fine for you guys," they would say when some of their friends convened for a cold one (and truly, they both knew that to be true, most people being able to stop after a brew or two), "but not for us. We have got to remember that difference. Enjoy yourselves, though!"

Not until Johnny had stayed sober for six months did his Mary come home. He got a job as a short-order cook—not his first job in this position—a couple of towns away, especially a couple of towns away from the tavern that still drew him like a hummingbird to red nectar. On more than one occasion he'd said to Edward Showalter over their sodas, "One day, ES, I'm going to have my own café. Nobody telling me what to do. I'm not going to serve booze or dinners. Just breakfast and lunch so I can be home with my family in the evenings." Edward Showalter, an electrician by original trade, promised Johnny that when he got ready he'd help him find a place and fix it up. It was like a covenant they made with each other. And one day at a time, they moved toward that "one day."

Then several months ago the old feed station property near Yorkville had gone up for sale. The building had been empty for years, some occasionally wishing the eyesore would just burn down. But it didn't. And one day Johnny called Edward Showalter and said he'd had a vision while he'd been at church that morning. "Don't know another way to explain it, but I saw me in the old feed station—of course it was fancied up—serving food to you and a fine lady. I think it's time, ES, that I put my money where my mouth's been all these years. I talked it over with the Missus and she said she believed it was time too. Of course we prayed, but she also said she just had a feeling. So we all but wiped out our savings and bought the place this morning! I'm taking you up on that offer to help me remodel since that's the only way we'll be able to afford to do it. I can't pay you much, but I'll give you what I can."

"I'd say rather than a vision you had a hallucination, Johnny, because I sure don't have a fine lady in my life. *Not that I wouldn't like to.* But that's not going to stop you from opening your restaurant or me from keeping my word." Other than the side job Edward Showalter had recently done for Gladys when she'd hired him to do the wiring and mount the new clock ensemble on the square building, Edward had worked full-time for Johnny helping him get ready to see his dream come true. It was the first longer-term job he'd had since he'd done all the updating to Tess Walker's old place in preparation for Dorothy's move. At Arthur's recommendation (who'd heard tell Edward Showalter was sober), Katie Durbin, who'd inherited the house when her aunt died and then worked a formal trade deal with Dorothy into her contract for Crooked Creek, had hired Edward Showalter to bring everything up to code, electrical and any other way. He was the genius who could do it all, and so he had, including some painting and helping Dorothy to create her vision of that four-poster bed made out of old dining room table legs from Swappin' Sam's.

And who would have guessed that within a short amount of time after Johnny and he had started working on The Piece, Nellie Ruth McGregor would be sitting right there across from him at a table. It wasn't but a few days after their work had commenced on the restaurant that Edward Showalter had received a call from Nellie Ruth, a mutual friend of theirs having passed on his name as somebody who could do some painting for her. Seems she'd had a "painting incident," is the way it had been presented. It had been an incident all right: she'd ended up sitting smack in the middle of a spilled gallon of Splendid Rose. "What were you thinking?" the entire Partonville Community Band wanted to know when she showed up at practice with rose-colored freckles and wads of paint in her cuticles.

So she'd called this Edward Showalter (*and why did everybody always call him by both names?* she'd wondered) they'd recommended. "You'll have to wait maybe a couple, three-four weeks, maybe a month or more," he'd said to her into the receiver. "I'm working full-time on an important job. Kind of a rush. Gotta stick with it." Nellie Ruth agreed that would be fine since she didn't perceive any other options and she was in no hurry. Then at the Pumpkin Festival dance, the mutual friend pointed her out to Edward Showalter. "That's the woman whose living room you're going to be painting."

"Really," he said rather than asked. Next thing he knew, his feet had walked him right over to her. "Edward Showalter," he'd said extending his hand. "Electrician, affordable, de-pendable, sober, and for you, a painter to boot. Jesus Loves You. Even if you don't see Him coming again, HE IS!" Aside from the painter reference, it was the same string of words that boldly appeared over the camouflage paint on the outside of his van.

"Oh! A *believer*!" Nellie Ruth said as she shook his hand. (If there was ever a prayer warrior, it was Nellie Ruth McGregor.) They'd spent nearly the entire evening twirling around the floor and talking as fast as they could, stopping only to have some punch and catch their breath. It was as though they'd been created to dance together: not once had he stepped on her toes; not once had she missed his lead.

Now here they sat across from one another at A Little Piece of NYC, Edward Showalter having just helped to seat her. "Truly, Edward, you are such a gentleman."

"Truly, Nellie Ruth, you wouldn't have said that fifteen

years ago. I was a drunken snake until Jesus got ahold of me and I got sober. Jesus and Johnny. What a duo!"

Nellie Ruth's heart sank when she heard the word "drunken." By the look on Edward Showalter's face, she could tell she hadn't hidden her reaction well, which was embarrassing.

"You better believe I *was*, as in *was* a snake. If you don't believe it, just ask Arthur Landers. He'll recollect my worst days and tell it like it was. Why, it's likely I still owe the man money for work he did on my car that I never, in my drunken stuporness, got around to paying him. And now that I've thought about it, I'm going to look him up this week and see if I can't square things away."

"You've given me no reason to doubt you. It's just that a long time ago. . . ." Her eyes shifted from his to the table to the front door, then back to the table. "Oh, never mind," she finally said making eye contact with him again. *Lord, let it be true that he is always sober now!*

Nellie Ruth had only been involved with one other person who drank too much and that had been her dad. Hearing Edward Showalter bring up *his* darker days brought back horrid memories for Nellie Ruth. Her father had died when Nellie Ruth was only a teen. He fell off a curb in front of the tavern and was struck dead by a passing car. Since her mother had already passed on, Nellie Ruth packed up a few belongings and started driving until the car ran out of gas, which is how she ended up in Partonville, Dorothy having found her asleep behind the wheel in the church parking lot. She took her in and the rest, as they say, was history.

Nellie Ruth had always hoped for a good man in her life, often bending God's ear about it. And yet, her history with her father left her wary of men. But her assistant manager's job at Your Store, playing in the community band and serving at church kept her happily busy. Besides, Partonville wasn't exactly a metropolis of eligible men her age—or any other age, for that matter. Up until the Pumpkin Festival, none had caught her attention. Edward Showalter's bold introductory statement of faith had pried something open. Now she hoped she could trust her growing vulnerabilities, for she was attracted to him. She looked at what appeared to be a fine gentleman sitting across from her and said another silent prayer for him, that his prior weakness would remain just that. She knew if he even so much as once flirted with a relapse that would be the last he would see of her.

"So tell me," she said, as she leaned back for Johnny to set the water glasses on their table, "what job are you going to tackle next, now that the restaurant is open?"

Edward Showalter rubbed his chin. "At the moment, only God knows. I've just got a couple little kinks left to work out here for Johnny," and he stopped talking enough for the two men to wink at each other, Johnny nodding his head toward Nellie Ruth making it clear he was waiting for an introduction, which Edward Showalter obliged him with.

"Vision!" Johnny said as he walked away.

"What did he say?" Nellie Ruth asked. "Sounded like he said *vision*."

"Hm." Edward Showalter was clearly going to offer no more, so Nellie Ruth let it go.

"You were talking about your next job," she said as her eyes began to cast around the menu looking for something that would radiate "New York City dish."

"Oh, right. I was saying that I don't have anything lined up just yet."

"What about my living room," she asked, disappointed he'd already forgotten.

"Of course! But I thought you were referring to a *paying* job. The only pay I will accept for painting your living room is the company of your beautiful self."

Nellie Ruth lowered her eyes, unaccustomed to outright flattery. She felt like a sixteen-year-old rather than the sixty-something woman she was. "Sixty-something and never been kissed," she'd sighed to herself on her sixtieth birthday. Even though it was true, she knew no one would believe it. When she lifted her eyes, Edward Showalter was studying her face to see if he might be speaking too boldly. She gave him a shy smile and they held one another's gazes so long it began to feel inappropriate so they went back to looking at their menus.

"What do you think is the best New York City dish Johnny has on the menu?" Nellie Ruth had no personal New York point of reference from which to draw and nothing seemed obvious. *Steak sandwich?* she'd wondered. *Could it be the cheesy hash browns with green onions in them, which surely is an unusual combination for these parts, even though they sound good to me?*

"New York City dish?" Edward asked, gleam in his eye. Then he broke out in a full-blown smile. "Why are you asking about a New York City dish?"

"Because of the name of the restaurant, silly!" *Do not be calling a grown man silly, Nellie Ruth! He'll think you're . . . silly. Oh, Lord! I just don't know how to ACT!*

"What's New York got to do with the name of Johnny's restaurant?" Edward Showalter already knew the answer to his question but he wanted to hear it out loud.

"You know, Little Piece of NYC."

A ripple of laughter flew out of him. "Is that what you thought the NYC was? New York City?"

"Who *wouldn't* think that?" she asked in all innocence, feeling sillier by the minute and not exactly flattered to feel she was the brunt of some kind of joke.

"Johnny! JOHNNY, come over here!" Edward Showalter belted in the direction of the kitchen. "Of course you thought that, Nellie Ruth. I told him!" he said to her. She was relieved to learn it wasn't she who Edward was . . . making fun of?

Johnny appeared from the kitchen. From terrific aromas and what looked to be tomato paste on his chin, she had the feeling something good was going on in there.

"Nellie Ruth here has proven me right. I knew it! I win! Pay up, buddy."

"Name of my restaurant, right?" Johnny asked Nellie Ruth flatly, then sighed.

"Right," she said. "But what's to win? It's A Little Piece of NYC, which so cleverly rhymes. And NYC is New York City. I mean even we Pardon-Me-Villers know *that*!"

Johnny just shook his head and pulled his wallet out of his back pocket. He rifled through the bill compartment and Nellie Ruth's breath caught in her throat. *So he's quit drinking and taken up gambling!*

"Here you go, ES," Johnny said as he handed Edward Showalter a piece of paper. "Paid in full."

Edward Showalter noticed Nellie Ruth straining to see how much the payoff had been, her face looking somber. If it was more than five dollars, she thought, she was out of there, no matter how flattering he'd been. Edward Showalter took note of her face and slid the paper over in front of her. She picked it up and began to read, then laughed out loud. It was a dollar-off matinee coupon for one of the theaters in Hethrow. "That's what you bet? Coupons?"

"Yes, ma'am," Johnny said. "We try to keep all aspects of

our lives on the up and up lest we stumble and head down the slippery slope."

"But what is that NYC on your sign outside if it's not New York City?" Nellie Ruth wanted to know.

"Go ahead and tell her," Edward Showalter said. "Go on." He uttered another *Told you!* under his breath.

"New Yorkville Cuisine. But a name that long wouldn't fit on the sign so we decided to just use the initials. We thought folks would notice the whole of it on the front of the menu, but I guess not."

"Told you," Edward said again while Nellie Ruth flipped her menu closed to study it. There it was, plain as day. NEW YORKVILLE CUISINE.

Nellie Ruth looked deep in thought. "I have an idea!" she spouted to Johnny. "If you can figure out what truly is a New York dish, you could cover all the bases. Just one thing. One really New York thing. But who can we find who's lived in New York City that can help us figure out that perfect dish?"

Johnny laughed his great booming laugh. "I have," he said. "Both Mary and I have lived in New York City. That's where we first met. And what a brilliant idea!" Johnny said. "ES, she's not only a living vision but she's smart to boot. Hang on to this one, Mr. Showalter!" he said as he headed back to the kitchen. Johnny's bold teasing embarrassed Edward Showalter, which is, of course, why he kept it up.

"*Vision,*" Nellie Ruth said. "There! He definitely said vision . . . ES." She was the first person aside from Johnny to ever call him that. "Do you mind if I call you ES?" No indeedy, he did not, and yes, indeedy-do, she'd purred his initials, he told Johnny the next day.

10

Jessie was making the bed, grumbling within herself about the pressure she felt to keep things tidy while company was present. If she left any little thing lying around, Vera wanted to know where she could put it for her, assuming that Jessie was as neat as she was, which she was surely not. In fact, if Herm and Vera weren't staying there, she wouldn't even be making her bed, but she'd noticed Vera glancing in their room when she'd pass by so she figured it wouldn't kill her since they would be leaving in . . . *How many days and hours is it?* A quick calculation let her know they'd be there at least another week and . . . *two* more weeks assuming they left the day after Thanksgiving, which surely they would. She fussed within herself as she tucked in the bottom corners of the sheet, something Arthur kicked out each time she tucked it in, saying his feet needed to breathe, so really what was the point of making the bed? When she was through she picked up Arthur's coveralls and socks. They were lying on the floor right where he'd stepped out of them last night (same as night before and night before), the coveralls looking like a collapsed denim slinky. She tried to run the numbers in her head that could tally how many times since they'd been married that she had picked up his pants, socks, underwear, newspapers, car parts he'd absentmindedly carried in from the garage. Too many decades, too many items to process without exploding her brain. *Too many for any woman, Arthur Landers!*

Worst of all, in the midst of her litany of pet peeves, she could not get Arthur's "won or lost" statement about the whole of their marriage out of her mind.

She smoothed the ripples in the soft quilted bedspread with her aged hand, noticing the accumulating wrinkles around her knuckles. *Where do the years go?* The bedspread had been a handmade gift from her mother after she and Arthur had married. It was a too-fancy-for-both-of-them item she got down from their attic only when company came. She'd always guessed her mom had hoped the beauty of the quilt might add a touch of softness to the harshness she already saw brewing between her tough daughter and her often gruff new husband, the two of them erupting into a fight as often as they exploded with laughter. "Two such fiery souls," her mother had said. Jessie pondered how swiftly and easily lives can change courses in the batting of an eye, the asking of a question after a ballgame, an impulsive answer.

As she continued to fuss with the bedspread, tugging it this way and that, finding herself working to get it perfectly squared up on the bed, she thought about how lives can just as easily change courses by what *doesn't* get said. Her memory locked on a brisk sunny day (pre-Arthur) when Lester had circled their conversation around to the topic of children, even recalling the exact feel of the sun on her left shoulder. She'd returned from a tournament on a Sunday (the grill was closed on Sundays) and Lester had surprised her by showing up at her door to take her out to the park for a picnic. He'd made them a late dinner of ham sandwiches, a light smear of mustard on each slice *(how did he even know that's just the way I liked it?),* and a special batch of not-too-much-onion potato salad just for her, separate from that he'd served on the day's luncheon menu. There was a large dill pickle each, carefully wrapped in wax paper. A jar filled with fresh-squeezed lemonade they drank out of two empty jelly jars. Everything neatly packed in a picnic basket, blanket thrown over his shoulder when he came to the door.

When they were finished eating Lester wiped his mouth and lay back on the blanket, shadows from the leaves dancing across his face. "Feels good," he said with contentment. "Doesn't it? Feels good to just be here." Jessie agreed that it did; she was bone tired and road weary. She, too, reclined. She placed her right hand behind her head, her left across her abdomen. "The only thing that will make this feel better one day," he said boldy, a warm tone in his voice, "is the sounds of a couple youngins playing right over there on the swing set." Although her eyes were closed, she could imagine him pointing. What she could not imagine under the hand on her abdomen was being pregnant. As soon as anyone in the traveling league even suspected you were pregnant, you were off the team. Marriage itself was frowned upon for just that reason, although if you were a good enough player, they'd squawk but put up with you. Competition was stiff and some of the gals on the bench were just waiting for their opportunity. The very idea of anything getting in the way of her ball career gave her chills and she'd instantly changed the topic as though she hadn't heard what he'd said. After all, he'd never even spoken of marriage. Now he was talking about *children*, a new tone in his voice. She was shocked; the man had barely kissed her!

But more importantly, at that moment she knew for certain that she did not love Lester in that way, nor had she ever. He was a good friend, yes . . . But Arthur had started calling and hanging around lately. Arthur. Impulsive, fun, animated, spontaneous, unpredictable Arthur. At the thought of him, she'd splayed her fingers wider over her abdomen. If she was ever to have children—which wouldn't be until after she'd retired from the circuit—that is whose child she could picture within her.

After she and Arthur had married and after she'd finally aged out of the traveling league, having been replaced by the latest kid wonder, she began to long for Arthur's child to be growing in her womb, nestling in her arms. Now here she was a childless old lady. *Wonder if Lester and I . . .*

"My, isn't that a pretty quilt!" Vera exclaimed when she appeared in the doorway.

"This old thing?" Jessie asked, staring down at the gift, wondering how their marriage had ever endured all these years. *Held together one miserable stitch at a time,* she thought when she noticed Arthur had carried the remote control to bed with him last night and left it on the nightstand. Again.

The ring of the phone startled her. It wasn't even 8 A.M. "Hello."

"It's Lester."

"Lester! I can't believe you're calling. I was just thinking about you."

"I bet you were." Silence. Silence.

"Did you want something?" Short silence.

"I'm sorry I sniped at you yesterday at the grill. There was no call for that."

"No, Lester," Dorothy said. "I'm the one who's sorry for bothering you at the height of the lunch hour. It was inconsiderate."

"Dorothy?" Silence. Silence.

"Yes, Lester?" Silence.

"If you're needing folks to cook up any food for the Thanksgiving dinner, just let me know. Turkey, dressing, green beans . . . anything." Throughout the years, Lester had learned that the wonderful grace of doing for others always helped take his mind off himself and that to pull back on a collection jar or a kindness just made him all the more miserable.

"I'll do that, Lester. Thank you for your offer. To tell you the truth, I was ahead of myself anyway; it's not even one hundred percent sure this event is going to happen yet. If it does, it'll be a joint venture with UMC and the St. Auggie folks. I'm waiting to hear back from them right now. I'll keep you posted. They'll be making the decision before noon today so I'll give you the word soon. But Lester, I won't be telling you during the height of the lunch hour." Dorothy chuckled. Lester smiled. It felt good to get that call off his chest; he'd felt guilty since he'd seen Dorothy walk out the grill's door yesterday, not to mention Doc Streator had pointed out to him that although he was sure he hadn't meant to, he'd spoken rather crossly with "that wonderful lady."

Nonetheless, Lester did not want anybody thinking about him as a charity case just because he was single. After a goodly long bout of rational thinking about it last night, he knew he was a blessed man. He had a fine home above the grill, his own business, and good friends—including Arthur. But honest-to-gosh, sometimes that man needed a good boot in the butt. Truth be known, he couldn't think of anyone more qualified to give him one than Jessie! *Match made in heaven!*

The candles had burned down about an inch already. It wasn't like Paul to be late for dinner, but then Jessica thought he might have said something about stopping to run an errand on his way home. She couldn't exactly remember; her brain was foggy about many things lately. Even though the fragrance of the baking meatloaf had turned her stomach, she'd pushed through it and made herself prepare her husband a meal fit for a man who had to endure what she was about to tell him.

It had been twenty-four hours since the truth had erupted in front of Dorothy. Ever since Dorothy had left she'd felt badly that her husband wasn't the first to know what she by now absolutely believed to be true. After all, her breasts were growing more tender by the moment, making nursing uncomfortable. She no longer even had enough energy to keep feeling guilty for her silence, so tonight was the night. Meatloaf and baked potatoes still warm in the turned-off oven; Paul's favorite green bean casserole in the Corning casserole bowl on the stove (she thought for sure she'd lose it when she opened the can of cream of mushroom soup); candles burning; Sarah Sue merrily entertaining herself on a blanket, her own mushy-looking dinner having long been consumed while her mommy swallowed and twice gagged at the site of the orange mess. And then, just like that, Paul was kissing Jessica hello. She hadn't even heard him come in, she'd been so zoned trying to find the perfect words to announce her news after dessert: tapioca pudding with a cherry on top. She'd spoken many variations of her announcement aloud throughout the day, just to see how they might sound. All versions seemed to come out the same way: a giant dose of bad news, no matter how sugarcoated she'd tried to paint them.

Paul backed away from his wife's heart-shaped mouth and looked at her face. "Oh, honey, I'm sorry. I didn't mean to startle you. I thought you heard me come in!"

"I'm pregnant." She uttered the words as flat and as common as a board, as if she'd told him they were out of toilet paper. Something about hearing him say the word "startle" just seemed to trip her get-it-over-with trigger. There was no good way to say it.

Paul stared at her for a minute, then he broke his gaze to smile at Sarah Sue, who, much to Jessica's surprise, he then walked over to and picked up, giving her a big hug once she was in his arms. And then he continued walking right out of the kitchen into the living room where he plunked down in his chair, Sarah Sue on his lap. Jessica's heart started racing a mile a minute. It raced so hard she thought she might faint. Throughout the day she had played out many possible reactions to the news, but never had she imagined this. She walked into the living room hesitantly. He didn't acknowledge her when she entered, so she perched her rear end on the arm of the couch, unable to bring herself to look casual.

"Did you hear what I said, Paul?" He leaned forward enough in his chair to deposit Sarah Sue onto the floor. Then he leaned back in the chair and folded his hands in his lap.

"Yes. I heard. It looked like dinner was ready. How about we go eat?" Without another word, they adjourned to the kitchen. Jessica sliced the meatloaf while Paul dished up a helping of the green bean casserole onto each of their plates. She got out the butter for the baked potatoes; he poured himself a glass of milk; she would have water with dinner, thank you. Then they were seated, candles burning between them.

"Mind if I pray?" he asked her, as though she would ever say anything other than "of course not," which is what she said, her voice cracking. It occurred to her that news of her pregnancy seemed to inspire prayers.

"Dear God, thank you for this food we're about to eat. Thank you for my wife and my daughter. And forgive me, God. Forgive me for not knowing what to say. You know I'm disappointed and I haven't handled this very well. Help Jessica forgive me too, and keep her well. And the baby, too. Amen."

When he looked up, tears were streaming down his wife's face. "I'm so sorry, Paul. I'm so sorry!" She began to violently sob causing her to immediately have to race to the bathroom, Paul right on her heels. When she was done depositing the cracker she'd eaten before dinner in hopes it would settle her stomach, she positioned herself in her usual recovery posture sitting on the floor, back against the wall. Paul sat down right beside her and put his arm around her.

"I'm so sorry, Paul," she whispered through her sobs as she leaned into him.

Paul put the knuckle of his index finger under her chin and tilted her face toward his. "Jessica, I love you. Please don't cry, honey." He grabbed a few sheets of toilet paper from the roll mounted on the wall next to him and wiped her eyes, then he grabbed a couple more sheets and held them to her nose. "Blow," he said. And she did, her face as red as he'd ever seen it. When she was settled down he said, "Stay right here. Do not move—unless you have to, of course." He smiled that endearing lopsided smile she couldn't resist, the one that had gotten her in this predicament to start with. He disappeared from the room, then returned with a plastic bag from Wal-Mart. Miraculously, Sarah Sue hadn't uttered a peep, which allowed the two of them to have this moment to themselves. "Open it," he said, then kissed her on the cheek.

She separated the sides of the bag and saw the most beautiful little teddy bear looking right up at her. "Oh, Paul!" She took the bear out of the bag and clutched the softness under her chin. "Sarah Sue will love it!"

"It's not for Sarah Sue; it's for you. I bought it for your first Pregnant Gift."

Jessica gasped. The day after she'd told Paul she was pregnant with Sarah Sue, he'd bought her what he'd called a Pregnant Gift. He continued to bring her a teddy bear, one more precious than the next, each month of her pregnancy—aside from the flannel nightgown with the teddy bear print on it, which he saved for her birth month. "Special for the hospital," he'd said with pride. "Button-down top for the . . . um . . . feeding." He'd built a shelf in their bedroom to house the bear collection so they could keep watch over her and the baby in her belly while he was at work.

"But I hadn't told you yet this time," she said to him as they continued to sit on the floor. "How did you know?"

"At first I didn't. At first I thought you had the flu. Then I worried you had something worse. Then . . . I just knew. Something about the look on your face. I just knew."

"When did you know?"

"When I left yesterday morning and told you to phone the doctor if you weren't feeling better. I looked at your face . . . I looked at *you*, and I just knew. I decided, since you were obviously having a hard time telling me, that I would make it easy for you tonight at dinner and have Bunky here," he stopped and patted the little bear on top of the head, "do the talking for me. And then you just blurted it out. I was disappointed Bunky couldn't do his thing—I couldn't have *my* big moment—and I'm afraid I didn't handle it very well after that."

"Is that what you were apologizing for in your dinner prayer?"

"Yes."

"Oh, Paul!" Both of them still on the floor, she awkwardly situated herself until she was sitting on his lap and wrapped an arm around his neck. "I love you so much! I just don't know how we're going to be able to afford this. And I don't even know if I have the . . ." He put his finger over her mouth.

"Shush, sweet wife of mine, and just give me a kiss."

Her eyes cast to the toilet bowl, recalling what her last action had been. "You crazy? This might be the grossest kiss you've ever experienced."

"I'm willing to take the risk." Just as he leaned his head forward, Sarah Sue began to cry and his wife bolted forward.

Ready or not, reality was setting in.

11

"**J**acob, it's Mom," Dorothy said into the receiver. "Did I catch you at a bad time? You sound like you're frazzled."

"It's been a wild day alright, but I'm really glad to hear from you, Mom. I was going to call you later in the week; sorry you beat me to it. Did you get my e-mail yesterday though? I usually hear back from you right away."

"Yup. Got it. Thanks for the update about your car. I'm glad the recall issue didn't apply to your model. I was gonna e-mail you back, then thought I'd call instead. I just wanted to hear your voice.

"Thanks, Mom."

"Any *real* news from Pennsylvania to tell me about? Famous cases? Will I see you on the ten o'clock news—although we both know I couldn't stay awake that long. HA!" Jacob was Dorothy's tall, dark and handsome attorney son. He was also her firstborn. Each time she thought about his age and position, she wondered where on earth the time had gone. Wasn't she just potty training him? Although he'd never married, his life had been a busy one. He was driven. Perhaps so driven to climb the ladder that he hadn't had time to settle down. But then, he was extra particular.

"Nothing that exciting or dramatic. Just two cases that are consuming more of my life than I barely have time for right now."

Dorothy's heart sank. She didn't think his response boded well for his ability to come home for Thanksgiving, even though she'd allowed herself to believe he would. "Any end in sight?" she asked, firing up her optimism.

"I'm hoping to have them wrapped up before the holidays."

"Which holidays would that be? Thanksgiving? Christmas?" The last thing she wanted to do was lay a guilt trip on a busy man, but still . . .

Jacob erupted in a hearty laugh, one that sounded like his father's—although when Henry'd been alive, he'd laughed far more often than his serious son and namesake, Jacob Henry Wetstra. Jacob knew his mom was hoping for the earlier answer from her mid-fifties son; she was sometimes as transparent as cellophane. "Thanksgiving, Mom. I'm hoping to be there for Thanksgiving and your B-day. I hated to miss all of Partonville's big festivities last month, especially knowing how much you put into it. From the sounds of your e-mails and phone calls, though, no doubt a good time was had by all without me. I'll tell you, I sure have enjoyed reading the Centennial Plus Thirty booklet! Thanks for sending it. I felt a real flare of pride when I read our family's short bio. Tell Doc and Eugene they did a great job on it."

He'd been thinking a lot about home lately. More than he hated missing the Pumpkin Festival, though, he had hated to disappoint his mom when he found out he couldn't make it. She was eighty-seven, almost eighty-eight now. He never knew when his last visit would be just that, and it always knotted his throat to think about such things. "Yup, it looks like if I don't sleep between now and Thanksgiving, I'll be able to make it home." When he'd said "home" he'd had to snap the image of the farm out of his mind, since the visual had gone there by default. He tried to remember what his mom's new little house even looked like. He decided referring to *that* as "home" was not right. What should he call it? "Your house?" All of these thoughts blindsided him as they reeled through his mind; he'd never been one to dwell on the sentimental.

It fretted Dorothy when she thought her son wasn't getting enough sleep. "Are you taking care of yourself, Jacob? I'd hate to think you're working night and day and not having a lick of fun. I'd rather you spend that time sleeping rather than traveling if you're overdoing it."

It took him a second to answer. "Nobody cares about you like your mother," he said gently, meaning every word. "Don't worry. I've been burning the candle at both ends a good deal lately, but I get caught up on sleep when I can. And I'm making sure I get to the gym at least three times a week, sometimes four. Helps the stress levels."

"You young folks and your gyms. We just used to take good long hikes down to the creek, or walk a mile or two to a neighbor's or play kick the can, climb trees . . ."

"Mom, I'm over fifty, not twelve."

"I'm talking about folks your age," she said. "Katie Durbin went on and on about how she couldn't fit her exercise equipment upstairs in the farmhouse." She instantly wished she hadn't mentioned Katie's name since she wasn't sure if Jacob had decided yet whether or not Katie could be trusted, their first meetings having gotten off on less than agreeable footing. "I'm talking about people doing things together rather than everybody getting on their own machines in their homes or at the gym and running as fast as they can and never actually going anywhere or seeing anything beautiful."

"This is beginning to sound like a mini lecture, Mom," he said with a chuckle—although Dorothy recognized a slight stiffening in his voice.

"Well, if it is, I'm talking to myself since *I'm* barely getting enough walking in. I just worry about you, honey."

"I know, Mom, and I love you for it. Let's change the subject, though. How are things *really* going for you in Pardon-Me-Ville now that you live in town? I know we've talked about it a few times and you always say 'fine, just fine,' but that's not enough of an answer for me to *really* know how you're doing."

"Always the lawyer, huh, son? 'That's not enough of an answer, your honor!'" Both of them chuckled, this kind of teasing an ongoing endearment between the two of them.

"Yes, your honor. How is my mom *really* adjusting after a few months in her new home?" *There, that's what I'll call it. Her new home.*

"You want the truth? My little Vine Street home is not the farm," Dorothy admitted flatly. Sigh. "But it's home now and I'm training myself to think of it that way. I *do* like being so close to May Belle and Earl. But oh, how I miss my barn and the land and Woodsy and . . . But I'm trying to make myself get more exercise since I can't take my daily constitutional down by the creek every morning. You know, replace old habits with new ones. Of course, I say that like I'm doing a good job of it."

"Back to exercise again? How'd you do that? Guess it beats talking about the weather, although I have to say we've sure had our ups and downs out east here when it comes to the hots and colds."

"Same here. One day there's not a cloud in the sky and the weather feels like Indian summer; the next it's damp and cold and makes you think snow is just over yonder and blowing our way."

"You been out to the farm lately?"

"No. No wheels, remember?" She pointedly worked to keep the hard knock of that loss of her independence out of her voice. "But I'm planning on going tomorrow if the weather holds out. Josh is picking me up. We're hoping to get in one last crawdad hunt before the season closes. I think we're pushing it now, though."

"So you and Josh are still buddies, huh?" Jacob thought back to the farm auction, how his brother Vinnie's sons had at first been jealous of their grandmother's relationship with Josh. But by the time they'd all spent a few days together—and especially after the crawdad hunt—Dorothy had made it quite evident who was her flesh-and-blood and who was her good friend. She'd also made it sparkling clear there was room for all of them. Same as she obviously tried to do when it came to Katie, Vinnie and himself—although like his mother, Vinnie was just naturally a more trusting type so he'd taken to the city slicker quicker. Even though Jacob and Katie had seemed to at least come to terms before they all parted ways, he still carried this niggling feeling of distrust about her.

"Well, I hope you get your one last hunt in, Mom, but to be honest with you, I have concerns about you wading in the creek. You know it can be slippery. And I don't want you catching a chill. You know . . ."

"Jacob Henry, this is starting to sound like a mini lecture. Is that what you're meaning to give?" Although he couldn't see her grinning, he heard it in her voice.

"Busted. Okay, we're even. I know you're capable of taking care of yourself, Mom. I just worry about you."

"Yes, and that's one of the billions of reasons I love *you*. Let me get serious a minute here, son. If you do get to come for Thanksgiving, how would you feel about helping to serve a Thanksgiving dinner at church rather than eating at my house?"

He gave it some thought. "Will Vinnie be able to bring his sons?"

"I talked to him just before I called you. He said he's coming no matter what, and that it *looks* like the boys will be with him. Although he wasn't one hundred percent sure, he said Joan was thinking about going to Cancun for the holidays. Apparently she's been seeing someone who invited her and the boys on this swell vacation. The boys declined. 'Refused,' was the exact word Vinnie used. Told her to go ahead and go if she wanted, so it sounds like that's what she's going to do, since she knew Vinnie would be glad to have the boys."

"Wow. How's Vinnie handling this, Joan seeing someone? Someone who has invited her *and* his sons on a vacation?"

"Same as he always does. Says 'To each his own and we're each owned by the same loving Father.'"

"Now where do you think he got that line?" he joked. Jacob had heard it fly out of his mom's lips time and again throughout his life, and his brother's—not to mention Caroline Ann's, his beloved sister. "What I wouldn't give to hear Sis say that again. I've been thinking about her a lot lately." A long silence passed between them.

"Me, too. Me, too, son." Caroline Ann had been the sibling who worked at softening Jacob, the sibling who could loosen him up, challenge him when he was being grumpy, make him laugh out loud. *All loved by the same loving Father. . . .* What was so loving about a God who would let someone die from breast cancer, he'd often wondered? The fact he questioned everything that way was probably why he was a good lawyer. And yet, he secretly longed for just a dose of whatever it was his family members had that made them so strong in their faith.

"Well," he said, chippering up his tone of voice, "I'm anxious to see everybody else! I'll let you know when I'm coming in. In the meantime, though, I better get back to work. Thanks for calling, Mom. I love you."

"Wait! Don't hang up! What do you think about my Thanksgiving idea?"

"Whatever makes you happy, Mom. Might be a good way for all of us to make the transition. I was already thinking how odd it would feel to not be out at the farm." Yes, it would be odd, indeed. And sad, they both thought, although neither spoke it.

Theresa Brewton, the daughter of one of Dorothy's oldest and now departed friends, said the St. Auggie's Social Concerns Committee was excited about the idea of a Thanksgiving Dinner, especially since *they'd* talked about the very same possibility a month ago but had just never gotten going on it. "I do believe," Dorothy said with joy in her voice, "that God is tapping us on the shoulder!" Theresa quite agreed, laughed, then said she would, however, like to talk to God about the extremely short notice—which set them both to laughing. Father O'Sullivan had said their building was pretty booked up with one meeting and another, but they all agreed if they could use the UMC basement, they didn't see why they couldn't pull this off! "But we'll need to keep the meal—the plan—simple," Theresa added. Dorothy agreed (silently *vowing* to keep Gladys out of it!); told her Lester had volunteered to cook whatever was needed; her family would do potatoes (unless numbers got so high they needed another volunteer); May Belle would do some bar desserts and that she was sure UMC would be good for a few turkeys. Then Dorothy popped the All Important Question: "You think you can chair the joint event, Theresa?"

"I don't see why not."

"PRAISE GOD FROM WHOM ALL BLESSINGS FLOW!" Dorothy sang in her tenor voice right into the receiver.

"Wow. That's quite a response!"

"You have *no* earthly idea just how happy that makes me!"

Jessie had to get some time to herself or she was going to explode. While the other three guests (*Arthur might as well be a guest the way I have to wait on him hand and foot!*) had walked back to the creek, she'd headed out Saturday morning and left a note on the kitchen table. Arthur wanted to point out to Herm and Vera the designated park area, the access road set to run right down the property line between Crooked Creek Farm and his property. Jessie told them to just go on ahead, saying she'd seen it all before. The minute they'd left she'd scrawled the note. "Need to run some errands. Help yourselves to anything while I'm gone. If I'm not home for lunch, eat leftovers or make yourselves some grilled cheese sandwiches." She wanted to add a P.S. to Arthur saying, "I'm sure Herm and Vera can help you find the refrigerator," but she stifled herself.

She fired up the sedan and headed down the lane wondering where she would go and where she'd say she'd been when she returned. All she knew for sure was that she needed to be by herself and that was all there was to it. Out of habit she turned right on the gravel road at the end of their driveway, which would lead her toward the hard road into Partonville. Realizing she didn't want to see anyone she knew, she did a gravel-spitting U-turn and headed toward Hethrow. From the field, Arthur noticed the rooster tail of dust kicking up like a land-born jet stream heading that-a-way, but before it had completely evaporated it came zooming back on itself then raced off into the horizon. Mostly he recognized the sound of the Buick's engine. He wondered where his moody wife had headed off to in such a hurry—she hadn't said anything about going anywhere before they left—and he wondered what in the world kind of bees were swarming in her bonnet.

Jessie stayed on the hard road all the way to the interstate where she hopped on and headed north. Twenty miles later she decided she better stop before she no longer wanted to, her journey now feeling more like an escape than a brief getaway.

Yes, it was time to S-T-O-P and consider what she was doing.

"From what I heard tell," Arthur said, still pointing his thick finger toward the bank of trees down the creek line toward Crooked Creek Farm, "this here so-called park ain't gonna go past them trees. Dorothy said they was talkin' 'bout puttin' in swings and such, but she's agin it. Said we don't need no playground when nature provides its own. 'Yup,' I told her. 'That is absolutely true.'" Herm and Vera nodded their heads in agreement.

"Reckon they'll even let the kids jump into the swim-min' hole the way we used to, what with everybody bein' lawsuit happy these days?" Herm stuffed his hands into his pockets, a faraway look in his eyes. He could remember countless youthful days they'd all gathered at Dorothy's named trees by the swimmin' hole and dropped like falling leaves into the creek from Woodsy's strong branches, only to climb back up and do it all over again.

"I hadn't thought 'bout that, but I bet yur exactly dad-gum right! Just leave it to them lawyers to ruin Dorothy's best intentions."

"Now, boys," Vera said, "no sense getting yourselves all riled up before something even happens. And Herm, you know getting riled up will not be good for your blood pres-sure." The men were both shaking their heads back and forth. It was hard to tell whether they were doing so because they thought she was wrong or to erase their own negative thinking.

"I know, Arthur, how about you play us a tune on your Hohner," Vera said in a gear shift. "I see it peeking out of your pocket. It's too nice of a day to be getting so wrought up about possibilities."

Arthur never needed much encouragement to play his harmonica. Within a wink he was playing a soulful rendition of "Unforgettable," which seemed like the perfect tune for the moment. He was good at that kind of thing, matching mood to moment. Even though it was a song with a happy lyric, he continued to grumble within himself about *them dad-gum dirty dogs that might keep kids from havin' their own memories. Insurances kin make things unforgettable before they're even dad-gum experienced!* After the last note was played and Vera was done clapping, Arthur shoved the Hohner back in its resident slot while Vera grabbed hold of Herm's hand to give it a happy squeeze. Herm entwined his fingers with hers in a familiar gesture, which Arthur eyeballed.

"Why don't you two lovebirds float a few sticks down the creek, just for old time's sake. I'm gonna go see what that woman is up to. Maybe she's got lunch on the table. If she does, I'll ring our old lunch bell." Although he hadn't heard her come back, the Buick might have made its way up the driveway while he was playing, his eyes having been aimed at Weeping Willy, Woodsy and Willoway.

"I believe we'll take you up on that, Art," Herm said to his cousin. "You go on ahead. I reckon I can recall a few more stories I haven't ever told Vera yet and I don't imagine they'd be ones you'd want her to know, so better ya don't hear me a tellin' 'em." Herm winked at Arthur but he doubted he saw it. Arthur had spun on his heels and headed toward the house before Herm's eye was even back open again.

". . . make yourselves some grilled cheese sandwiches." Arthur had read every word of Jessie's note out loud. "What errands?" he asked aloud. "We've got company, woman! And it's lunchtime! Ya don't ask company to git their own lunch!" He wadded up the note and stuffed it down deep in his pocket. He opened the refrigerator door and stared at all the containers and jars. He closed the door and decided to just wait it out. Surely she'd be back before Herm and Vera were. He marched into the living room, plopped into his La-Z-Boy and turned on the TV.

Herm and Vera continued holding hands as they strolled along the creek. Herm was indeed recollecting many memories, most she'd heard before. She didn't mention that to Herm, though, because it did her heart good to see her husband enjoying himself. She'd been raised on a farm, too, but a dairy farm. Her farming memories were more attached to the endless hard work and long hours. Up before dawn; to bed practically right after dinner; do it all over again the next day. You just couldn't decide to put off milking a cow to go swim in the creek if you wanted her to continue earning food for the table. Skip a milking or two and the cow could quit producing.

Vera loved Herm's ability to tell such happy stories. She could almost feel the cool creek-water splashes, hear the boys shouting Annie-Annie Olson free—or whatever that phrase was. She chose not to interrupt Herm to ask him, even though she *still* didn't understand what the phrase was, even though he'd just said it. When she was a girl she just mumbled whatever when it had been her turn. No, she didn't wish to spoil his reverie; the more stories he told, the more he'd remember, one leading right into the next.

At some point, though, Vera wondered when she'd stopped listening and begun to wonder what was going on between Arthur and Jessie. What had really seemed to set Jessie off, and she couldn't blame her, was Arthur's insensitive statement about not knowing whether he'd won or lost. Kidding aside, it was an inappropriate comment and she didn't blame Jessie for being mad about it.

"What did you say, Herm?" She realized rather than just talking, he'd asked her something.

"I said, what do you reckon is going on with Arthur and Jessie?"

"Why do you say that, Herm?" It gave Vera the goose bumps to think they'd been thinking about the same thing—not the first time.

"Because she hightailed it down the road right after we got to the creek. I don't know what Arthur's trying to pull, acting like he's goin' up ta see if lunch is ready yet. She ain't returned."

"How do you know she left?"

"I know the sound of a unique Buick when I hear it. And you didn't notice that big rooster tail of dust comin' and goin' this way and that?"

Vera just sighed. No, she hadn't heard or noticed anything about a car; all engines sounded alike to her. She had noticed, however, one of the same things Herm had, and that was the lack of a ringing dinner bell.

12

Josh and Dorothy gabbed nonstop all the way to Crooked Creek Farm, their chatter as lively as the clatter of the rocks on the undercarriage and the patter of the gentle rain that let loose for the last mile of their journey. Of course, that wouldn't dissuade them from a creek adventure since, after all, part of the fun was "accidentally" getting wet anyway. By the time they pulled up next to the farmhouse, Katie was out the back door to greet them. Dorothy carefully stepped down from the tall SUV and moved back in front of Sheba's door. "Do you remember this trick?" she asked Sheba, holding her arms out in front of her.

Sheba came flying through the back window right into her arms. Although it unsteadied Dorothy, it also thrilled her to pieces Sheba still *did* remember. It was, after all, the same way Sheba had exited The Tank nearly all the years of Sheba's eight-year-old life before The Tank died and Dorothy made the decision she needed to quit driving. Josh broke into applause and Katie followed suit, although they'd both caught their breath when Dorothy had wobbled.

"What a grand welcome!" Dorothy said, setting Sheba down—who immediately hightailed it toward the barn and back again, then around their legs. "She thinks we've finally come home," Dorothy said wistfully. She leaned down and patted Sheba's head when she flew by. "Enjoy it while you can, Sheba. That's just what I'm intending to do!" Dorothy opened the SUV's rear door to retrieve her backpack. She slung it over both her shoulders and jostled it around until it settled on her back. Josh tried to talk her into letting him carry it but she told him she was a tougher old bird than he might think. She promised she'd turn it over if it got to be too much. The rain had stopped and she was ready to rumble. "Ready you two?" she asked Josh and Katie who were watching her gear up. "Let's get this show on the road before the rain comes back. Oh, that little bit of rain will have awakened the earth's aromas. I can hardly WAIT!"

"Don't you want to come in and have a sip of something before we head out?" Katie asked.

"And have the call of my flabby old bladder cut the hunting short? Not on your life!"

"Let me grab my jacket," Katie said. "You two go ahead and start down; I'll catch up." They didn't need to be told twice; they were merrily jaunting that way before Katie had reached the door to the back porch.

Before Josh had gone to pick up Dorothy and Sheba, he'd laid out the hunting supplies near the edge of the barn so they could just grab them on the way: his extra pair of shoes, a couple of towels—just in case, a small net (although hands were always better and Dorothy would say he was cheating if he tried to use the net anyway, but nonetheless, he had it too—just in case), a giant bag of potato chips and three cans of soda. He'd packed it all in an old waterproof army surplus bag his dad had once given him. Said he'd had it around for years (couldn't even remember where he'd gotten it) and that his wife, Chloe, Josh's stepmom— although he just called her Chloe—had been cleaning out the garage. Bruce thought Josh might like it. This was the first time Josh used it; it wasn't the type of backpack you'd want to be seen with at school. Certainly not the upper-class Latin School he attended in Chicago when his dad had given it to him, and not Hethrow High either. Sometimes he didn't think his dad knew him at all. Nonetheless, his dad had thought of him, so he'd kept it. After Josh shrugged on the backpack, he and Dorothy turned to see if Katie was on her way yet. Although she wasn't, they kept moving toward the creek. "She'll find us," Josh said. Sheba was already near their destination, feet flying up behind her like they were paddling through the air, squirrels and other critters flying this way and that at her sudden intrusion.

Katie put on her expensive windbreaker and thought how dumb it was to wear such a good jacket to a creek, but it was the only lightweight jacket she owned. She recalled Jessica having teased her one day, asking her if she'd been shopping for barn clothes yet.

"Barn clothes?"

"You know, the type of thing you wear to . . . get dirty."

"You can actually shop for barn clothes? Is that a brand or a style or . . ."

Jessica's face had turned beet red before she broke out laughing. "Oh, Katie! No, barn clothes aren't a brand or a style, unless you count old, worn, stained jeans and sweatshirts a style. And if you do, then for the first time in my life, I am on the cutting edge!" she'd said looking down at her dowdy attire. "I'm just talking about old clothes you own that you don't care one way or the other if they get grubby. I was just teasing you about actually shopping for them!"

Grubby was not one ounce Katie's style; she had no desire to look like she *belonged* in a barn. She decided some people just weren't born to dress down and she was one of them. She picked up the file folder on the kitchen table and ran it upstairs where she slipped it onto her closet shelf next to the box of letters sent between her mom and Aunt Tess. The box of letters that had ultimately led her down the trail to her paternity. She closed the closet door to keep her real estate file out of view; there was no point in talking about something before its time. The only thing it was time for at the moment was to pretend she was interested in slimy, wiggling, clawed little beasts. "Mice and crawdads. What am I doing here?"

After having decided she needed to stop herself before she *never* turned back, Jessie pulled off at the next exit and traveled the overpass toward the ramp leading back in the opposite direction—the one that led home—but she simply could not make herself turn the wheel of that Buick toward the ramp. She drove right on by it and pulled into one of those roadside combination gas station and convenience stores. She eyed a spot as far away from the pumps as she could and backed the Buick in. As she was shutting off the engine she thought, *I'm backed into a corner all right. That's* exactly *how I feel.* She let her head thunk back against the headrest and closed her eyes. She wished she had a pillow to stuff behind her neck. Nothing about her life was comfortable right now. Nothing. Her skin didn't even feel like it settled over her arms correctly and she fussed around repositioning them, first letting her forearms rest in her lap, then draping her hands over the steering wheel, allowing her now wiggly arms to dangle. *Who would have thought? Who would have ever thought I would come to this?* What she really needed was something to throw. But what? And at whom?

She idly watched people pull their vehicles up to the pumps, exit the car, slip what looked to be ... credit cards? ... in and out of the slots. Then they studied some type of a screen before doing anything; Jessie couldn't see the details of what it was all about—drat her fuzzy eyes! Since she and Arthur never left town and the only place Arthur would ever buy gasoline, or allow her to, was at By George's in Partonville—and by George, By George did not have such newfangled equipment as credit card slots and such—she was clueless about what was going on. George simply came to the car, smiled, asked you what you wanted and gave you everything you asked for. Simple. No contraptions.

When did I start allowing Arthur to allow *or* not allow *things in my life?* She lifted her head forward and banged it back against the headrest again, as though to knock some sense into herself, then repeated the action. She watched a woman approach the screen, push a few buttons, slide her card in and out, stare at the screen, walk back to the gas cap and then realize ... something. She saw the woman's mouth moving as though she was chastising herself. *Good. I've got company.* The lanky woman leaned inside her car and did something and the cover to the gas cap popped open. She came back and unscrewed the cap, allowing it to dangle from a cord. It reminded Jessie of Edward Showalter's wallet he kept attached to his belt with a chain. The woman lifted the nozzle, pulled up a handle, stuck the nozzle in her auto's gasoline shoot, then pulled the trigger. She must have snapped on some kind of pumping lock because the woman cleaned her windshield. *She doesn't have to talk to anyone. She depends on nobody to help her travel to wherever she's going next.* The longer Jessie watched, the more appealing this idea became. Maybe By George's had helped contribute to her . . . dependency? *Is that what I am? Dependent? And if so, whatever happened to Mugsy knock-'em-dead McGee?* She determined the next time she needed gasoline she would drive clear out of town to one of these stations and pump her own. But first, she guessed she'd have to find out how to get a credit card. She and Arthur had never owned one, Arthur believing you should pay your way as you go. Not that she'd been opposed to that line of thinking, mind you, but Arthur had made that decision for the both of them. *No more!*

She'd surely paid her own way as she went, she decided. She'd paid—yes, it had cost her *plenty*—to go absolutely nowhere. Now here she sat.

She wondered what time it was. She'd never been one to wear any jewelry, not even a watch or a wedding ring. Since she was playing ball when she and Arthur married, she told him not to bother with a ring since she'd have to take it off to play and she was afraid she might lose it. That was the truth, but it was also the truth that she figured she could never ever get used to some bobble on her finger. She looked at her left ring finger and tried to picture anything there. Her nails were ragged and somewhat dirty. She chewed the edge off one that looked particularly uneven. Decided that looked better, but then, who cared? She leaned forward to look at the sun's position through the windshield and decided it was past one-thirty. She lifted her buttocks off the seat a bit so she could ram her hand into her jeans pocket and retrieve her money she kept in a money clip, just like a man. Twenty-two dollars. That wasn't going to take her very far. She noticed a sign in the window of the station. When she got close enough, she saw it said Vienna Dogs and went and got herself one—she was excessive with the mustard, which always annoyed Arthur—along with a self-serve soda, lots of ice. All that ice annoyed him too. Said she never got her money's worth of soda with all that ice. She added two more cubes before snapping on the lid and paying. She carried her lunch out to the car and set the soda right on top of the hood, no napkin beneath it. That would bug Arthur. She hoped it made a ring and he saw it. She leaned her backside against the hood and ate her dog, thinking. Thinking she didn't have enough money to do anything but head home, which made her mad until she realized she'd *have* to go home anyway—at least for now—since the Happy Hookers would be coming to her house for bunco come Wednesday. *Not yet.* She wasn't ready to go home *yet.* She better stall for at least another hour if she wanted to make sure she didn't have to serve them all lunch. She tossed her garbage in the can and got back in the car, but after two minutes she knew she couldn't sit still any longer so she fired up the Buick. But she had to go home with something or where would she say she'd been? *Getting a hot dog in . . . Gads! I don't even know where I AM!*

13

As Katie stepped onto the back porch to head for the creek, the phone rang.

"Katie! It's Jessica. You busy?"

"I was just on my way out the door. Dorothy and Josh are probably already down at the creek; they're going crawdad hunting and you know how much I love *that*!" They both laughed at the absurd notion. "In fact, I was just thinking about you a minute ago when I realized I still don't own any barn clothes—and that I don't care if I ever do." She waited to hear Jessica's lively chuckle but there was only silence. "Jessica? You still there?"

"Yes. I'll let you go. You're busy."

"What's up? You sound . . . different."

"Not much is up. No, *everything* is. I was gonna take a ride out to the farm if you weren't busy; I have something to tell you. But go ahead and enjoy your company. And tell Dorothy I said thank you. She'll know what I'm talking about."

"Why don't you come tell her yourself? I'll wait up here for you. If I'm lucky, by the time you get here they'll already be back and I won't have to deal with the creepy critters at all!" Again Katie laughed but Jessica did not. "Jessica, is everything okay with you?"

"Yes. No. Well, I'm sure it will be."

"Okay, you're driving me crazy, not to mention worrying me now. What is up?"

"I don't want to tell you over the phone."

"Then get yourself over here and *now*. I'm not going to be able to enjoy myself for wondering what's going on. Or should I just ask Dorothy?"

"NO!"

"Then bring Sarah Sue, and Paul too. He's off today, right?"

"Yes. He's off. He finally had time for me to give him a haircut, which was long overdue. I shaved a little too close over one ear and he didn't say a word and. . . . Honestly, he is so patient, so kind to me." Her voice hitched. "He's the one who told me to get out of the house and 'go out to Crooked Creek and talk to your friend.'" Katie warmed to think Paul considered her in that way; she was still trying to get to know him better. She could never decide if he was perhaps a little shy, or just quiet, or what. Jessica said he was always "running on tired," due to his mining hours and all the responsibilities around the Lamp Post—not to mention being a daddy. That could account for it too. But some people were just naturally more elusive than others; maybe he was just one of them. He definitely loved his wife and daughter, though, which made him one man Katie could give her approval to.

"So do it. Get on over here! What are you waiting for?"

After a short silence, during which time Jessica tried to think of a good reason not to go—other than that she might be sick—she realized that the truth was that her need to share her news was stronger than her embarrassment over barging into someone else's gathering. And if she puked, well, she'd puke. And if it had been anyone else but

Dorothy . . . "I'm on my way. Don't wait up, though. Head on down to the creek. I'll find you."

"Are you kidding? I've already taken off my jacket. I'll be right at this kitchen table where things are cozy with my new fabulous rug runner, there are no clawed critters, there is no dirt . . ." Her eyes landed on a mousetrap. "Okay, there are mousetraps but no dirt, and I'm waiting for my best friend. I'll put some coffee on right now."

"NO!" Jessica realized she'd been a little too emphatic once again, but the mere thought of the smell of coffee rumbled her stomach. "No," she said in a quieter voice. "Thank you, but I just don't have a taste for coffee."

"Okay then, I'll just sit here and watch the mousetraps." However, the idea she might actually see action rumbled *her* stomach. "On second thought, I'll slip my jacket back on and wait for you on the front porch. I don't think I've sat on the porch swing since . . . I can't remember when."

"Bye!" Jessica said just before she slammed the phone into its cradle. The mere *thought* of swinging made her nauseous.

Josh held the brown wiggling critter high over his head. "Check the size of THIS one! This ought to score me double!" Dorothy was bent over at the waist and in the middle of lifting a rock. They'd barely begun and already Josh had scored? She straightened up a little too quickly and lost her balance.

"Dorothy!" Josh let the crawdad plunk into the water and leapt to her side, grabbing her by the elbow just in time to help steady her before she went down. Dorothy shivered while she got her bearings, the combination of the cool air, water and the incident taking their toll. The heel of her wet shoe (it was just too nippy for bare feet) slipped on a mossy rock and again she almost went down but Josh held her steady. Rather than cave in to the drama of the moment, she straightened herself and took Josh's hand in hers.

"What big one? I don't see a big one. I think you said that just to distract me from the one I was surely about to nab." She laughed. Josh smiled but his gaze did not leave her face. While still holding her hand, he slid his free arm around her waist. He thought she was, as she had recently proclaimed, the toughest old bird he would ever meet in his life, and yet, sometimes she seemed so fragile it scared him.

"Right. That's exactly what I did," Josh said in a quasi repentant voice. Josh noticed Dorothy shiver again, the dampness clearly getting to her. "What say we call the hunt a tie and head back to the house; it's colder than I thought it was. I don't think Mom's gonna make it down here anyway." Dorothy agreed with his suggestion. Josh ushered them both back to the big log where they'd left their gear. He held both of her hands as she sat down, then he sat down beside her while they changed into their dry shoes and socks, which admittedly felt good to both of them.

"Dorothy, do you think Pastor Delbert would like to get to know me and Mom better?"

Dorothy finished tying the last bow of her new pink shoelaces she'd just this morning laced into her Keds. She sat up slowly and studied Josh's face. *Wonder how long that question's been on the end of his tongue? Such a kind and tender boy. So vulnerable. Just like my Vinnie at this age.* "Yes, Joshmeister. I think he'd like to get to know the nephew he never knew he had."

"Then why hasn't he called us?"

"Have either of you called him?"

He looked a little sheepish. "I can't speak for Mom, but I don't think so. And no, I haven't phoned him either. I just figured the adults needed to make the first move."

Dorothy chuckled. "Are you admitting you're not an adult yet?"

"I hate trick questions, especially from adults," Josh teased. "I can tell this is going to be a no-win answer for me."

"Here's the thing, Josh." Dorothy stuffed her wet shoes into a plastic shopping bag and rearranged a few items in her backpack, stalling to find the right words as she silently prayed for a good answer. "Situations like this take time. I'm sure Pastor wants to get to know you. Both of you. After all, he's never had the chance to experience what it's like to have a sister . . . half sister . . . and a nephew."

"Half of a nephew," Josh said, trying to lighten the moment.

"Right. Half of a nephew, although I wonder which half he'd choose right now," she said, smiling while looking him up and down.

Josh took note of his muddy pants. "I think he'd choose the half with the ears and the cleft in the chin since they both look exactly like his."

Dorothy thought about the attributes of her sons—physical and otherwise—that were like their dad's. It always felt like such a miracle to see so many pieces of Henry and his father before him living on in a son's smile, the shape of a fingernail bed, things they'd all commented on at one time or another. It was hard having her children live so far away, not getting to see her grandsons that often—another reason she was grateful to God for filling in some of the gaps with this lovely child. Something positive to do with her longing. "Yes. You do share those features, Josh. It's obvious you've studied him well. He's probably noticed those exact same similarities."

"Think?"

"I think it's highly possible. You'll have to ask him yourself one day."

"You know, Dorothy, it feels good to me. It feels good to know where my ears and chin came from. I mean I know I look a lot like my dad, but there's always been something different than either my mom *or* my dad. And I've also noticed that Mom and Delbert have the exact same color of eyes. I know she's noticed, too, since I caught her staring at her own eyes up close in the mirror one day."

"Did she say anything about them?"

"No. But I knew what she was thinking. I see that same look on her face when she studies her dad's, my *real* grandpa's, pictures. That's okay to call him her dad, my grandpa, isn't it?" It felt odd since neither his mom nor he had ever met the man before he died.

"Yes, it's fine to call him that, since he is." They were silent for a moment. "Do you and your mom ever talk about this?"

"No. Not really. I've brought it up a couple of times, just wondering when we all might get together."

"What does she say?"

"She says these things take time. They can't be rushed or forced. Then she changes the subject."

"She's right. Be patient, with both of them."

"So you don't think I should stop by and see Pastor Delbert? Uncle Delbert?"

"I didn't say that. No sir-ee, I did not *say* that." She winked at him.

Josh studied her face. She looked right inside of him somehow, and he thought how good it always made him feel when she did. Like she knew him better than he knew himself.

Josh stood and offered her his hands to help her stand. She took them, he gave a gentle tug and up she came. By the time she'd completely righted herself, she stood before him—both of them exactly five feet and ten inches tall—still holding his hands. She gave them a good squeeze and his eyes a big smile, letting him know she approved of what she knew he would soon do.

"You know," Josh said, "I really did have a giant crawdad. I really did win."

"You'll never be able to prove it by me. I'm thinking we'll have to have a hunt-off in the spring, don't you?"

"Yup. And maybe Alex can join us."

While Josh pictured the three of them together, splashing away, Dorothy wondered if God would keep her on this earth that long. She sure hoped so. After all, there was a huntin' tie to break. *Just one more summer, Lord. Just one. But Thy will be done. Thy will be done.*

◇◆◇

"I am so tired of blubbering." Jessica took the tissue from Katie's hand, wiped her cheeks, then gave a hearty blow of her red nose. Her entire newsflash—including Paul's endearing Pregnant Gift—had spilled out with barely a breath in between sentences aside from some hiccupping sobs made all the sobbier by the retelling of Paul's tenderness. The only thing she hadn't mentioned was Dorothy's drop-by. "Well, aren't you going to say something?" Jessica finally asked Katie after she settled down and their eyes met.

"Yes, I am." Pause. She wanted to throw her arms around her and say *Congratulations!,* but after carefully studying her

sweet friend's face during her entire emotional rendering, realizing how worn and torn Jessica was about the news, Katie
gave herself time to consider her response. "Yes, I am going
to say something, Jessica." Katie's tongue rolled around in
her mouth finally settling between her lower gum and cheek
like a wad of chewing tobacco. She mindlessly tapped her
finger against the protrusion like she was checking to see if
her tongue was still awake in there. "You look like Rudolph
the Red-Nosed Reindeer." Pause. "Only not as good."

Jessica's eyes widened. Then her bottom lip began to
quiver. Then she busted out laughing so hard she nearly
made herself sick *and* wet her pants. The laughter Katie had
hoped to elicit caused her to begin laughing, too. The two
of them sounded like a laugh machine, one picking up
where the other left off. Every time they'd start to simmer
down, one of them would burst out again. "Oh, Katie!"
Jessica managed to get out between bouts. "You could not
have said anything more perfect! Boy, did I need to laugh!"

"Well, that's a happy sound!" Dorothy studied Jessica,
her long slender legs stretched out in front of her on Katie's
mud-colored, kit-leather couch, tennis shoes off her feet
and neatly tucked under the coffee table. Dorothy raised
questioning eyebrows at Jessica, who nodded an affirmation. "Well, at least you're finally laughing about it. I'd say
that's mighty fine progress."

"So you know, too, Dorothy?" Katie asked.

"She kind of found out by accident when she stopped by
and I had to run to the bathroom and heave. She was so
kind . . ."

"Is that what you wanted me to thank her for?" Katie
asked Jessica.

"Yes, but I guess I can do it myself now."

"Pish-posh on the thank-yous. I'd say from the laughter that Katie had the better medicine anyway, whatever it was. Yes indeedy-do, laughter is always a good medicine."

"Argh! Don't say medicine, Dorothy!" Jessica grabbed her stomach just thinking about it, which caused Dorothy to laugh, which set them all into hysterics again.

Katie looked up and saw Josh standing in the doorway to the living room. He was leaning against the doorframe on his elbow, arms crossed in front of him. He looked puzzled and . . . for whatever reason funny to all three of them, who continued to guffaw until they were absolutely spent. Giddiness, they concluded, was a wonderful, cleansing gift.

"Oh, my sides hurt from laughing so hard," Jessica said. "I can't believe all that jiggling around hasn't made me sick."

"Give it time," Dorothy said somewhat under her breath. And again, they laughed.

"I have a feeling I've missed the punch line here," Josh said, having no idea what on earth was causing such chaotic howling.

"You missed more than that," Katie said, sniffing through her laughter. "You missed the biggest news I've heard for some time!"

"And that would be . . . ?" Josh's eyes cast from woman to woman waiting for someone to answer.

"I'm pregnant again!" Jessica blurted out in front of another hysterical laugh as though it was the funniest joke she'd ever had played on her. "Isn't that a hoot?" And then she laughed until she broke down and cried again, not knowing which of the two felt better.

❖◆❖

Jessie arrived home just in time to find Vera at the sink washing up the lunch dishes. Jessie was carrying a bag of potato chips in one hand and a six-pack of bottled root beer in the other. "Root beer tasted pretty good the other night," Jessie said. "Thought we might need us some more." Vera gave her a kind smile, then pulled the drain plug in the sink. While Jessie reconfigured the refrigerator to accommodate the six-pack, the sounds of water gulped and swirled down the drain.

"I take it you made the boys lunch." It was a statement, not a question, and it had come out of Jessie's mouth with an edge of sarcasm.

"It's the least I can do to help you out while we're staying here, Jessie. There wasn't anything to it, you had so many nice leftovers in the fridge. Did you get lunch? I can . . ."

"Yup, I ate" was all she said, feeling no need to explain her Vienna Dog in *whereverland*, which now seemed more like a visit to the Twilight Zone than reality. An awkward silence hung in the air while Jessie put the chips in a cabinet. "Where are they?" She didn't really need to ask since the television was blaring from the living room.

"The boys?"

Jessie bit her tongue, several other descriptions flying through her head. "Yes."

"Napping in front of the TV, at least I suspect that's what they're doing. I haven't heard a word since they walked in there. Herm usually shuts his eyes for a few minutes in the afternoon. Does Arthur?"

"Arthur shuts his eyes to lots of things," she said, then was sorry for having said it. "I mean he can sleep through just about anything if he's in that dang La-Z-Boy."

Vera studied Jessie for a moment and looked like she was

debating something. "I think I'll go up to our room and give you a little peace and quiet. I brought a couple of magazines," she said, folding the dishtowel over the cabinet door under the sink, just the way she'd found it. Jessie said nothing in response.

Awkward. Awkward. Pull yourself together, Jessie. Arthur isn't her fault. "If that's what you'd like to do," Jessie replied. Forcing herself to brighten her tone of voice, she added, "Otherwise we could maybe play a little crazy eights."

Vera's eyes brightened. "Crazy eights? Why I haven't played crazy eights for so long!" She tried to decipher if Jessie wanted to play cards or was just being obliging. Then she decided even if Jessie was just trying to cheer her own self up, a few good rounds of cards might be just the ticket. "That would be right fun!"

"I'll get the cards. How about you pour yourself a root beer and open a bottle for me."

"You got it." Vera went to work on the beverages and Jessie disappeared around the corner. She kept the playing cards in the dining room buffet, same place she kept the bunco dice and score cards, poker chips and a very old game of Sorry, the box ripped at all four corners. *Sorry. Exactly,* she thought, as she pushed the board game aside to get to the deck of cards that had made its way to the back of the shelf. *We are one sorry excuse for a couple. But right now, there's nothing I can do about it but play crazy eights. Perfect.* By the time she returned to the kitchen, Vera had everything set out, including a bowl of potato chips.

"I hope you don't mind if I opened that bag of chips," she said somewhat sheepishly. "I tell you, they looked so good when you brought them in that I haven't been able to stop thinking about them. Even though I am not one ounce hungry, they just seemed like the right accompaniment for a card game. I can't remember when I last had a potato chip! Herm says it sounds like my head's empty when I crunch, so rather than annoy him, I just stopped buying brittle snacks."

Jessie pulled the worn-just-right deck of cards out of the box. She remembered when this deck was brand new and it was all she could do to keep them from flying this way and that, they were so slick. She lifted half the cards off the deck and began to shuffle with determined vigor, whapping the deck on the table, cutting them in half and reshuffling again and again until she set them down and scooted them in front of Vera. "Cut?"

"Nope. They're fine," Vera said, tapping the top of the deck with her index finger giving it the customary seal of approval.

Jessie began the deal, one to Vera, one to herself. Pause. "So let me get this straight," Jessie said—slap of card, slap of card—"you quit eating something you like because Herm doesn't like the way your head sounds when you chew? As though you could possibly do anything about that? As though he has a right to"—slap, slap—"keep you from"—slap, slap, slap—"enjoying potato chips?"

Vera began to pick up her cards one at a time and fan them into her hand, arranging and rearranging. Jessie plunked the rest of the deck on the table and set about fanning her own cards. Vera opened her mouth to speak but then shut it and moved one card way on the right to the far left of her fan. She stared at Jessie over the top of the five of clubs, then popped a chip in her mouth and chewed, mouth closed, as though she was proving something. As though Jessie would now see why she'd quit eating them.

Jessie didn't look up. "Sounds fine to me."

Vera picked up another chip and popped it into her mouth, this time chewing with her lips slightly parted. Jessie fingered through the top of the bowl until she reached the biggest chip. She popped it into her mouth and started to chew, but decided to add one more. Then she chomped. "Your play," she said, a couple of crumbs falling out of the right side of her mouth before she swiped at them with her knuckle.

Vera stuffed two chips into her mouth and chomped. Crunchcrunchcrunch. "These are the best potato chips!" She'd chewed, swallowed and had gone for two more before she made her play.

"Euchre anyone?" Herm asked through a yawn as he walked through the doorway and noticed them playing cards. He rubbed his hands together in anticipation of the possibility.

Although it flicked through Jessie's head to say NO!, *we—the WOMEN*—are playing cards here, suddenly the idea of her and Vera against Herm and Arthur held quite an appeal. She folded her fan and without asking snatched Vera's cards out of her hand. She flipped through the entire deck one card at a time, removing everything but nines through aces. Then she started to shuffle. "Go get your cousin!" she demanded. "Girls against guys." *And isn't THAT the truth?* "Game on!"

"Arthur!" Herm yelled as he pulled out one of the chairs between them and seated himself. "Arthur! Get in here. Euchre!"

"Herm," Vera said in a sterner voice than she usually used with him. She lowered her volume and softened her tone. "No need to yell."

"You tried talkin' to him lately? I believe ol' Art is in need of a hearing aid."

"You tell him that?" Jessie wanted to know.

"You tell him?" he fired back.

"About a million times."

"What does he say?"

"He either doesn't hear me or he just grumbles. Has a million excuses, like 'I wasn't listenin'' or 'you mumble,' or my personal favorite, 'Yur not sayin' nothin' I wanna hear anyway.'" She was shuffling the cards so fast it was a wonder they weren't smoking.

"You call?" Arthur asked as he sidled up to the table scratching his right armpit.

"Sit down," Jessie commanded. "Euchre. Vera and me against you and Herm."

"Where'd we get the tater chips?" Arthur asked. He hadn't seen any of those around for a good long while. He always preferred the popcorn Jessie made. Cheaper and fresher. Said he always suspected there weren't any real potatoes in those bags of potato chips anyway—which is, of course, why she'd purchased them before her return.

"From me," Jessie responded as she winged them each their cards, dealing in multiples of two, then three, then two . . . her fingers flying, dispensing them like she was a professional dealer, or a robot, or one who could, if she got a mind to, zing a card three feet off the table and decapitate someone like she'd seen in one of those kung fu movies on TV.

"Hmm" was all Arthur said in response, figuring getting chips was what she must have been up to with those rooster tails of dust. Maybe. But he doubted it; she was gone far too long for that.

As the rest of them studied and fanned their cards, Jessie got up and topped off the bowl of chips, scooted it right next to Vera's elbow, then poured a second bowl full, setting this one down between her and Herm. She sat down, fanned her cards, repositioned a couple, then grabbed two chips and stuck them in her mouth, crunching down on them with unnecessary energy. She chewed and smacked. Smacked and chewed. Herm just stared at his cards. Jessie noticed Vera hadn't touched the chips since Herm had come to the table. Jessie continued to cram one chip after another into her mouth until she finally caught Vera's eye. Jessie opened wide her mouth and stuck a chip in, flaring her eyelids wide open and nodding her head, trying to force Vera to do the same with her chips. Which she didn't.

When Jessie finally wiped her hands on her pants and turned the top pile card over, it was a three of hearts. "What do ya say we call clubs trump," Arthur said to Herm rather than asked. "Let's whip 'em good right outta the shoot."

Jessie held back a groan, having not a single club in her hand, in fact, nothing over a ten aside from one queen of an off suit, then picked up her bowl of chips and held it across the table in front of Vera. "Here. Have a chip, Vera." Just to be polite, which Vera always was, she took one, gave a glance to Herm, then reluctantly set it down on her napkin next to the bowl near her elbow. Jessie snorted through her nose loud and strong enough to blow out a candle, had one been burning.

Arthur led with an ace of hearts, feeling very clever since he was left holding both the right and left bower, the two highest cards impossible to beat, and the ace and king of clubs. If there'd been a television commentator giving the call, he would have said, "It's only possible for him to lose one hand, and that's if someone has to trump his ace. The rest are his." Which, cutting to the chase, would mean the men would get the first point. Of course, only Arthur knew what he held at this juncture, but Jessie knew Arthur well enough to know what his grinning mug meant. He and Herm were going to take this hand, no doubt about it. And that's just what they did in very short order. They high-fived and acted like goons, repeating this childish performance the next four hands in a row. Although the cards were with the men this evening, Jessie thought, the adults lived in the *female* bodies.

With determination, Vera, who had been lusting for more potato chips all along and who had suddenly had it with Herm and Arthur's smugness, picked up two chips and crammed them into her mouth. CRUNCH! Chomp-chomp. More chips. Chomp-chomp-chomp. Jessie did the same. Within a few minutes, both bowls were nearly empty. But still, the boys won. And they war-hooped now along with their high-fiving, acting plumb nuts, if Vera didn't say so herself, which she did when the guys won the whole enchilada.

But in the end, Jessie felt victorious, even if it wasn't for herself. "Vera," she said, "some things matter more than who wins or loses a lousy game of cards." She put the rest of the chips in a Zip-loc bag, retrieved the other bag of chips she'd purchased and packed them both in a grocery bag, which she handed to Vera with a triumphant smile. Although Jessie wondered if Vera would have the strength to crunch on her own once she and Herm went home, it really didn't matter. All that mattered was that at least for a moment, she had set another captive free from an over-bearing Landers man.

14

"That was a right nice picture show, don't you think?" Edward Showalter asked his Saturday matinee date as they left the theater, the theater at which he'd used the dollar-off matinee coupon he'd won from Johnny. He held the theater door open for Nellie Ruth but not with an ounce of suave. He couldn't remember whether you walk in front of a woman to pass through first so you can hold the door open from the outside, or just try to jostle from behind her to push it open, her leading the way—which is the route he decided to take but which was awkward at best and left her having to push it open the rest of the way, wide enough for her to actually pass through since his arm wasn't seven feet long. He felt like a klutz ("nerves will do that to you," Johnny later told him) and wondered how on earth they'd finagled their way into The Piece the other day without this difficulty. He managed to get the van door open and she scooted right into the front seat. "Buckle up!" he said. "Wouldn't want a lovely lady to take any chances!" *My* lovely lady, he wanted to say but didn't, the endearment feeling way too presumptuous.

New relationships, he thought, were complicated.

Although his faith and ongoing sobriety boosted his self-esteem, the constant knowledge of how quickly and how low one can fall held its own doubled-edged sword of insecurities when it came to a relationship with someone who didn't know firsthand the evils of addiction. Edward Showalter cringed each time he recalled some of his lowest moments involving booze and fast women. Cringed. Nellie Ruth was such a *lady*, a lady worthy of his best attempts at suave, no matter how bumbling they may be, so on he would charge.

He eagerly jogged around the front of the van and slid in behind the wheel to sit beside her. Twice during the movie their fingers had touched while reaching into the shared "Large Popcorn, Comes With Two Drinks" special, neither entirely sure their touch had been an accident. One or the other, and usually both, would extract their fingers like they'd been snake-bit, whispering, "Go ahead." "Sorry!" "No, you go ahead." But they both still remembered the tingly feeling brought on by the slightest of touches as they rode side by side in the camouflage-painted van.

Edward Showalter had spent the entire morning cleaning his van after feeling quite embarrassed about it during their last date. He'd seen Nellie Ruth cast an eye over her shoulder the first time she got in and he wondered why on earth he'd never noticed the mess before. He'd since tossed out two empty McDonald's bags, extracted numerous rags into a pile to be washed, gathered a pair of beyond-stained painters' pants he kept for quick-changes on extra-dirty jobs (couldn't remember the last time he'd washed them), discovered three empty Cheetos bags, four empty Coke cans and . . . He'd have to start eating better if he was to get in tip-top shape for Nellie Ruth, he decided. And while he was at it, he'd also have to try scrubbing some of those varnish stains from his fingers and get a new razor (old single-blade just wasn't doing the job) and spit-polish his good shoes—all of which he'd managed to accomplish before picking her up for the movie. All the activity had not only spruced him up but helped him work off some of his nerves. He was doing everything he could to make himself appear worthy.

Nellie Ruth had spent an inordinate amount of time before her Saturday date staring in the mirror, wondering what was becoming of her that she would take a day off of work. Since when did an assistant manager shirk responsibilities? She *always* worked on Saturdays, and at a cash register to boot! But yesterday, when ES had mentioned the possibility of a matinee, she immediately called one of the checkers who usually had Saturdays off and asked her if she'd like to trade days with her, Nellie Ruth taking the woman's Thursday spot, which she agreed to. Now she had to phone ES to tell him it was a go. She still had a difficult time believing a woman should call a man. It's not the way things had been done in her era. Even though she'd never actually dated as a teen—or as an adult, for that matter—she'd learned the protocols.

In order to clean his van within earshot of his telephone, Edward Showalter had pulled it right up onto his front lawn, right up next to the front door of his house, which he propped open. Once in a while he'd even stop crumbling papers and tossing cans just to make sure he wasn't missing a ring-a-ling. When she finally did call, he was happy to learn the matinee was *on*. He barely finished up all his cleaning, chores and personal scrubbing before it had been time to pick her up.

And now, all too soon, the show was over and he was driving her home. It was as though time had speeded up on him and he wondered how he might slow it down the next time they were together.

"You never did tell me how you liked the movie," he said, turning his head toward her for a flash, then looking down at his speedometer only to realize he was barely going fifteen miles an hour. Still, he didn't push down one lick harder on the gas pedal.

Mmmm. What was that aftershave fragrance? "Yes, the movie was great. I can't think when I've last been to a movie."

Edward Showalter was smacked with an outrageous thought and his heart began to hammer at the risk, but he decided to walk the plank and follow through with it anyway before he chickened out. "Maybe we oughta make it a regular date. You know, our Saturday Afternoon Matinee date?"

"That would be so nice, and believe me when I say I'd like to say yes." (Shot down, he thought.) "But the truth is, Saturday is my scheduled workday and I doubt I could find someone to permanently trade with me. Wilbur counts on me, being the assistant manager and all."

"You're the assistant manager of the whole of Your Store?" he asked, suddenly feeling even more intimidated to be dating someone in management, odd-job man that he'd become.

Never being one to sound braggart, she replied, "Oh, it's just more of a title than anything, you know, something Wilbur gave me one time instead of a raise. Not that he isn't good to me! He certainly is. And for the most part, I like my job."

"For the most part, huh?"

"You know what I *do* love about the grocery business?" She closed her eyes as if to envision it. "I love the order of the neat rows of shelves, the bright colors of the fruits and vegetables right down to the different shades of peppers:

red, green, yellow . . . those that are green but have tinges of
red in them. . . . I love the sound of the cash register, even
just pushing the buttons on it, as silly as that sounds. I like
the idea I'm helping to feed a town of people I've grown to
love." She opened her eyes and stared out the window, realizing she was closer to her home than she'd like to be and
suddenly feeling quite embarrassed to have prattled on
about such silly things.

"Sounds like you like all the parts. Sounds like the hum
of a grocery store is like music to you."

She turned her head straight toward him. "How poetic!
That's exactly it! But, of course, nothing is perfect."

Well, don't I know that *about myself!* "What parts or part
don't you like?" he asked. "I mean about your job."

She drew another fragrant breath of his aftershave, then
released it, feeling a little nervous about the intimacy of
what she was revealing, yet realizing she trusted sharing it
with him. "I wish we had more variety in the store. Lately
I'm just kind of bored, or restless or something with some
of our selections. I've asked Wilbur if we might not carry
a few scented candles along with the utilitarian ones, maybe
a wider variety of tea bags. Just some little things like that."

Edward Showalter didn't know a thing about scented
candles or fancy tea bags. He had nothing to say in response. He knew about wattage and switches, painting and
hammering. Staying sober. Cheetos. He knew about *Cheetos*
for goodness' sakes!

"I worry if we don't modernize just a little that we won't
make it. I already hear people talking about shopping at the
big supermarkets in Hethrow because of the variety. But the
truth is," her voice saddening, "we could never be one of
them."

"No, you can't be. But look what you *are*. Look at all the older folks, like Dorothy, for instance, who can't drive anymore. How would they get their groceries if it wasn't for Your Store keeping staples stocked at a place folks can walk to, or have deliveries right to their doors when they're no longer able to walk? I would venture to say that not a one of those big fancy places would bring groceries to your door. Not a stinkin' one. Or know exactly where you live without telling them. Worry about you if you don't come to the door. Why, look at what happened with Tess Walker! If it hadn't been for her grocery delivery—you know, the day she didn't come to the door—why who knows how long she might have been in there by herself, dead in her bed."

"I guess you're right. That does make me feel better. And yet, Partonville itself has got to keep going to support a grocer who will do all of that, and with not many young folks sticking around or coming back, how long can we keep on?"

The van turned right and crept along toward Nellie Ruth's place now, like it was sneaking up on something in its camouflaged splendor; but if he drove any slower, he thought, he wouldn't be moving at all. Finally it came to rest in front of her house. He shut off the engine and stared straight ahead, wondering why he hadn't made it a Saturday *night* date since they could have taken in dinner and a show. And why hadn't he thought to ask her for dinner before this date? It would seem too . . . spur-of-the-moment now. Inappropriate. Like he was taking it for granted she had nothing else to do. *What's a dollar-off coupon anyway compared to time spent with Nellie Ruth!* He felt cheap. He looked at his watch; it wasn't even 4 P.M.

Out of the corner of Nellie Ruth's eye, she saw him looking at his watch. She suddenly felt badly for bringing such a gloomy topic to their date and figured he was bored out of his gourd. *No wonder he's looking at his watch!* "Goodness, ES, I'm so sorry to have bored you with my ramblings." She reached for the door handle, her face turning crimson.

"Don't you DARE touch that handle, ma'am!" He pulled open his door and jogged around the van to do the honors. With each step he chastised himself for having brought up *a dead person, for goodness' sakes! A* dead *person! What were you thinking bringing up a DEAD PERSON when she was talking about her beloved groceries! You fool!* No wonder Nellie Ruth was in such a hurry to get out of his van. And if she thought he always drove that slowly, she'd probably never want to ride with him again.

"Thank you," Nellie Ruth said as she slid down off the seat.

"I'll walk you around." Silently but way too swiftly for both of them, they ended up at the bottom of the staircase to her private entrance, which was around to the back of the large home Bernice Norris owned. Nellie Ruth had rented the upstairs of Bernice's place for thirty-five years. It was the bottom-of-the-stairway spot she'd told him to meet her for each of their previous dates. It just didn't seem appropriate for him to come up those steps. Although neither of them mentioned it, they'd both seen the curtains in Bernice's living room move slightly each time they came and went. No, Nellie Ruth did not want to have Bernice listening to two sets of footsteps going up the back stairs to her house. Not until Edward Showalter, professional painter, was painting, and then, well, he'd have to come up. That would be official business.

❖⬥❖

Immediately after his mom, Dorothy and Jessica had launched themselves into their last fit of laughter, Josh headed up to his bedroom to check his e-mail. He was going to give Shelby a call if he didn't have a message from her, but he decided not to since, at least for the moment, all women seemed more than he could understand. Instead of booting up he threw himself on his bed right after turning on the television on top of his dresser. It had been a long while since he'd watched Saturday cartoons.

Downstairs the voices had finally settled into conversation, Jessica having to excuse herself only once to be sick, and then she thought it was because she'd laughed herself sick rather than actually succumbing to a pregnancy queasiness. At least for the moment.

"Since I've got the two of you here," Dorothy said, "let me tell you about something in the works. Jessica, although this *officially* has to do with you, let me just say right now that I do not expect you to be involved in any official capacity. None. You've got enough on your hands." Jessica had a puzzled look on her face as she worked to keep track of her official involvement, or not, in whatever Dorothy was speaking about. "Well, I guess that sounded rather confusing, didn't it?" Dorothy said. Jessica's head nodded, as did Katie's. "Bottom line: It's now official. The Social Concerns Committee at UMC, which you are officially on, which is your only official part, has teamed up with the Social Concerns Committee at St. Augustine's. We're going to host a Thanksgiving dinner for the community, right down in our church basement! We thought it would be nice to offer a meal to folks who either don't have any family around or might otherwise be too financially hard up to put out a Thanksgiving spread."

"What a nice idea," Jessica said, "but it doesn't seem fair for me not to do anything. Since I'm on the committee I ought to . . ."

"I will not hear another word about it, Jessica. You are hereby officially absolved. Period. Theresa Brewton is chairing the event and I believe we're going to have plenty of cooks and volunteers." Jessica started to open her mouth but Dorothy put a finger to her own lips. "Hush, child. You just cook up that little one there, okay?" She then turned her head toward Katie. "Katie, I've been wanting to talk to you, too. I thought perhaps you and Josh might like to help out. That is if you don't have any other special doings. It might be a right nice way for you to get to meet a few more folks around here. And I know Josh and my grandsons will have a good time together again, no matter what they're doing."

Katie hadn't given much thought to Thanksgiving since her last conversation with her ex. In fact, she'd tried to block the entire holiday out of her mind; all it produced was visions of her lone stranded self sitting at her own kitchen table, just waiting for the sounds of a mousetrap to trip. In fact, she'd already picked up a Healthy Foods frozen turkey dinner the last time she'd gone to the grocery store in Hethrow, the Hethrow store offering far more in terms of an organic section, health food aisle, larger and more exotic fresh fruits and vegetables than Your Store. When the cashier had wrung up the frozen dinner, Katie thought how pathetic her little Thanksgiving dinner for one looked on the conveyor belt. She held her own brief pity party when she got home, stepped around the mousetraps and put it in the freezer. "Just another day here in paradise," she'd said to herself, then quickly added, "but snap out of it, Katie! That whole Pilgrim thing was a long time ago anyway. Who cares?" And thus, she'd stuffed down any emotions she might have harbored about the holiday—until this moment.

"Oh, Dorothy," Katie said, her dejected voice revealing her feelings for what she was about to say. "I guess Josh didn't tell you yet. He's not going to be here for Thanksgiving. It's his dad's turn to have Josh for Thanksgiving. Josh asked me if I wanted to go to Chicago with him, maybe visit with friends or start my holiday shopping with the throngs. I thought about it, but there's really no one in Chicago I'd want to spend Thanksgiving with *(nobody to invite me)* so I told him to just go ahead and take the SUV."

Dorothy's face fell. After all her thinking about her own grandsons and the wrangling that had gone on about their Thanksgiving, she hadn't even considered Josh might be with his dad, whom he seldom mentioned. "Oh, honey. No, he didn't tell me. But do you mean to say you were just going to sit at this farm all by yourself? On Thanksgiving Day?"

Katie nodded but she forced herself to paste on a bright face. "It won't be that bad. I can read and do whatever I want. No loud music and banging doors, no smart-aleck answers and cleaning up after someone for a few days." She smiled, but suddenly everything that made her nuts was just the list of things she realized she'd miss in the wake of her son's absence.

"I won't hear of it!" Dorothy said. "You know you're always welcome to spend any holidays with me and my family. Always. And this year we're spending our dinner in the church basement. Sure, we'll be serving, but we'll no doubt eat ourselves silly and have a good time doing both."

"Did you say your sons were both coming in?" Jessica asked.

"Yes! I'm so happy! I wasn't sure Jacob would be able to make it; he's got some big cases going on now. But he assured me he'd be here to celebrate my birthday. And I'm just thrilled my grandsons get to come, too! They were maybe going to be off with *their* mother." She cast her eyes toward Katie, a sudden pang in her heart. "But you know, Katie, the sadness in your eyes helps me remember I need to pray for her, too." Katie swallowed a couple of times.

"Katie, you hadn't even told *me* you were going to be alone on Thanksgiving!" Jessica looked like she might burst into tears on her friend's behalf. "You shouldn't keep things like that to yourself. I've just learned the hard way that doesn't work well—along with what a relief it is to finally share . . . whatever." A sheepish grin crossed her face.

"Lord," Dorothy said, closing her eyes, "we thank You for the wonderful gift of friends to help us share our loads." Katie swiped at her lower lashes with the back of her knuckle. "And to be with us to help celebrate the good stuff!" She paused for a moment, then opened her eyes. "And I am most happy to report, friends of mine, that all of my guys said they thought it would be great to help out at the church. To tell the truth, we were having a hard time picturing us having our own dinner anywhere but here at the . . ." Dorothy stopped short her words, not wanting to make Katie feel guilty for living in what was now her own home, as well as being sad about not seeing her son for Thanksgiving. *Lord, shut my mouth!* she prayed as she slammed her lips together.

"Your birthday?" Katie asked, shifting gears to help move them all along.

"Oh, didn't you know?" Dorothy asked, realizing her mouth was already back open, but then, *She did ask me a question, You know Lord!* "I was a gift of Thanksgiving to my parents." Dorothy sprouted a warm smile, then shared how many birthdays and Thanksgivings her mom and dad had so beautifully and prayerfully and thankfully woven that message into her grateful heart.

Jessica's eyes welled. "Oh, Dorothy, I sure pray I can leave that kind of a feeling with Sarah Sue." Then she put her hands to her abdomen. "And this little monkey." A veil of guilt fell over her for being upset at the news of this child within her womb. *A gift of thanksgiving, from God. Now if I can only remember that during the next few—make that many—wild years.*

Katie's body temperature began to rise and her cheeks flushed. "Is it warm in here or is it just me? Or are we just too emotional?" She, after all, used to be a woman of controlled emotions. What on earth was happening to her? Although she'd been warmed by Dorothy's lovely Thanksgiving birthday story, she hadn't been moved enough to break out in a sweat over it.

Dorothy smiled. "I hate to tell you, Katie, but honestly, you look like you're having a hot flash. Have you had any of those before? Or do you know if you've started through the change?"

There it was. Hot flashes. Mood swings. What she'd been trying to ignore: The Change. Swirling in the room in the midst of them. Swirling in the room along with all the crazed hormones of a newly pregnant mom and the memories of a well-seasoned and long-gone-through-it older woman. Katie picked up a nearby magazine and began to fan herself. Just as Josh was heading down the stairs, they all broke out in laughter again. He turned around and marched right back up the stairs. "Women!"

15

"**I**'m sure by now you've all seen the notice in the *Partonville Press* and this week's bulletin about the upcoming Thanksgiving dinner co-sponsored by the joint Social Concerns Committees of our own UMC and St. Augustine's." Pastor Delbert Carol Jr. hoped his enthusiasm made up for his lack of knowledge about the details regarding the event. He pushed his glasses up his nose, raked his hand through the top of his thinning hair and glanced at the hand-scrawled note from his wife he held between the thumb and forefinger of his left hand. He squinted a moment, trying to decipher her handwriting, then nodded appreciation to her; she'd handed him the note at the last moment. "Dorothy, would you like to say a few words for us?"

Although Dorothy was taken by surprise at Pastor's offer, she stood—as did Gladys, who yanked down the bottom of her blazer, turned to face the rest of the congregants (front pew, remember—always) and instantly began booming her voice back across the pews. "As head of the Social Concerns Committee here at UMC," she said, giving an authoritative nod to Dorothy, who politely smiled and sat down, "on behalf of *both* of the churches, I'd like to offer a welcome to anyone who would like to attend. Although I am not in charge of the *event*, per se, I do know we will be starting with a Thanksgiving prayer promptly at three P.M.

and serving turkey, dressing, potatoes and a few as yet un-
named side dishes immediately following the prayer. But
here's what we need you to do, besides show up on time.
We co-sponsors need you to let us know—and at this point
I believe it is Sue Johansen or Theresa Brewton you are to
call and their numbers are in your bulletin—by this Friday
at the latest if you're coming and how many there will be in
your party. As you can well imagine, we need to be able to
thoughtfully plan such an undertaking. PLUS," and she
paused to center the buttons on her blazer by shifting it
slightly to the left, "don't forget that we'll be taking up a
freewill offering, so come prepared." When Gladys's backside hit the pew, Dorothy's simultaneously sprang up off
hers. It happened with such perfect timing it reminded
Pastor of one of those old pound-a-peg toys: pound one in;
another pops out. That old wooden toy had been one of his
favorites when he was a child, then one of his son's as well.
He glazed over for a moment wondering what had ever become of it now that his son and daughter were several years
beyond the pound-a-peg phase. Then he wondered if he
needed some of that dinko (or was it ginko?) stuff he'd seen
advertised on the television. Something that might help
him stay focused.

Dorothy felt impatient with Gladys; for someone not in
charge, she was having trouble acting like it—not to mention sounding more militant than thankful. Without thinking about it, she'd lurched up off her pew. "But folks," she
said loudly enough for them to hear, yet tenderly enough
to accompany her message, "please don't let the idea we're
going to be passing the hat, so to speak, keep you from
coming." A chuckle rippled through the pews. "This meal is
a gift of Thanksgiving for all that God has done in our lives.

If you can or feel led to give, fine. If it is simply your turn to receive, that is just as wonderful! And if, at the last minute, you haven't signed up but wish you had, please do not hesitate to come join us. Come as you are. Everyone is welcome around our Thanksgiving table!" Down she went and up popped Gladys, who opened her mouth and looked around at everyone for an awkward moment.

"That's right," she said, then plopped herself back down.

Pastor looked at Dorothy, waiting to see if there would be another volley but she shook her head. "Well, then . . ." He paused to push his glasses up his nose and raise questioning eyebrows one last time toward Gladys. Nothing. "Thank you both very much for that report. Both I and Father O'Sullivan feel blessed to watch our generous parishioners (a couple *congregant* eyebrows raised at the *parishioner* referral) combine our resources and offer this dinner. We will, I have no doubt, be *doubly* blessed by *all* those who come."

Dorothy was glad to see Jessica in church with Paul and Sarah Sue. They sat in the back pew, though, just in case Jessica had to make a quick exit. Jessica had asked Dorothy to please not tell anyone her news, although she knew Dorothy would never breach a confidence. "It's just that I haven't officially been told yet," Jessica said, looking sheepish. "I'm going to wait a couple of weeks to make my appointment, hopefully with Doc Streator since I haven't met the new doctor yet. But I've already started taking an extra vitamin a day—fat amount of good it does since I usually can't keep it down."

Dorothy smiled and touched Jessica's cheek. "You just take care of yourself, hear?" Although Jessica's parents didn't

live more than a hundred miles away, Dorothy knew it was
a pain in Jessica's heart that she and her mom, Naomi,
weren't closer. Not in terms of miles, but heart connections.
Yes, on that level she wished they were close enough to be
discussing life-altering issues like this.

Naomi, born and raised in Partonville, had gone away to
college to study business. She couldn't wait to flee Partonville. She'd told everyone in her senior high school class
that she wanted to make something of herself. When she'd
told her mom the same thing, her mother brushed her long
hair out of her face and back behind her ears. "You are a
wonderful young woman, Naomi," assuring her that she already was somebody. Somebody special. Naomi pushed
her mom's hands away from her face and loosened her hair
from her ears so it could drape back around her face the way
she liked it. "You just don't have a clue about me, Mom." It
was a familiar scene for the two of them, one that would
play many times over before graduation day.

Naomi, who always hated her old-fashioned name and
took to introducing herself as Natalie in college, met
Jessica's dad at a dance her first week away at college, where
she'd gone on a full scholarship, which was the only way it
would have been possible. One of the things that had attracted her the most to Christopher (never Chris) was his
determination to make something of himself, too. It showed
in the way he carried himself, the way he managed to hold
everyone's attention when he told a story, the way he appreciated her bold statements about being her own woman.
Soon they were on the fast track to success, together. Natalie and Christopher this, and Christopher and Natalie

that. They were a duo. By graduation, their top-of-the-class grades, well-honed forensics prowess and calculated maneuvering had landed them jobs less than two miles from one another. It turned out they would be settling in St. Louis, not too very far from Partonville, yet far enough away to be in another world. It about crushed Naomi's folks to learn their daughter would not be returning to her hometown. "A hundred miles away might as well be five hundred, for as often as we'll probably get to see you," her mother had said. "But I understand you need to make your own life."

After Jessica came along—and she had definitely not been in Naomi and Christopher's plans, the pregnancy landing in the one percent failure rate of the birth control pills Naomi faithfully took every morning—they enrolled her in nurseries and day care so Naomi could maintain her corporate climb. Depending upon who had the heavier workload for the day, either Naomi or Christopher dropped Jessica off. And at least one weekend a month they would make two roundtrip treks to Partonville to drop off and pick up Jessica. While Jessica spent the weekend with her grandparents, Naomi and Christopher adored their freedom and entertained in their glamorous home, took off for exotic weekends away *(What's the point of making all this money if we don't spend some of it on ourselves?)* or just lolled around in their peace and quiet.

Jessica grew up loving her visits to the little circle-the-square town where her warm and inviting grandmother lived. She and Grandma would go to the nursing home daily to visit her grandfather, who, due to a severe stroke, could not move other than to smile his dear smile at her with one-half of his tender face and lift a finger toward them—so removed from the grandfather she remembered when she was younger who tossed her high in the air and gave her rides on his back, bounced her on his knee and read her stories. Partonville was also where she learned to love the church, the meaning and importance of the body of believers who had so rallied around Grandma after Grandpa's devastating stroke. She felt more herself in Partonville than anywhere else.

Jessica vowed she one day would like to raise her own family right there in Partonville, maybe even right next door to Grandma. She loved baby-sitting as a teen since she adored children, and would do so both in her neighborhood and in Partonville. And she spent hours crocheting and painting and all the other crafts her grandmother taught her from the time she was old enough to pick up a needle or paintbrush. She couldn't imagine wanting to be anything other than a wife and mother. Happy. Content. The way her grandmother seemed to be with her homespun lifestyle. No business suits or day-care setting for her or her children. Ever.

But Jessica's own mother simply could not understand (like her mother before her had not understood her own daughter) any woman not wanting to make more of herself than a homebody, and over time, they just grew further apart. Oh, not that they didn't love each other, for they did. But since Jessica's natural bent was toward the creative and cozy and her mother's was driven, store-bought and upscale, it sometimes left massive and awkward gaps in their conversations and overall relationship, especially when Jessica's mom would continually nudge Jessica to go to college.

Her parents were beside themselves that their only child had, during her senior year in high school, fallen for a guy from Partonville whom she'd met at church and who more abhorrently worked in the coal mines. "That's what we get for getting that child her own car," Christopher had said to Naomi one night when they were quarreling about their daughter's ongoing visits to Partonville, long after they'd tired of the weekend drive. "Too sentimental," her dad had said about Paul after they'd once met him. "A man with seemingly no voice of his own. And certainly no ambition to get out of the coal mine." But no matter how much they tried to dissuade her, Jessica and Paul stood strongly together.

As soon as she and Paul married, not long after Jessica graduated from high school, she moved to Partonville and they both lived with her grandmother while they looked for a place of their own. Grandma's offer to the sweet couple whom she'd spent so much time with—witnessing their love for one another and growing to love Paul like her own—had put nearly a final blow in her relationship with her own daughter. Three generations of women pried apart by differing visions of what and how a woman should be.

"You could at least take night classes at Hethrow's Junior College and get yourself an associate's degree," Naomi told Jessica after the college came into being. "I mean it's right there in your backyard. How will you ever take care of yourself if Paul should leave you?" When she and Paul bought the dilapidated Lamp Post motel with a meager down payment—a move that baffled her parents no end since the couple hadn't even consulted them—Naomi put on a full press for one of them to get some college, offering to pay for it, saying they'd never make a go of a business if one or the other of them didn't get some business education. Naomi simply could not understand why her daughter had chosen to become what she perceived to be nothing more than a glorified maid. "Really, Jessica, you come from better stock than that!" It crushed Jessica to the core that her mother didn't understand that her heart wasn't that of her mother's and that she and Paul were very proud to set down stakes right on the main road into Partonville. And she wasn't a maid; she was a business partner with her husband and one of her duties just happened to be that of cleaning the rooms.

It nearly did Jessica in when her grandmother, who loved and supported and cheered her on, had died shortly after they'd celebrated the grand reopening of the Lamp Post from its long-neglected slumber and moved into the little attached dwelling. It was difficult for them both to watch Jessica's grandmother's little house, which was right next door to the Lamp Post, be sold for the assets that would pay the nursing home bills until her grandfather died, six months to the day after her grandmother. What little was left was willed to Paul and Jessica, who spent the meager monies for two memorial benches for her grandparents in Partonville's Community Park.

But the one thing no one could take away from Jessica and Paul was their desire to make a go of their new business on their very own with no help from her parents (and they wouldn't have accepted any now should it be offered), which, in their hearts, had been made possible by the love of her grandmother. So far, they had. Yes, money was always tight, and now this pregnancy . . . But overall, neither Jessica nor Paul would change a thing about the paths they'd chosen because they'd led them to each other.

"Your folks love you as best they know how," Dorothy had told Jessica when Jessica had said how much it hurt her that her parents hardly ever came to visit, not even their own granddaughter, and how they didn't seem to even notice all of the wonderful improvements they'd made to the Lamp Post the last time they did swing by. And how they refused to stay even one night in one of the newly decorated rooms—*"Number Eleven, the best out of the twelve"*—she and Paul had been so proud to offer them.

But the hardest thing for Jessica to bear was that Naomi had, from the moment she'd found out her daughter was pregnant with her first baby, coached Jessica to please train her child *not* to call her Grandma, which was for old ladies who knit, she'd said. "Your baby can just call me . . . Natalie, okay?"

Yes, Jessica was very happy for Dorothy's presence in her life, and May Belle's, and that of any other older woman who had ever helped nurture her natural self (and be joy-filled surrogate grandmothers to her daughter) since she'd lost her beloved grandmother, whose endearing presence had been such an affirming force.

She didn't even want to think about the comments her parents would make when she told them she was pregnant again.

When church was dismissed, Gladys bustled around reminding everyone on the Social Concerns Committee that Theresa Brewton had invited them to St. Auggie's for a brief meeting. After Edward Showalter reminded Nellie Ruth what set Your Store apart from the mega places, she had decided there was no *way* she would miss this meeting; she wanted to make sure Your Store, *her* store, got the business for the dinner. Although she hadn't officially asked Wilbur yet, he always offered a discount for these types of things and it would be a good thing to remind community folks about that.

16

Katie sat in the SUV in the church's parking lot after the service waiting for Josh, looking from her wristwatch to the digital clock in the Lexus and back no fewer times than once a minute. She didn't know whether to go in and round up Josh from whatever he was doing—and what on earth could it be since Dorothy had scurried over to St. Augustine's and Shelby didn't attend church, at least not this one—or to lay on the horn, which was her impatient instinct, although she curbed it. After five minutes passed she decided to go in and find him. She didn't have to look very hard. When she opened the church door she nearly ran smack into him, Pastor Delbert beside him, his hand on Josh's shoulder. They were apparently just getting ready to come outside.

"Oh! There you are!" Katie gasped. She looked from Josh to Pastor and back again, just like she'd been doing with the clocks, an awkward silence suddenly filling her mouth.

"I was just walking Josh to the car," Pastor said. "No need to keep you standing outside in this cool weather." The three of them walked in silence to the SUV. She got in and buckled up. Josh stopped outside of his door and extended his hand to Pastor, who gave it a hearty shake.

"Thanks for stopping by, Josh. I'm looking forward to getting to know you better, too. Dorothy brags on you all the time. You've obviously got her under your spell," he said with a smile. Josh felt an inexplicable surge of happiness flood though him.

"See you next week!" Josh said through the window after he got in and buckled up. "Mom, did you know Delbert and his wife and kids have decided to come to the church's Thanksgiving dinner? Isn't that just the coolest? He said it was his wife's idea and that he thought maybe she just didn't want to cook. But he laughed, so I'm sure he was kidding. He's funnier than I thought he was."

"You're not even going to be in town for Thanksgiving, Josh."

"I know. But *you* will!"

Aside from Gladys, everyone on the UMC portion of the joint Social Concerns Committee was shocked at how efficiently and calmly a meeting could run when Gladys wasn't in charge of it. There were, of course, a couple of things Gladys commented on after they were out of earshot and one was the lack of refreshments. It was a fact: everyone at UMC had been spoiled by May Belle. Her sweets were such a natural part of every meeting that it never occurred to them anyone *had* a meeting without refreshments.

"Had I known about their lack," Gladys said somewhat indignantly, "I would have gathered up a few cookies and such from the meet-and-greet time we had to miss."

"Wasn't a morsel left on our table when we headed out," Dorothy said. "Wanita's two rascally boys had their pockets full, I think."

"I don't know why that mother doesn't make those two boys have better manners rather than just letting them run wild."

"They're just boys," May Belle said. "It makes me happy they enjoy my cookies and that they *are* so healthy and rambunctious." While Gladys gave a harrumph, May Belle thought of her own quiet Earl, how far back in the corners he stood when he was little, uncomfortable with crowds and loud noises, strangers and the other children his age. Of course, she'd loved him just the way he was. Still, it was hard to hear anyone complaining about boys who were just being boys. But then, Gladys could complain about anything—the other thing being Jessica's sudden and shocking departure from their meeting, her hand over her mouth. "I sure hope I don't catch whatever she's got! Why on earth do people go out when they're sick?" Dorothy had to swallow down a laugh. "Oh, I doubt very much you'll catch what she's got, Gladys," she said while thinking it would take a miracle unlike any she'd ever see again!

Although Nellie Ruth was silent during all of this, she was smiling, too, but for a different reason. She'd not only convinced the joint committee members that she was in the best position to do the shopping ("just give me a list!"), but she was already picturing herself gliding along delivering all the beautiful groceries tucked in ES's spiffed-up van.

When Tuesday night bedtime at the Landerses' rolled around, Arthur announced he was going to Harry's for breakfast Wednesday morning. Said he was gonna be there at 6 A.M. sharp and if nobody was up he was going by himself. Said they'd all be worried about him at the grill since it had now been over a week since he'd been there for breakfast and that their late appearance last week didn't count because all the regulars had already come and gone.

"Hard tellin' what all mischief might be a goin' on in town. Got to keep up with things," he declared as though he was speaking about the state of the union. "Besides, yur gone too long and all they's talkin' bout is you."

"But you get the *Partonville Press,* Art," Herm said. "Seems to me they don't leave many a stone unturned. And from what I recall, there'll be a new edition right in your paper box come tomorrow, it being Wednesday and all. Still got that visitors column? Wonder if we'll be in it!"

Arthur sucked air between his front teeth. "I said I'm goin' to breakfast at six A.M. No, let me correct myself. I said I'm gonna *be* at the grill at six A.M. tomorrow. I ain't waitin' around fer you lazy bones to make yur brunch appearance at the table. Fella's gotta start the day off early and get some bacon and eggs in his belly before the sun starts settin'. Anybody wants to come along, they better git up and have their britches on by five-forty cuz that's when the taxi's leavin'."

Although he'd sounded pretty crabby, he also sounded like his usual self so nobody batted an eye.

Truth be told, Arthur was counting on the fact that nobody would be moving by five-forty. Although he enjoyed visiting with Herm and Vera, sometimes a fella just needed a little space. Time to be alone in his truck. Think about things, like what in tarnation he was gonna do with Jessie. *Like there's somethin' anyone* could *do with that woman!* He didn't think she'd spoken one civil word to him since shortly after Herm and Vera had arrived. Of course, Herm and Vera's endless chatter made up for any voids. *Don't those two hand-holdin' jabber boxes ever shut up?* And what was up with those near violent euchre games, he wondered. Sure, euchre was always lively, but these nightly games felt more like war, like there was an ax to grind. But what? As soon as the women had the dinner dishes cleared every evening, out came the cards. He thought maybe it was time to talk to Herm about just letting those two old hens win for an evening so they could be done with the euchre wars for now. And thinking about being done with things, it was time they were done with those endless dang bags of potato chips they keep runnin' to Your Store to buy. Both of those women were liable to lose all their teeth if they kept pounding down on chips like that, and Jessie was gonna plumb cause them to go broke if she didn't start making popcorn again. He was gonna just *tell* Jessie to make them all some popcorn if they had to suffer through another night of cards. And Herm, well, he'd done some of the dumbest bidding he'd ever seen last night. It was a miracle they'd still been able to win.

What was wrong with everybody?

Much to Arthur's chagrin, by 5:10 A.M. every light in the house was on. The one thing he'd forgotten was that tonight was Wednesday night and the Happy Hookers were coming. The women wanted to get an early start on "preparations," they'd called it. What preparations he couldn't figure out since it seemed to him all they needed to do would be to put out a few bowls of the remaining potato chips (that would get rid of them!) and there you'd have it. But all the way to Harry's, the women sat in the backseat yappin' a mile a minute about little things they needed to do, like vacuum and get out the card tables and chairs and run into Your Store again for bridge mix and stop at the doughnut store for a dozen mixed for dessert and Oh, NO!

Jessie hadn't thought about prizes yet! Maybe they'd have to run to Hethrow, Vera suggested. After all, she hadn't had a chance to study any of the new development Arthur had talked about all week. "Wal-Mart will have what I need, Vera," Jessie said, nipping that excursion in the bud. She didn't much like shopping. "Nothing fussy. I don't know why they buy such fussy, useless bunco gifts anyway. Just more things to dust. I'm gonna keep it to a few practical items." *Yap, yap, yap,* Arthur thought.

When they were nearing the grill, Arthur's rude won-or-lost comment during their last visit sprang into Jessie's head again—for the billionth time. *That MAN!* She wondered if Lester had heard it. It would be pretty embarrassing if he had, which made her kind of dread seeing him. She hoped the Landers men would have better sense this time than to bring it up again.

"Not a one of the Hookers phoned that they can't come?" Vera asked Jessie with a pout while Arthur was pulling them into his usual parking space, trying to keep his ears slammed closed to protect them from the absolutely *endless* yappety-yap. Vera loved playing bunco and had been hoping she'd be able to substitute for somebody. Jessie didn't answer right away; she was busy peering around Arthur's head to see if Lester had opened up yet. No, the CLOSED sign was still on the door.

"Nope. No cancellations yet. Never can tell, though, Vera. Might be a last-minute something or other. If they all show up, you can still pull up a chair and visit with everyone. Got a couple new Hooker members since you were here. You'll get to meet our new neighbor, the famous, or infamous, depending on how you see it, Katie Durbin, who owns Dorothy's old place now. You know, the one who drives that big fancy SUV."

"Foreign car," Arthur said to Herm with disdain.

"You need say no more," Herm said in response. He shook his head with remorse.

"In spite of her L-E-X-us, I like Mizz Durbin okay," Arthur said to nobody in particular. "She don't bother me none. She's got spunk and I like that in a woman." He turned his head to wink at his cousin. "Course too much spunk can be downright annoyin', not to mention naggin' and irritatin'," he said, casting his eyes to his rearview mirror knowing he'd find Jessie's eyes burning right into it, which they were.

"Who's the other new Hooker member?" Vera asked, trying to change the subject. Just then, Lester flipped the sign from CLOSED to OPEN.

"Saved by Lester!" Herm said. "Sorry to interrupt this stintilatin' (as only Arthur could say it) conversation, ladies, but it's time to go eat!"

Arthur managed to be the first one in the door. He walked right over to his usual stool and gave the seat top a tap to pay it his respect. "Not yet, honey," he said to the red vinyl disk. "Maybe another week or so."

"Arthur Landers, sometimes you worry me," Gladys said.

"Feelin's always mutual, Queen Lady," he responded with a Cheshire smile.

"Arthur! Good to see you!" Harold Crab said from across the U. "I was beginning to think you didn't love us anymore. I heard tell your cousin and his wife were here though. Hope you don't mind; I mentioned it in the visitors column, even though you didn't officially ask. I imagine you've been visiting up a storm." Harold slid off his stool and walked over to the table where the rest of the Landers clan was seating themselves. He extended his hand to Herm. "Herman, right? You probably don't remember me, but about a million years ago—maybe when you were twelve or so—we got in some trouble together down by the creek during one of your visits. Of course, I'm a few years younger than you boys so you probably might just remember me as the pesky tag-along brother to my cute, long-legged sister, who you might very well remember." He stopped and smiled. "But still, I never once told what *really* happened in that outhouse, even though I heard my sister talking about what she'd overheard from my brother once."

"And you are . . . ?" Herm asked as they shook hands.

"Oh, how remiss. I'm Harold Crab."

"This here," Arthur said to Herm as he pulled out his own chair at the table, "is the esteemed editor of the *Partonville Press*. You'll be happy to know," he said, casting his eyes at Harold, "that my cuz here thought we oughta stay home today cuz we'd learn jist as much out of your rag of a paper as we'd learn here today. Set him straight, Harold. Set the poor man straight."

"I'm highly complimented, Herman, that you understand my role in this town, even though others do not." He shot Arthur a look. "But as much as I hate to admit it—especially since *Arthur's* the one who said it—he's right: if you want to learn it first, come to Harry's every day. I usually either learn here what needs to be in the paper or what folks are saying about what I've already put in it."

"Your eggs are up!" Lester hollered to Harold.

"It was nice to see you again, Herman." Harold spun on his heels and headed back to the counter, tossing a "Hi,

Jessie" over his shoulder. Then he realized he had not even acknowledged the woman who must be Herman's wife and came back to give her a quick greeting. "Vera, right?"

"Just like *Cheers*," Herm said. "Everybody knows your name!"

"And your business," Jessie said half under her breath. Just then Lester appeared with four coffee mugs, two mug handles in each hand. He always brought mugs to the tables since they were easier to carry. He slid them onto the table, made eye contact with no one and said, "Let me know when you're ready to order." Off he went. Herm didn't dare say a word about anything other than food to the man; Vera had warned him before they'd even gotten out of bed. He thought she was exaggerating the episode but he kissed her on top of her head as she nestled in his arm and said he appreciated and respected her suggestions. Always had, always would.

Jessie ended up seated at the side of the table that faced the U. She watched Lester's back as he broke eggs. Like most in town, she marveled at his egg-cracking trick. She looked at Vera who was staring at her with her eyebrows pinched together. They both cast their eyes back on the makeshift menu on the table between them. The boys had already decided what they wanted (of course, it was a no-brainer for Arthur) and had slid the table's only menu to their corner.

"How's Lester's French toast?" Vera asked Jessie.

"Wouldn't know. I'm not one for sweets in the morning."

"I think I had it once back in the seventies," Arthur said. "Didn't kill me so I guess it was okay."

"I think I'll try it," Vera said. "What are you having, Jessie?"

"Two eggs over easy, sausage patties and rye toast," she said looking at the menu.

"Want breakfast spuds with that?" She hadn't realized Arthur, in his impatience, had waved Lester back over. Lester had already written down her order on his tablet. When she looked up they made brief eye contact, then both veered their eyes in other directions. *Yup, he'd heard Arthur's dumb comment during their last visit. She could just tell.* Her cheeks reddened with anger at Arthur and embarrassment for herself as she cast her eyes toward her husband, who was looking at Lester. Lester veered his eyes toward Vera and waited for her order, pen perched over the pad.

"How many pieces of French toast do you serve?" she asked.

"How many ya want?"

"Two."

"Then I serve you two," he said, his hand scrawling on the pad. "Side?"

"Side?" Vera asked him back. "Side?"

"Side order," Arthur said. "Like a side of bacon or ham, sausage or . . . Side order, Vera."

"Oh. Well, I think I'll have . . . Where are the sides listed?"

"Along the bottom," Lester said, who locked eyes with Jessie again for the briefest of moments and ever so slightly wagged his head at his growing impatience with Vera. *Nah,* Jessie thought, shaking her head at her own thoughts. *He didn't hear Arthur's dumb comment.* Her cheeks darkened, having embarrassed herself imaging such nonsense. *Even if he did, he's as used to Arthur as I am!*

"Oh. I see," Vera said running her finger under the word "sides." "I'll have . . . ham! Yes. Ham sounds wonderful. Wait. Is it off the bone?"

"Is there another place a pig can grow it?" Lester asked sarcastically, which was just his nature. But Herm didn't know Lester *that* well and he was thinking his tone of voice was not an appropriate one to use with his wife.

"Well . . . ," Vera said, putting her finger to her mouth in a thoughtful gesture.

Vera could be so exasperatin'! Arthur thought. "She wants ham," he said, trying to end their misery while taking note that Lester was looking at Jessie again (since she was shaking her head, causing Lester to wonder if she wanted to change her order) causing Arthur to wonder why he was looking at Jessie when he was waiting for Vera's order. And why, Arthur also wondered, was Jessie shaking her head at Lester like that? "And I'll have the usual," he barked. "What about you, Herm?"

"Three eggs scrambled, bacon crispy, potatoes with onions and whole wheat toast. Get that?"

"Yup. Arthur's usual." Lester was gone before any of them could respond, but not before glancing at Jessie one last time. (Of course, he'd glanced at each of them to make sure they were done with their world's-longest-bout of ordering, but Arthur didn't know that.)

Arthur stared at his wife, a prickly feeling climbing up his neck. Her cheeks were pink. He turned and looked at Lester behind the U. When Lester turned around with a plate of something in his hands, he glanced over to their table, wondering why Arthur was staring at him, if Arthur had perhaps called him back and he hadn't heard him. Arthur, however, thought he saw Lester's eyes flash toward his wife again. *Is somethin' fishy here?* He looked from Lester to Jessie and back at Lester again. If he didn't know better, a fella could wonder if Lester was making googly eyes at his wife. *Nah.* Then, like a seed that had just sprouted to life, Herm's question from his last visit rang into Arthur's head, once again causing a flashback to the *last* turn of events that had followed his question some six odd years ago. *'Aren't you the guy old Art here stole Jessie from?'* Well, *come to think about it, he IS the guy I stole Jessie from.* . . . Arthur uncharacteristically began chewing on his bottom lip. *Surely it can't be! But gist look at those two . . . and . . . where DID that woman go when she run off the other day, was gone fer hours and only came back with a bag of potato chips? POTATO CHIPS!*

Vera, in her typical fashion, started chattering nonstop about the Hookers' meeting and progress, Hethrow and the amount of rain they'd had this year. In the midst, she noticed Arthur was chewing on his bottom lip, his eyes darting between his wife and Lester. Jessie look flushed or something, and neither of them seemed to be paying a lick of attention to what she was saying. Her mind took to racing like a bumblebee in a flower bed, landing a moment here and another there. Something wasn't right.

OH! Surely not . . .

17

"Oh, sweetheart. I feel so bad. I wish I could throw up for you a few times just to relieve some of your burden."

"That is one of the sweetest things you've ever said to me, honey."

Paul stood in the bathroom next to his wife, who was in her usual position on the floor. His dented metal lunchbox was in his hand; it wasn't even light outside and he was already heading to work. "Have you made a doctor's appointment yet?"

"I thought we talked about this yesterday after I had to flee from the joint Social Concern's meeting, never to return. You know we've stretched our funds as far as they'll go right now. I am ninety-nine-point-nine percent sure I'm pregnant. I don't really need a doctor to tell me that right this minute. And the sooner I go, the more co-pays we'll have to make. Maybe if I just wait a month or so . . ."

"You will do no such thing, Jessica!" Paul never raised his voice with her. It had shocked both of them. "Honey, I don't care how tight the budget is, we're not going to mess around with your health or the health of our baby. God never lets us down. Remember how your grandmother always used to say that? We have to believe that now. Finances will work out."

"I just wish we hadn't purchased the new sign out front

and. . . . Well, I mean I am glad we have it since it sure makes us more visible, but the timing is just bad."

"Maybe the timing is more perfect than you know. Maybe it's the new sign that will draw in a few more folks who like to take the back roads and they'll be just the paying guests whose money pays our co-pay. Don't forget our new ad!"

Jessica and Paul had deliberated a long time before deciding, for the first time ever, to spend money on advertising. A young salesman had appeared at the hotel a few weeks ago, briefcase in hand, and told them about the new startup publication he was pitching called *BackRoads Illinois*. He'd been raised by parents who loved to travel the back roads, he'd said; it was just in his blood. He decided to try to make a living out of doing something he loved to do. He'd majored in journalism and minored in business and (the more he shared, the faster he talked) one day it just came to him, he said: travel the way you like, pitch to the tourism industry to get distribution and gather the ads. Surely there were still enough folks left on this earth who weren't in a hurry, he'd said.

If he'd tried to pressure Paul and Jessica in any way to "buy now," that would have been the end. But instead he'd left them with a mock-up of what was soon destined to be his first issue. Said they could get in on the ground floor and that he was selling annual space at discount prices to those willing to take the first risk. Paul and Jessica had enjoyed the little paper, reading it from front to back, even making note of a few places they'd never heard of and would like to visit one day.

Although Partonville used to be on what would have been called a pretty main drag back in its day, the expressway now ran through Hethrow. Aside from people visiting Partonville residents, there wasn't much cause to be meandering through Partonville and staying overnight, unless you simply enjoyed the meandering, and Paul and Jessica had decided when they bought the little hotel that surely there were people who liked to bypass the expressways. In the end, they'd transferred some funds out of their nearly depleted savings and written the salesman a check. New answering machine; new sign; new advertising. Now to pray for the payoff—and continued prayers that they hadn't been ripped off. When Jessica had bubbled on to Katie about *BackRoads Illinois* and the great opportunity they'd bought into, rather than being excited for them, Katie had asked her if they'd done any homework on this guy who just showed up at their door. "Any business references or proof he even was who he said he was?" None. "How long ago did you write him the check?" Long enough ago that they couldn't cancel it within the thirty-six hours of the change-your-mind law. Katie had sighed while Jessica groaned.

Paul leaned down and kissed the top of her head. "What's done is done, hon," he said referring to . . . everything that was useless to fret about, from the check to the pregnancy. "I gotta go. I'll see you tonight. I sure hope you have a better day and that Sarah Sue cooperates. If you don't feel up to making dinner, just let it go. I can find something. The only thing I for sure want you to do today is to make that doctor's appointment, hear?"

She slumped back against the wall and sighed. Even though she was coming around to accepting the idea and even though she had such a supportive husband, and even though he was so reassuring, there was still a chance the doctor would say, "Whoops! Just a gas bubble!" and she would instantly belch and . . . But once she made that appointment and a real doctor told her otherwise, there would be no turning back. "Fine. I'll make the dumb appointment." Although she'd acquiesced, she'd done so with a sigh and a pouting face. The cutest pouting face Paul thought he would ever lay eyes on.

"That's my girl," he said as he hurried off to make his journey down into the earth.

"God, take care of us," she prayed aloud. "Take care of us both." The last thing she'd needed to hear last night was the news report of a group of coal miners trapped in a mine out east. There was already enough to worry about without renewed fears of *that*.

The minute Josh was off to school, Katie ran up the stairs and got her folder down from her bedroom closet shelf. She had a few more numbers to run, another reference to check out about that *BackRoads Illinois* publication and a building inspector to meet. She'd made up her mind there was going to be no better place or time to unfold her plan than at the Happy Hookers' meeting tonight since most of her key players would be present. There was a part of her that dreaded the announcement; she'd spent plenty of time figuring how to deliver it—no *present* it—in the best light. She'd strategized how to defuse any hot spots, parlay any doubts into positive thoughts. Yes, she'd need *all* their support if she was to make this happen profitably. And that was the thing that scared her the most: she didn't like relying on anyone else. Not anyone. If it all came to pass, this would be the exception to her rule about not mixing business with friendships, which she hoped she wasn't jeopardizing.

Although the real estate portion of the deal was sound—barring any surprises by the inspector—relying on others was definitely out of her comfort zone. Reliance made her vulnerable and she was allergic to vulnerable. And, of course, Gladys would probably hate everything about it since it wasn't her idea, but Katie had been working on a way to bring her around, too.

May Belle couldn't remember ever having had such a backache. Whatever she'd done to it—and it started the day she'd climbed up on the step stool to rehang her bedroom curtains after washing, starching and ironing them, although her back had already been tired from all the baking—those mid-back muscles were determined to stay clenched, especially along her right side. She'd asked Earl to rub some Vicks VapoRub on it for her since she couldn't reach the area that hurt the worst, it being too far up the small of her back. Earl had done his best in the awkward situation. But he wasn't much for contact and nothing had really been rubbed in with a good friction, which May Belle was sure was the trick. Maybe she could take Dorothy aside at the Hookers' meeting tonight and have her rub in a good dose of it. She put the jar in her purse, just in case.

Vicks VapoRub had been one of her lifetime favorite antidotes for all kinds of things, especially colds and sore muscles. Living on limited funds, she'd grown accustomed to items in her medicine cabinet—and everywhere else—serving double duty. But Vicks was at the top of the list. Her fond attachment to Vicks dated back to the days her own mother would rub a Vicks-smelling liniment on her chest when she had a cold, but not before first holding an old cloth diaper over a steaming kettle of water. Her mother would smear her entire chest with a thick layer of the product, rubbing it in real good, clear up over the top of her shoulders, up her neck to her chin, then quickly put the warm, damp cloth on top of the love rubs. "It always feels better with the warm cloth on top of the love rubs," her mom would say. Sometimes on days when May Belle was filled with memories, she would find herself drawn to the jar of Vicks and she'd rub a little under her nose, just because. Cleared her sinuses and her head, she thought. Helped bring the memories into a three-dimensional focus.

Aside from Vicks, though, she wasn't one to take much to any kind of drug. She'd rather suffer through a headache than to swallow a pill any day. Not only did she not like putting things like that in her body, but she'd always had trouble just getting pills to go down. "My swallower just does not want to swallow them," she'd told Dorothy once when she'd had to give in years ago and get a round of penicillin from Doc Streator for a terrible bronchitis. "Pish-posh on your swallower," Dorothy had told her. "Do like I do with Sheba and just put the pills in a wad of braunschweiger and eat it. You won't even know it's in there." Dorothy had been worried sick about May Belle's horrible cough and threatened to hog-tie her and put the pills down her throat with her turkey baster if she had to.

"What if I don't like braunschweiger?" May Belle asked somewhat defiantly, not wanting to ingest the drugs but knowing she had to if she wanted to get her health back (and what would ever happen to Earl if she didn't?), Vicks VapoRub not having done the trick for the last week—ten days, if she'd been honest with the Doc.

"Then put them in a marshmallow or roll them up in one of your wonderful gooey oatmeal raisin cookies."

"I don't have any cookies."

"Want me to bake you some?"

"Anybody but you," May Belle had teased before going into another fit of coughing, since Dorothy's strong suit was certainly not her baking. "If there'd be a prize for the worst pie crust at the county fair, I'm sure I could claim it," Dorothy had joked, although it was surely the truth. About the only sweet she made on a regular basis—and most often it was for breakfast—was white toast smeared with butter and sprinkled with sugar. If she was feeling extra hungry for dessert for breakfast, she added a light dusting of cinnamon.

Eventually, of course, May Belle got her pills down and healed. But now, as evening drew closer, May Belle wasn't convinced she could bear to sit at a bunco table since sitting was the worst for her back. She could hardly stand to even think about missing a Hookers' gathering since the Happy Hookers were not only her closest friends, but the evening was always her social highlight each month. A chance to just let her hair down, although she never literally did. She kept her hair up in a silver-white bun on the crown of her head, loose silvery strands often flying around her face. She imagined her hairdo looked quite the sight now since stretching to reach her hair was so uncomfortable that she'd just pulled the long thin strands to the back of her neck, put a rubber band around it and left it in a ponytail all day. Earl all but did a double take every time she came within his vision. This did not look like his mother. No, he was used to her looking a certain way and this wasn't it. The more she got to thinking about how she looked, the more she decided to see for herself. When she turned on the bathroom light, she could hardly believe it. She looked like an octogenarian hippie! All she needed was a string of beads. "I cannot show up at the Hookers' meeting tonight looking like this and be unable to sit through even one round of dice, Earl," she said on her way to the phone. As soon as she was done dialing, she tried to rub her back again while the phone rang.

"Yup," Arthur said into the receiver.

"Oh, hello, Arthur. It's May Belle."

"May Belle who?"

"May Belle Justice."

"I know it's May Belle Justice. I was jist pullin' your leg."

"Well, Arthur, I wish you wouldn't because my back is too sore for a leg pull today." Arthur heard the smile in her voice, but he also could tell she was in pain. "In fact, that's why I'm calling. As much as it breaks my heart, I cannot make it to the Happy Hookers tonight. May I speak to Jessie, please?"

"Welp, now, you might could if she were here, but she ain't. She and Vera are out spendin' my money for you gals tonight."

"Will you please give her my regrets, Arthur? Assure her I'm going to be fine so she doesn't worry. Just tell her I've got a backache that's making it too difficult to sit. I hope she understands. I hate canceling this late."

"Yup. I'll tell her when she gits home, if she ever does. Ya put a couple hens in the car together and set 'em loose to get ready for a pack of wild women and ain't no tellin' what time they'll be back!"

"Oh, Arthur. How you talk," May Belle said, covering her mouth with her hand as she laughed. "I'm sure they'll be back in short order. Jessie's not the type to run away for too long." In light of Jessie's recent disappearance (yes, he'd blown it up into that), Arthur thought May Belle had used an odd choice of words. If something *was* going on with Lester and his wife—and he was becoming more convinced of it by the imaginative moment—did everybody in town know about it?

"I'm beginnin' ta think I don't know that woman at all," Arthur said with an edge of anger in his voice. "I'll tell her ya called. Bye, May Belle." And he hung up.

He wandered back into the living room where Herm was napping on the couch, his usual pattern right after lunch. He wondered if Herm had noticed anything peculiar like about Jessie's or Lester's behavior this morning, like how pink her cheeks were. Looked like she was wearing rouge. Since when did his wife wear rouge? And Lester, well, he just couldn't seem to keep his eyes off Jessie. Arthur had even noticed Vera was looking kinda suspicious-like at the two of them. *Something ain't right. It ain't right at all.*

He took the TV remote and turned up the volume. Herm didn't stir, so he turned it up again until it was nearly full volume. Herm's eyes flew open and he sat up.

"You know, Arthur Landers, Jessie is right."

"What are you talkin' bout?"

"She said you needed a hearing aid and now I *know* you do."

Arthur turned down the volume until there was only an unintelligible faint mumbling of voices wafting from the set. "How's that for ya? Kin you hear that? I kin hear it just fine."

"Yup. I hear 'em just fine, too."

The two of them sat there watching the man and woman on the soap opera. They appeared to be yelling at each other, although neither man could make out a word they were saying.

"Such nonsense, these stories," Arthur said. "Who'd believe a word of it?"

"I don't know if this is the one Vera watches or not." He sat up on the edge of the couch to take a closer look. "Yup, I believe it is. That doctor there looks familiar." The scene had changed to a crowd of people in a hospital waiting room.

"Herm, did ya notice anything funny at breakfast today?" Arthur asked, still looking at the set.

"Like what?"

"Like Jessie. Or Lester. Notice anything peculiar like 'bout him? Or her?"

"Can't say as I did. Lester looks exactly the same although maybe a little thinner hair on the top of his head, but that's about it."

"Notice anything . . . odd about his service?"

"He was a little impatient with Vera, I thought, if that's what ya mean."

Who wouldn't be, Arthur wondered. "I was thinkin' more along the lines of how he acted with my wife."

"Is that right. Can't say as I did." Although Vera certainly had, and she'd whispered her speculations to him when they were in the bedroom. He'd poo-pooed her crazy suggestion until she'd talked about Jessie's cheeks being so red, which he *had* noticed, like she was wearing rouge or something. He'd never seen her cheeks look like that before. He'd only seen Vera's look something like that once when she'd bought some new fandangled compact that came with two cheek colors in it and she'd put them both on at the same time and then asked him how she looked, which he thought was a trick question because he assumed she wanted him to say fine, or wonderful, or glamorous, but she did not since she looked like a clown but he couldn't say that either so he didn't say anything. He just stared at her, which upset her. She'd skulked out of the kitchen, where she'd come to parade her new rouge while he was drinking coffee and reading the paper, and then after she skulked out during his silence, he'd heard the water running in the bathroom for a long time. Then he heard her crying. Then more water. And when she returned, he heard something hit the garbage can. When she sat down across from him she was no longer wearing the makeup but she'd scrubbed her cheeks so hard they were redder than the makeup and he started laughing and she ran out of the room again. He felt like he was kind of in that same situation right now with Arthur. There just wasn't a good way to respond.

"How he was?" Herm asked, playing dumb, hoping Arthur wouldn't want to dig any deeper.

"Yeah. How he was. How he looked at her, for one dern thing."

"He looked at all of us, Art. We all look at each other all the time. Look, I'm looking at you and you're looking at me right now." *Dumb.* Where was Vera? He didn't know how to do this. Now he felt *his* cheeks getting red—which made Arthur wonder if HERM knew something!

"Ya don't think he was givin' her googly eyes?"

"Googly eyes?"

"Herman Landers, ya know what I'm talkin' 'bout. Stop playing dumb. It was as plain as day and we all saw it!" Arthur clicked off the TV and slammed the remote down on the coffee table.

"Arthur Landers, I do *not* know what you're talking

about." *Lie, lie.* "But it sounds like you're accusing Lester of . . . flirting with your wife. Surely you don't mean ta tell me *that.*"

"I mean to tell ya ex-act-ly that! That scallywag was flirtin' with my wife. I wonder 'bout the way he looked at her, Herm, and I'm beginnin' to wonder if there ain't somethin' a goin' on here!" Now Arthur's cheeks were turning red. In fact his whole face looked like he was holding his breath, just like when he'd imitated Jessie's rampage.

"Now simmer down, Art. Simmer down. For cryin' out loud, you're both old men! And Jessie, well, she's no spring chicken. You're talking like a teenager here."

"Ya sayin' my wife is too old to have somebody flirt with her? Or that she ain't pretty enough for some old codger to give her a second look?" He'd taken a step toward Herm. Not a dukes-up step, but a step. Herm stood up and put his hand on Arthur's shoulder.

"No, Art, I didn't say no such thing! Your Jessie is a fine woman. A darn fine woman!"

"Darn fine enough for that Lester K. Biggs to still be carryin' a torch for her after all these years?"

Just like Vera's rouge. Danged if he said she was, and danged if he said she wasn't. "I think, Art, that you're making something out of nothing here."

"Nothin', huh? I'm the one with a wife who disappeared for an entire afternoon—and when she had *company,* no less—and then came back with nothin' more than a bag of potato chips—POTATO CHIPS!—and some root beer—actin' crazy suddenly playin' euchre war games and . . ."

"Slow down, Arthur. Just slow down and calm down. You are inventin' things now."

"You kin tell me for a fact my wife didn't run off to see Lester the other afternoon?"

"No, I cannot tell you that for a fact. But wasn't Harry's open when she left? Wouldn't Lester have been working? And good Lord, Arthur, I don't think you could hide something that was happening right there in the grill, a place you and Harold both just told me was where everybody learned everything."

Arthur thought back to the day she'd run off. It had been . . . Saturday. Yup. The grill was open, and one thing you could count on was that Lester would have been there and been open from 6 A.M. to 6 P.M., just like clockwork. But she'd been gone until mid-afternoon and the grill wasn't usually busy then. They could have been there alone.

"That scallywag!" Arthur stormed out the back door and headed for his truck.

"Where you goin', Art? Now just calm down and get back in here before ya get yourself in trouble."

"I'm goin' to give that scallywag a piece of my mind. That's where I'm a goin'!"

"What if you're wrong, Art? You're gonna make a fool out of yourself!" Both men were next to the truck now, one on each side. Arthur got in and so did Herm. "I am not letting you do this, Art." Arthur cranked over the engine and, before Herm even had his door closed, the truck was on its way down the driveway. It was all Herm could do to latch the door.

18

"Let's see. I think that does it," Jessie said peering into the Wal-Mart cart. She'd placed the prizes on top of a few other items. "Most buncos gets the beige dish towel; most wins, the black oven mitt; booby prize, the nylon scrubber."

"Need wrapping paper?" Vera asked, hoping they could get out of the kitchen department and into something a little more fun.

"Nope. Got sandwich bags at home. They'll do just fine. And, they can be used again. All that fancy paper is such a waste. Now where was I? Oh, gotta go to the doughnut shop and then to Your Store to get the bridge mix since they were out of it here. I don't want to listen to those women if they don't get their bridge mix."

"Oh, I haven't had bridge mix for so long!"

In the checkout line Jessie said, "The only thing left to do at home is set up the card tables, get out the dice and scrap paper for scoring and clean the bathroom again. No doubt those men have made a mess of it while we were gone. I don't know what I was thinking cleaning it before we left. I swear, Arthur just waits until I put out the clean hand towels to dip his hands in axle grease, then wipe them on my towels. Is Herman like that?"

"Aren't all men?"

They finished their in-and-out stop at Your Store (which

was also out of bridge mix) and were heading around the square to turn toward the Kmart on the outskirts of Hethrow when Vera asked Jessie if she wouldn't like to stop and get a cup of coffee, maybe a piece of pie. She'd noticed the dessert tray on Lester's counter at breakfast and had been thinking about it ever since, which she told Jessie. What she did not tell Jessie was that she'd just like to see how she and Lester behaved together—when Arthur wasn't around.

"We should probably get on with the rest of our errands and hightail it home to get things done so we're not running around at the last minute. We still got supper to cook since no doubt Arthur and Herm haven't decided to become chefs while we were gone."

"Oh, come on, Jessie. Let me treat you. After all the cooking you've done for us while we've been here, I insist. Pull on over to Harry's. Look, there's a spot right in front!" Vera was being so insistent that Jessie veered into it just to settle her down.

"Alright. But we can't stay long. Just a quick coffee and dessert and we're on our way."

"Got it." When the ladies entered, not another soul inhabited the place, so Vera plunked herself down at the counter so they'd be close to Lester's work area. "I haven't sat at a counter since the dime store shut down in our little town. They used to have the best soda fountain. Cherry sodas. That's what I loved. It's kind of fun sitting on a stool, isn't it?" Jessie just looked at her.

"What'll it be, ladies?" Lester asked while swiping a damp cloth in front of Vera, who had selected the only seat at the U that hadn't been wiped down after the last customer.

Vera (on high alert for signs) thought he seemed more animated than usual and tried to decide if that meant anything. "I'd like black coffee and a piece of that pecan pie I saw in your dessert case there," she said pointing.

Lester turned his eyes to Jessie. "And you?"

"Just coffee for me, thanks."

Vera's first bite of pecan pie was on the fork tines two inches from her mouth and Jessie was watching coffee stream out of the decanter and into her cup when Arthur burst through the door, Herm quick at his heels.

"WELL, IF THIS DON'T TAKE THE CAKE!" Arthur boomed as he planted his hands on his hips and stared first at Lester, then at his wife.

"Don't have any cake today," Lester said in a voice as flat as a fritter. "Pie and tapioca pudding's all I got left. No pecan either. Vera got the last piece. Just apple."

"I ain't talkin' 'bout no desserts!" Although Arthur had lowered his voice, it was still loud. "I'm talkin' 'bout my wife sittin' right there big as you please while some termite makes googly eyes at her."

"Googly eyes?" Lester asked Arthur, trying to get it to register. He stood as still as a post, coffee pot poised over Jessie's mug. Vera's forkful of pie was still in front of her lips; Jessie's cheeks turned beet red with anger over what was clearly Arthur's ridiculous insinuation; Herm looked like he might faint. Arthur and Lester—who had now figured out what Arthur was talking about and whose own cheeks had reddened—stared one another down for what seemed to Jessie like an eternity but which really amounted to only a couple of seconds.

Herm tapped Arthur on the shoulder and squeaked out of his dry throat that it was time to go. Unbelievably, Arthur turned on his heels and said, "Fine! I spoke my piece!" and out the door the Landers men went, one tromping and the other scuffling behind him. Vera looked at her bite of pie and decided there was just no sense in not putting it in her mouth, so she did. She didn't dare look at Jessie who she was sure was mortified. And she sure wasn't going to look at Lester. But, of course, she couldn't help it. She needed to see if he looked guilty. Her glance revealed he looked shocked, dismayed and angry. Now she couldn't help but look at Jessie, whose lips were sucked inside her mouth. To Vera's instant chagrin, it was perfectly clear she'd been dead wrong in her speculations. What on earth had she been thinking? She was sorry she'd ever mentioned such a ridiculous thing to Herm. And now, had he gone and told Arthur? *Oh, Lordie, Lordie!*

Lester finished pouring Jessie's coffee, scribbled up their bill, ripped it off his pad and set it between them, then disappeared back into his storeroom, not to return. Thank goodness nobody entered the grill during any of this time. As though nothing had happened, Vera took one more bite of her pie, then said she thought she better save room for bridge mix and doughnuts and why didn't they just pick up a bucket of chicken or something on the way home so nobody had to cook or clean up. Jessie nodded her head, her lips still inside her mouth, as though if she let them out they might say things too terrible for anyone to hear. Vera picked up the ticket, looked at it and left a five-dollar bill on the counter. Lester could keep the change. He'd earned it. Without another word, they exited Harry's Grill.

After Jessie backed the car out of the slot, she tromped on the gas pedal and laid a patch of rubber, right there on the square. It was the first time she'd ever been glad Arthur insisted on big engines. She squealed around the first corner of the square, then got hold of herself, slowing down before the next corner and exit off the square. Killing herself wasn't the answer. Killing Arthur . . . now that was another thing.

Vera kept her hands clutched together all the way to Kmart. Although Jessie wasn't speeding by much, they were going plenty fast, according to Vera's standards, who always did five miles an hour under the limit, just to be safe. Thank goodness Kmart had the bridge mix, but Jessie thought she'd never get Vera out of the housewares aisle where she'd disappeared the moment they entered the store. Truth be told, Vera was trying to stall, just to catch her breath and to keep Arthur and Jessie apart from one another. But sooner than later, Jessie got them moving toward home. When Vera saw the sign advertising Long John Silver's, she suggested they stop and get to-go food, her treat. It seemed the least she could do, she said—although she never explained about what. Aside from a little conversation in Long John Silver's about the choices in side dishes (during which time Jessie thought she would lose control more than once), they'd barely spoken a word to each other since the scene in Harry's.

When they arrived home, thankfully Arthur's truck was nowhere to be seen. Vera let out a loud exhale, realizing she'd been holding her breath all the way up the drive. The one thing she feared for sure was that Jessie and Arthur might get in a knockdown, drag-out fight if they saw each other too soon, before her apologies could be rendered in front of both of them.

The women went straight into their preparations and suppertime came and went and the men never showed up and suddenly it was time for the Hookers to arrive. Although for obvious reasons they were both glad the men weren't around, Vera wasn't used to not knowing Herm's whereabouts. He'd always been so good about such things; it was just one more thing she loved about him. For him to be stuck with Arthur in that kind of a mood—it was no telling what they might be up to, which fretted Vera as much as anything else. But mostly, she sure hoped Arthur didn't come storming into the Hookers' meeting tonight and cause a ruckus. Now wouldn't *that* be something!

Dorothy phoned Maggie Malone for a ride to the Hookers' meeting soon after Jessica called to tell her she wouldn't be attending so she couldn't pick Dorothy up. The very moment Dorothy and Maggie arrived at Jessie's, the phone rang. It was Jessica phoning with huge personal apologies that she was giving such last-minute notice, but Paul had to work late and there was nobody to watch Sarah Sue. Although that had been the truth, Jessica was also too tired to drag herself out anyway, even if she did feel better—which she didn't. She'd learned from her humiliating exit from the meeting at St. Augustine's that it was best just to bow out of things until she was past this phase—or at least until everyone knew. The women would ask too many questions. Figure it out. She didn't want word spreading until she was absolutely for-sure positive, which would, at this point, undoubtedly be confirmed after her appointment next Tuesday morning with the new young Doctor Nielson since Ellie, both the young and the old doctors' receptionist, had informed her that in Doc Streator's bid to begin bowing out of his practice, he was no longer seeing new maternity patients. Although Jessica was highly disappointed she'd have to learn the news from someone she didn't know—

who didn't know her—at least she'd kept her promise to Paul and made the appointment.

When Jessie got off the phone with Jessica, Dorothy and Maggie said their hellos, having spent the first few moments chatting with Vera, who was just learning from them that Jessica couldn't attend. Vera hoped she looked sad enough, although she was really cheering inside. Dorothy'd already noticed the box of doughnuts on Jessie's kitchen counter. Had there been any doubt as to who was hosting the Hookers this evening, the doughnuts would have been a dead giveaway. Jessie served the same thing every time—and usually right out of the box—which was fine since Dorothy liked doughnuts any way they came at her. But she knew she'd have to listen to Gladys say, "Doughnuts, again?" That would be okay, though, since what could Gladys be if not Gladys? And, as usual, the prizes were lined up on the counter in a neat little row of brown paper lunch bags with small words written on the outside like "Booby prize."

Seventy-two-year-old Maggie, sole owner and designer at La Feminique Hair Salon & Day Spa, eyed Vera's hair and noted how thick it still was for a woman of experience, which is what Maggie referred to rather than age. Maggie's own hair was at this particular moment in time—although it could and did change on a whim—a chestnut color, her eyebrows the exact same shade of pencil. It was clear, Maggie thought to herself, that Vera did her own home color, but it wasn't bad. "You ought to come in to the shop if you're looking for something to do before you go home. I could give you a Thanksgiving trim, wash and set. Got a dollar-off coupon in this week's *Press*." Maggie had heard all about the length of Herm and Vera's stay from one client or another, each speculating how none of them would care to have company for that long. She'd also heard from two clients who'd witnessed Jessie laying a patch of rubber when she'd left Harry's, Vera riding shotgun. She wondered if the two women were at each other's throats. One had even asked Lester about it but said he'd been closed-mouth like he always was.

"I just might do that," Vera said. "Maybe Monday or Tuesday? Think you might have anything then?"

"I bet I do. Just give me a call," Maggie said, retrieving her metal card case with the flip-top lid from her giant hand-bag, which had long shoulder straps and a pumpkin made out of sequins appliquéd on it. She flipped out a card and handed it to Vera. "Here ya go, honey. Even if I'm booked solid, I'm sure I could squeeze you in. What with the holi-day everybody wants to look her best for family gatherings, but I'm used to working longer hours then. And if Jessie al-ready tossed the paper, I'll give you a dollar off anyway, since you're a guest and all. We ladies have got to keep up our appearances, right?" Maggie had cocked her hip, placed her hand on it and tossed her head back when she'd said the word "appearances," as though to strike the perfect pose to depict them. She was wearing black slacks and black suede flats with a black sweater festively embroidered with colorful turkeys. Vera thought she'd seen one just like it at the Wal-Mart in her hometown. Too flashy for her, she'd thought at the time, but it looked terrific on Maggie, whose earrings purchased at the Pumpkin Festival craft fair dan-gled all the way down to just above her shoulders. Vera no-ticed that the turkey on Maggie's sweater looked like he was watching the bottom round bauble of her earring sway, as though he were thinking about nabbing it.

"Knock-knock," Gladys said as she walked in. She'd no longer closed the door than out of her mouth came "Doughnuts. Could have guessed. I was hoping you'd have May Belle bring something, like her snickerdoodle cookies."

"May Belle! Hey, where's May Belle?" Jessie wanted to know. "Didn't she ride in with you and Dorothy?" she asked Maggie.

"Why, didn't Arthur tell you?" Dorothy asked.

"Tell me what?"

"That May Belle can't come. She's laid up with her back, poor thing. And you know it must be terrible sore for her to miss a Hookers' meeting. She said she left a message with Arthur. And speaking of Arthur, where is the rascal, who obviously did not do his job very well? Think I'll give him a piece of my mind." Dorothy and Arthur had always been swell friends; she was one of the few people Arthur would listen to, should somebody need to talk sense into him.

"He's out with my Hermie," Vera said, jumping right in. "Who knows what those two are up to!" She only hoped it didn't involve Lester!

19

When Nellie Ruth arrived at Jessie's, Dorothy smiled at the gentle glow of love she recognized shining in Nellie Ruth's eyes. Even after all Dorothy's years of widowhood, she could still remember the warmth of the man who had made her life so lovely, her cool November evenings so much cozier. Gladys's booming voice interrupted Dorothy's reverie. Gladys was looking at her watch and counting heads. "Where's the rest of the Hookers?"

"May Belle's down with a sore back, Paul's working late and Jessica can't get a sitter, so we're two down," Jessie said. "But Vera here is subbing so we're only one short. We'll just play with a blind."

"Where's Ms. Durbin?" Gladys asked. "I mean she lives right next door. Goodness, you'd think she could be on time." Just then there was a loud knock at the door. Jessie ushered Katie right in.

"I'm here, Mayor," Katie said to Gladys, her voice having been heard loud and clear through the door. "And by my watch I'm right on time," Katie said, checking her expensive trim wristwatch as she spoke.

"You've got perfect timing, Katie." Dorothy sidled up to greet her and take her coat. "I guess those of us who have been in the club since the beginning of time are just used to everyone showing up early," she said over her shoulder as she headed toward Jessie's bedroom to put it on the rest of the pile.

"I'll do better next time, Gladys. I promise." Gladys pursed her lips and nodded her head in approval. It occurred to Katie how easily Gladys could be manipulated.

"Shall we get to it?" Jessie asked as she led them toward the living room where the card tables were set up.

This was Katie's first time in the Landerses' home, which she'd already started surveying. Although it was relatively clean and the decorating was sparse (not a tchotchke in sight), aside from two cheap halogen floor lamps, it was like stepping into a time warp from the seventies, with shades of the fifties thrown in for good measure. Although she felt cramped in her mouse house since it was so much smaller, or at least chopped up, than her spacious and open brownstone in Chicago had been (she'd had extensive remodeling done on the brownstone the moment she'd moved in, turning two units into one), the Landerses' home was considerably smaller than Crooked Creek Farm.

As everyone was being seated, Katie took note of the missing spots of plaster and the worn carpet, the uneven floors. Should the Landerses decide to sell and move into town, since they didn't seem like the Florida type, this would undoubtedly be a knockdown for sure, although it would be worth it to hold an estate sale first. The kitchen table and dining room sets, she observed, were so old—and yet not antique—that they were currently popular in the retro trend. She'd seen them in a store in her Chicago neighborhood selling for outrageous dollars. And yet in this setting they just looked outdated. She also knew that if a demolition sale for this house were held in the Chicago area, solid bucks would be shelled out for some of the stunning moldings. It would be a shame to see them go to waste. She doubted, though, that anyone in Partonville had a clue what things were going for in the city. As she scooted her chair up to the table she concluded this whole place, molding aside, didn't have near the character as the mouse house, which was, it occurred to her, the first time she'd thought of her home as *having* character.

"Okay, let's see who goes first," Jessie said. Of course, Gladys had seated herself at the head table. Dorothy said Vera got to be Gladys's partner first since she was a guest. Nellie Ruth and Maggie teamed up to form the other head-table pair, leaving Katie and Dorothy paired at the second table. Jessie said she'd play with the first blind, or ghost player, or whatever they were calling it. Maggie said she thought it would be more fun to say she was playing with an imaginary friend, a handsome friend, which was what she was planning to do when it was her turn with "the blind—as in blind date. I think he'll be six-foot-two, eyes of blue and have huge biceps and curly blond hair."

The highest roller at each table would start the round. Jessie spoke as she picked up the dice and rolled a two. "Maggie Malone, you are too old to be dreaming up things like that. Too old," she said as she passed the dice to Katie.

Back at the head table, Maggie picked up the dice, cupped it in her left hand and topped it with her right. She blew into a space between her thumbs, then said, "Come on, honey! Mama needs a six!" She turned her head toward Jessie. "If I get a six, I can have any imaginary friend I want." She shook her hands together and gave the dice a side-winding roll. "SIX!"

"I'm telling Ben," Dorothy quipped.

"Well, in case you don't recall," Maggie said, "I just described Ben to you! I never said my imaginary friend was young now, did I?"

"No men allowed at a Hookers' meeting," Dorothy teased. "And that is that." Everyone had a good chuckle while Jessie and Vera hoped it was the truth.

Now that Katie was done rolling the dice and Jessie was keeping score for their table, she had time to think about her announcement—which was off. Jessica wasn't present and she was too good a friend to end up the last to hear. In fact, Katie was a little miffed at herself when she realized she hadn't already called her. She made a mental note to never let business get in the way of her new friendships. She'd already lived too many years in Chicago doing just that.

Suddenly Dorothy hollered BUNCO! having rolled three ones in one roll. Nobody could believe how quickly sounds of that first yelping BUNCO! had introduced itself into the evening. One for the record books, Nellie Ruth declared. While they were chitchatting, changing tables to begin rolling for twos, Katie's eyes landed on a Victrola pushed right up against the front door. "Does that old Victrola still work?" she asked Jessie, who was her partner this round.

"Nope. Hasn't worked for decades. It's been sittin' there so long the door probably doesn't work anymore either. That Victrola," she said, pointing at it with one of the dice she'd picked up, "used to be Arthur's folks and he just can't seem to get rid of it." She picked up the remaining die and gave them a quick shake and roll. Nothing. It flashed through Jessie's mind that as cantankerous as her husband could be, he was equally as sentimental—although he didn't reveal that side as often. He showed it most, she thought, in how attached he was to his old coveralls, his old chair, how when she'd aged out of the ball league he'd hung her old baseball mitts on display in the back bedroom, collected all her programs in a box . . . slept in the hospital chair beside her when she'd miscarried their only pregnancy and packed away the baby things before she'd arrived home. The box was probably still in the attic; she'd never asked.

"See that old sheet there next to it?" she asked Katie, pointing at the tower up against the Victrola. "It's covering a stack of four dusty boxes of old 78s we inherited with the broken Victrola." Jessie was trying to sound disgusted, but her voice betrayed other feelings. "Arthur says he can still hear his dad singing along to those scratchy old things. Says they're the reason he started playing the harmonica. Says he's gonna find somebody to fix that thing one day, listen to every single one of those records—one right after the other—until he can play them all on his Hohner." It was her turn to roll again. She picked up the dice, gave an aggressive shake (as if to shake her anger back up), then all but slammed them to the table. "But then Arthur says *lots* of things now, doesn't he?" Her head gave a frustrated wag as she shot a glance at Vera, who was just picking up the dice at the other table and was briefly hurled into a bout of guilt, which she tried to shake off before rolling, lest it give her bad luck.

"Is there no one in town who does repairs on such things?" Katie asked, popping a chocolate-covered raisin in her mouth, one of the three small pieces of chocolate she would allow herself this evening.

"I haven't heard tell of any such person," Maggie said, "and I pretty much hear tell about everything in the shop!" A burst of laughter rippled through the room. It was amazing,

Katie mused, how women could jabber away, roll the dice and add the scores all at the same time. "I have an old grandfather clock I'd love to get repaired," Maggie said. "Oh, I suppose there's a clock repair person in Hethrow, but you ladies keep me so busy with your beautifying and my great-grandkids keep me so busy with their lives that I just never seem to get around to looking one up." While the dice bounced on the tables, the women came up with a litany of broken antiques and collectibles they'd hung onto, thinking they'd get them fixed one day. Things they just couldn't part with no matter how many pieces they were in.

"Sam Vitner doesn't do repairs?" Katie asked.

"All that Sam Vitner knows how to do," Gladys pronounced in judgment, "is to tell a good story."

"Apparently stories good enough to talk you into buying that old wheelbarrow you've got in your front yard, the one you put your boulder collection in." Dorothy's eyes twinkled with mischief. "What was his story on that wheelbarrow, Gladys?"

Gladys's lips drew tight across her teeth. She picked through the bridge mix until she found a caramel. Before she put it in her mouth she answered, "That it was big enough to hold my boulders."

Josh hung up from talking to Shelby—forty-five minutes, something he'd never get away with if his mom was home—then checked his e-mail. Good! One from Alex. All it said, however, was "SCORE! Landed a date with Jennifer. Will keep you posted." He decided to send Dorothy an e-mail. Anything but do his homework. Besides, he was feeling a little punk and talking to Dorothy always made him feel better.

Dear Outtamyway,

Mom said you didn't know I wasn't going to be around for Thanksgiving. Sorry I hadn't mentioned it. Guess I just didn't think about it. Mostly what I've been thinking about is how strange it is mom's letting me take the SUV by myself. First solo road trip. I feel ready for it. Too bad you and Sheba can't hop a ride. We'd hammer down all the way to the windy. Might be the best part of my holiday. Probably would.

Sounds like you're all going to have a big time, like you call it. Busy but big. I'm gonna spend the whole weekend with my dad and his Daily Kids. I think I've told you I call them his Daily Kids cause they're the ones who are with him every day. I guess they're my half brother and sister but they don't feel like it. (I think I've got more halves of relatives than anyone I know!) They just feel like his kids. They're okay, I guess.

Anyway, I'm hoping to get to see Alex one of the days. Maybe Friday or Saturday—although dad's family usually likes to go look at the Christmas windows at Marshall Field's on the Friday after Thanksgiving. Ever seen them? They have these scenes like from movies or whatever. Kinda cool but never seems worth the hassle to me, not since I got past ten years old, I think. I'd rather go to a movie. We'll see. Gonna e-mail Alex next to see what his schedule looks like. Hard to tell since he finally got a date with Jennifer. He's been working on that since kindergarten I think. Good for him. Now maybe he'll stop razzing me about Shelby.

Speaking of Shelby, she told me to tell you hi. She said you'd be seeing her "Grannie M" at bunco tonight

and then for your "pink scalp appointment." (Shelby
said YOU call it that. I think it's mean. You have hair.
Just not much of it.) Guess Mrs. Malone mentioned it to
her because she said she's always happy when it's your
day since you're fun. Of course I agreed.

   Wonder if Shelby's gonna be at your Thanksgiving
dinner. Forgot to ask her. Doubt it though. She's got all
those relatives. I'll miss her over the holiday. (How
sappy is THAT?!) I'll miss you too. And mom. (Okay,
Sap Overload.)

   Gotta study. Talk to you soon, before I leave, I hope.
   Your pal,
   Joshmeister

After Arthur had stormed out of the grill he and Herm had
spent the first hour of their torturous streak just tearing
around in the truck, Arthur's anger causing the truck tires to
kick up gravel on the back roads or lay a patch on the hard
road a time or two as he tromped on the gas pedal as fast
as his mouth was flying. There'd been a time during their
youth when laying a patch of rubber would have made them
both proud. All it had done this night was to make Herm a
nervous wreck. Herm didn't know it, but Arthur had scared
himself a little, although, of course, he'd never admit it.
Herm's feet had been pressed into the floorboard and his
hand frozen to the door handle as though it had rigor mor-
tis. That's when Herm had suggested they stop by The Tap
and play a game or two of shuffleboard, maybe have a
Schlitz to calm their nerves. Since the Hookers would be
gathering, Herm didn't think they should go home, so for

lack of anything better to do, Arthur pulled into the parking lot of The Tap and in he'd stomped.

But Arthur's anger made his beer taste bitter. After two swallows, he'd left it on the bar, not even carrying it over to the shuffleboard table with him. To make matters worse, here he was trying not to think about Jessie and there she was, her eyes looking at him from a dozen different pictures hanging on the wall. Since The Tap sponsored the Wild Musketeers baseball team (and had the best Friday night fish fry in the county, including the one served by weasel Lester), there was last season's winning team photo right on the wall next to his end of the shuffleboard, right along with about a dozen other years' worth that spread the entire length of the entire shuffleboard. And since Jessie was the pitcher, she was always front and center in the photos. A dozen sets of her feisty eyes were looking right at him while he tried to finesse the puck down the board toward his target. The same eyes Lester had no doubt found so attractive. The same eyes whose determination and spunk had, so many years ago, lured them both to her front porch.

Dad-gum it! A man can't fault another man for havin' been attracted to her, kin he? I mean, just look at her! His eyes scanned the nearest photo one more time. *But dad-gum it, one man got her and the other didn't and that's the way it's gonna stay—even if I have to fight for that yelpin', throwin', cantankerous woman!*

It struck Arthur that his wife might be a lot of things, but gol'*dern* she'd never been a *sneak.* He figured if she got it in her fool head she liked another man better, she'd have just told him. Just like that. Jessie didn't tritsy-foot around. *She'd a zinged a few words at me just like she was pickin' off somebody at second base, and that would have been that. Right?*

"Let's go, Herm," Arthur said after intentionally sliding the pucks down the shuffleboard and into the end gutter with a thunk. "Let's get out of here." Herm didn't have to ask what was wrong; he'd caught Arthur looking at those pictures time and again even though it was clear he was trying not to.

While the ladies were shopping he and Herm (after trying to entertain themselves playing shuffleboard) had made their way back to the house, hidden the truck in the old shed-turned-garage-turned-shed (Herm's idea to avoid any confrontations until Art calmed down), hiked down to the creek and seated themselves down near the fire pit. Arthur sat on a stump staring toward the creek water, which was all but invisible since the sun had long ago set. As much as he hated thinking about this whole gol-dern predicament, he had to sort it out. His gut felt like a rolling boil of confusion. What was he to do—if anything? He thought back to when he and Jessie were first married, how every evening she wasn't on the road playing ball they used to jaunt down to the creek, Jessie saying she had to keep her bending and springing and moving legs in shape. She'd jump the narrow crossings of the creek and on the heels of her landing stop to do a few toe touches and deep squats or toss her arm as though she was throwing a zinging pickoff play to second. He'd always been attracted to Jessie's enthusiasm and competitive nature, her "giddyup and go-go-go," he used to call it. They'd started their creek ritual early in their marriage and if he hadn't been so . . . *whatever* . . . he would have smiled at the memories. When she'd finally wear herself down, they'd sometimes sit on a couple of stumps and watch the sunset together. Now it was dark and cold and damp and he was sitting across from his cousin who was getting on his very last nerve and who, by the way, might have started this whole dang mess!

When had he and Jessie stopped taking their evening constitutionals? His brain hurt. Must have been at least . . . well, maybe now that he thought about it, maybe a decade or two since they'd walked down to the creek together. *Surely it ain't been that long!* Visions of Herm and Vera's creek-side hand-holding rifled into his head. He picked up a twig and cracked it in half, then he yelled at the creek to "shut up so as I can think!" The bubbling wasn't soothing like it usually was; it sounded more like blurping and slurping that was mocking him, keeping him from concentrating on the matter at hand, which was the state of his marriage. Just the other day he'd heard some television talk-show guru ask a couple about "the state of their marriage" and he'd jokingly said to the guru, "Such hogwash. But if I had to pick I'd say ours is a wind-whipped Nebraska." Now the question didn't seem funny. When had he ever—ever?— during its nearly sixty years of existence considered the state of their marriage? A marriage just *was.* That was a girlie-guy thing to think about.

Lester aside, what *was* the state of his marriage? *The state of my particular marriage. I'd say it's a gol' dern, belly-achin' annoyin' mess,* he thought, but he had no earthly idea what to do about it. What if she really *was* seeing Lester? *Then* what? And if she wasn't (which he was more inclined to believe now that he'd spent some time calming down and trying to sort it all out), well, he'd made a mess out of things now, with both his wife *and* Lester. Herm had tried to warn him. *Me and my hot head.* Then again, there *were* all those signs.

"Arthur," Herm said after his cousin yelled "Shut UP!" to the creek for the second time, "I think you're having yourself a nervous breakdown—or worse—over something that you are plumb imagining." Herm felt like a broken record, but what else was there to say that might help calm his cousin who was sizzling like the lit wick of a firecracker.

"You sayin' I imagined Lester's googly eyes? You gonna tell me you didn't see 'em? You gonna tell me my wife didn't disappear for hours and blame it on a bag of potato chips? You gonna . . ." He suddenly found himself with nothing else to add, having said it all time and again in the last hours, so right out loud he told *himself* to just shut up, which saved Herm the effort.

"Art," Herm said, exhaustion plaguing him now, "even if Lester did smile at Jessie, you smile at people all the time yourself and it don't mean a thing. Why, you smile at Vera and you don't see me getting all huffy, do you?" Herm pushed the button on his Timex. The illumination behind the hands let him know he'd been yawning for an hour already and it was only 9 P.M. He was cold from sitting on a stump in the damp night air, the coldness seeping through his clothing and radiating down to his arthritic knees and up to his bursitis-laden elbows. And he was hungry and tired. And he was sick of listening to Arthur. Enough was enough. The alarm had gone off at 5:15 A.M. to get them ready for breakfast at Harry's, and most of the day since had been filled with tension. He was done in. And Arthur, although he might be crackin' up, had at last finally run out of words.

But bunco sometimes didn't break up until 10 P.M. or so. Where were they to go if not to the house? It was their only option.

20

The last time Katie and Gladys were paired up for the evening was at the head table. "I understand you've volunteered to help with the Thanksgiving dinner," Gladys said as she rolled the dice.

"That's right."

"Have you ever worked at anything like that before?" Gladys asked, sure Katie had no idea what she might be in for. Gladys scored three points before having to hand the dice off to their opponents.

Katie wanted to respond with her long litany of volunteer projects, which had drawn the top socialites in Cook County, made millions of dollars and at which she'd worked her tail off coordinating all the committees *and* served the hors d'oeuvres. But that would have been an out-and-out lie. The only thing she'd ever actually volunteered for was to head up a commercial Realtors' committee on urban development and then, all she'd really done was appoint people to do the work. She hadn't even called the caterer. "No, I have not. I'm sure you'll have much to teach me," Katie said ever so sincerely to Gladys, continuing to grease the axle of the one woman she figured could rally the troops to make her new venture miserable if she set her mind to it. She also knew if Gladys was on her side, she could help jump-start the project since she was well connected and also good at appointing people—and she was relentless when making sure they were doing their jobs. She recalled Dorothy had once said she and Gladys might become "good buddies" one day. Although Katie saw no opportunity for that, when it came to getting things done, it almost stung to think she and Gladys might be more alike than she'd care to imagine.

"She'd teach you if she could," Dorothy said to Katie, "but it will have to be another time since she's not going to be working on Thanksgiving Day either." Figuring she'd made her counterpoint when she noticed Gladys huff and jerk down her blazer, she added, "That's because Gladys is blessed to be able to spend the day with her family, which is wonderful." And it was, they all agreed. Especially Katie. This time not to grease Gladys's cooperation, but because she wished she could say the same about her own Thanksgiving day.

Katie scored the last four points to give her and Gladys the win for the final round of the evening. After everyone tallied their scores, Gladys discovered that the last win had secured her the prize for the most wins. Had it been anyone other than Jessie who'd purchased the prizes, she might have been more filled with anticipation, but just the same, she did love being a winner. Nellie Ruth took most buncos and Vera was absolutely thrilled to win the booby prize, even though it meant she had the worst scorecard.

When the ladies were handed their bags, Gladys opened hers first and said, "A black oven mitt. Black. Well. At least it won't show the dirt, I guess." Nellie Ruth opened her bag next and did her very best to hide her disappointment. A beige dish towel would definitely not go with her Splendid Rose kitchen paint. Even though ES had yet to begin, she'd already picked out a colorful floral-print kitchen tablecloth with a black-and-white-checked gingham border.

"Gladys, what would you think about trading? That mitt will go *perfectly* with my new kitchen colors when we're done. I'm afraid I've burned so many holes in my old mitt that there's now more hole than fabric." Gladys, who had raised an eyebrow at Nellie Ruth's mention of "we," as in "when we're done," took one look at the beige dish towel—beige being her favorite color—and the swap was made. Of course, Vera didn't have to open her bag to know a nylon scrubber awaited her, and yet she couldn't remember exactly what color it was. She stuck her hand in and took out her prize. "What an interesting shade of . . . would you call this green?"

"I'd call it something that gets the job done," Jessie said. "What difference does it make what color a scrubber is as long as it scrubs?"

"Right," Vera said. "That is exactly right." *I'll keep it under my sink.*

"You gals stay seated," Jessie said, looking at the cuckoo clock. "Vera and I are going to bring the coffee and dessert right to you." They scurried off to the kitchen. "You get the Styrofoam cups and bag of napkins," Jessie instructed. "I'll grab the doughnuts." When they got back to the living room, Vera set about giving each lady a cup and a napkin. Jessie came around behind her plunking a doughnut on each of their napkins. At least, Gladys noted, she'd used tongs. Last time she'd used her fingers. (Of course, the tongs had been Vera's idea.) Katie started to take a pass, then realized it would look rude. She also started to ask for a knife, since a half of the frosted greasy-looking doughnut before her would surely be worth heartburn and five pounds, but there was no knife. She decided she could just quietly eat what she wanted and leave the rest. Jessie set the box containing the last of the dozen doughnuts at the table in front of Gladys and went back to the kitchen to get the coffee pot, sugar container and the mug of spoons she kept on her counter. She'd wait to see if anyone asked for cream, which she hoped they did not because she forgot to buy some. She and Arthur didn't use cream—and neither did Herm and Vera—so she hadn't given it a thought when they'd been running their errands this afternoon. She went from table to table pouring the black brew into the cups hoping to get the evening wrapped up.

"This is decaf, I'm assuming?" Gladys asked Jessie.

Jessie stared at Gladys for a moment, then waited until Gladys had gulped in a mouthful. "What's the point of drinking coffee if it is?" she said with perfect timing. Gladys realized it was too late to do anything but swallow. Jessie held back a grin. It occurred to her she was behaving like a brat, but her ire was up enough to decide *all* the bullies should get their due. Gladys opened her lips to enter into her oft-repeated "can't sleep" diatribe. "Just kidding," Jessie said flatly. "Bought a half-pound bag of decaf just for tonight, just for you bunch of lightweights. Anybody who wants can take the rest of the bag home. Nobody'll drink it here." Since the coffee-and-cream situation had reminded her about Arthur again, she looked at the clock—again. It was 8:47. She wondered how long it would be before Arthur and Herm came home. Surely it wouldn't be much later; Arthur was usually heading for bed about now. "And speaking of going home," she said, feigning a yawn, "I've had a long day." Vera's mouth fell open. The tone in Jessie's voice nearly demanded they hurry up, eat and leave. Although Vera was going to breathe easier once the Hookers were gone, she would have never had it in her to be so . . . obvious.

"Well, for goodness' sakes, Jessie! It's not even nine yet!" Gladys, who was reaching for a second doughnut when Jessie snatched the plate away, sounded completely put out. "I was going to have a short discussion about the Thanksgiving dinner plans before we left." With that, everyone seemed to leap to their feet to head down the hall to collect their coats. "I guess I'll phone you volunteer workers tomorrow since we don't have time for it tonight." Gladys was definitely puffed up, but much to Jessie's relief, moving down the hall.

"That'll be fine with me, Gladys," Nellie Ruth said. "Thursday is my day off. . . . OH! NO! Wait! I traded with someone. I *will* be working tomorrow. It's a good thing we *are* breaking up early. I almost forgot! I'll be around tomorrow evening, though, Gladys. Just let me know anything I need to know. Or stop by the store, if you want. Honestly, I don't know what's wrong with me lately."

"I'd say absolutely nothing," Dorothy said, nipping anyone else's snide comments about Edward Showalter in the bud. Nellie Ruth gave Dorothy a hug and kissed her on the cheek. "Thank you," she whispered into Dorothy's ear. "Thank you for always being in my corner since the day I arrived in this town."

"The real crunch is going to start after we tally up the reservations on Friday. Try to get yourself together by then," Gladys said, "since you're doing the shopping. That is no small task, one that I hope you haven't underestimated. If nothing gets purchased and delivered, nothing can get cooked. We sure don't want United Methodist to look like it's dropped its end of the ball. I hope you've cleared all of that delivering with Edward Showalter."

"Yes, Gladys. Yes, I have. He's happy to be helping us. He just wishes he could come work Thanksgiving Day, too, but he's having dinner with Johnny Mathis and his family. Kind of a tradition with them."

"Johnny Mathis?" Vera asked. "The well-known . . ."

"Not that Johnny Mathis. This Johnny is a dear friend of . . . Edward Showalter's." She almost said ES but had promised herself to keep that endearment just for him. "He owns The Piece."

"The Piece?" Vera looked more confused than ever.

"Oh, it's really called A Little Piece of New Yorkville Cuisine. It's just shorter to call it The Piece. Kinda cute, don't you think?"

"I thought it was A Little Piece of New York City," Maggie said.

"No," Nellie Ruth corrected softly. "It says A LITTLE PIECE OF NYC on the exterior sign. We all just *assumed* that meant New York City. Inside, on the menus where the whole clever name is spelled out, you can see it. A LITTLE PIECE OF NEW YORKVILLE CUISINE. You'll have to stop by and check it out. Edward Showalter helped Johnny rehab the entire building."

"This is all just dandy," Jessie said, "but really, it's time to go." She spread her arms and worked like a border collie with a bunch of sheep to corral them out the door and into their cars, Vera right on her heels.

"I'm glad to hear someone in the area has sprouted a trendy little restaurant," Katie said as she pushed the button to unlock her SUV's door. "Do you know if they serve any vegetarian dishes?"

"Oh, I don't know about that, Katie," Nellie Ruth said. "I do know the restaurant smelled delicious when we were there. Very cutting edge."

"Well, goodnight!" Katie said, slamming her door. Soon all were in their cars and headed down the lane. And it was perfect timing since Arthur and Herm were just making their way along the fence with a flashlight. Thankfully, Arthur had had enough sense to grab it out of the garage before they'd hiked down to the creek. Both men were relieved to see the stream of taillights, although Herm wished there had been just enough lag time between the ladies leaving and them returning to have allowed the womenfolk to have gone to bed. But on they tromped. They were too tuckered out to do anything else.

21

Lester lay in bed on his back in the pitch black, eyes wide open. How he had managed to get through the rest of his day after the Landers clan left the grill was a mystery, if not an out-and-out miracle. Arthur had appeared, spoken his astounding accusation and left so swiftly that Lester had barely had time to react, other than to seek shelter in the storage room to pull himself together before the early dinner crowd started arriving, which was only a ten-minute lapse. His mind had been a complete mess ever since. It was all he could do to keep flipping the burgers, dish up the special for the day (he'd set three orders down in front of the wrong people, something he never did), then lock the door at 6 P.M.—and he'd been watching the clock, its hands seemingly stopped—wash the dishes, clean the grill and climb up the stairs to his home. Once he'd locked the door behind him, he'd leaned back against it for a couple of minutes, his body finally releasing the tensions his mind hadn't had time to digest. He plopped on the couch where he remained until he'd undressed and crawled into bed at nine.

Vera and Jessie were folding up the card tables when they heard the kitchen door open. Since it was right on the heels of the ladies leaving, the last car probably not having got to the end of the drive yet, they assumed someone had forgotten something. Jessie walked back into the kitchen fully expecting to see a Hooker, but there stood the cousins. All three froze in place, Arthur's arm midair over the counter, flashlight dangling from his fingertips; Herm halfway through the door, cold air blasting in from behind him. Jessie and Arthur stared at each other, a thick blanket of wariness cloaking them. Much to Arthur's surprise, what struck him was the intensity in Jessie's eyes, the same intensity in every single photo on the wall at The Tap. What struck Jessie was that Arthur's eyes looked sad. Not since The Tank was dying had she seen Arthur with sad eyes. She dared a glance at Herm, who looked utterly terrified. He was shivering. He needed to close the door.

Vera walked into the kitchen and made the first sound. It was a loud gasp. And yet, nobody moved. After what felt like a silent testing period to see if anyone was going to throw out a fiery word (or if Jessie might reach for something and wing it), in silence, they each set into action, Herm being the last to move and thankfully close the door, sending a sign he'd decided it was okay to stay—although his eyes weren't sure. Vera put the dice and scorecards away; Arthur brushed his teeth. Herm scrounged in the suitcase for the tube of Ben Gay; Jessie rinsed out the coffee pot. While she was setting it in the drainer she peaked out the kitchen window. Arthur's truck was still nowhere to be seen. And there was that flashlight on the counter. Had they been hiding? Listening? When on earth—and how—had they arrived home?

Herm and Vera finally closed the door to their bedroom. They embraced for a long while. Her arms wrapped around him, she stroked his back; he kissed the top of her head.

They were very happy to see each other. Even though they had much to share, they were simply too tired to speak. They crawled into bed, snuggled even tighter than usual and were soon both fast asleep.

While Jessie was still in the kitchen, Arthur stepped out of his coveralls and walked over to the photo on his bedroom wall, a photo he hadn't taken note of for years. It had hung in the exact same spot since Jessie'd quit playing ball, her team's manager having presented it to her upon her retirement. It occurred to him that maybe the familiarity of things caused a blind spot, the spot in which this picture— just like the ones in The Tap—had disappeared for so long. Although Jessie never liked pictures of herself (she hated every last one of them in The Tap), this one had always been special. She was in her late twenties. She wore a ball cap, a catcher's mitt and a stiff-looking uniform. It was her official semi-pro photo that had appeared in one program or another. She was smiling. She had been married for two days.

Arthur sighed, then heard a sound behind him. He turned swiftly enough to catch Jessie watching him study her picture, her eyes now holding questions rather than fire. They stared at each other for a moment, the wariness having followed them into the bedroom. Her eyes glanced to the floor, to his coveralls. He followed her gaze but didn't make a move to pick them up. She sighed, folded back the fancy wedding-gift bedspread and turned out the light, leaving Arthur standing in the dark in his skivvies. She sat on the edge of the bed, removed her clothing, put on her cotton pajamas she kept under her pillow and slid under the covers. In the dark, she heard rustling sounds and the distinct click of the metal clasps on Arthur's coveralls. She felt Arthur knock into the bed, trying to feel his way in the dark. She heard the clinking sound of the clasps again, then the light weight of Arthur's coveralls across her feet as he laid them on the end of the bed. She felt the familiar bounce of the mattress as he slid in beside her. Anticipated the toss and tug of the covers as he rolled to his side, his back toward her. He always slept on the right side of the bed, she on the left. He took a huge breath and released it and she felt the slight rise and fall of the sheet against her right arm. Aside from the weight and position of the coveralls, it was all so familiar . . . Nearly six decades of familiar. Surely that had to be worth something.

Maybe, she thought, it was everything.

Dear Joshmeister,

The Happy Hookers ended early tonight so thought I'd boot up before bed. (I just told you something you probably already know since your mom left at the same time as I did and she had a shorter drive.) I didn't win any prizes. (Maybe you know that, too.) This was one of the more boring meetings we've ever had (not just because I didn't win), but then I guess sometimes boring is relaxing. It was good to see Arthur's cousin's wife Vera, though. (Have you met his cousins yet?) I hadn't seen her since their last visit years ago. Maybe being from out of town makes you lucky; she won the booby prize. Then again, you only win that because you lose the most, so . . . Then again, I lost and didn't win *anything*. (enough pouting)

Best thing that happened in my evening was to see an e-mail from you! And such an informative one. I've read it twice now. Thanks for taking the time to catch me up! The first thing that caught my imagination was to picture the three of us (you, me, Sheba) tearing down the highway toward Chicago in that big SUV. If it's as chilly as it is tonight, though, Sheba would have to keep her head in the car so we didn't catch our death of colds.

I imagine we could get in all kinds of trouble together on a road trip. Probably a good thing we can't go. ;>) But I can't WAIT to hear about your trip when you return. I'm already wondering about Alex (tell him I said Hi) and Jennifer.

Yes, I have seen the windows at Marshall Field's. Henry and I took the children there twice when they were old enough to appreciate it. Mid-fifties or so, I'd say. We stayed overnight both times with my friend Selina who lived out west of the city a ways. All three of my kids would sleep on a feather bed mattress she'd yank off her bed and toss on the floor in the living room. We'd make the drive in one day, visit, have dinner and go to bed. Bright and early the next morning, downtown we'd go! Oh, the kids would get so excited when they'd start seeing those forty-two giant golden trumpets hanging on the outside of the building! First we'd creep along in the big line of people waiting to see the windows. (I'd be praying nobody had to go to the bathroom! ;>))

I remember the kids always wanted to stand and look longer at each window but the smash of people behind us kept us moving along. Then we would wait in line for hours to eat lunch under the tree in Field's. I think the restaurant was called the Walnut Room, although I don't remember any walnuts. Then we'd

drive home, the kids sound asleep in the backseat.
We'd have to save our pennies for months to afford
that trip, but it sure was exciting, for *all* of us.

Of course there weren't computer games and e-mail
then, or cable TV, or super highways. You kids see so
much so early now that I imagine looking at windows
might seem boring. If you have to go, though, try to
make the best of it. Maybe the Daily Kids will enjoy
it and you can enjoy watching your half of them.
hahahahaha (Hey, halves of relatives are better than
NO relatives!)

Shelby's Grannie M (what a corker!) was decked out
in her usual splendor tonight. I (my pink scalp and not
much hair, but thanks for noticing what I *do* have)
always look forward to seeing her, too.

I'm fading to tired now. Must sleep. Must sleep. . . .
Good night and don't let the bedbugs bite!
Your friend, Dorothy

In the wee dark hours of the morning without a moment
of sleep padding his restless mind, it became stark clear to
Lester that this was one of the main differences between
him and Arthur: Arthur acted on impulse and emotion,
and he, well, he had to take time to think about things after
they happened. Figure out what he even thought, and what
course of action, if any, should be taken in response. He'd
always needed to take time to lay a plan. *It's just like football.
Arthur leads a spontaneous offensive life charging headlong into
whatever. And me, well, I lead a defensive life, reacting to things.
Takes both sides to play a game, though.*

But now, Lester didn't even know what kind of game

Arthur was playing. Arthur had rallied his ridiculous charge on . . . what? *Nothing, absolutely nothing. You old fool!* He certainly wasn't about to duke it out with Arthur since that might falsely indicate he was taking a stand for another man's wife. And if he said or did nothing, it might look like he'd admitted to something since he wasn't willing to counteract the accusations.

And what would Jessie think about him should he do something . . . or nothing? Did she need him to step in to defend her, set the record straight? Or more likely, he thought (Lord help them all), did Arthur need help against Jessie, who might be throwing sharp objects at him by now? The recent image of Arthur's demonstration of Jessie's cleaning rampage actually set him to laughing out loud at the thought of her giving that old geezer a good what's for. Who better to do it than Jessie!

Laughing helped give him some perspective. After he'd finally settled himself down, he knew it was time for him to take the bull by the horns, strategize, assume the offensive for a change. And truth be told, after this fiasco, he was glad he didn't have *any* woman in his life since love just seemed to make some folks plumb nuts.

22

Dorothy was relaxing at Maggie's shampoo station, head back in the sink as Maggie worked over her, elbows extended out to the sides, fingertips gently running up and back along the curves in Dorothy's cranium, thumbs massaging in little circular motions just above her ears. Then the rinse. Of course, the entire process only took a minute due to Dorothy's lack of hair, but it was always a heavenly dose of contact. Maggie worked her magic when it came to fulfilling a need for touch. Dorothy and May Belle had often talked about the multiple gifts Maggie dispensed, and touch was at the top of their lists, along with good company, a boost to their femininity and the unending string of surprises concerning Maggie's latest cosmetic and fashion adventures. Maggie's exuberance alone was worth the stop since it was catching. It was amazing how relaxed and yet energized clients felt when they left La Feminique Hair Salon & Day Spa.

"What a boring Hookers' meeting Wednesday," Maggie said as she coaxed Dorothy to sit up. Maggie wrapped a towel around Dorothy's head. The towel was still slightly warm since the dryer had turned off just before Dorothy had arrived; the warmth was comforting. "I can't remember when we've had a more boring night of bunco." Although it was Friday, this was the first time Maggie had seen Dorothy since the Hookers had gathered.

"That's exactly the same word I used when I e-mailed Josh with my recap. Boring. Not that Jessie didn't put out a nice spread."

"Her usual spread of doughnuts, black coffee, no cream and bridge mix, you meant to say."

"Didn't have to. You said it. Still, who of us really needs more than that?" Dorothy patted her stomach through the plastic drape.

"There wasn't even any juicy gossip. We might have been able to enjoy more of it if Nellie Ruth hadn't showed up," Maggie said laughing. "She and Edward Showalter are sure one of the talks of the town right now. Isn't it just . . . Isn't it ro-man-tic," Maggie said, breaking into the vintage song and twirling herself around a couple of times.

"Watch out now. I don't want you to go down before you're done beautifying me! It was good to see Vera," Dorothy said, ignoring the chance to gossip, which she didn't much care for. Maggie and Dorothy were both on the move now, over to Maggie's wash-and-set chair, the other chair reserved for colors and perms.

"After what I heard tell about Jessie laying a patch of rubber on the square, I expected to feel more tension between those two Landers women. That's a long time for company. But they seemed to be getting along just fine."

"A patch of rubber?" Dorothy asked, the words bumping out of her as Maggie rubbed the towel over her head.

"You didn't hear? When the two of them left the grill the other day, bunco day, I believe it was, Jessie laid a patch of rubber after she backed out of her parking spot. You can see it for yourself, if you go look when we're done here. Why, I heard tell she even squealed the tires around her first leg of the square!"

"No!"

"Yes!"

"That big old Buick must have just gotten away from her," Dorothy said. "I hope she's not the next one who has to think about giving up her driving. I tell you, Maggie, it's one of the hardest things. . . ." She cut herself off, determined to quit whining about a circumstance that was not going to change. "I'm surprised nobody mentioned the incident at bunco. But then if they thought Jessie and Vera had been quarreling, I understand why they didn't."

"Ben told me he saw Arthur and Herman tearing around town in Arthur's truck the same afternoon. He said he figured those two old buzzards were reliving their youth." Ben was Maggie's husband, the two of them as crazy in love as the day they'd married more than fifty years ago. Maggie pumped Dorothy's chair up a few notches and rearranged her drape. "Isn't it something how when men do that, they're just reliving their youth and when women do it, we think somebody must be mad or the car just got away from them?" Maggie gently combed through Dorothy's wispy locks as they pondered the injustice of it all.

"Josh mentioned Shelby when he e-mailed me," Dorothy finally said, both women feeling the entire gender thing wasn't worth getting fired up about, especially since they seemed to be feeding it. "Guess those two are still going strong?"

"You betcha! My granddaughter said she's not sure which was worse. Worrying her tomboy of a daughter might never have a date (although Shelby was Maggie's great-grandaughter, Shelby had never called her anything but

Grannie M), or knowing how crazy gaga she is over the first guy she's ever dated for serious—especially since he's got that big old SUV."

"Oh, I remember that fretting so well! If my Caroline Ann had done half the stuff I feared she might be doing when she was one minute late. . . ."

Maggie spun Dorothy's chair to look right into her eyes instead of talking to her in the mirror. "Who's to say she wasn't?" Maggie teased. She spun Dorothy back toward the mirror after they'd both laughed.

"Well, only Caroline Ann and God know for sure now. If she was sitting right in that chair today," Dorothy said, her finger peaking out from beneath her drape as she pointed, "we could have asked her. But sometimes cancer has its way. Then again, if I did have the chance to ask her, maybe I wouldn't want to know! I can assure you Vinnie and Jacob spend far too much time tormenting me by telling me things they used to do, things I wished I'd never heard." Maggie, small round brush in one hand, dryer in the other, turned the hair dryer on with her thumb, which put an end to their conversation. The minute Sheba, who always came to the shop with Dorothy since Maggie loved her to pieces, heard the loud whir of the motor, she scurried back to the laundry room and disappeared.

"YOU'D THINK SHE'D BE USED TO THIS AFTER ALL THESE YEARS!" Maggie hollered, holding the dryer up in the air.

After Dorothy's finishing touch of spray, she paid Maggie, stuck a dollar in her hand and said to Sheba, "Come on, girl. Let's go see for ourselves just how good a job Jessie did layin' that patch, then we'll stop by and see if we can't do something for May Belle, poor thing. I imagine Earl's worried to pieces, his mom being down this long."

Nellie Ruth was straightening the rows of cucumbers when she felt a tap on her shoulder. She turned, expecting to see either Wilbur, her boss, or Gladys, who she figured would be stopping by to check if she had all her reservation numbers tallied. Instead, Edward Showalter's grinning face greeted her. He had his hands behind his back.

"Pick a hand," he said playfully.

Nellie Ruth bit on her bottom lip and said, "That one!" She pointed to his left arm. He whipped his hand in front of him, empty, then quickly swung it behind his back.

"Pick again." He jostled his arms as though he might be switching things around.

"That one again!" she said, pointing to her last selection.

"HA!" he said, once again revealing his empty left hand, then zinging it behind him. "Pick again!"

She stood staring at him, trying to telepathically read his mind, but mostly getting lost in the arch of his eyebrows, the bold curve of his nose, the way his ears stuck out—but just right.

"Hey! You gonna pick?"

"Oh! Sorry. Yes. I pick . . . um . . . LEFT AGAIN!"

This time he carefully brought his left hand forward, a little package in it. She could tell he'd wrapped it himself, the electrical wire "ribbon" being a dead giveaway. "I know the wrapping is kind of . . ."

She cut him off. "The wrapping is *perfect* for you! What's inside?" She grabbed the package and gave it a squeeze.

"How about you open it?"

She unwound the wire and for lack of anything else to do with it, she wrapped it around her wrist, then she slid the tissue off her gift. It was a scented candle. "VANILLA! Oh, ES!" Two ladies standing by the tomatoes craned their necks to see what she'd been squealing about. Seeing the candle, they smiled first at Nellie Ruth, then at Edward Showalter. Then they put their heads together and whispered to one another as they took off down the aisle, one of them pushing the cart, the other looking back over her shoulder to get another gander at giddiness in the produce aisle.

Suddenly Nellie Ruth maneuvered the candle and paper into her left hand, picked up a cantaloupe with her right and set the candle and paper in its place. Then she quickly built a pile of cantaloupes around it until not a sign of her gift could be detected. Edward Showalter appeared to be shrinking on the spot. *I thought she liked it!* "Hello, Gladys!" she said over his shoulder. "Good to see you. Gladys, I'm sure you know . . . Edward Showalter."

"Yes. Of course I do," she said as though Nellie Ruth was daft. "He installed the new square building clock for me, remember? I hate to interrupt you while you're *working,*" she said, shifting her eyes to Edward Showalter.

"I was just leaving, ma'am. I just dropped by to"—his eyes veered to the pile of cantaloupes, then back at Gladys—"say hello and to assure Nellie Ruth here that I'm looking forward to helping her on Monday with the food deliveries for Thanksgiving. I'm glad I have a chance to express that to you myself."

Gladys looked from one of them to the other. Something felt suspicious but she didn't have time to figure it out. She needed to collect reservation numbers from everyone (she decided she'd talk to Nellie Ruth later when Edward Showalter wasn't hanging around to interrupt) and check in on May Belle to make sure she was going to be up for her end of the workload. "Well," she said, yanking down on the bottom of her blazer, "I have to be going." She started to walk between Edward Showalter and Nellie Ruth, her eye set on a cantaloupe. Quickly Nellie Ruth closed the gap, pressing her side up against Edward Showalter's. Her face turned bright red when Gladys's eyes flew, yet she didn't move. She was stuck to Edward Showalter like cling wrap, not an air bubble between them.

"The cantaloupes aren't that ripe yet, Gladys," she said in a rush. "You'd be better off waiting a couple of days." As soon as the words—which weren't exactly untrue but which did stretch the fact a hair—were out of her mouth, Nellie Ruth silently apologized to God, her entire face now turning every shade of the red peppers in the display bins across from her.

Gladys shook her head and chugged her cart down the aisle. Over her shoulder she said, "I'll call you tonight, Nellie Ruth, and you can give me your tally of reservations. And Nellie Ruth," she said, stopping her cart and turning around to speak, "I must say your jewelry leaves something to be desired."

Nellie Ruth had no idea what Gladys was talking about. She grabbed her ears. No earrings. She put her hand to her neck. No necklace. Then she looked at her wrists. The electrical wire said it all. "Poor Gladys," Nellie Ruth said with a grin, "she doesn't know a new fashion trend when she sees one."

❖◇❖

Every time Lester heard the grill door open, he snapped his head to see who was coming in, afraid it would be Arthur. For a guy who'd decided to make a plan, after two whole days of trying to come up with one, he'd failed. *I am who I am.* At first he'd fretted that Arthur might be spouting his accusations to others, but although he'd heard a few folks laughing about the patch of rubber out front and Cora had tried to shake the grapevine bushes a few times to glean the status of things with the Landerses' company, Lester hadn't heard a peep about anything unusual, so Arthur must have been keeping his business between the two of them, which would be in keeping with the Arthur he knew—at least the one he knew up until a couple of days ago. He tried to convince himself no news must be good news since surely if all-out war had broken out between Arthur and Jessie, he would have heard about it by now.

BANG!

Lester ducked. When he heard no screams and saw no blood trickling at his feet, he turned around. "OH!" Earl was standing right there not one foot from his face. "Earl! You liked to scare the breath out of me!" Earl reared back. He looked like he might bolt. "I'm sorry, Earl," Lester said, forcing a soft kindness into his voice. He knew Earl wouldn't hurt a flea. "I just . . . I just wasn't expecting you to be standing there. The sound of the door slamming surprised me, buddy. I'm sorry, I didn't mean to yell at you." Earl blinked a few times. The warming sound of Lester's voice was making more sense to him than the words. Earl didn't understand why he should frighten Lester when Monday through Friday he came in at lunchtime to deliver phone-in meals.

"Do you have any deliveries for me yet, Mister Lester?" Earl asked almost in a whisper, not wanting to frighten

Lester again. Lester looked at his little pile of call-in orders, then at the clock. "If you don't mind waiting, Earl, I'll have them ready in a jiffy. How about you sit down at the counter and I'll get you a soda."

"No, thank you. I'll just wait." Earl continued standing in Lester's grill area, a place nobody else was allowed to roam, but like the slamming screen door, some behaviors Earl just wasn't going to change.

Lester went to work on the sandwiches: one ham sandwich with the works for Rick Lawson (Partonville's only attorney at law), and another, lettuce only, for his secretary in his law office; one burger basket for T.J. Winslow at Richardson's Rexall Drugs. "Only got two stops today, Earl, at least so far." For more than twenty years, Lester had "hired" Earl to deliver food. His pay was per delivery, not time, as occasionally Earl had a way of getting sidetracked. Lester paid Earl fifty cents per delivery and the people on the receiving end usually slipped him a quarter or so. Nearly all deliveries were to store owners on the square, although sometimes he'd walk as far as By George's or the doughnut shop a few blocks off the square. "Earl, you need to close the inside door, please. It's chilly out there today." Earl did as he was told, then came right back behind the counter to wait.

"How's your mom's back?" Lester asked, having heard about May Belle's condition from Gladys.

"Fine."

"Oh, is she better then? Up and around and baking again?"

"No."

Lester stopped spreading mayo and looked at Earl. "Is your mom in bed or laying on the couch, Earl?"

"Yes."

"Where is she, Earl? Where is your mom? On the couch or in bed?"

"In bed."

"Has Doc been out to see her?"

"No."

"Has anyone been by to see her?" Lester sounded concerned.

"Yes."

"Who?"

"Dearest Dorothy. She was visiting when I left." Earl called everyone by Mister or Missus plus their first names, aside from his Dearest Dorothy. He'd called her Dearest Dorothy since he could speak.

"Good," Lester said with relief. "That's good that Dorothy's there. And make that three deliveries today, Earl. I'm going to whip up Dorothy and your mom a couple sandwiches. One for you, too."

◇◆◇

"Oh, Dorothy," May Belle said to her dear friend who was seated in a chair next to her bed, "I'm so glad you convinced Earl to get busy with his job. Honestly, if you hadn't stopped by, I didn't know how I was ever going to get that son of mine out the door. He's been so nervous since I've been down. I keep telling him and telling him I'm fine, that I just need to rest a few days, but he paces around here until I feel so bad for him. It's dug up all my worries about what will ever happen to him when I. . . . I mean just when I think he'll be okay on his own, I see how nearly paralyzed he becomes when I'm down. You're just what he needed— what we both needed."

"He loves you, May Belle. You're so rarely ill he just

doesn't know what to think about it when you're not in the kitchen. As for the other, God's got His eye on Earl, so don't you worry about it—although I know that's much easier to say than to do."

"I know God's watching. I know. And I thank God every day for my health and Earl's, too. But you can bet I'm having a few chats with Him about my back! Of all the bad timing!"

"You're undoubtedly right; you probably about wore it out with all those oven calisthenics for the Pumpkin Festival. No *way* should you now start hefting turkeys in and out of your oven and baking batches of bars. Not even if you're feeling better in a week."

"Don't be silly. I'll be fine," May Belle said as she struggled to turn on her side to better face Dorothy, then realized the pain was too bad so she settled back into her original position.

"Oh, I can see that plain as day! You're about ready to launch out of that bed like a spring chicken!" Dorothy teased. Then her expression turned serious. "Have you phoned Doc yet?"

"What do you think?"

"I think I smell Vicks VapoRub and I imagine you've already gone through a truckload of it by now and you're still in bed. How have you even managed to get it rubbed into your back when it's as clear as a bell you can't even turn over?"

"Earl tried to do his best, bless his heart. I'd packed it in my handbag to bring to the Hookers' meeting Wednesday hoping to get you aside in Jessie's bedroom to give me a good dose. But then I realized I just couldn't sit through bunco. You know how many times we have to get up and down."

Dorothy scanned the nightstand for the jar. "Where is it now?"

"I left it in the bathroom on the sink. I tried to reach my hand back there last time I made it to the bathroom."

"I'll be right back." Within a moment Dorothy appeared with the little blue jar. "Now then, how are we going to get you on your side?"

May Belle fidgeted and winced, then finally said, "You push me, okay? That is if you can get me turned over far enough without ending up having to give yourself a nitroglycerin tablet! Aren't we a fine pair? I'll help as much as I can." Although May Belle moaned a few times during the process and ended up doing more work than Dorothy, between the two of them, they got her turned and her nighty pulled up for the application.

Dorothy dipped two fingers into what remained of the contents in the jar. "This all you got?"

"No. I've got another bottle or two in the medicine cabinet."

"Good. I'll probably need it." She began gently rubbing the Vicks into May Belle's back. "Tell me exactly where, okay?"

"There! Right there."

"I hope I'm not hurting you. Is this pressure okay?"

"Just right, dear." Dorothy swiped her fingers around the bottom of the jar a couple of times to collect what remained, then began to focus her rubbing on the zone. "Why does it hurt so good when you push on a sore muscle?" May Belle asked.

"May Belle Justice, if you're not up and around by day after tomorrow, which will be Sunday, I am going to send

Doc straight to your house after church, and I don't care what you say!"

"I bet this'll do the trick."

"I'm not convinced."

May Belle hated talking to the wall, but it's what she was facing. "How about you call in the Big Guns with one of your bazooka prayers, okay?" Dorothy didn't need to see May Belle's mouth or eyes to understand her request. She laid both her hands flat on May Belle's back and began.

"JUST DO SOMETHING, GOD! Right *here's* where she needs it," she said, spreading her fingers and gently pressing them into May Belle's back. "Amen."

Just then there was a knock at the door.

"Do you think God has shown up just like that?" May Belle asked.

Dorothy could hear by the tone in her voice that May Belle was smiling and that was a good sign. She peaked through May Belle's curtains. "Oh, no. I see Gladys's car out there. You stay put. I'll send her away."

"What day is this? Friday? Oh," May Belle said with a fretful tone in her voice, "she's here to see how many reservations I have! I've let the phone ring a half dozen times in the last two days."

"Don't worry. Folks wanting to come will have called the next person on the list. Some of them probably already called me; I've received several reservations the last two days. How many did you have before you got down with your back? I'll give her your report."

May Belle's fingers began to move as she spoke the names and counted them out. "Not counting Earl and me, let's see, that's six adults and four children."

"Got it." Dorothy pulled down May Belle's gown and rearranged her covers in case Gladys stormed the place. She scooted through the house, opened May Belle's front door and, after a quick greeting, said, "May Belle's back is still bothering her. But she's treating it and she's asked me to tell you she has taken reservations for a total of ten people, not including her and Earl. Six adults, four children. I'll only be here a little while more, then I'll go home and tally up my reservations. I hate to rush you, Gladys, but I'm sure you're working hard to round up all the numbers to give to Theresa and I don't want to hold up that important process. Good-bye." She closed the door. Gladys whirled on her heels.

"There must be something in the air today," Dorothy overheard Gladys saying as she tromped down the sidewalk, visions of slamming doors and Nellie Ruth and Edward Showalter glued together at the hip playing in her head.

23

Considering the accusation that had been made, it had been a quiet two days at the Landerses' house. In the wake of the wild scene at Harry's and with company around, Arthur and Jessie both felt the uncommon pull of restraint as well as an ongoing loss for where to even begin addressing the issue at hand. Every once in awhile they'd accidentally make solid eye contact, intentionally holding it until one or the other looked away, realizing that no amount of staring, not even straight into a person's eyes (not even when giving them the evil eye), could reveal a window into his or her thoughts.

"Maybe familiarity is everything" kept running through Jessie's mind like an unbidden mantra. More than once she'd studied her own photo on their bedroom wall and recalled how happy she'd been playing ball. How happy she'd been to look into the bleachers and see her handsome new husband standing in the midst of an otherwise sitting crowd as she'd walk into the batter's box, hear his voice cheering her on, "Give 'er a good rip, Mugsy!" Arthur had never once made her feel like she should quit, a request Lester had—with and without words—pinned in the air. She couldn't imagine not having had the opportunity to freely travel and use her talents to the best of her ability for as long as she'd been able. She couldn't imagine not having had Arthur by her side, cheering her on, sharing her victories or whipping out his Hohner and giving her a few bars of "You Are My Sunshine" before the games and after the defeats. "My Action Jackson Jessie," he would say when he gave her a bear hug. "Ya gave 'em all ya had but they jist had more today!"

Arthur continued to waffle between wanting to kick himself in the behind for jumping to conclusions and feeling like throwing something at somebody. *(Maybe Jessie's been on ta somethin' all these years!)* But mostly he was stuck tripping over memories: planting the annual gardens, Jessie dragging the hoe and he dropping in the seeds, she too impatient to disperse them; hearing the roar of the throngs of She-Bats fans as they leapt to their feet to cheer Mugsy McGee Landers; how they'd stuffed down the sorrow at the continuing monthly discovery that once again there would be no child—and the day they'd silently stopped waiting.

But then, then there was this past summer when she'd pitched her way to the senior citizens' league championship for the Wild Musketeers. More than once in the last couple of days he'd thought about the kiss he'd spontaneously planted on his wife's lips after that game (right there in front of everybody), such was his joy in her victory, such was the exuberance of the resurrection of long-buried emotions. (He wondered if Lester had paid special attention to *that,* the googly-eyed weasel!) He smiled in spite of himself thinking that even during all the times Jessie had winged *whatever* at the outhouse while he was "hiding" in there, pelting it until he thought his eardrums would break, his marriage felt alive.

Now he could picture it: the state of his marriage was alive.

About the only thing he couldn't seem to picture was Jessie having spent twenty-four hours a day, seven days a week with Lester, whose life ran by the clock and the day's special. She was *still* too much of a wild spitfire for that kind of a routine. Herm was right: he'd imagined everything!

Herm and Vera had spent their sparse private moments since the incident sharing the gritty details of their observations. Herm talked about Arthur's erratic behavior after his explosion at Harry's, including tearing around town, staring at the photographs above the shuffleboard and then his bizarre yelling at the creek to shut up. "Oh, Hermie!" Vera had exclaimed with a hushed voice before unfolding the details about Jessie's patch of rubber and how she hadn't said a word, really, about the actual *incident* at the grill. They both vowed they didn't want to do anything to cause more strife, which ultimately led them to make a pact that they would not butt in, no matter how tempting. "Mum's the word" concerning the incident. But most importantly, Vera admitted she'd grown "a strong intuitive feeling" that *nothing* was, nor had ever been, going on between Jessie and Lester and she was sorry she'd ever mentioned it. "Hermie, sometimes I think I just talk out of my head. I don't know why you listen to me," she'd said, a tone of remorse lacing her whispers. He'd pulled her close and given her a squeeze. "Well, sugarplum, we all have our moments."

In light of all the tensions and private thoughts—especially after Herm asked everyone if they'd like to play a game of euchre and he thought all three of them were going to pummel him—the men and women had spent most of the past forty-eight hours paired up avoiding one another. The women had twice driven to Hethrow to browse, Jessie hating every minute of Vera's aimless shopping but finding it more tolerable than dealing with Arthur. They'd even stopped by The Piece for lunch, their curiosity having been piqued at the Hookers' meeting. Vera asked Jessie if she saw anything on the menu that looked to be a New York City dish. Jessie shrugged her shoulders, but when Johnny came to the table, she challenged him—and there was no other word for it—to point it out. He said he was glad word was spreading and that the New York City special would soon be unveiled. He encouraged them to come again next week since it was sure to be in place by Tuesday. As soon as they left, he wrote a giant note to himself and posted it in the kitchen: "CREATE NEW YORK CITY DISH! NOW!!!" For lack of anything else to do to keep them busy, the women had also done a little grocery shopping for their Thanksgiving meal, including picking up two cans of French-cut green beans, Durkee onions and a bag of bread cubes for the stuffing.

While Jessie and Vera were busy hopping from one place to another, Arthur and Herm took long wandering drives in a twenty-mile radius to check out the county's "progress" (or lack, thereof, they decided), stopping for an occasional beer break and a few games of shuffleboard at The Tap wherein Arthur's eyes never once looked up at the wall of photos. They'd also spent a couple of leisurely hours prowling around Swappin' Sam's. Sam had nearly talked their ears off about a rolltop desk he'd "procured just yesterday." He claimed it was from a mansion on the East Coast but didn't explain how he'd found it or how it had arrived since he hadn't left Partonville. When the cousins pulled away from the store, Arthur said he never did trust a man who would use a snakey word like "procured." Herm agreed.

"There are regular-type words that are just trustworthier, like hows about 'I bought it' for instance." The two men nodded their heads for the next eighth-mile. "But I still find Sam and his stories entertaining," Herm said, which was followed by another eighth-mile of head nodding. The teen from Hethrow driving behind them mused over how the two old codgers reminded him of the head-bobbing hula girl he'd once seen when browsing with his mom at Swappin' Sam's.

Friday evening all four of the Landers clan went to the show in Hethrow, none of them having been for . . . well . . . they couldn't even remember when. Arthur never wanted to pay for a theater ticket when television was cheaper and his La-Z-Boy was more comfortable, and Jessie admitted to having trouble sitting still in movies. But Herm and Vera had not only talked them into it ("I heard tell there's a vintage Buick in the chase scene, Art"), they'd continued talking nonstop all the way to the theater and back, so uncomfortable were they to find themselves all locked up in the car together—a little fact Herm and Vera hadn't thought through before recommending the outing. Arthur and Jessie both wanted to slam their hands over their ears during the drive. They were neither one used to nonstop chatter. That night in bed Herm told Vera he swore he could "see electrical arcs of air cracklin' between them two." He said he had never in his life been so glad to get out of the car and into the theater. The whole time they were in there, though, he said he'd spent more time dreading the ride back than paying attention to the movie. He had to ask Vera how the guy in the Buick had actually managed to escape in the midst of all that shooting, then he bemoaned what a waste of a good car it had been when he learned the car had burned in that fiery scene near the end. Vera confessed to Herm that she, too, had been tense throughout the picture show, dreading the ride home. And yet, she said with a hopeful tone in her voice, her intuition told her the waters were calming. "Time and prayer—and I've sure been praying!—work more miracles than we might imagine, Hermie," she said, patting his stomach as she snuggled up to him. "It's probably a good thing we're here just to help them keep a lid on their emotions until they're both thinking more clearly." She kept her mum's-the-word promise by not adding, "especially since you ignited this mess to begin with."

Katie leaned her head back on her terry-covered bath pillow and pondered the iridescent light in the blanket of bubbles that skimmed the bottom of her chin and covered her body, aside from her bent knees which protruded like mountain peaks rising out of a sea of clouds. One thing she did adore about the mouse house was this deep old claw-foot tub. Her mind wandered from Josh's upcoming first long-distance solo car trip to her first Thanksgiving at her ex in-laws' house. She'd hated creamed peas ever since. Her thoughts finally settled on the wave of lonesomeness that continued to engulf her when she pictured herself this holiday. Although she was glad to have the distraction of serving the Thanksgiving dinner at church, she had concerns about her first honest-to-gosh volunteer job—and what gene was she missing that *that* was the case! She was especially happy to know she would at least spend a good portion of the day around Dorothy. And her family. Her grandsons. Her sons, Vinnie and Jacob. Jacob, whom she pictured carving the bird. As if to erase that thought she blew at the bubbles, a few breaking free and slowly drifting toward her feet. Before the bubbles even burst she'd shifted her thoughts to how good the familiar thrill of a new commercial real estate and business endeavor felt. But such a *mix* of emotions. . . . As prepared as she'd been going into her meeting with Colton, what she'd done afterwards—equally prudent, hope-filled and risky—had blindsided her like a cold water balloon to the back of the head. *What's up with me?*

Colton moved toward her, his hand extended, perfect pearly whites gleaming through his tan, deep green eyes flashing streams of sparkles right at her. As wily as that man could be, there was no doubt about the fact he was drop-dead gorgeous. Gorgeousness aside, however, they were meeting today as adversaries. She quickly zipped up any feminine responses and put on her game face, even when he complimented her on her suit, for which she cordially thanked him as though she'd barely noticed what she'd thrown on this morning. After briefly glancing at their menus, they each ordered a specialty salad. While they waited for their food, they engaged in casual touch-bases about how long it had been since they'd last connected, who had moved where, built where, retired, moved up and on, gone bust after a bad gamble.

By the time their food arrived, Katie had made it clear she'd conducted a recent study of the whole of Hethrow and its surrounding areas. She shared a few earnest accolades about his and his brother's shrewd planning. "We enjoy what we do," he said with ease. "Of course, we had a few more plans, but then. . . ." He winked. He had of course been referring to Crooked Creek Farm. She raised her eyebrows and smiled.

"I can't help but wonder if you're enjoying whatever it is you're doing out on that farm, Kathryn. You never seemed the farm type to me." Katie noticed a slight change in the tone of his voice. Although he was, of course, digging, he was also teasing her. He asked if she was becoming a modern-day version of Eva Gabor in the old television show *Green Acres*. She bit back her recent mouse-and-boredom saga and shrugged, as though she had no need to explain her life to him—which she did not. The conversation then quickly moved from one thing to the next as they ate their salads and circled each other, testing the waters of their intent, knowing the reason for the meeting was at hand as soon as their plates were cleared and coffee was served.

"So, what's on your docket, Mr. Craig? I imagine you and your brother have your eye on your next expansion project. In fact, I have no doubt that's why you phoned me."

"My dear Ms. Durbin, can't a man phone a woman just because he's a man and she's a woman?" His eyes leisurely dropped to her necklace, moved to her lips, then back to her eyes.

"Of course he can," Katie said, casting her eyes to the napkin she rearranged on her lap, keeping them there until she could earnestly look up with a make-no-mistake-I-am-here-to-do-business look and tone in her voice. "But in this case, this woman holds title to the topic of the day so let's get down to it." He crossed his arms over his chest and smiled at her with admiration. She was a worthy opponent, always had been. He knew there would be no casting Kathryn Durbin under his spell—which, of course, made her all the more attractive to him as a woman. But he loved the game as much as she did, and for now, the game was on. He'd concluded by the fact she'd returned his call that she was in the market to deal and now here they were. Why else would she have purchased that place to begin with if not to make a profit—from him?

"How much?" he asked flatly, sitting as still as a post.

She pulled a bulging file folder out of her briefcase. "I'm not sure it's for sale—at least not quite yet. For right now, it is simply my property."

"*My* property," he said. "Sounds like you've not only moved in but staked claim."

"Not so much staked permanent claim, perhaps, as become a launching pad for possibilities." She opened the file but kept the top sheet of blank paper in place. "What do you know about the National Register of Historic Places's relatively recent announcement that the . . ." She shifted her paper to the side and ran her finger down a few lines until she found the sentence "that 'the General Services Administration's Center for Historic Buildings, Office of the Chief Architect is partnering with the National Park Service to digitize records of listed GSA properties to make them. . . .'"

"Whoa! What's the National Register of Historic Places got to do with Crooked Creek Farm? Crooked Creek Farm has certainly not been . . ."

"Well, I'm sure you're familiar with the Preservation Easement Program and how charitable remainder trusts can . . ."

"Kathryn Durbin, stop." He held up his palm like a stop sign as he shook his head. What on earth kind of a wild goose chase was she off on here? She was smarter than this. That acreage was a gold mine for development, not preservation and. . . . He studied her face. "Historic places? Preservation Easement Program? Surely you're not thinking about trying to *block* development?"

"Possibilities lend value," she said with obvious pleasure. And yes indeedy, she had been exploring all of these possibilities because one day, all the land *around* Crooked Creek would be up for sale—including the Landerses'. The more pearls like parks, historic sites, possibly greenways that could separate Hethrow from Partonville—and Crooked Creek Farm was certainly that gateway, as he very well knew—the more valuable everything around it would continue to become.

In the wake of her silence, Colton's eyes cast up and off to the left. Katie knew he was trying to get in her brain, envision her strategy. Then something struck him like thunder! She knew he was probably already running surrounding per-acre figures in his head and subdividing them. He looked at her, smiled, then with intent and control—and in order to try to smoke her out—allowed his face to relax into something between neutral and disgust.

"From what I hear and observe," he said flatly, "the whole of Partonville and most people in it could be declared historic. But as you well know, old does not always lend value, Kathryn. In Partonville's case, I'd say old simply means 'useless as is.' There is nothing either historically valuable or quaint about that town that might otherwise attract investors or residents. No drawing card, schools. . . . The biggest drawing card Partonville has right now is its potential to be an upscale suburb of Hethrow, offer larger estates, a gated community." Although that's what he said, what he didn't say was, "unless one day *another* town begins to boom to Partonville's west," which is exactly what Kathryn Durbin had figured out and he knew it! She was a worthy opponent, to be sure. More worthy than he had bargained for.

Katie blinked. Even in the midst of her major moment (during which time she should have been inwardly gloating to have caught him so off guard), she was astounded to find herself feeling personally offended by his "useless as is" remark about Partonville. But she refused to allow any portion of her face to twitch.

"Useless as is?" she asked, her tone revealing nothing. "Certainly you don't mean that the way it could be construed."

"Oh, come on, Kathryn. You're too savvy to not see the writing on the wall. (He would give her nothing if not a challenge.) Partonville is all but over. Ready or not, progress is poised to march right over it. Flatten it. Create something new out of the ashes."

"So you see no value in the town . . . or its people?" she asked.

"Hold on now. I don't recall saying the people of Partonville have no value. You've got to admit, however, that most of them are choosing to live in a time warp. The days of Andy of Mayberry went out with black-and-white TV—although you do have Acting Mayor Gladys of Pardon-Me-Ville, as I've heard her and her town referred to." He laughed. "Having met her a time or two and cruised through Partonville recently. . . ." He laughed again, but he took note of the fact that Katie was not joining him in his laughter. He felt her drawing a line in the sand—in the topography.

Yes, Gladys irritated Katie and the square was dying. But Katie had also come to realize that as annoying as that woman was, she'd cared enough for her town to fight for it with her Centennial Plus 30. She'd rallied the troops, fired up their pride and, like Arthur had said, in the end "done them all proud." She thought about Dorothy's love for the land, May Belle's goodness, Delbert's concern for the people in his church—and their budding relationship.

"The square," Colton said, busting into her stream of thought, "has become nothing short of a stop-gap to progress. I still remember the recent fiasco when your mayor decided to change the direction of traffic on that square in the middle of the night. What'd she call it? 'Moving forward in time'? The *Daily Courier* had a field day with the gridlock."

Katie fought the urge to cringe. That had indeed been a fiasco reported in all the surrounding papers, including the *Daily Courier,* Hethrow's largest circulated newspaper. And yet . . .

"It's time," Colton continued with a tone of finality, drawing his own line in the topography, "that the square get replaced with a four-lane. Although I admire the large net you believe you're casting, I repeat, there's nothing in that town or on that main drag that is either historically valuable or that can survive more than a year or two and you very well know it. Come on, Kathryn. Partonville is obsolete. What have you *really* got in that town but a gas station that isn't modernized, a grocery store that can't compete with a Super Wal-Mart, a laughable little motel that probably sits empty most of the time now that Hethrow has captured interstate travel. . . ."

Katie didn't hear what he said after that. Her blood was beginning to boil. To call all the hard work Jessica and Paul had put into their motel laughable crossed a line. She opened her mouth to defend her friend, then realized that to do so would mean she would lose control of the game. He or she who responded out of emotions lost. That's the way it went.

It struck her that quite unaware she'd become attached to this place and its people, and that a town could not be separated from the people since a town, a community, *was* the people—and like it or not, ready or not—OHMYGOSH!—she had become one of them.

"Interesting thoughts," she said quietly, maintaining outward control, "but nonetheless thoughts that are sadly lacking vision."

"Really," he said, obviously taken back a little. "I've been accused of many things in my life, but I don't believe I've ever been accused of lacking vision, Kathryn."

She'd once heard Dorothy explain how she had to occasionally talk to her smile. As much as Katie did not want to smile right now, she knew it was essential. *Come on, smile.* As if on command, every possibility she'd been exploring solidified into a personal commitment, and with it a genuine smile sprouted from ear to ear. "Oh, but Mr. Craig," she said, her voice as silky smooth as his could be when winding around a target, "I accuse you of nothing. I'm just stating my opinion."

"Sounds like an opinion with monetary value," he said, egging her on to say more.

"Exactly. Monetary value."

"And that would be?"

"A monetary opinion with value," she said. She flipped her folder closed and stuck it back in her briefcase. She took a look at her wristwatch. "Would you look at how time flies when you're in good company," she said. She delighted in watching Colton make the slightest of gestures to straighten his posture. Abruptly she stood and extended her hand. "This has been delightful and I do hope you'll call me again, *man* to *woman*. (What goes around comes around, she thought.) I've already made arrangements to pick up the lunch bill. Next time you can buy." She didn't give him time to say another word. She was gone before he knew what had hit him.

She drove straight to the independent Realtor on the cusp of Hethrow and Partonville. She needed to do some wheeling and dealing and fast. Close the deal on something she'd been speculating about, never mind she hadn't found the right time to talk to the rest of those on whom in large part she would have to rely. She couldn't think when she'd ever been more excited, determined—or scared. If, in the end, this tip-of-her-iceberg plan didn't work, Kathryn Durbin, Development Diva, would never be able to face Colton Craig again. She was either firmly belted into the driver's seat or precariously perched at the precipice of a slippery slide.

Katie had to figure out another way to bring all the key players together to get their support and back up her leap of faith; the tub was as good a place as any to strategize. She pulled the plug on her tepid bath water and let a couple of inches drain out before replacing it with straight hot water. As the steaming water streamed into the tub, she sat up and swished her hands around her like fish fins to blend it in. With Thanksgiving coming, not to mention Christmas, her time was running short. Just when she turned off the faucet, it hit her: perhaps the small-town grapevine could be her friend. Maybe she should just talk to Jessica and Dorothy, then maybe—if she dared—make an appointment with Maggie at La Feminique Salon & Day Spa and let a few things "slip." (A slippery slide could just as easily be a shortcut to success! she told herself. Isn't that how it went in that old board game Chutes and Ladders?)

As she slid back into the depths of the renewed bubbles, the double-edged sword of her business venture, spurred on by Colton Craig's pompous attitude, seized her again. But in her heart of hearts she knew that her financial risk and professional image weren't nearly as weighty as proving something far bigger to herself: who she *really* was and what she found worth fighting for.

24

By Friday night at nine Gladys had her reservation totals. After passing them along to Theresa, she also had a headache. By the time they'd added in the volunteers and allowed for a few late reservations (which she was already hearing murmurs about) and last-second walk-ins (although she would have *never* encouraged those, but too late now), their numbers would undoubtedly be in the forties, and Lord help them all if they verged toward fifty! But what concerned Gladys most was that May Belle was still down with her back; Jessica was still ill and had, under Dorothy's command, deferred doing *anything* causing Gladys to speculate Jessica had some dreaded disease—although after hearing how the numbers had swelled, Jessica had, at the last minute, volunteered (out of sense of guilt, no doubt, Gladys thought) to "cook and drop off one turkey" which now only caused Gladys to fret she would be *spreading* her dreaded disease; and Nellie Ruth, well, Gladys hoped she could get her mind off that odd Edward Showalter long enough to focus. United Methodist Church seemed poised to be humiliated on their very own turf. Any committee chair worth her salt, Gladys thought, would have been dogging these folks; Theresa did *not* take firm enough control of things.

"The worst thing that will happen," Dorothy calmly said to Gladys, "is that we'll all be gathered together to give thanks." Dorothy had found Theresa's leadership by faith so refreshing and inspiring that she was determined to back her up. "Remember the loaves and the fishes story from the Bible, Gladys. I'm sure God will provide. We'll all just do our part and it'll work out fine. Have a little faith." Then Dorothy'd hung up and fired fervent bazooka prayers that got all the more fervent when she stopped by May Belle's Saturday morning and May Belle said she thought her back felt worse instead of better. "Oh, Dorothy, what am I going to *do* about that Thanksgiving dinner?"

"Don't worry, May Belle, it's all under control." *Lord, HEAR MY PRAYER!* Dorothy sat next to May Belle's bed; Earl stood right behind her wringing his hands. "May Belle, how about we just figure out how much of what we need on UMC's end and I'll pass the information along to Theresa so she can add it to Nellie Ruth's shopping list. Monday will be here before we know it and that's the day she and Edward Showalter are supposed to be delivering the food. Let's just concentrate on one thing at a time and not get ahead of ourselves with worry. You know, Mary Crowley said it best when she said, 'Worry is a misuse of the imagination.' So, let's imagine a wonderful dinner with just the right amount of food."

Dorothy said over her shoulder, "Earl, honey, would you please get me the tablet of scratch paper your mother keeps near the phone. Oh, and a pen. And a *pencil*," she said more loudly as she heard Earl's footsteps already padding down the hall. "THANK YOU, DEAR!" Earl went fast to work on the request and returned in a jiffy. "Okay, let's see now. Let's start with the turkeys." Just then May Belle's phone rang. "Can you answer that, Earl?" Dorothy asked over her shoulder since Earl had once again positioned himself near her back.

Earl only answered the phone when someone asked him to. He did not like talking on the phone and in fact usually didn't. The phone made him nervous since he couldn't see who was talking. He'd pick up the receiver when instructed, listen and be silent. Most folks in town understood the situation and would patiently wait for May Belle to come to the phone, knowing she'd likely been getting something out of her oven or putting something in when the phone rang. At Dorothy's instruction, this time Earl disappeared and picked up the receiver within one ring. "TELL THEM TO HANG ON," Dorothy hollered. She didn't hear any talking. Pretty soon Earl was back.

"Do you know who it is, Earl?" May Belle asked.

"I think it's Miss Nellie Ruth," he said.

"Tell her I'll . . . Never mind," Dorothy said as she set her supplies on May Belle's nightstand and headed down the hall. May Belle heard quiet mutterings from the other room and after awhile Dorothy was back. "Earl was right. It was Nellie Ruth. She wanted to know if she was supposed to buy the ingredients for the things Lester is cooking or if he was taking care of that himself. She said since Your Store isn't open on Sundays it was mobbed today and she was worried they might run the shelves bare, making pickin's too slim by Monday. She was going to start setting a few things aside. I suggested she phone Lester herself right now since it's between the breakfast and lunch crowds. She hadn't thought about phoning him, she said. I instructed her to phone us back after she spoke with him and let us know. If we don't hear back from her within an hour, I'll give him a call myself. As much as I hate to admit this, Gladys is right: Nellie Ruth is a little scatterbrained lately. But it's just so wonderful to see that child all aglow that I can't help but be happy for her. I mean, who would have ever thought?"

Ninety minutes later Dorothy phoned Harry's. "Lester, it's Dorothy. First of all, thank you for the lovely lunch you sent us yesterday. We gobbled it right up."

"Yup."

"Did Nellie Ruth call you?"

"Yup."

"I realize you're probably busy with lunch customers now but could you just tell me who's buying your ingredients? You or the joint committees? Of course, we'll reimburse you if you buy."

"Me. I'm donating all ingredients for the dressing and a big mess of green beans. I told Nellie Ruth that. What's wrong with her anyway? She seemed . . . flustered or something." Dorothy heard his hand go over the receiver as he assured someone their order would be right up.

"I do believe Nellie Ruth has been bitten by the lovebug, Lester."

"Well, believe you me when I tell you it is now official, Dorothy: love makes folks plumb nuts. I gotta go." Clunk.

Since Katie had arrived at the Lamp Post, she and Jessica had been talking a mile a minute. Paul, Sarah Sue in tow, smiled when he passed through the kitchen, happy to see his wife lively and distracted, at least for the moment. Four more days and they'd know for sure, he thought. He nodded a howdy do to Katie, then disappeared.

"He's such a nice guy," Katie said after Paul was out of earshot. "It's good to see a father so involved with a child," she said wistfully. "I'm hoping Josh's Thanksgiving vacation goes well with his dad. Sometimes he comes home kind of sullen."

"Good thing Paul *is* good with kids," Jessica said splaying her fingers over her belly. "But you said you had something to tell me when you called. What's up? I'm so sick of me that it will be good to hear about somebody else's life for a change."

"You're not going to believe where I'm heading after I leave here; well, that is after I stop by May Belle's since Dorothy said that's where she'd be this morning. But first I have something big to announce and you are the first to know. And," she said, after chuckling, "it officially *officially* involves you, too! Fasten your seat belt, though; this is news that will shock you."

"Don't tell me *you're* pregnant!" Jessica laughed.

"Impossible. I haven't even had a proper *kiss* for decades."

"Katie!" Jessica said, her face turning red. "So what is your news?"

I've taken on the Craig brothers, she thought. "Jessica, I'm bored and I need a project. Commercial real estate has always been my passion and my area of expertise so why not use them both to help revitalize Partonville. I'm going to start by opening a business—a collection of businesses, really, and what better time to launch a project like this than right after the Centennial Plus Thirty when you've all been reminded we have something here to be proud of."

"What?!"

"You heard me. I'm opening a collection of shops all under the same roof. One of them, the cornerstone of the businesses, will be a boutique of sorts, a gift shop, if you will. And guess who's going to provide some of the product and help me decorate?"

"The Merchandise Mart in Chicago?" Jessica's heart skipped a beat just imagining the colors, the fabrics, the designs of . . . whatever. She'd dreamed about visiting the Merchandise Mart since she'd first heard tell of it.

"Wrong. *You* are! You and your wonderful bookmarks and baskets and gifted squinting eyes . . . and every other crafter and artist in the area who'd like to put their things on consignment and earn some income. I was even thinking about asking May Belle if she'd like to sell some of her baked goods. You know how she always wraps them up for bunco prizes with cellophane and those curly ribbons? You know how they sell those oblong caramels wrapped up in waxed paper near so many cash registers around the country?" Jessica shook her head no; she had no "around the country" base of experience. Nonetheless, it didn't thwart Katie's enthusiasm. "On my way over here I thought, why not put some of May Belle's wrapped goodies near the checkouts!" Jessica's eyes were growing ever bigger. "Of course, along with everyone's handmade things I'll also do wholesale buying, or hire a buyer, which might be a better choice since merchandising is not my area of expertise." Katie was more animated than Jessica had ever seen her, waving her arms around, pacing. . . . "I could even ask Maggie Malone to lend us some of her, um, exotic flair since my taste is definitely conservative and we'll want to have something for everyone. And she's certainly a one-woman advertising agency. And speaking of Maggie, heaven help me, Jessica, I'm going to La Feminique right after I talk to Dorothy and May Belle and I'm getting a 'wash and set', as Maggie called it. Please do not *ever* tell Jeffrey at Gregory's in Chicago or I'll be barred. But I figure Maggie's place is as good a place as any to start the buzz. It's never too early for good buzz."

"Oh, Katie. Honestly, I don't mean to rain on your parade, but do you *really* think something like this can work here in Partonville?" She blushed, realizing she was being a little presumptuous since after all, Katie was a rich businesswoman and she was, well, not. "I'm sorry. I'm sure you know what you're doing, Katie. I'm sorry."

"Stop that, Jessica! It *is* a fair question. And don't think I haven't asked myself that several times. But remember how everyone was talking at the Hookers' meeting some time back about how they wished Partonville had a good browsing store? Dorothy brought it up, I think."

Jessica just stared at Katie. She'd been talking too fast. And had she understood Katie correctly, that *she* would be expected to supply things to sell in her store, and to help decorate it, too? She could barely stay awake right now, let alone keep her head out of the toilet. And she had a baby, and another one on the way and. . . .

"You feeling ill again?" Katie asked, noticing the change on Jessica's face.

Dreaming was wonderful, but reality had to be faced here. "To be honest, Katie, I'm overwhelmed. I've got my hands full right now. I don't know when I'm even going to find time to brush my teeth once this second one arrives." Katie slumped in her chair. Jessica wanted to be encouraging, but Katie had been talking so fast . . . it was all too much to take in. "Where are you planning on putting your store?" she asked in an effort to at least engage with the idea. "Are you going to build somewhere?"

"Okay, this is not the exciting response I'd been hoping for." *Banking on, literally.* Katie felt like the cold water balloon to the back of the head had once again arrived. "I purchased the old Taninger building. You know, the building straight across the square from Harry's? The one that used to have a furniture store in it?" Jessica nodded her head. "From what I understand, it's been empty for nearly six years now, having been the first store—not to mention the largest store—on the square to go out of business after Hethrow built up."

Jessica studied her friend's face, then allowed her mind to envision a gift shop on the square. A shop with her crafts in it appropriately tagged JESSICA'S JOYS. She'd meant to make decorative stickers like that for her bookmarks sold at the Pumpkin Festival craft fair, but never got around to it. She'd gotten so excited the day she'd come up with that wonderful play on her name, Jessica Joy, and the thrill of it rippled through her again, along with a slight wave of nausea that once again snapped her back into reality. "Oh, Katie, your idea does sound wonderful, and I can almost picture it," she said, her eyes in a slight squint. "And I wish you well. But honestly, I don't know when I'll have an ounce of time to do crafts again. Ever." She looked like she might cry.

"Jessica, you're *way* too talented to ever let that creative part of yourself shut down just because you're a mother! When are you due?"

"I don't have my appointment until Tuesday, so nothing official yet. But from the best I can figure, this baby will arrive in late July or early August."

"Well, that gives you several *months* to whip up a few things to begin with! And don't put so much pressure on yourself, Jessica. It's not like you need to fill the whole store; just one little display, just for your product. You'll be one of *many* talented people to step forward once word gets around." *Please, God.*

"For your sake, Katie, I sure hope so." Wanita jumped into her mind. Oh, wouldn't she be excited to know she had a year-around place to earn a few extra dollars with her crafts!

Katie leaned toward Jessica. "To tell you the truth, the size of that building is the one thing that almost held me back from making the purchase. That's way more space than we need *and* it needs tons of work. But," she said, rallying her energy, "it's structurally sound–I had it checked out every which way–and it's *on the square,* which is important to me. And the price was certainly right since it'd been on the market for so long that the Taningers had already moved to Idaho. They were more than ready to unload it. I figure I can subdivide the downstairs, open our shop and rent the other portions–including the upstairs–to unique types of businesses. I've been thinking about several alternatives. Things like maybe a bath shop or," she eyed Jessica's abdomen, "a children's store. Kite shop. Types of trendy little stores that would be good complements to a gift shop. You know, create like a boutiquey mini mall of sorts in one building. After listening to the Hookers the other night talking about the need for antique repairs and thinking about my mother's old dented pan and hearing Dorothy talk about how that awful eyesore of a Swappin' Sam's is actually a *drawing* card, I even picture an antique store in the building as a possibility, or maybe a clock repair place or something like that. I know," she said, feeling incredibly alive for the first time in several months, "maybe even a tea room since Nellie Ruth and Maggie are always talking about teas!

"Partonville is ripe for possibilities. It just wouldn't take that much to bring a solid quaint factor (as much as she hated to admit it, Colton had been right about the square's lack of quaintness) to our (oh, GADS! she'd said *our*) town. Give out-of-towners, including Hethrow people, a reason to want to come to Partonville just to spend a few hours browsing, have a bite of lunch. Hey, maybe we could even put in a little bagel place that serves veggie dishes. If something like this could grow on itself, it might even help draw other new businesses to the square, not to mention to the Lamp Post! And speaking of the Lamp Post, the mini mall—and we'll have to think of just the right name for it—will run full-page ads in *BackRoads Illinois* right next to your ads for the Lamp Post." Jessica's eyes widened. "I've done research on that paper and you and Paul were definitely smart to get in on the ground floor."

"Oh, Katie! Thank *goodness*! Even though Paul tried to get me to let it go, we've fretted about that ever since you mentioned it!"

Although Katie wouldn't tell Jessica this, at least right now, she'd been so impressed with the guy's business plan that she'd decided to invest in his venture. If *BackRoads Illinois* made a go of it—which she was pretty sure it would—she perceived it could one day expand into a *BackRoads* for every state. On top of that, it would be a natural place to advertise anything, including acreage, should she be in the market to buy—or sell.

"What on earth brought all this on, Katie? I've never heard you talk about *anything* like this before."

Katie looked at her watch. "Honest, I don't mean to be evasive, but right now I've got to swing by and tell Dorothy and May Belle about it, then get to Maggie's by . . ." She glanced at her watch a second time. "I've got to go right now! I hope I don't chicken out before I get to Maggie's. Nobody but *nobody* touches my hair but Jeffrey.

To tell you the truth, I think this appointment is scaring me more than any business risk!"

The Craig brothers worked with a fury. They had been conducting conference calls and Internet researches on farm preservation, preservation easement programs, conservation reserve programs (a voluntary program for agricultural landowners in Illinois), anything and everything that might give Kathryn Durbin the ability to set herself up to stop them cold in terms of commercial real estate development to the west of them. They'd long been in the business of buying up farms to transform into urban sprawl, not *preserve* their acreage. What they needed to get a feel for at the moment was how likely or not this preservation type of trend might be—or become.

What they both believed, however, was that Kathryn Durbin was interested in nothing but preserving her own potential. Her actual ability to get Crooked Creek Farm on the National Register of Historic Places (perhaps she was talking all smoke and mirrors) was somewhat difficult to discern, given they weren't completely familiar with Crooked Creek's history; they'd moved into this area from Chicago only a couple of decades ago when their development projects began. Although no plans would be as optimal as buying the contingent Crooked Creek, if push came to shove, they felt assured they could find ways around it—but they wondered if she'd already been consorting with others in the area, planting her wild ideas about preservation. Lots of question marks.

No matter, they decided. They knew of many farmers in the area on the brink of retirement who weren't as much interested in preserving their farms as they were in feeding themselves once they aged out of the ability to continue doing the hard work. Farmers had taken a bite the last many years and there weren't as many family members willing to stick around to take over. And no matter what some folks thought about the march of progress, the Craig brothers had, in fact, been thanked by many of those sturdy folks after a deal was done. What was to preserve? Aging into poverty? They'd received healthy dollars for a move, retirement security and enough to pay for health insurance and supplements—a longtime worry. Development had brought more hospitals into the area, a junior college, more jobs. . . . "It's not like we're the devil," Colton told his brother. "Everyone can be reasoned with when it comes to finances, including Kathryn. That's why she's in this game; we just have to find her price."

After laboring over their investigative results, possibilities and several hours of running the numbers, they came up with an offer for Crooked Creek Farm, one they knew she could not refuse. The offer was, in fact, exorbitantly higher per acre than what Crooked Creek Farm would be worth "as is" on the market today—even higher than it would bring after the park was open. She could make her financial killing now without having to invest—or waste—another cent of her time and resources. Yes, their offering price was outrageously high, but they believed the risk of the investment was worth it. (Risk was the name of commercial real estate development. You didn't get into the business without being willing to risk, and high stakes at that.) They were willing to risk whatever it took to stop Kathryn Durbin. If indeed she had been talking to other farmers, once they saw she'd sold out, that would be the end of this preservation nonsense.

25

Katie's heart was in her mouth. If it was humanly possible, she was, she thought, perhaps even more nervous about letting Maggie Malone work on her hair than she had been about meeting Colton Craig for lunch or ultimately taking him on. Of course, it was ridiculous since hair was only hair (but then it was appearances!) and money was only money, but if she added up all the money she'd spent on hair vanities at Chicago's most posh salon during the last five years, it would be shocking. One thing she knew for sure was that the only thing she would allow Maggie to do was to wash and . . . blow dry. At least she hoped the woman had a blow dryer, since she'd put her down for that "wash and set," which was a throwback to her mother's era. She could always go home and redo whatever Maggie did, and after all, her next all-day Chicago spa appointment was only a couple of weeks away.

As she drove to the salon the one thing she felt confident about was her scheme. Dorothy had literally cheered at her new venture (she'd even teared up at what she called "the goodness in it"), and May Belle was thrilled to think that once she got back up to snuff, she might be able to add some much needed income to her coffers by selling her baked goods in a tea room, which, as the creative energies spun between the three women, had now become an absolute part of the master plan—never mind that Katie knew nothing about running a food-service business. (She had the money to find someone who did.) Although Katie had originally hoped to get the first of the mini-mall shops open by Christmas (and the mini-mall idea had now become *The* Master Plan), she realized after looking at May Belle's pained face, digesting everyone's responsibilities for the upcoming Thanksgiving dinner, recalling how strained Jessica looked, knowing how crazed *everyone* got with the Christmas holidays (not to mention the building needed substantial amounts of work), it had been an unrealistic wish—even as much as she longed to smack Colton Craig right between the eyes with her Christmas-season grand opening. A spring opening, however, made the most common sense, and if she did things up in the grand style she was beginning to envision, even that might be pushing it, but she hoped not. She wanted to be able to give the Craig brothers *something* definite when next they spoke, though. She knew they were probably spinning all the preservation possibilities right this minute, which made her very happy since all they would really be spinning was their wheels. Whether or not she acted on any of the preservation possibilities remained to be seen, but for now, the only thing she knew for sure—at least for the moment—was that she was keeping the farm, setting up a business and buying every piece of real estate that became available within three blocks of the square.

And—yikes!—getting ready to enter Maggie's. She parked the Lexus around on the side street hoping nobody would associate her with La Feminique Hair Salon & Day Spa, locked it up, took a deep breath and entered. To her shock, Gladys McKern was sitting in the color chair, her head a

matt of Brunette Brown dye, aside from the few sprigs
Maggie hadn't yet smeared with her giant color brush she
held in her rubber-gloved hand. It was hard to tell who was
more shocked at the appearance of the other, Gladys or
Katie. Maggie hadn't warned either of them, not wanting to
rob herself of the chance to witness their shock.

"Come on in! We don't bite in here," Maggie said, noting Katie had hesitated in the doorway. Gladys was the last
person Katie would want to witness her being Maggie-ized,
as Dorothy had called it. But Dorothy had also tried to encourage Katie by assuring her she might be surprised to find
out just how talented Maggie really was since she attended
those hair shows up in Chicago every year. *Right.*

"Please close that door. The cold air will set off my
arthritis," Gladys said, pulling the bottom of her drape
down around her knees.

Katie stepped in and apologized for her delay. Her mind
was reeling. Rather than being distressed about Gladys's appearance, she was beginning to realize she couldn't have or-
chestrated a better opportunity!

Her eyes cast around. To her surprise, the shop was quite
trendy. She'd pictured décor about like the Landerses, but
this, well, this was actually quite chic, for Partonville.

"Make yourself at home," Maggie said, waving the goop-
laden brush as though it were a magic wand. "I've got chai
tea bags out today, right back there," she said, pointing to
her tea cart.

"It's too odd for me," Gladys said, "but I guess *some*
women like it."

Maggie frowned at Gladys; she was sure Katie was a
woman of finer taste. "Water's still hot in the pot. You
might enjoy browsing my supply of aromatherapy on the

counter there, too." Maggie's aromatherapy display was one of her favorite things. It thrilled her to think somebody had arrived who might not only appreciate the offering, but be able to afford a bottle or five.

Katie walked over to the small rack of tiny bottles. Black velvet cloth was artistically wrapped around the base and decorative diffusers and a few shiny glass blobs were scattered here and there with perfect aesthetic balance. Maggie definitely had an eye for presentation. Katie tucked the piece of info into her mental mini-mall bank. She picked up a sample bottle and held it to her nose. *Lavender!* It reminded her of her last massage in the city. Michelle had laced the massage lotion with lavender to help soothe her frazzled nerves. *Maybe a massage therapist could rent a space in the mini mall or open up on the square!* Katie set the bottle down and noticed that both Maggie and Gladys had been watching her every move in the mirror. "Sell much of this?" she asked Maggie, picking another bottle up to read the label.

"I wish," Maggie answered. "I can't seem to convince my regulars there even *is* such a thing as aromatherapy, and it is just so . . . so delicious! Oh, well. Their loss, I tell them," and she averted her eyes to Gladys for one quick nanosecond. Gladys mumbled "hogwash" under her breath loud enough that they could both hear it. Katie repositioned the bottle while thinking how well the aromatherapy would probably sell in a boutique location with fresh clientele. She smiled at both of them, allowing her eyes to linger on Gladys. She noticed the very corners of Gladys's lips turned upward, just a tad.

"So," Gladys said, "you're here for . . . ?" assuming it wasn't an appointment since she'd heard tell about Katie's trips to Chicago for day-long salon treatments. *Of all the wasteful things!*

"A wash and style," Maggie answered.

Style, Katie thought. *I've been moved up to a style instead of a set. Thank goodness!*

While Katie made herself a cup of tea *(mmmmm, imagine a whole tea room . . .),* seated herself and began flipping through a magazine, Maggie studied the shape of Katie's head, the width of her jaw, trying to picture the perfect do. She didn't imagine Katie would give her much rein, but then again, maybe that's why she was here, for a *change*! Although Maggie adored all her steady and long-term clients and friends, no one ever wanted to brave one of the new tricks she'd learned at the annual styling shows.

She finished Gladys's final application, then put a plastic bag over her smeared mess of hair. Without instruction, Gladys rose and planted herself under one of the two dryers. Once the dryer was turned on and Maggie had set her timer, she sighed with relief and turned her attention to her next client. (Gladys didn't need to be under the dryer at all for her processing, which took forty-five minutes of waiting; but since she didn't wait well, the "air only" setting for the first twenty minutes or so helped cool her jets, so to speak, and offered Maggie a short respite on Gladys's color days. It was, Maggie thought, one of the best survival tricks she'd ever invented—especially today since there always seemed to be tension between these two women; Maggie wanted to be flowing free in her creative zone when she worked on Ms. Durbin.)

"Alrighty then, Katie, set your purse there by the style chair and take a seat at the shampoo station." With a slight hesitancy, Katie decided to abandon her handbag. Odds were high against anyone rustling this place—another positive thing about a business investment in a town like Partonville, she thought. Gladys raised an eyebrow, she being one to always hold her handbag tight to herself. Katie thought her heart would hammer out of her head, she was so caught up fretting about her hair. She arranged herself in the chair and Maggie put on her drape, adjusting the Velcro around her neck to the perfect tension. "Just lean back and unwind," Maggie said, clearly noting the woman was a nervous wreck, her back like a ramrod, "and leave the driving to me."

Quicker than she thought possible, Katie relaxed into Maggie's able and generous scalp-massaging hands. Before she was ready, it was time to sit up. Maggie wrapped the towel around her head and ushered her to her styling chair. Katie noticed Gladys watching their every move, the angle of the mirrors being just right to see everything anyone was doing in the small shop. Maggie began towel drying Katie's thick red hair, which, Maggie had already noted with her well-trained eyes, was color enhanced to cover the sparse gray—a few of the roots beginning to reveal themselves under her discerning study. (She remembered that Katie had a few roots showing the first time they met at Dorothy's during Katie's Aunt Tess's funeral dinner.) While the towel was draped over Katie's head Maggie said, "So, what's new with you since the Hookers' meeting? You know, I don't think I've ever had a chance to ask you how you're adjusting to life out at Crooked Creek Farm. That must be some transition for you." Katie had her eyes closed, enjoying the feeling of hiding under the towel, wishing she could melt away into the floor.

Suddenly Maggie whipped the towel off her head and spun her chair around. Katie felt exposed in her thoughts.

"New with me?" she blurted, lifting up her face to the mirror. Her eyes flashed from Maggie to Gladys and back again, then she remembered she was on a mission. She smiled at them. *Time to forge ahead.* "Interesting you should ask. Something quite amazing, really, and something that will affect both of you." Katie noticed Gladys had scooted down in her chair enough to lower her head almost out of the dryer, no doubt straining to hear. (Katie decided Dorothy's suggestion had been perfect: "Make your announcement proudly, Katie, and for *goodness'* sakes, get *Gladys* on your side!") "If it doesn't disturb her color, you might want to turn off Gladys's dryer for this, Maggie, so she doesn't miss anything." Maggie's eyes sparkled; Gladys's widened as they both stared at her. Gladys lifted her dryer and feigned innocence. "Were you talking to me?" she asked.

"I was about to make an announcement and I didn't want you to miss it," Katie said with enthusiasm, "since after all, *you* are partly responsible for my decision. I'm so glad to have caught you here since you'll now be among the first to know. I'm opening a new business in town! Mayor McKern, I want to thank you for proposing such a wonderful idea a couple of Happy Hookers' meetings ago." Never mind that Gladys had all but sounded off against it when the ladies had bemoaned their lack of a good browsing shop. One thing was certain, Dorothy had told Katie, Gladys would remember it as her idea if everybody else loved it and gave her credit for it. "My whole undertaking was actually inspired not only by your idea for such a business, but by your dedication to keeping Partonville on the map with our Centennial Plus Thirty." It was clear from the look on Gladys's face that Dorothy's suggestion to butter up Gladys was just the right ticket. Katie unveiled her visions for the mini mall and how important Gladys's input would be since she was, after all, the mayor. Within a few more sentences, both Gladys and Maggie were beside themselves with enthusiasm (each spouting their own ideas for shops ranging from Partonville giftware to lingerie), especially after Katie told Maggie she would rely on doses of her input and sense of flair, and how could anything like this be successful in Partonville without the *mayor's* endorsement! Katie had them wrapped around not only her little finger, but dedicated to her unspoken purpose to prove Colton Craig wrong about their town.

By the time their chatter reached a fevered peak, they had carried on for so long without any beautifying going on that Katie's hair had nearly air-dried. Maggie checked her watch and rinsed the color off Gladys's hair so as not to fry it; it had been one of the fastest forty-five minutes she'd ever experienced. Gladys plopped back down in the color chair since Katie was in the styling chair. Maggie asked Katie if she minded waiting while she finished up with Gladys, who already had visions of a mini-mall ribbon-cutting ceremony dancing in her head. Within fairly short order, Gladys was out the door, all but chirping a good-bye to Katie, encouraging her to keep in close contact with her about the mini mall's progress. When the door closed, both Maggie and Katie let out a sigh.

Maggie spritzed Katie's hair before combing it this way and that, taking note of how Katie's cowlicks (two of them!) handled, how her forehead looked with her hair on and off her face, how much natural wave she had, which was plenty. Katie was so caught up in the fabulous way things were shaping up that she forgot herself during the briefest of moments when, in the middle of a sentence about the new business venture, Maggie asked her if she minded if she gave her a little trim. Before Katie, who was turned away from the mirror, knew what had hit her, Maggie was snapping the scissors next to her right ear.

Following her latest bout of upchucking, Jessica had assumed her familiar position, buttocks on the bathroom floor, back against the wall. JESSICA'S JOYS. She said the words aloud, designing stickers in her mind with happy stars on them while her stomach settled. "Paul! Come here! Quick!"

Paul rounded the corner on the fly, her call having scared him. "WHAT IS IT!?"

"You'll never guess what!" She was breathless. "Katie's going to open a mini mall on the square and one of the stores is going to be a *boutique*! She wants me—*me*, Paul—to help her decorate and to give her my handmade items on consignment! Wouldn't it be just wonderful if I could launch a line of handcrafts called Jessica's Joys? Oh, Paul! Think of the extra income!" And then she stuck her head back in the toilet bowl.

Dorothy stood by the church door waiting for May Belle and Earl to show up, but when the church bells began to ring and she didn't see them coming down the sidewalk, she knew May Belle was still down, at least down enough to be unable to handle a hard church pew. Dorothy prayed while she found a seat. *Lord, please comfort and heal my friend. Calm Earl's heart and help him to find ways to help his mother. Give May Belle the good sense to rest as long as she needs to. And*

help us figure out what to do about our dinner. Fill in the gaps. You already know I've taken two nitroglycerin tablets this week and if I get myself down, we'll really be in trouble. DON'T LET ME BE DUMB! By the time the church bells were done ringing, Dorothy, who gave a happy smile to Paul, Jessica and Sarah Sue in the back row, had seated herself next to Doc. Doc always radiated calm and that's sure what she needed right now. His greeting smile and gentle hand pat were just the ticket.

During announcements, Pastor asked if the Social Concerns Committee would like to give a report about the Thanksgiving dinner. Nobody moved. Dorothy expected Gladys would rise, but she did not. Gladys folded her hands across her chest. If UMC's ship was sinking, she wasn't going to be standing at the helm when it did.

"Anybody?" Pastor asked. After their last bobbing exchange, it was hard to believe neither one of them had anything to say. Reluctantly, Dorothy finally stood, smiled and gave a brief report. "The joint committees of St. Augustine's and we here at UMC would like to thank God and the citizens of Partonville for helping to fill up our Thanksgiving tables; it looks like we might have as many as fifty or more folks gathered together!" A few low whistles and a light band of clapping raced around the room. "You probably all know that reservations are officially closed, but don't forget that if you decide at the last minute this is where you'd like to be, don't hesitate to come. That's what our Lord taught us. Come. Come as you are. And if any of you feel nudged to lend a hand with cooking or serving, please see me after the service today or give Theresa Brewton a call. Her number's in your bulletin again this week. I'm sure we're going to have a blessed time." *Lord, hear my prayer!*

Dorothy slipped out of the service early to put on the coffee for the Meet and Greet, a task May Belle would usually have handled. She also knew she'd have to listen to everyone whine that there were no sweets. If The Tank had been parked outside, she could have just made a run to buy some doughnuts. It was terrible to not have that type of mobility. *Terrible,* she thought. Even though she'd often promised herself she wouldn't complain about giving up driving, she'd still find herself grumbling. Oh well, coffee would just have to do.

What she hadn't banked on, however, was that when the Meet and Greet folks gathered, they were so busy buzzing about the new mini mall that city slicker was bringing to town (proving the grapevine was alive and well), they barely noticed there was neither a cookie nor a piece of coffee cake to be had.

26

By Sunday, the beginnings of conversation had sprouted between the Landers men and women. Perfunctory things, to be sure, but nonetheless words. Herm and Vera, who never missed church at home, prowled through the Yellow Pages. They'd decided since the ice had at least been broken between Arthur and Jessie, they'd go ahead and attend a Baptist church just at the edge of Hethrow. (According to Herm, if it wasn't a good ol' alter-callin' Baptist church, it didn't count, and Vera believed she needed to get herself right up there and repent of her unfounded gossip!) They'd have to trust that God would keep Arthur and Jessie from pummeling each other while they were gone, and in fact determined to pray so during their drive. Of course, they'd each been praying plenty for them already. Arthur and Jessie didn't attend church and they weren't about to start now, no matter how much encouragement Herm and Vera gave. "I mean, come on, Herman the Vermin! What kind of God would let the Buick Wildcat go out of production!" Arthur thought he'd cracked quite the joke, but there were times he really did wonder. Although Herm tried to keep a lightness in his voice when he responded, he actually meant what he said. "Better watch yourself talkin' 'bout God like that, Art. He can smite the likes of us rascals as quick as He can take out the Wildcat!"

When Herm and Vera drove away, hoping to make the ten-thirty service, Jessie stood in the driveway waving good-bye. She was relieved to have her house back to herself for a couple of hours, but on edge about her and Arthur being alone for the first time since the incident at Harry's. She needn't have worried, since before Herm and Vera had seated themselves in the car, Arthur had mumbled something about taking a walk down to the creek. When she went back in the house he was gone. She figured a creek walk was his way of further avoidance.

But this standoff just could not go on much longer; it was not only wearing thin, it was wearing her out. *How would, how could it end?* Jessie wondered. Neither one of them had figured a way to address it yet, the air still thick with the possibility for an explosion. But with Thanksgiving only four days away, Jessie reckoned maybe it was time she broke the ice, let Arthur know his accusations were a bunch of hooey. She considered the options. Do and say nothing or do what she'd always done: step up to the plate and take her swings. Since when had she ever stepped out of the batter's box and declined to get back in? She donned a jacket, her Wild Musketeers baseball cap and headed toward the creek.

Batter up!

Dorothy marched straight to May Belle's after church. May Belle said she thought she maybe felt the slightest bit better, but she was still in bed. Dorothy made them all a sandwich, then announced to May Belle that Doc would be by in short order since she'd told him at church May Belle needed a drop-in, and pronto. May Belle started to protest but truth be told, she had no choice and Dorothy had made that clear. When they were finishing their lunch, Doc arrived. He checked May Belle best he could under the awkward circumstances and without x-rays, then prescribed a muscle relaxant. "Let's see if this does the trick. I wish you could get this filled today, but as you very well know, Richardson's Rexall Drugs isn't open on Sundays. Earl," Doc said, handing the prescription over to him, "you go to the drugstore first thing in the morning and get this filled for your mother, okay?" Earl stared at it, then nodded his head. Although the pharmacy in Wal-Mart at the edge of town was open on Sundays, they didn't know Earl there, but more important, he didn't know them.

As soon as Doc was gone, Dorothy phoned Josh. "I need you to do me a favor, okay?" Within thirty minutes he'd picked up her and Earl and off they'd gone to Wal-Mart. By 2 P.M., May Belle had swallowed her first dose. As much as Dorothy wanted to support her local drugstore and her old music student who ran it, there was no sense in May Belle having to spend one more hour in pain than she needed to now that she'd finally moved past the Vicks VapoRub.

Early Monday evening Nellie Ruth and Edward Showalter pushed a piled-high shopping cart each through Your Store. She was reading off the master list, double-checking to make sure they had everything. She was going to check out the groceries herself and she and Edward Showalter would try to bag and organize them according to their delivery route. All told, including her own home, they had eleven stops, which wasn't as bad as she might have thought. They began their route at 7 P.M.

Gladys had warned them they better check May Belle's status before dropping off her groceries. Edward Showalter waited in the van while Nellie Ruth went to the door. When Earl opened it, Nellie Ruth knew she had her answer.

"IS THAT YOU, NELLIE RUTH?" May Belle hollered from her bedroom.

"YES, MAY BELLE! IT'S ME AND EDWARD SHO-WALTER!" Earl flinched and Nellie Ruth lowered her volume. May Belle's house wasn't *that* large. "Where would you like us to take your groceries?" she asked in a strong but non-yelling voice.

"If you could just put them on the countertop, Earl can put them away. Hear me, Earl?" Earl didn't verbally respond but he nodded his head, keeping his eye on Nellie Ruth.

"Earl's nodding, May Belle! Hold on, I'm going to flag Edward Showalter on in." She leaned out the door and waved her arm to motion him in.

"That's good, Earl. Show Nellie Ruth and Edward Showalter to the kitchen."

"May Belle! Are you going to be okay to cook?"

"I'm not sure yet. Doc gave me some pills. I'm feeling a little better. But if I can't, Dorothy said she and her sons would use my kitchen as well as hers."

"GREAT!" This time Earl covered his ears. "Oh, I'm sorry again, Earl." She lowered her voice. "Everything's under control then!" Silence. "Well, as under control as it can be right now." Edward Showalter was beside her, a bag in each hand. She gave him a shrug.

"Mom," Josh hollered up the stairs, "it's Colton Craig on the phone!"

"I'll get it up here!"

Josh had been thrilled to learn about his mother's mini-mall plan. Several kids at school had even talked to him about it already, the Partonville grapevine having spread its tentacles all the way to Hethrow. Shelby thought it was the coolest thing ever and said her Grannie M was "nonstop excited." He'd never been more proud of his mom. But to hear Colton Craig was on the phone made him nervous. He just didn't trust that guy, and he hoped if his mom was talking to him that her intentions for the mini mall were nothing less than the way she'd presented them. She'd said she wanted to do this "to help breathe new life into Partonville." He hoped it wasn't simply her next scheme to breathe new life into her bank account.

"I got it, Joshua," Katie said into the receiver with her business voice. Reluctantly he hung up.

"Colton. What may I do for you?"

"I received a call from one of my Realtor scouts today informing me he'd heard you were bringing a mini mall, or some such thing, to the square in Partonville." Katie did not respond. She hadn't thought about the grapevine *over*reaching quite this quickly. She wouldn't make this easy for him, though. But still, she wished she had a grand-opening date in place, the name of a famous tea-room chef (Was there such a person? She'd have to find out!) to roll off her tongue or something else equally impressive. After a few more moments of silence, he continued. "I told him he must be mistaken."

"I've heard Scouts never lie. Isn't that why they say 'Scout's honor'?"

"Is this your idea of a monetary opinion with value? To bring a new mini mall to a dilapidated building in a dying town?" Again, she did not respond. She would let him have to think about his next words, his next move—while she fought to dismiss what he'd said.

In the silence his mind ripped through a dozen ways she might be playing this. Surely she wasn't trying to drive up the price of Crooked Creek Farm or further set the stage for her preservation nonsense by first attempting to give a lift to a stale business district. *Surely.* Or maybe she just bought the rundown building to make him think that. What was Kathryn Durbin up to? What did she know that he didn't? The only thing he knew for sure was that it would be financially lethal to underestimate her.

"Can you hold on, please, I have another call coming in," she said abruptly. Without waiting for a response she put him on hold and looked at her wristwatch. She counted the seconds until forty of them had passed, then she flipped back to him. "Colton, I hate to cut this short, but I have another call I have to take."

"Well, I . . ."

"I'm sorry, but I really do have to go. I'll get back to you hopefully before the holiday. I've got a pretty full plate right now. If I don't talk to you before Thanksgiving, though, I hope you have a great weekend."

"Kathryn," he said, his voice firm enough to command a few moments more of her time, "let me just say that Craig & Craig Developers is prepared to make you an offer for Crooked Creek Farm, one we feel is beyond generous and one we feel you'd have to think twice to refuse." While he was talking he was already upping the offer in his mind. "We believe we can work *together* with you as one of our visionaries and we're prepared to pay more than top dollar for not only the farm, but your partnered services." He went on to state numbers so staggering that they made her legs go weak.

She opened and closed her free fist and leaned her forehead against the wall, gently bumping it against the hard surface a couple of times. One of the most powerful Realtors in the state—one who had for decades been her rival— was offering her not only a lucrative partnership, but as much money as she'd ever closed in one deal. She straightened her spine and steadied her voice. "I shall take that under advisement," she said as flatly as she could considering her throat had gone dry, "but right now I have to go." She thought she honestly might faint. She hung up the phone and ran her hand through her hair . . .

Her HAIR! How could she keep forgetting! What on earth kind of a black hole had she stepped into this last week? She walked to her bedroom mirror and stared at herself. She had never looked so . . . *different* in her entire life. She stepped in closer to the mirror and studied herself. Her eyes, so like her father's and brother's; her chin, as stiff as her upper lip right now—her hair, as short as a schnauzer's.

"Who are you, woman in the mirror?" she asked aloud. It was as though she was looking at a stranger, both inside and out. "Are you Kathryn Durbin, butt-kicking commercial real estate developer who knows when she has the opportunity to make a financial killing, then take the money and run far away from this one-horse town? Or are you Katie Mable Carol Durbin, a *Green Acres* city slicker of a woman ignorantly investing in a dilapidated building on a dying square in a Podunk place called Pardon-Me-Ville?"

◇◈◇

Jessie walked along the creek with vigor, stopping every twenty feet or so to skip a rock, which didn't really skip in the creek, but nonetheless felt like a good exercise to keep her pitching arm in shape during the long off-season—and help her fight her nerves. She'd kept her eyes peeled for Arthur but there was no sign of him. She gathered a small pile of twigs, sat down on a big rock and began tossing the twigs into the water, watching them rush away. "Where's that old coot gone?" she wondered aloud. Arthur, who was sitting in the crook of a tree a ways back from the creek, and who had been watching her move toward him, settling not ten feet from him, couldn't help but feel a twinge of pleasure. That woman would never give up throwing things. Never. After she'd let her last twig fly, she stood and brushed off her pants, turned and for the first time saw him.

"How long you been sitting there?" she asked.

"The whole time ya been flingin' them rocks and twigs."

"Why didn't you say something? You knew I was looking for you!"

"How'd I know that?"

"What else would I be doing down here?"

"Why would I think ya'd wanna find me? Maybe ya'd rather just as soon find me a floatin' as a sittin'."

"Arthur Landers! I would want no such thing!" She noticed his eyes brighten just the slightest. "For openers, you're too big for me to have to drag your dead body all the way back to the house." The light in his eyes quickly extinguished, giving her a pang of guilt. "Well," softening her tone in the slightest, "of course I was looking for you. If you've been sitting right there all along I'm sure you even heard me ask where you'd gone!"

"I thought maybe ya was lookin' for *another* old coot," he said.

Jessie wondered if he'd been inferring anything about Lester, which he had. "No, Arthur, for better or for worse, *you're* the old coot I was hunting."

For better or for worse. Jessie's turn of a phrase struck them both as the truth of the bottom line. Did it get much worse than this? They started talking at the same time, Arthur intending to ask Jessie point-blank if anything was going on between her and Lester (even though he'd decided there wasn't, he needed to hear her say it); and Jessie just wanting to say it's time they talked (or maybe she'd finally just give him what's for!), then see where it went from there. After stepping on each other's words, they both fell silent.

"You go," she said after a long pause.

"Jessie, I reckon the reason I went to the grill was ta ask Lester straight out if he still had eyes for ya. Then when I saw him standin' there right in front of ya . . ."

"Arthur Landers, *dang* your stubborn head! I don't know where you got such a wild idea! Lester was doing nothing but pouring me a cup of coffee!" Rather than retaliate, which she expected, Arthur's expression went from sheepish to hang-dog.

"For better or for worse, Arthur, here we are. And to tell you the truth, the last few days I've been remembering some of the better, and here's the plain truth, Arthur: I wouldn't have *had* the better—the best—of my years without you."

Arthur was stunned, as stunned as Jessie had been by her own admission. He wasn't one for fancy words or explaining himself either. Never had been. He felt inadequate to respond, the words binding and twisting themselves up inside of him. But speak he must. "Jessie," he began, then he lowered his voice and repeated her name. "Jessie, ya know I've always been proud of ya, don'tcha?"

"Yes, Arthur," she said, her voice quaking the slightest bit as she tried to fight the unbidden emotions ("emotions are not to be trusted") rising up in her throat, "I know that."

He started to take a step toward her but stopped. "What about Lester, Jessie? Do ya ever regret not marryin' him?" His eyes searched hers, his vulnerabilities laid bare.

She stood silent for five seconds, carefully choosing her words. "For one thing, Arthur, he never asked me. And for another thing, I never loved Lester. *Never.* I chose to marry *you* when *you* asked me, Arthur, and I didn't have to think twice about it. For close to sixty years now, come hell or high water, we've stuck it out. I know some of it hasn't been pretty, but we've stuck it out. That must mean *something,* right?"

"I reckon it means somethin', but Jessie. . . ." Arthur wanted to ask his wife if she *loved* him, which she hadn't exactly said. He wanted to ask her if she reckoned memories were enough. He wanted, through his now blurring vision, to grab her in his arms and plant a claiming kiss on her lips.

And so he did.

Before he'd barely backed off he whipped out his Hohner and played a chorus of "It Had to Be You," the music speaking what he simply could not. After the last note silenced, Jessie opened her mouth and out squeaked, "Me, too." Then for the first time ever she simply allowed herself to bawl.

When Herm and Vera returned from church, they were stunned to find Arthur and Jessie sitting at the kitchen table, the deck of cards laid out, a bowl of freshly popped popcorn on the table.

"Euchre?" Arthur asked Herman. Herm's eyes darted to Jessie, then to Vera, who was looking at Jessie.

"Me and Arthur against you and Herm," Jessie said. And then she winked. Although Arthur and Jessie went on to lose the game, old memories and the fact they were just, by golly, used to each other, made playing the game—on the same team—enough of a victory in itself, at least for now.

27

By Tuesday morning, May Belle's back had improved enough so that she could plant herself on the couch and make short journeys to the kitchen and bathroom without wanting to scream. Dorothy had phoned a couple of women on UMC's Care Committee who saw to it that casseroles were dropped off at the Justice household. Here May Belle was supposed to be baking up a storm for Thanksgiving and people were serving her instead. She wasn't used to that, but it also helped her realize how good it made others feel when she'd done the same for them; she could see it on their faces. What good was it to love giving if there were no grateful recipients? She concluded this was a good, albeit difficult, lesson God was teaching her and she gave thanks. One thing was evident, though, and that's that she was not even *near* well enough to start cooking and baking up a storm. And if she tried, Dorothy said she'd come over there and hog-tie her before she'd allow her to set herself back. May Belle knew she'd do it, too. It was a difficult call to make, but she donned a cloak of humility and picked up her phone.

"Dorothy, I'm giving in. Thank goodness I am better and getting around a bit, but I need to let people know *today* that I'm not up to handling the big duties for our Thanksgiving dinner at church. When did you say your family's arriving? And how will we work this?"

"Oh, May Belle! This is such good news! You're on the road to recovery! Now just *do-not-overdo-it*. I have spoken my piece. As for my family, much to my delighted surprise, Jacob arrives late this very afternoon! We just hung up! He said things wrapped up quicker than he thought they might, his hardest case settling out of court. Vinnie and the boys will be here late tomorrow night. He couldn't get them out of school any earlier. He was a little worried the airlines might be overbooked, but he assured me they wouldn't accept any amount of bribing they might offer them to give up their seats. Don't you worry about a thing either, dear. It's the Wetstra clan to the rescue! And we're all darn happy to do it. It's just what we need to help us get over not being at the farm this year."

"Oh, bless you, my friend. Bless you and yours. I've already started explaining to Earl that other people might be coming into our kitchen to cook and bake. He says he understands, but we'll see. I know you'll handle it just right, though. He'll trust them all if you're with them and I'm sitting nearby. Of course, he knows your boys, but he doesn't see them that often, and teenagers change so much as they're growing up that he might not recognize your grandsons, but he'll be okay." Dorothy knew May Belle was working to convince herself.

"Jacob and me will come by in the morning and see what you've got on your list, and if you don't have one, since you're up and around now, make one. And be specific. I'm not sure what we'll do about the desserts. You know I stink at baking. But never fear, we'll figure out something. Is that turkey thawing in your refrigerator?"

"Yes, ma'am. Since it was right at sixteen pounds—and goodness, if they're all this small we're liable to be in trouble!—

I had Earl put it in the fridge when Nellie Ruth dropped it off. I gave it a little nudge with my finger just a while ago. It's still got a ways to go, but it should be just right by Thursday morning. Probably a good idea to get it in really early so it has time to set before we slice it. I think it would be best to take it to church already sliced."

"Look how smart you are: that is exactly what Theresa told us to do! I tell you, she's a real crackerjack! But don't you think about any of this. You just concentrate on getting well and we'll do whatever needs to be done the best way we figure to do it. And you know, that reminds me: I have to phone Katie to see if she'll cook Jessica's turkey. Jessica called me on the verge of tears this morning saying at the last minute the hotel had booked up for the holiday and she thought she'd have her hands too full to do a turkey, which was the only thing she took on. I tried to keep her from volunteering in the first place but you know how conscientious she is. Poor thing, she is having such a time. . . ." Dorothy remembered that today was Jessica's doctor's appointment and she hoped it went well for her with the new Doctor Nielson.

"I better go, May Belle. I've got my own chores to accomplish, too. I better not get so busy checking in with everyone else that I forget my own to-do list! First off, now that Jacob's coming in tonight, I've got to finish getting my house ready for my family. They said they all want to stay here with me and they don't care how crowded we are. This ought to be something. I'm going to let them figure it out since I can't. There's my double bed, the double bed in the guest room, one couch and one rollaway bed I've borrowed in case none of those men fit on the couch—and I sure don't want to sleep on it either. I reckon this whole entire house is gonna look like one giant pile of puppies when we get ready to go to bed!"

Katie hung up the phone after talking to Dorothy, then phoned Jessica to assure her it would be no trouble at all for her to cook the turkey. She would, in fact, come and pick it up since she had something to show her anyway. When Jessica asked if it was her hair, Katie simply moaned. "You have to promise me you will not laugh." Jessica reminded Katie she had a doctor's appointment and told her not to stop by until after four-thirty. Katie tried to guess what Jessica's reaction to her hair might be, then she pictured Jacob looking at her head and . . . Perhaps that rat of a Colton Craig had, after all, reminded her that she *was* a woman since Jacob kept popping into her mind.

But wondering what anyone would think about her hair was the least of her frets: she'd never cooked a turkey before. She assumed they came with directions, though. If not, there was always the Internet. She for sure wasn't going to ask Jessica how to cook it, though, since sick or not, stressed to the hilt or not, Jessica would take the job back. No, she'd handle this one on her own.

When Doctor Nielson saw how long it had been since Jessica'd had a checkup, he insisted on giving her a quick once-over along with a pregnancy test. He didn't chat with her like Doc Streator always did when he'd examined her. She found getting a physical embarrassing and Doc's casual conversation had always helped her relax. This doctor just went straight to work, only asking her questions that pointedly pertained to her health. Nothing about her daughter—who Doc would have asked about, or more likely chatted with in the reception area—or how the motel was doing or . . . It just wasn't the same.

When Doctor Nielson was done with the examination, he said he was going to step out for a few moments to collect the lab results. He instructed her to go ahead and get dressed. He told her to open the door when she was ready, which she did. He sat on the stool and rolled it over to the end of the examining table where she'd climbed back up, legs dangling over the end. This left him looking up at her, which felt uncomfortable since he was the doctor and she was just the patient, but she was trapped.

"Jessica Joy," he said, looking at her chart, "you are a healthy, pregnant woman." He looked up and smiled. It was the first she'd seen him smile and it completely changed his face. She'd been so expecting to hear the words confirming her pregnancy that to actually hear them didn't faze her. "I see by your chart you have a five-month-old daughter. Physically you are in fine shape, and as you undoubtedly already know from your last experience—since I see Doc made a note here that you had it pretty bad during your first pregnancy—the morning sickness will probably soon subside and you'll get your energy back. I'd like to ask you, though, how are you feeling emotionally about this pregnancy? Was it planned?"

Jessica's face turned crimson. *Such a personal question.* "No," she said, the sound barely escaping her mouth.

"How do you feel about it?"

"I have good days when I know everything will be okay

because God will provide, and I have bad days when I just feel sorry for myself." There. She'd shared a basic truth with the new doctor, who, upon hearing her words, broke out in the widest smile yet.

"That's a healthy answer that lets me know you are in touch with not only reality but your own emotions." He stunned her by whipping a tape recorder out of his pocket and jabbering into it about his findings. It felt odd to hear herself described in terms such as "white, healthy . . . female coming to me with symptoms of . . . pregnant . . . asked patient to return in one month . . . will be starting her on. . . ." He clicked off the recorder, rifled it back in his pocket, looked at his watch and then at her. "Any questions?"

"Kind of," she said, wishing she hadn't.

"And they are?"

"Do you talk into a tape recorder about everyone you see?"

"Yes, ma'am. Then I pay a medical transcriber to type it up and put the notes in your file. That way everyone, including me, can *read* my findings, since my writing tends to verge on scribble when I'm working to stay on schedule." He took another quick look at his wristwatch just to make sure he *was* on task. "Anything else?" She shook her head. "I'd like to see you back in a month."

"Yes, I heard you tell that to your recorder."

"Right." He extracted his prescription pad from his pocket and neatly printed on it. "These are for . . ."

"I heard it when you talked to the recorder. Take one a day. Vitamin plus iron."

"Do you have a problem with me talking to my recorder, Mrs. Joy?" Although he didn't have a stern tone to his voice, it held an authoritative note.

"Not at all," Jessica said apologetically. "I'm . . . I'm just used to Doc Streator talking to *me*."

It was a statement the young Doctor Nielson needed to hear. He couldn't stop thinking about it the rest of the day. Maybe *that* was the secret to gaining the trust and acceptance of his new patients here in Partonville.

Throughout most of Jacob's plane ride to Chicago, then on the puddle jumper to Hethrow, and again during the brief rental car ride to Vine Street, he fought a subtle grief about his family's first-ever Thanksgiving away from Crooked Creek Farm. But he was glad he could come in a day early and had, since his last conversation with his mom, worked hard to clear the decks. If he had any luck at all, he'd be able to stay a whole week after Thanksgiving; it all depended on Monday's phone call from his secretary. He hadn't mentioned this possibility to his mom so she wouldn't be disappointed if it didn't come to pass. His mind wandered from one thing to the next as memories of Thanksgivings past paraded by. He recalled how his father carved the turkey, always beginning with V slices to the breast with the bone-handled knife, which he hoped hadn't gone in the auction. He smiled at the crisp vision of him and his brother racing around the house as cowboys, each straddling an arm of the couch when it was time to ride, their baby sister whining she didn't have a horse—their father bouncing her up and down on his leg. *I still miss you, Sis.* He'd loved the way that first taste of pumpkin pie slid down his throat when dessert was *finally* served, which was not until his dad finally said he thought everything had gone down the hatch far enough to make room. He smiled remembering the day he'd first tasted May Belle's pumpkin pie and realized his mom's had really been awful. But nonetheless, his dad always said, "A little slice of heaven, honey." Yes, he was anxious to see his brother and mother, to dwell in the land of shared memories, if only for a little while.

Visions of his mom downing those nitroglycerin tablets during his last visit appeared like annoying pop-up screens on his computer. She was eighty-seven, almost eighty-eight. She had already outlived the national averages. He needed to spend more time with her while he could. On the plane ride, he'd come to grips with the reality that he was *lonesome* for family, if not just lonesome, period—something he didn't like thinking about. He'd looked out the airplane window at the top of the billowing clouds and wondered, was it his age? *Is fifty-five making me sentimental, sappy or . . . smart?* Was he lonesome because he'd lived a half-country and more away from his family? Or maybe it was his last in a long string of failed loves, most women not living up to his expectations in the end, the one who did having crushed his heart to bits.

WELCOME TO PARTONVILLE, the familiar old road sign read. In a few short minutes, his mother was opening her front door. He wrapped his arms around her waist and picked her up off the floor as he hugged her. "Jacob Henry," Dorothy said into his ear, "don't you go throwing *your* back out now. That's all we'd need!" Jacob gently lowered his mom to the floor and backed up a step to take a good look at her. More creases in her neck, he thought. A little less hair than three months ago maybe. Definitely more age spots on the hands he gripped tightly in his own. But his mom's eyes still twinkled with mischief and spunk, which had always been one of his favorite things about her.

"I'm so glad you're here, son," she said, hugging him again. "It feels more like two years since I've seen you than a few months. Of course, we had so much to do the last time you were here, what with the auction and everything. In some ways my whole life has changed. . . . I feel kind of bad you're coming back to a project again. But you know," she said, her voice brightening, "life is the way it is."

"Don't feel bad about anything, Mom. I'm here and I'm glad we've *all* got something distracting to do. But I'm most glad to see you alive and kickin', as Dad used to say."

"Well, I don't know about kickin', but I'm definitely *alive!*" she said, tossing her hands in the air. "Bring your things on in and let's have us a nice glass of iced tea. I brewed some special for you this morning right after you called and said you were coming in."

Jacob walked out to the street to retrieve his suitcase from his rental car. Just as he turned around and slammed the door, bag in hand, a cashmere-colored Lexus SUV went careening by, the driver all but gunning the vehicle as it approached him. He recalled Katie Durbin owned a light-colored Lexus SUV and he doubted there was another vehicle like that big LX450 in Partonville. But he hadn't gotten a look at the driver's face. Considering the vehicle was now already two blocks away, though, from the distant rear this driver looked more like a man. Maybe it had been Josh. He remembered an e-mail where his mom had mentioned "the Joshmeister has his license now."

Katie checked her SUV's digital clock when she hit the WELCOME TO PARTONVILLE sign. Four-fifteen. Jessica probably wasn't back from the doctor's yet. She might as well get used to people seeing her looking like this so she decided to swing by Dorothy's to give her the first chance to faint. It wasn't until Katie got nearly all the way up to the curb in front of Dorothy's house and that guy with the nice rear end backed out of the car that she recognized Jacob. She took one hand off the steering wheel and placed it on top of her head. Next thing she knew, she'd all but floored the accelerator pedal.

Katie sat in her vehicle in front of unit number six at the Lamp Post. She was waiting for Jessica's car to appear. She looked in the rearview mirror at her head. She was going to have to cancel her spa day. She simply could not let any of them see this . . . *this*. People at the salon would laugh her out of the place. When she first saw Jessica's vehicle, her instincts were to flee, but she forced herself to stay the course, get out of the SUV and step up behind Jessica, who was now leaning into the car unbuckling Sarah Sue's safety belts. When Jessica turned around, her eyes flew open and she screeched.

"I know it's bad, but I didn't think it was *scary, too!*" Katie wailed.

"You stunned me is all; I didn't know you were standing right there!" Jessica, Sarah Sue on her hip, stared at Katie's head and face, then spent what seemed like two years circling her. Katie stood frozen, waiting for the laughter. When Jessica returned to face Katie, her eyes brightened. "It's the most perfect haircut for your face—your whole *head*! I mean it's taken five years off you!" Jessica's face reddened. "Oh, I didn't mean to imply you looked old before, it's just that this is the most perfect thing I've ever seen! Maggie has outdone herself," she said, nodding her head with approval. She hitched Sarah Sue higher on her hip and reached a hand around to Katie's neckline, fluffing the little wisps of hair with her fingertips.

Katie's voice sounded like doom. "What? Did you find two hairs she forgot to cut off? You don't need to placate me, Jessica. Friends tell friends the truth."

"Placate? I'm not sure I know what that word means. But if it means I'm just trying to tell you something nice and I don't mean it, I am not placating. I promise you. Katie, I'm not kidding; this haircut makes your beautiful eyes just *pop*! It's uncanny."

Katie studied Jessica's face. One thing Jessica could not do was to lie. It was true: she really liked it; it was clear by her expression. The sound of a vehicle pulling in behind them went unnoticed until they heard a loud wolf whistle. They both turned to see Paul, window down, little fingers still in the sides of his mouth from the whistle.

"Thanks, honey!" Jessica called out. "Nice to know this pregnant wife still has it! . . . Or maybe he's whistling at you, Katie?"

Paul got out of his car, lunchbox in hand, and strode to his wife and daughter with his arms open. "Oh, honey, that's wonderful news! I'm happy for us, aren't you, Sarah Sue? You're going to have a little sister or brother," he said, gently chucking his daughter under the chin with his knuckle, then giving his wife a kiss.

"Jessica!" Katie said. "I'm so caught up in my own hair that I didn't even think to ask! I'm happy for you, too!" Paul unleashed his wife so the two women could hug; he just knew they were going to.

28

It had been exactly a week since the scene at the grill, and over two weeks since Herm and Vera had arrived from Indiana. Miracle of miracles, the Landers clan was getting along. Herm and Vera were starting to miss their home, however, and had announced they'd be heading back at eight-thirty on Friday morning in order to beat the weekend traffic. Before they'd gone to bed last night, Arthur said he thought they should all have breakfast at Harry's one last time. Herm asked him if he thought that was a good idea and Arthur said he needed to set the record straight with Lester. "After all, it's Thanksgivin'."

When they arrived, Lester was at the grill, his back to the door. He was caught up in his usual routine of one-handed egg cracking. "Arthur!" Harold Crab yelled. "We thought you'd left town!" Lester swung around so fast the guts to one of the eggs he'd just cracked went flying and splatted on the floor. Arthur grabbed hold of the bill of his cap and gave Lester a nod. He didn't exactly smile, but it was a friendly gesture. Lester, plenty wary, finally turned his back on Arthur and went about cleaning up his mess, which was easiest done by pouring a huge dose of salt onto the egg. Helped congeal it.

"Don't think I've ever seen you hit the floor with an egg before, Lester," Sam said as he watched the cleanup.

"First time for everything," Lester muttered in response. "Hope it's the last—for *lots* of things."

While Arthur made his rounds at the counter slapping backs, swapping insults and curtseying to queen lady Gladys, the rest of the Landerses seated themselves. Lester stayed aware of Arthur's movements, until he was at last settled at the table with the rest of his kin. Vera was already reading the menu to Herm. It was *definitely* time for those two to head home, Arthur thought, but he was determined to play nice.

A minute later, Lester arrived with his pad in his hand. "Me and Art will have his usual," Herm said with more perkiness than was called for, but oh, how he was trying to make up for what couldn't be talked about, ever again.

"You?" Lester said, looking to Vera.

"Let's see . . . I just can't make up my mind."

Arthur rendered a dramatic sigh. "How about ya jist go with our special and end the pain," he said. Jessie's impulse was to kick him a good one under the table, but she decided it was a tad too early in their fragile peace for such a move.

"You know, I think I will," Vera chirped. "What a good idea!"

Then Lester's eyes diverted to Jessie, but only for a flash of a second. He stared at his pad real quick-like. "I'll have the special, too," she said, not looking up.

"Aw, fer Pete's sake!" Arthur said, banging his hand on the table. Everybody froze. "Jessie, this here's Lester. Lester, this here's my wife, Jessie. And *me*, Lester, well, I guess I've been yur friend fer so many years I'm just stuck with ya as a friend till we both die." After a brief moment, there was a group exhale. It dawned on all of them at the same time that they'd just heard an apology of sorts, and as far as Arthur was concerned, that was that.

Thanksgiving morning Katie stood at the back of the house and watched her baby drive away in the SUV. Although they'd originally planned for him to leave Wednesday after school, Katie had heard on the news that there'd been a major pileup on I-57 northbound and traffic was backed up for seventeen miles. Travel the night before Thanksgiving was always terrible; one wreck and it was impossible. Josh hadn't even argued when she suggested he wait until early Thursday morning to head out since the way it sounded from the news, he probably wouldn't arrive at his dad's until then anyway. Besides, that would give him a chance to swing by Dorothy's Wednesday night—with Shelby, of course—and say hello to Steven and Bradley, Dorothy's grandsons, whom he was sorry to miss spending time with. *Next time,* he thought. *I hope Christmas.*

As it turned out, their plane had been late getting in from Colorado and Josh was going to have to get up early, so it was a quick visit. Before Dorothy's grandsons opened the door after hearing the knock, they took note through the window that Josh was holding Shelby's hand. "Still going strong with those two, huh Grandma?"

"Thicker than molasses soaked into a buckwheat pancake," she quipped.

Steven opened the door and extended his hand. "Good to see you, man! You, too, Shelby. Come on in. Grandma tells us you're heading back to Chicago to see your dad," he said as they passed through the door. When he was shutting it behind them, he quipped, "Bet you're sorry you have to miss all the cooking." Everyone chuckled, including Jacob and Vinnie, who were sitting on Dorothy's couch. Dorothy scurried over and gave Josh and Shelby a hug.

Josh looked around Dorothy's living room. Suitcases were piled everywhere and the air was laced with the fragrance of Dorothy's crock-pot spaghetti. Dorothy was positively beaming. He saw how happy it made her to have her family around and he wished he could stay and be a part of it. "Gathered for the big day tomorrow, huh?"

"That we are," Vinnie said, getting up along with Jacob to shake Josh's hand and extend a greeting to Shelby. "The boys and I were no sooner in the door before Mom here," he nodded his head at her and gave her a playful smile, "was reading us the timetable and the list of things we gotta do tomorrow. She sounded like a drill sergeant." He gave her a quick salute.

"Wow!" Josh exclaimed. "I thought *I* was the only one with a sergeant for a mom!" Since Dorothy's sons were grown men, it always felt funny to imagine them in the role of the . . . sons. "Now that cracks me up," he said, breaking into a big laugh. "I'll see you in a whole new light from now on, Dorothy!"

"Come on and sit down," Dorothy said. "Let me take your jackets."

"We can only stay a minute. It's late and I've got to get Shelby home before *her* sergeant mom comes looking for her," he said, grinning at her. "I've got to be up at the crack of dawn anyway so I for sure make it to Chicago for my dad's dinner."

Their visit was indeed a short one, but it was so energized that more than ever he hated to have to tear himself away from the swirl of happiness, drop off his sweet thing and head out alone tomorrow, but such was life. By 11:30 P.M. he was pulling into the driveway at Crooked Creek, his good-bye kiss from Shelby still lingering on his lips. He realized being with Dorothy's family had actually made him a little anxious to see his dad. He hoped they'd have a good visit; sometimes watching his dad with his Daily Kids made him jealous, or lonesome . . . he wasn't sure what it was. He tried to imagine Dorothy's sons missing their dad, whom they could never see again, and Steven and Bradley having to be away from their mother. . . . He guessed life was complicated for everybody.

As instructed, though, while he'd been at Dorothy's he'd passed along a hello to all the Wetstras from his mom, who didn't come along but said she'd see them all tomorrow. He also said his mom wanted to remind them to send somebody out to get her tomorrow since she wouldn't have a car; Jacob told Josh to tell his mom not to worry, that somebody would be there at the specified time— whatever it was.

When Dorothy had asked Josh about his mom's hair, Josh hesitated before he answered. Shelby filled the gap. "I stopped in the shop just when Grannie M was finishing Mrs. Durbin. It's really s-e-x-y. Grannie M outdid herself!"

"Gross," Josh said. "Moms don't have sexy hair. They have mom hair." He wasn't sure *what* he thought about her new haircut, to tell the truth. Moms were supposed to look a certain way—at least *his* mom always had. This new haircut looked so different that he wasn't sure if he'd ever get used to it and he kind of hoped she'd grow it out again, get herself back to normal.

As soon as Josh was out the door, for lack of anyplace else to put them, Dorothy's sons piled all the suitcases in front of the closed front door to make room for the rollaway, then began making the decisions about who was going to sleep where. Everybody was tired and tomorrow was a big day. They quickly settled down but livened themselves back up again rambling through their own personal spin of a "good-night, John-Boy" routine. Dorothy's heart was so happy listening to it that she couldn't help but get up off the rollaway (Vinnie and Steven had landed in her bed; Jacob in the poster bed and Bradley on the couch) and make one quick walk through her house to give them each a kiss on the cheek. She'd been right; they did look like a pile of puppies. *Her* pile of puppies. *Lord,* she prayed as she moved from one to the next, *even though I do miss the farm, I THANK You for gathering my family together. This,* it became clear to her as she circled around again and kissed them each on the other cheek while brushing tears from her own, *is what makes a home a home.*

The mom who had been described as the one with the sexy hairdo, the mom of the kid who was leaving on his first long-distance solo road trip on Thanksgiving Day, stood in her driveway crying and waving. She'd held back the tears until she was sure Josh couldn't see them; she'd walked halfway down the drive, still waving, before she could no longer fight them. She cried and cried and then sobbed her way back into the house. "Please, God," she'd said aloud after entering her kitchen, "look after my baby." A brief wave of satisfaction washed through her to realize she'd progressed enough in her "prayer life"—although that was a huge exaggeration—to spontaneously talk to God at all. Maybe she was her pastor half brother's half sister after all. She smiled at that bizarre thought as she blew her nose. She would see Delbert today at the Thanksgiving dinner. She would see him and his wife and her half of a niece and nephew, as Josh had reminded her when he told her to tell them all "Hi and Happy Thanksgiving" for him.

But first, she had to wrestle with the turkey. She needed to get it out of the freezer and read the cooking directions she'd spotted on the back of the package yesterday. *I remember Mom used to start early.*

The smell of roasting turkey wafted throughout homes in Partonville and the surrounding countryside. The Landers clan was cooking a stuffed twelve-pounder, Jessie and Vera having put it in the oven early, none of them liking to eat too late. They'd already decided they could have turkey sandwiches later in the evening while they played one final round of euchre.

The smell of the giant mess of bacon and onions Lester had sautéed for the green beans momentarily offset the aroma of the twenty-two-pound turkey he'd ordered after he heard through the grapevine that the number of reservations continued to swell. Worst-case scenario, they wouldn't need it but he could serve turkey and gravy sandwiches for his Friday special and turkey soup on Saturday. Two large pans of dressing were being readied. Even though the sign on the door at Harry's Grill said CLOSED, he was glad to be fast at work within, looking forward to sharing a meal with people he'd grown to care a great deal about over the years. Thanksgiving had always been kind of a down day for him, but the joy of cooking and knowing he would be part of a crowd made his heart happy. He hoped the Landers clan had a nice day, too—every single one of them. And he meant it.

Gladys was in the church basement in a dither of a tither bossing around the setup and serve volunteers. (She just couldn't keep herself away.) Vincent, Bradley, Steven, two men and two teen girls from St. Auggie's tried to get the tables, chairs and table settings to her liking before she took off for her family's celebration. Twice she had them rearrange all the tables—no small task—realizing she couldn't get her own backside through the far corner with the tables at a T like that and, "NO! We can't *possibly* orchestrate any order in here if we try to do a square inside of a square! Who's crazy idea was THAT?" Vincent held back his response since he was the one looking at the scrawled diagram she'd handed him. It looked like a square inside a square to him. Theresa Brewton just bit her lip since even though she was supposed to be overseeing things, she was on Gladys's turf. While Gladys was busy with the tables and chairs, Theresa quietly redirected the food lineup into a more sensible formation. Vincent couldn't help but notice his sons hadn't complained once about all the work, especially since the girls had shown up. Much to the boys' mortification, he bragged to the girls how great his sons' baking efforts had been that morning, he and the boys deciding they'd rather eat their own attempts at May Belle's recipes—instructions thankfully written out in great detail—than to endure their grandmother's baking. (The three of them had actually had a grand time together, a time they would go on to talk about for years.)

Although May Belle and Dorothy had both tried to encourage Earl to go to the church to lend his strong self to the setup project, he wouldn't go until someone he knew well—like his mother or Dorothy—would go with him. This wasn't a part of his routine. Jacob, Dorothy, Vincent and the boys had been in and out of his kitchen several times already as they whisked back and forth from Dorothy's house and oven to Earl's. It was all too unusual, Earl thought, all this coming and going, and it unsettled him. May Belle did her best to sit at the kitchen table as long as her back would allow, trying to reassure him everything was fine. It just about drove her crazy to be unable to help, but she kept remembering God's lessons about receiving. Dorothy kept Earl as busy as she could, sending him on missions between the houses to get one thing or another, Sheba fast on everyone's heels. Even though it was chilly, Sheba's little tongue was hanging out from all the exercise. It occurred to Dorothy that she wasn't the only one who missed those daily jaunts down to the creek!

Both the Wetstra and Justice households' turkeys were already sliced in large deep baking pans and covered in foil in ovens set at low. Sweet and mashed potatoes were now the project at hand. Since they were up to fifty maybe sixty reservations, this turned out to be a much bigger job than Dorothy had bargained for. (She had phoned Theresa on Wednesday and asked if she thought she could recruit one extra large pan of each on such short notice and Theresa had told her she'd already covered that base—just in case.

Thank you, Lord, for our supporting role and for giving us Theresa!)

Dorothy's arthritic fingers were bothering her and Jacob told her not to worry, they'd manage without her. He turned out to be a peeler extraordinaire, thank goodness. She sat at the table across from May Belle and they joked about being supervisors—or maybe they'd just gotten old enough to be benched, Vinnie teased. "Oh, like THAT would ever be possible with you two," Jacob said to the women, handing them each a small slice of raw white potato to nibble on—a Wetstra tradition. "May Belle, your most difficult job today is keeping the birthday girl out of my hair!"

Earl had finally relaxed enough with the boys to try his best to help with the peeling when he was invited, which made his mom smile. She noticed Jacob giving each of Earl's peeled potatoes a little spruce-up before he sliced them. She appreciated his ability to honor Earl's attempts. Under May Belle's supervision, Jacob had also done a rather artistic job of arranging the sweet potato slices, butter and brown sugar dotting the tops of the dishes just waiting for browning. "Not too bad for a collaboration between a lawyer and a gimp," Dorothy quipped.

Dear Birthday Girl (and Steve and Brad and Sheba and everybody else),

I made it! Maybe mom already told you since I called her—like she *demanded* I do (Yes, sergeant!)—the minute I arrived. There was more traffic than I expected so early in the morning (guess everybody had the same idea) but we did keep moving, even though it was WAY slower than YOU would have wanted to be going, Dorothy! Sheba's ears wouldn't even have been bouncing some of the time, let alone flying. ;>)

We're eating Thanksgiving dinner late here. Dad's wife's folks are coming over at five and so is one of her sisters who has two small children about the ages of the Daily Kids. (More halves of relatives—although I guess since they're dad's wife's, they're not BLOOD halves! Whew!)

We ARE going to look at the windows at Marshall Field's tomorrow and I'm going to do my best to remember the stories you told me. It's fun to picture you there with your kids—although I wish I had some pictures of you then. I can't imagine you without gray hair. Know what I mean?

Gotta go. I'm being called to help set the table.

HAPPY THANKSGIVING and HAPPY BIRTHDAY! Hug everybody for me when you see them. I'll be home Saturday night to avoid Sunday's traffic and we'll celebrate your birthday then. Got your present wrapped already. Alex and I are either going out Friday night or Saturday morning for breakfast. Gotta see what time we get back from the window thing. I'll give you the full report when next I see you.

Gobble-gobble and hip-hip-hooray to the BIRTHDAY GIRL,

Joshmeister

29

"I will not panic. I will not panic," Katie said aloud to the rock-solid frozen enemy she had, in a fit of wrestling with the unwieldy thing, mindlessly started calling Sir Thomas Turkey. Sir Thomas Turkey weighed seventeen frozen pounds, which was right near the line of two chart weight brackets and would, according to not only the directions printed on the plastic wrap, but three of her cookbooks, take somewhere between two to four days of refrigerator thawing (depending on which weight bracket she believed) and six to ten hours in cold water. *Why didn't I read this before!* Her microwave directions didn't recommend trying to thaw anything that heavy and, besides, the turkey wouldn't fit into it; she'd tried. Several times. She'd nearly frozen her own navel propping the bulk of him to the microwave door with her abdomen while twisting and turning him with her hands. If she had had hair long enough to grab, she would have pulled it all out by now.

According to all directions, Sir Thomas Turkey would, after he was thawed *(HA!)*, take somewhere between three and four hours to cook at 325 degrees, which was recommended. She was to have the sliced beast (oh, and don't forget letting him SET for twenty minutes after he's roasted before slicing!) at the church at two-thirty, which was now less than six hours away.

So much for starting early.

Surely there was another way, a more modern and sensible—and efficient and *expedient* way—to slay Sir Thomas into juicy serving slices. She booted up her computer and began to surf the Net; she would not humiliate herself by making phone calls. She could handle this. Thank heavens she came across a site that warned her about the bag of what sounded to be *gross* inner body parts stuffed inside one of Sir Thomas's orifices. Although she discovered a few ways to expedite the roasting itself, like the baking bag method (and, of course, she didn't *have* a baking bag) and the high-temp foil wrap approach (but still, the bird needed to be thawed), and don't forget the deep-frying (but she had no deep fryer), nothing she found led her to a victorious way to speed-thaw and cook the bird within her timeline.

Too bad she didn't own a chain saw, she thought. That'd fix Sir Thomas! She'd saw his frozen contrary self in half, thaw his halves in the microwave and then . . . then she'd put one half in the microwave and the other in a high-temperature oven and voilà! In her panic (which she continued to repeat she would not succumb to) she actually phoned Sears in Hethrow, hoping they were open. She'd talked herself into believing the chainsaw method—which, as wacky a thought as it was, seemed her only option—might really *work. Why not?* ". . . closed for the holiday" the recording said. It went on to encourage her to arrive at six A.M. for the early-bird shopping specials on Friday.

She'd probably be dead by then, she thought, having been knocked out cold by her seventeen-pound adversary as they both flew to the floor in their final round. She imagined every word in the *Partonville Press*.

BALD WOMAN SURROUNDED BY MOUSE-TRAPS FOUND DEAD NEXT TO PARTIALLY THAWED TURKEY. Although authorities at first assumed it was an accident, suicide is not being ruled out since witnesses close to Katie Mable Carol Durbin have stepped forward to disclose her recent questionable business investments.

Joshua Matthew Kinney, Durbin's son and only heir (although she is reported to have been survived by many halves of heirs), discovered his mother's body late Saturday evening when he arrived home from a trip she ill advisedly allowed him to take on his own. (He was only sixteen, folks!) He suspected his mother had been dead since Thanksgiving when she was reported by an undisclosed Partonville resident to have been cooking a turkey. Her son, riddled with grief, wondered if foul play (har, har) wasn't involved since he said, "I don't think my mom knew how to cook a turkey."

Acting Mayor Gladys McKern calls the loss a sorrow for the whole community, especially for those who showed up at United Methodist Church to share in a Thanksgiving dinner only to find they were out of turkey due to Ms. Durbin's death.

She couldn't even run away from home—she didn't have a car! And she wasn't getting picked up until it was time to go to the church, with Sir Thomas.

At 2:20 P.M. the church basement was a buzz of activity laced with eau de Thanksgiving fragrances. Cooks and volunteers were arriving en masse and Gladys had popped back in for a brief moment away from her family gathering

just to make sure there were no fatal flaws. Although she hadn't intended to make another appearance, the more she sat at her son's and thought about Theresa Brewton's lack of leadership ability and how she didn't want the Catholics to be able to lord it over the Methodists about whose fault "it" was, the more she couldn't help but make one final check. While Steven was off picking up Katie, Jacob, Vinnie and Bradley ran up and down the stairs hauling in their turkeys, potatoes and desserts. When Lester arrived, he happily accepted their assistance. Edward Showalter dropped off Nellie Ruth but didn't leave for Johnny Mathis's until he'd made sure she had everything she needed. Although their parting was difficult, they both knew they were each going to be where they belonged for the day, Nellie Ruth telling ES she would give thanks for him every time she glimpsed her electrical wire bracelet—which would be often since she was serving up the potatoes onto each plate.

At 2:40 P.M. Earl and Dorothy escorted May Belle down the stairs. (Gladys made an exception for May Belle's early seating on account of her back.) Earl stood by his mother's side, her elbow in his hand; Dorothy walked in front of her in case she fell, which May Belle said was a joke since she'd take Dorothy down like a bowling pin. Jacob walked in front of Dorothy, just in case. When May Belle got to the bottom of the steps and saw the bounty of food, her eyes welled with tears at God's provision—without her ever having to lift a finger. Although she knew she was pushing the envelope by tackling the stairs, she'd promised them all she would tell them when she needed to go if they would just let her at least come be "in the blessing."

"Where's Katie Durbin?" Gladys bellowed at 2:50 P.M. "Isn't she supposed to be bringing a turkey? We can't keep folks waiting at the top of the stairs for more than ten minutes! We told them three o'clock sharp and three o'clock sharp it will be!"

"Why don't you go on ahead and join your family," Theresa told her. She had the sweetest voice. "Didn't you say *you* were eating at three?"

Gladys looked at her watch for the eleven-billionth time and reluctantly headed for the stairs. "Well, I hope she shows up is all I have to say!" Of course, nobody believed that would be all Gladys would have to say, but to their surprise, it was. Up the stairs she went.

At exactly 3 P.M., Nellie Ruth and Dorothy powwowed and decided Gladys was right; they needed to let folks come on down. Nellie Ruth made the announcement that everyone was now welcome to come join the festivities and start finding their seats. They figured Steven and Katie would be arriving momentarily anyway. To Dorothy's delight, in with the surge of people came Jessica, Paul and Sarah Sue. Fifteen minutes earlier Paul had looked at his tired wife and said, "Jess, all of our customers are checked in and doing their own Thanksgiving things. You look exhausted. Let's just stop what we're doing, put a sign on the office door that says BACK AT FOUR and join the Thanksgiving dinner for an hour—even if you can't eat it. I can't stop thinking about Dorothy reminding us that Jesus said 'Come as you are.' Let's just do it, honey." After a few protests from Jessica about how she'd feel too guilty since she hadn't even cooked the turkey she'd said she would, Paul convinced her that Katie had control of everything, that that's what friends were for and that she always felt better after she was around Katie for a little while anyway. "She is one more thing we can give thanks for today." And so off they'd gone.

By the time traffic started flowing down the stairs, the teens had just finished lighting the last of the candles set around the fall decorations on each banquet table; the room was warm, inviting and filled with gratefulness.

After everyone was seated for ten minutes or so, Pastor looked toward the stairs one last time, as did Dorothy and Jessica, who began to fret the moment she learned Katie hadn't arrived yet and that Steven—teen driver Steven—had gone to pick her up. While Vincent was chastising himself for not sending his cell phone with his son, Pastor and Father O'Sullivan quickly and silently prayed they hadn't experienced any difficulties. From what Pastor so far knew about Katie, she wasn't one to be irresponsible. But alas, the meal and the guests were readied; the banquet had to begin. Theresa told Dorothy they really couldn't wait any longer, especially since she'd overheard the Joys' story about closing down for only one hour.

"You're right," Dorothy said with resignation. She shifted her eyes toward Pastor. "Who gets the pleasure of giving the blessing today, you or Father O'Sullivan?" The men gave each other an awkward glance realizing that between all the committee members, nobody had made this decision, or at least not told them about it.

"How about Father O'Sullivan leads us and I'll give the Amen," Pastor Delbert said. Everyone bowed their heads.

"Lord God, giver of light, hope and all things of love, we gather together today—and OH, LORD! it is so special for us *all* to be gathered together!—to share in a meal in Your house to give thanks for our bounty. Yes, what a special day it is when people of different faiths can come together in Your name!" His exuberant voice, familiar to some and new to others, was much heartier than Pastor Delbert's. Not that

Pastor Delbert's voice and prayers were ever flat or boring; it just wasn't his natural style to boom prayers the way Father O'Sullivan did. His words rang with such honest joy and cheerfulness—you could hear the smile behind them—that it inspired Pastor Delbert to reach over and pat him on the back, right during the middle of the prayer. He'd always loved Father O'Sullivan's prayers and felt especially blessed and glad his congregants got to experience them on this Thanksgiving day.

"Lord, give a special blessing to the hearts of the cooks, the servers and everyone who will partake of this meal.

"Be with those we love who cannot share this table with us today." He thought of one of the couples he'd seen arrive whose son was serving in the military. "Hold them safe in Your arms, as secure as You hold us here now. Bind us together now, Lord." He paused for ten seconds (something St. Auggie's parishioners were used to but that caused the UMC folks to wonder briefly if he was through and they'd missed the Amen) to allow all in attendance to focus on the experience, the shelter, the peace—aside from Wanita's twin boys whose chairs scraped on the floor while they socked each other.

"Thank You for the beauty of our tables, the nourishment in the food and the grace You extend to each and every one of us." He gently elbowed Pastor Delbert, who unleashed a heartier than usual "Amen!"

"Pastor, Father," Dorothy said, "we'd like for you two and your gathered families to head up the line today. We are especially grateful for your dedicated service to your flocks."

"Well, I couldn't . . ." Pastor Delbert started to say.

"Well, I could!" Father said, followed by a hearty laugh.

He waved over his sister and her family; Pastor Delbert then motioned for his wife and children. Nellie Ruth insisted Theresa and her family jump in next, then Dorothy and her family. Dorothy beamed at the sight of her little clan lined up like a row of big ducks. Her heart was so grateful, and yet, she carried an underlying worry about Katie and Steven.

Dorothy told Bradley to go tell the Joys to get in line next, since they were on a timeline. Jessica looked pale and tired and expressed concern for Katie. Dorothy assured her all was well while her husband rubbed a small circle on her back. "Katie is one of the most determined women I've ever met. They'll get here any moment. Just you wait and see!" Dorothy chirped in a tone convincing enough to convince herself.

May Belle asked Earl to fill her plate for her while she remained seated. "You know what I like, honey." He looked a little nervous but got in line behind Vincent, who, since he now lived out of Partonville, reminded Earl that they'd grown up together. "My mom brags about you all the time, Earl, about how much you help her with so many things, how you've been her groundskeeper . . . I'm so glad you'll be near her this winter to shovel her sidewalk. That's a relief to me and Jacob. Thank you, Earl. You are one of the many people I'm giving thanks for today."

Like his dad before him, Vincent had always had a warm and expressive way with his words. Although Earl didn't maintain eye contact with him, he did listen to everything he said. When he arrived back at the table with his mother's plate of food, he looked like his buttons might pop. May Belle had seen Vincent from across the room chattering on, and she thanked Vincent for whatever he'd said to her son. "I just told him how grateful we are he's here to help our mom, and I meant it," Vincent said. May Belle's eyes welled with tears. *Thank you, Lord. I give You thanks for a son who loves me and for those who love him.*

By the time the last person was served, Lester had, in the joint committee's eyes, become the hero of the day—although Dorothy was sure he'd responded to *God's* obvious nudgings after all her desperate prayers. In light of Katie's turkey's absence, his unsolicited bird was the one that not only finished serving everyone, but allowed second helpings to the few who chose to circle back. Good thing he hadn't made up the cards for the grill with Friday's special on it yet since it sure wouldn't be turkey sandwiches. No matter, Fridays were meant for fish anyway and he'd probably hear grumbles from the regulars if the usual all-u-can-eat fish fry wasn't the . . . usual.

Dorothy looked at her watch. She was beginning to *really* fret about Katie now. This wasn't like her. She speculated maybe Katie'd been so sad about Josh not being home that she just couldn't face everyone. She wondered how Steven would handle her if she was distraught. Or maybe the rental car had broken down or . . .

"You mentioned your cell phone awhile ago, Vinnie. Do either of you boys have one on you?" They both reached for their belts and simultaneously tried to hand her a phone. "Will this cost you an arm and a leg if I try to call Katie?"

"No. Just call her, Mom," Vinnie said as she wrapped her fingers around the surprisingly little contraption.

"Is the church office phone turned on?" Jacob asked. "I wonder if they've tried to call us?"

"We do have an answering machine; I'll check it if I don't get through to her." She was staring at the phone, realizing she had no idea how to use it.

"What's her number?" Jacob asked. He flipped open his phone. Dorothy spoke the number slowly as Jacob punched each keypad. He handed the phone to her while she passed Vinnie's back to him. All she got was Katie's answering machine, which now left her more worried than ever. She hoped they hadn't had an accident on the way to the church, or that something hadn't happened to Josh on the way to his dad's. With all their preparation she hadn't checked her e-mail today and now wished she had since Josh said he'd be sending her a birthday greeting as soon as he arrived at his dad's.

"Good idea about the church phone, Jacob," Vinnie said. "Bradley, run upstairs for Grandma and check the answering machine. Mom, tell him where it is." But the machine produced nothing.

By 4:10 P.M. action was big at the dessert table and Pastor talked everyone into singing "Happy Birthday" to Dorothy when she got her pumpkin bar. Theresa had made the decision while folks were eating to go ahead and cut them up, putting slices on individual little paper plates. She'd wrapped helpings for the Joys to take with them when she saw them ducking out to get back to the Lamp Post.

Dorothy was just ready to send somebody out on a search party for Katie when they heard the door open and slam shut at the top of the stairs, then heard footsteps in the stairwell. Steven appeared first, then in walked Katie. Brown mascara marks streaked down her face, she had an unreadable look in her eyes, a giant plastic bag in her hand and . . . that *hair*. Dorothy had to look twice to make sure it *was* her—as did everyone else. A hush fell over the room. Dorothy scooted herself back from the table and made her way to Katie's side.

"Oh, *honey*! What's *happened*? Is Josh okay?" Dorothy was sure from the looks of Katie that she'd been wrestling with some kind of a terrible demon, never mind her hair.

"I . . . I. . . . " Katie moved the plastic bag from one hand to the other as she swiped under her eyes, then looked at her fingers, noting she must have cried her mascara clear down her face. She glanced around the room and saw everyone was already eating dessert, which made her feel all the worse. "Sir Thomas . . ." she muttered, as yet another hot flash snuck up on her and an unbidden band of new tears poured down her cheeks. (She was starting to hate her very own hormones.) Dorothy cast her eyes around for Steven. Maybe he could explain. But he was already at the table piling food on his plate, clearly starving and looking somewhat annoyed.

"Sir Thomas? Goodness gracious, Katie! Who is Sir Thomas? What has happened?" Dorothy's heart was pounding now; Jacob had stepped up beside her.

Jacob! Oh, no! Katie thought as she fanned herself and sniffed and tried to pull herself together. She must look a sight! Her eyes darted from Dorothy to Jacob and back again a couple of times. Jacob's eyes were flicking from her hair to her mascara-streaked cheeks to her eyes and back to her hair again.

"Speak to me, honey!" Dorothy demanded.

Katie opened her mouth and then . . . had an out-of-body experience wherein she got a good look at herself, plastic bag in hand, hair missing, face a mess—the disaster she'd left behind in her kitchen. She couldn't help but to start laughing at herself, which several months ago, before she moved to Partonville, would have been impossible. She laughed and laughed until she finally caught her breath and said, "Sir Thomas is *dead*" (Dorothy gasped, which made Katie laugh all the more), "but his cousin, Colonel Chicken, is here to take his place," she said, now doubled over with laughter, as she held out the plastic bag, especially when she noticed Pastor Delbert had rushed over wearing his most concerned pastorly face, having overheard the word "dead."

Jacob leaned over and whispered in his mother's ear, "Does she have a drinking problem, Mom?" Dorothy shot him a look.

"Katie, I don't know what you're talking about, but I'm assuming everything is okay . . . with Josh?"

"Yes. Oh, *yes*, Dorothy! I didn't mean to frighten you! Josh made it just fine." She was pulling herself together now. "I tried phoning the church office from my cell phone to tell you I was going to be late but I got the recording and didn't figure anyone would be checking for messages. Steven couldn't remember his dad's cell number. We got here as soon as we could. I am so sorry I worried you."

"Who, may I ask, is Sir Thomas? Obviously someone close to you, from the looks of you when you first got here."

"I'm sorry, this is going to sound like I'm daft."

"You can say that again," Steven mumbled as he passed by her with his piled-high plate.

"Sir Thomas Turkey. Sir Thomas the frozen turkey that, even though I tried to dismember him with a hacksaw I found in the barn, refused to thaw enough for me to cook."

"You tried to hacksaw a frozen turkey?" Bradley, who had by now joined the group, asked. "With an actual hacksaw?"

"I had no choice. Sears was closed." Jacob, Bradley, Dorothy, Pastor and Father O'Sullivan, who had stepped up, looked blankly from one to the other, then back at Katie again.

"Did you have enough turkey for everyone without Sir Thomas?" Katie asked.

"Thanks to Lester," Nellie Ruth said, who had now joined the growing band of folks everyone was staring at. "God provides! Not to worry!"

"Oh, I'm so glad," Katie said with relief, "really. Guess you don't need this now then." She removed the giant carton of chicken from the plastic bag. "Poor Sir Thomas was so dismembered—it was such a hopeless mess, really—that I finally gave up on him. When Steven arrived, I *made* him drive us to Hethrow. You can't imagine how many places we cruised until we finally found one open! Something for . . . tomorrow's lunch for your family, Dorothy," she said, handing her the carton, then chuckling. "Steven was a real champ!" Katie said glancing his way. Dorothy turned and looked at Steven, who shrugged his shoulders as he shoveled another bite of potatoes into his mouth. He was famished and disappointed to have missed eating Thanksgiving with his dad but glad to be sitting with him now.

"Take your coat off and come relax, Katie," Dorothy said as she accepted the carton. "I think you need to eat something yourself. Chicken?" she asked with a twinkle in her eye, holding the carton in front of Katie, which set them all to laughing.

Katie fixed herself a plate of food from the bounty of turkey, dressing, green beans and scrumptious-looking sweet potatoes, one of her favorites. It all smelled and looked delicious.

May Belle slowly rose out of her chair when Katie returned to the table with her plate. "Oh, honey, I'm so sorry to leave just when you've arrived, but I need to go lie down. You can have my place right here." Vincent stood, which was the first time Katie had noticed him. "Vincent! It's good to see you again," she said as she seated herself, "although I must be a sight to behold."

"Well, I must admit you look different, that's for sure." He laughed and Katie noticed he had the same twinkle in his eye as his mother. He quickly turned his attention to May Belle and asked if he could give her a ride home.

"No, you stay and visit. Earl will escort me on the walk home. To tell you the truth, getting in and out of the car is harder than just taking my time and walking."

"Let me help you up the stairs then," he said. She took him up on the offer, Earl close on their heels. Katie seated herself in May Belle's chair while she watched Vincent's act of kindness. He was built completely different from his brother. Not as lean, but such broad shoulders. When she turned her attention back to her dinner, she noticed for the first time that she'd seated herself right across from Jacob.

"I agree with Vinnie; you sure do look different. New haircut," he said without revealing what he thought about it.

"Yes," she said, "*cut* being the key word *here*." She wished she could crawl under the table, but at least her hot flash was subsiding.

"I like it," he said.

"I must look a wreck," she said, unable to get past her self-consciousness, but laughing just the same while she smoothed down the little twerps of hair that served as a neckline. She'd never get used to it.

"You look (he glanced at her mascara-stained cheeks again) unusual but nice." He sounded sincere but she didn't know him well enough to know if he meant it or not. "You seem more . . . relaxed, for lack of a better word, than when I last saw you." (Clearly, Katie thought, he is measuring his words, making it all the more difficult to tell if they were sincere or not.) "But then I guess after one has spent a day hacksawing a frozen turkey named Sir Thomas, one is at the very least tired, if not relaxed." He couldn't help but grin.

Pastor set his second dessert down next to Katie and slipped into what had been Earl's chair. "I'm so glad you could make it, Katie—without your hacksaw, of course." Josh's reference to Delbert's sense of humor zipped into her thoughts. She wondered if she'd be lucky enough to become known as the town's hacksaw lady who owned the mini mall, rather than the city slicker.

"Yes, Pastor Delbert, I'm quite glad to have left my hacksaw behind for my late arrival—which I'm sure was stunning enough without it," she said smiling, looking into those eyes that appeared even more like hers now that her hair was back off her face.

"*Please* just call me Delbert, Katie," he said, pushing his glasses up his nose with an exasperated sigh. "You ever wear glasses?" he asked.

"Not yet, although I imagine I'll be aging into them pretty soon." *Surely they arrive right after hot flashes.*

"I've worn them since I was a kid," he said in a confessional tone. "I have to admit to disliking them."

"Ever try contacts?" Jacob asked.

"Don't have the courage."

"I did have the courage," Jacob said, feeling compelled to slightly readjust his glasses now that Pastor had done so with his. "Didn't like them. Nothing wrong with glasses."

Katie studied Jacob's dark eyes. Jacob and Vincent were each handsome, she thought, but not alike. Vincent was lighter in skin tone, fuller in the cheeks, and yet, there was something that looked the same about their faces. She turned her attention back to Delbert.

"Josh is one of the neatest kids I've met in a long time," Pastor said. "He's so honest. Refreshing, really." Katie wondered what her son had said, what he'd revealed about *her,* maybe. "He's big on family. I like that," he said with a smile. Family. Such a simple word, Katie thought. Such a meaningful word. *Thank You, God, for my son. Bring him home safely.*

Delbert finished his dessert, patted his stomach and bid his adieu. Pastor's wife and kids walked over and gave Katie a friendly greeting. "We'll have to have you and Josh come for dinner one night," she said to Katie.

"That would be nice." *Thank You again, God. Baby steps . . .*

Before long, everyone was starting to take their leave, some stopping to make a contribution to one of the envelopes on the table or pick up a tinfoil doggie bag Nellie Ruth had whipped up. Seeing the contribution envelopes, Katie reached into her handbag and grabbed some bills. She decided since she'd given up on Sir Thomas and hadn't even served the chicken, the least she could do was to help underwrite the day.

"Time to clean up," Dorothy said. "Earl was going to be one of the main helpers, but I'm glad he's home with his mom. Nellie Ruth and Lester, you two have done more than your share. You head on home—or to wherever you might need to go next," she said, winking at Nellie Ruth. "Let me and the boys and the rest of St. Auggie's cleanup volunteers take over now. Katie, I reckon you're needing a nap after your harrowing day. Why don't you swing on by to May Belle's tomorrow. She said we'll have my birthday lunch at noon, even if I have to bring it." Dorothy pointed to the chicken. "Looks like you've already supplied the party!"

"If somebody can give me a ride home later, I'm going to stay and help clean up, too," Katie said. "It's the least I can do after not showing up with the turkey. And as far as your birthday party tomorrow, that would be wonderful. But again, I'll need a ride. Boy, depending on people to haul you around is a pain."

"Sure is," Dorothy said. Katie clicked her tongue, realizing the insensitivity of her statement in light of Dorothy's recent loss of her wheels. Dorothy reached out and patted her arm; it was obvious Katie was chastising herself. "It's just the way things are for me, dear. Not your fault. When you get your son and your car back, enjoy them both while you can! As for that ride home after the cleanup, I'm sure somebody in my household can get you back to the farm. They're all itching to visit it anyway."

"You sure?" Katie was not in a hurry to get home. She wasn't sure which would be more disturbing: her empty house or Sir Thomas's now scattered—and oh, no!—partially thawed parts.

"I'm sure. By the way, now that I'm used to looking at it," Dorothy said, "that is one handsome hairdo, young lady."

"I second that," Vincent said, having stepped up behind her.

"I thought the same thing," Jacob said.

Hm, Dorothy thought as she looked from one of her son's faces to the other, both of them beaming right at Ms. Durbin.

30

Dorothy couldn't remember when she'd enjoyed a finer birthday party. Her belly was full of chicken and yesterday's leftover mashed potatoes; she was flanked by her family, May Belle, Earl and Katie, who felt like family; and the best part was that she was about to blow out the candles on the lemon chiffon cake in front of her, which—*Thank you, Jesus, for the miracle of drugs and Your touch*—her best friend in the world had felt well enough this morning to bake. She drew in a deep breath to make her wish, then held it while deciding to pray it instead of just wish it. *Lord, help me remember this wonderful moment after my family has all gone back to their homes—and help them to get there safely,* she added as she exhaled and blew out all six candles Earl had placed on top of the cake in a lopsided circle. Everyone clapped and cheered. "Nice to know you're still full of hot air, Grandma," Bradley teased. Dorothy reached out and touched his cheek. "Like Grandma like grandson," she said. "But for goodness' sakes, let's stop jawin' and get this cake cut! After eating nonstop now for two days, I'm about to starve to death!" She patted her stomach while May Belle removed the candles and took hold of her pearl-handled cake cutter. Dorothy noticed a quick shadow cross May Belle's face when she handed it to Jacob and asked him to do the honors. May Belle had pushed the edges of her healing back far enough this morning. *Help us* all *to remember, Lord,* Dorothy prayed, *what it is we need to remember—including when it's just time to enjoy!*

Dorothy watched the cake plates pass from one to the next in utter awe of a God who had not only planted the seed of the idea for the Thanksgiving dinner into the hearts of His daughters, but had taken care of every detail—*and* she was having lemon chiffon cake to boot! She raised her glass of water high in the air and said, "I'd like to make a toast." Everybody grabbed what they had in front of them, from coffee to cake, and raised it. "Happy birthday to me and may we remember to have hearts of thanksgiving every day of the year!"

By Friday morning at eight-thirty sharp, just as Herm had predicted, he and Vera had loaded up Henrietta and were tooting the horn as they pulled away.

Suddenly Henrietta came to a halt, then began to back up to where Arthur and Jessie were standing side by side, having stopped waving—and sighed—when they saw Henrietta's brake lights come on. Herm rolled down the window after he'd backed right up next to them.

"I've GOT IT!" he shouted. "Herman the Vermin says good-bye until we meet again—to Art with a Heart! Who would have ever thought!" he said, laughing like a hyena. Once again, Henrietta began to roll down the driveway, the sounds of her horn toot-toot-tooting until she was clear out of sight.

THE END

A Note from the Author

In my last Note from *Dearest Dorothy, Help! I've Lost Myself,*
I wrote to you from the bustle of Partonville. This evening
I type to you from my silent home office.

Okay, it's morning now. (And isn't that the way of life?!)
With a gust of surprising strength, last night the fine folks of
Partonville drew me back, back into their lives in order to
make sure I hadn't misquoted any of them. Then suddenly
(time passes like a finger snap when I am in Partonville),
"Oh! It's past my BEDTIME!" ("Now I lay me down to
sleep . . .") Eyes blink open, my senses awaken. A glass of
iced tea. Yes, it's *morning* now and I am back at my computer,
Celtic music whirling out of my speakers, encircling me, in-
fusing me with energy. And here's all I can think about: the
mystical and magical way music "plays" its way into a story,
influencing moods, temperaments and thus the story itself.

For this book, my fingers most *often* typed to the rhythms
of either vintage standards or Celtic. When Arthur whips
out his good ol' Hohner Harmonica to give us a tune (yes,
in my mind's eye, he plays for *me* too), I recall the songs
my parents loved. Songs they sang together during all my
growing-up years, right out loud, right there in our home.
And then they would kiss. Songs that were "their songs."
Songs that are now mine—and Arthur's.

When NEW LOVE is in the air (OH! Edward Showalter
and Nellie RUTH!), I hear the vigor of the happy Irish
flute, the power and vulnerability in uilleann pipes.

A couple minutes have passed since my last sentence. I don't even remember what I was going to say. A Celtic tune so JOY-FILLED spirited me to stand and dance, to lift my arms and twirl. (Just like that, the mystical, magical powers of music have changed *my* story.) But then, when it is The Day you have completed a labor of love *(Thank you, Big Guy!),* what more fitting thing can one do!

Charlene Ann Baumbich
www.welcometopartonville.com